SUSTENANCE

BY CHELSEA QUINN YARBRO
FROM TOM DOHERTY ASSOCIATES

Aristo

Better in the Dark

Blood Games

Blood Roses

Borne in Blood

Burning Shadows

A Candle for d'Artagnan

Come Twilight

Commedia della Morte

Communion Blood

Crusader's Torch

A Dangerous Climate

Dark of the Sun

Darker Jewels

An Embarrassment of Riches

A Feast in Exile

A Flame of Byzantium

Hotel Transylvania

Mansions of Darkness

Night Pilgrims

Out of the House of Life

The Palace

Path of the Eclipse

Roman Dusk

States of Grace

Writ in Blood

SUSTENANCE

A Novel of the Count Saint-Germain

CHELSEA QUINN YARBRO

A TOM DOHERTY ASSOCIATES BOOK
NEW YORK

Fic
Yarbro

This is a work of fiction. All of the characters, organizations, and events
portrayed in this novel are either products of the author's imagination
or are used fictitiously.

SUSTENANCE

A Tor Book
Published by Tom Doherty Associates, LLC
175 Fifth Avenue
New York, NY 10010

www.tor-forge.com

Tor® is a registered trademark of Tom Doherty Associates, LLC.

The Library of Congress Cataloging-in-Publication Data
is available upon request.

ISBN 978-0-7653-3401-5 (hardcover)
ISBN 978-1-4668-0772-3 (e-book)

Tor books may be purchased for educational, business, or promotional use.
For information on bulk purchases, please contact the Macmillan Corporate
and Premium Sales Department at 1-800-221-7945, extension 5442,
or write to specialmarkets@macmillan.com.

First Edition: December 2014

Printed in the United States of America

0 9 8 7 6 5 4 3 2 1

For
JOHN
who is my cousin

and

NANCY
who is my friend

AUTHOR'S NOTE

Although few of the books in this series take place within living memory, this one is one of the exceptions, concerned as it is with the anti-Communist hysteria that consumed much of America from the end of the Second World War until the collapse of the Soviet Union, although vestiges of it still linger: China practices its version of Communism, and there are people in this country who are worried about that, and see danger in China's economic policies. This story deals with the beginning of the strident period between 1949 and 1952, when there was a great juggling for power in the wake of the death of Franklin Delano Roosevelt; this was most—and most unobviously—apparent in the emergence of security and watchdog agencies, for the Second World War had made it plain that intelligence could tip the balances where ordnance could not. Many security bureaucrats—some moving from the FBI to the newly emergent CIG/CIA—took full advantage of the country's anti-Communist hysteria to set themselves up in unusually secure positions within the new organization, being at pains from the beginning to carve themselves out niches that would keep them employed for decades. The watchword *security* is still the favored explanation for anything the government/security industry/international business community wants that needs protection for being outside or beyond the law, a rubric to get around acts that are clearly unconstitutional without having to answer for committing a crime.

The early stages of such shenanigans developed when J. Edgar Hoover gained control of the Federal Bureau of Investigation in the two hectic decades between World War I and World War II. Hoover, with the determined support of the Religious Right of the time, started lobbying/pressuring/blackmailing Congress to extend the powers of the FBI to include foreign intelligence-gathering, as well as all domestic. When the matter came before Congress, shortly after the death of President Roosevelt, President

Truman refused to go along with the plan that was presented to him; instead he joined the talented spies and other intelligence agents like code-breakers and code-makers, linguists, engineers, and those possessing a variety of skills from several different departments of government who had been the backbone of intelligence-gathering outside of this country during the war, making it the heart (if that's the word I want) of US espionage that was being fashioned into a new and separate body, one with experience of working in foreign countries. With the men and women from General "Wild Bill" Donovan's OSS, and some code-breakers for Army and Navy intelligence, Truman granted the successor to the OSS a new agency for that work, the Central Intelligence Group, later agreeing to change the name to the Central Intelligence Agency. As soon as the limitations on both services were established, the feud between the FBI and CIA was off and running. As these two organizations were often used as figureheads in intelligence work, the government created more of them, most of them considerably less visible than these two behemoths of covert activities. Early in its existence, the CIA had a number of satellite offices, such as the one in this story in Baltimore, a leftover precaution from World War II, which made sure there were backups and bolt-holes for its agents in as many places as was practicable. The anonymity of a suite of offices in a commercial building was also supposed to guard against being targeted by enemies. But as technology made long-distance spying as reliable as anything humans in enemy territory could accomplish, a significant portion of espionage became an exercise in electronics, the results of which are still ongoing today: much of the groundwork for our present eruptions of scandals was laid by various forms of electronic snooping carried on with questionable legality against US citizens during the formative years of the CIA. Later, President Eisenhower put the CIA to work in ways Truman never even considered, but those developments are beyond the time of this novel, and are not part of it.

A great many people remember or know about the House Un-American Activities Committee witch-hunting in Hollywood, which began at the end of the 1940s, and the resulting Black List, which put paid to the careers of actors, writers, directors, and other mainstays of mass media. Even Sterling Hayden, a major leading man, and someone who had worked for Wild Bill Donovan in Europe during World War II, was unable to hold his own against HUAC. The Congress loved it. The government got oodles of publicity, which was more the goal of this pillorying than it was an appropriate response to any threat films represented. With the help of Right Wing reporters, a great outcry against Godless Communists and other so-called traitors arose and terrified the public into cooperation—the witch-hunt was under way! Right-leaning congressmen up in arms about immigrant policies that they felt were not strict enough because an occasional Nazi might slip through the barriers and everything would come tumbling down endorsed the investigations. The populace was mesmerized primarily because real life was suddenly as exciting as the movies. And all those famous faces! Big-name movie stars assuring the Committee they were four-square for the USA, and praising the Committee for the work they were doing, was a triumph for the Committee, and it went to their heads, eventually. The power of public opinion this subjugation of the entertainment media gave the HUAC was intoxicating to the legislators, who, until then, were not often nationally recognized persons, but after the broadcast and televised hearings became familiar and famous. It was heady stuff: all the innuendos and accusations about these face-famous men of stardom and glamour, icons of popularity, brought low by the Committee, which ruined careers and lives. And men they were: very few women were ever brought up on any subterfuge charges or innuendos, so very few women testified—for although women were part of the intelligence community, not only as secretaries but as agents and code-breakers and archivists, among other things, the Committee did not want to be seen to be bullies, and so—to mix the metaphor—they soft-pedaled their visible pursuit of women, and settled for rumor to be enough to scare most of the suspected women away from the film industry. HUAC had used the same technique early in their inquiries on academics, and it had worked splendidly, driving professors away from their universities and colleges, scientists out of their laboratories, and sometimes out of the country.

The entertainment industry was just the visible tip of the iceberg. Most of those whose lives were pulled out from under them were much less illustrious, and so did not attract the kind of awe and attention the big names of Hollywood did. For the teachers and union officers and engineers and journalists and other ordinary folk, the wreckage was done quietly, out of public view, and those seeking redress of wrongs had difficulty getting any court of law willing to protest the hearings; these less visible people often found themselves in the company of those already suspect, and subjected to the same oppressive investigation: in the first few years after the end of World War II, universities and their faculties took tremendous hits from the Committee, and like the accused in Hollywood, many academics, no longer able to teach or pursue their studies in the United States, fled to Europe or other parts of the globe to wait out the craziness, and to find a way to support their families in the process. Some of them never came back, having found a place where their work was more valued by those countries that took them in than it had been at home.

To make this clear, this is not a roman à clef: the characters are not real people in clever-but-penetrable disguises; the characters have elements of real people's experience in them, but not as a one-on-one transmogrification. Actual persons are mentioned in passing for context and for accuracy in the story, but please keep in mind that it is called a novel because I made it up from events that had a major impact on my grammar-school years. In the name of full disclosure, I was born in Berkeley, California, during World War II; I grew up there. I went to school there. I have/had relatives who were under HUAC investigation—and they didn't live anywhere near Berkeley—which is why, when I was in the fourth grade, I was followed by the FBI for over a week. I know: it looks nuts to me, too. It took me more than thirty years to find out what it was all about: the FBI wanted to scare my immediate family and our other relatives into rejecting the ones who were under direct suspicion; it had the opposite effect. I also had friends and parents of friends who lived in Berkeley, and who were compelled to leave the country rather than continue in either the University of California, or the then-called California State Teachers' College System, now the California State University System: the Ex-Pats' Coven in this story is very loosely based on a group of American academics whose newsletter was made available to US academics living in Europe, although it came out of London, not Paris, and for the most part served to help find jobs and apartments for those unfortunate enough to need them. To reiterate: all the various difficulties encountered by the Coven members in this story are based on incidents that actually happened to someone I knew, directly or indirectly, in that group of parents/friends/relatives; they are altered and condensed, for the average amount of time the actual people were away from the States was eleven years and this tale takes place within two and a half years, but—with the sole exception of Charis' loss of Saint-Germain's Jaguar—they all reflect actual experiences, though reinterpreted for the sake of the story. This period has left its mark on our history; we are still hearing echoes of it today.

So special thanks to Alain, Bernadette, Daniel, Ed and Ed's dad, Gordon, Jim, Lucius, Marco, Merrinel, Perpetua, Rollin, Sidney, Ulrich, Veronica, and Waring for access to diaries and journals, opportunities for interviews, telephone conversations, e-mails, photos, clippings, and all manner of personal memorabilia and other records of the real lives of real people dealing with the anti-Communist zeal of the time, with special thanks to those three who actually took an active part in post–World War II espionage and allowed me to interview them.

Another interesting problem that arises with a book so close to the present day is checking hard dates when certain events happened, for we have a lot of documentation for World War II to the present day, and that imposes its own demands. Such things as catchphrases and slang may have some of the same meaning and use now as then, but it is surprising how much has changed, and how rapidly. There is also the matter of what you have and don't have available in terms of high-tech—1950s style. There are three national television channels, period. There are a few local independent stations scattered about the country as well, and PBS is working its way into the national viewing market. No iPads, no cell phones, no desktops, laptops, notebooks, or other in-home computers. No smart phones. Very few electric typewriters. Only the military and intelligence groups have the ancestors of modern computers—huge, noisy, temperamental machines that would seem intolerably slow to computer users today. Color television is just becoming affordable. A very early version of a microwave oven is on the market, but not selling well. There are no Miranda Rights. There are no weather satellites. The space program is just barely beginning. There is no vaccine for polio or measles. There are no Toyotas or Datsuns/Nissans on the streets of America. The smallest eavesdropping bug you can plant is about the size of a nickel and has a cord. Transgender surgical protocols have yet to be developed. Homosexuality is illegal in most US states. The Civil Rights Movement, the Women's Movement, the Environmental Movement, the Gay Rights Movement are embryonic and easily dismissed by linking their goals with Communism. Most US cities have at least two daily newspapers, and some have as many as ten. Rock and roll hasn't fully arrived yet, though it is beginning to develop. In parts of the country, swearing in public can get you time in jail. Almost all stores are closed on Sunday. Engineers all carry slide rules; there are no calculators. The interstate highway system has yet to be built. The commercial jet airliner is just beginning to be a reality. One of the most sought-after additions to a house is a bomb shelter in the basement or backyard. And on and on. Those apologists who, in the last decade or so, have taken to saying that all the dismay over McCarthyism and HUAC excesses was exaggerated and incorrect have not examined the events of that time as those who lived through those years experienced them. There are vast amounts of information available that have bearing on this fearful epoch in what was a profoundly strenuous century, the 1950s being more tumultuous than they were seen as being while the decade was happening. On the surface everything was prosperous, everything was fine, everyone was happy, all problems were minor ones, etc., etc., etc. The Fifties were prosperous in most technologically advanced cultures, economies widened the job market, unions fought for—and got—better working conditions and more benefits for their members. Housing was booming. The birth rate was up. But there was also tremendous social pressure for conformity, which was justified by a number of complex religio-political catchphrases in popular music and in television shows—my ironic favorite is *and the people all said siddown! Siddown! You're rocking the boat.* With the emphasis on conformity, many Americans found it difficult to pursue expansive working projects in new fields in a way that did not appear to challenge the preferred conduct that society enforced, all of which was subtly and not so subtly reinforced by the shows on radio and television. Technology was welcomed only because it was demonstrably part of the security everyone was supposed to desire; otherwise the country was going through one of its periodic lapses into pronounced anti-intellectuality. So far as I'm concerned—and I admit I'm biased—although mass media made the anti-Communism frenzy worse for a while, mass media also served to break the witch-hunt's stranglehold on the American public: Edward R. Murrow was willing to take on Senator Joe McCarthy, Murrow's network was willing to stand behind him to a point, and everyone could watch it on television.

THERE ARE thanks and metaphorical bouquets to hand out, as well as making note of the background and environment of the story: so flowers and cheers to Wiley Saichek, my incomparable online publicist, for the resurrection of the Chelsea Quinn Yarbro Newsletter; posies and applause to Gryffyn Phoenix for her contributions to the Newsletter, and all her help with Internet publishing. A large bouquet and applause to my agent, Howard Morhaim, who has kept a careful eye on Saint-Germain. Many thanks and long-stemmed roses to Jack Leavitt, who handled a legal matter with steady good sense. Peonies and lilacs to Robert Black, Hazel Ryefeld, and Christopher Travers, my recreational readers on this book; more peonies and a round of applause to Libba Campbell for her eagle-eyed help with the manuscript. Random bouquets and applause to

Elizabeth Miller, Sharon Russell, and Stephanie Moss for their continuing interest in the series. A mixed tub of day- and tiger-lilies for the Yarbro chat group on Yahoo.com. Wreaths and cheers, in no particular order, to Charlie and Peggy, Maureen and David, Mary-Rose and Patrick, Megan, Alice, Steve, Marc, Brian, Shawn, Cheryl, Suzy, and, at a distance, Peter, Ingrid, Eggert, and Mark. And a large wreath of lavender and night-blooming jasmine, just because, to Joy and Christine, and a smaller one to Glenn, my acupuncturist, for keeping so much of the old body working. As always, catnip and mice to Butterscotch and Crumpet, for reminding me that the secret of the universe is: Cats Are First.

On the publishing side of things, thanks to Melissa Singer, the longtime editor of this series; to Tom Doherty, the heart of Tor/Forge/et al., for backing this series for a couple of decades now; to the bookstores whose owners put this series on the shelves for their customers, and order more of them. And—saving the best for last—special thanks to you, the reader, who has bought this book—may you find it was money well spent: you're the one who keeps the series . . . um . . . alive (if that's the word I want).

CHELSEA QUINN YARBRO
Richmond, California
31 July 2013

Part One

❖ ❖ ❖

CHARIS LUNDQUIST TREAT

TEXT OF A NEWSLETTER REPRODUCED BY MIMEOGRAPHY
BY WASHINGTON YOUNG IN PARIS, FRANCE, AND
DISTRIBUTED TO MEMBERS OF THE EX-PATS' COVEN ON
SEPTEMBER 8TH, 1949.

THE GRIMOIRE

newsletter for Autumn 1949
Washington Young, printer and publisher
Volume 2, no. 3

MORE BAD NEWS from the States: the Committee continues to wreak its havoc, pursuing their policy of forcing those who disagree with their political positions to lose their jobs, their positions in their communities, and any chance of following their established professions in the United States of America, all in the name of freedom. The press has supported their hysteria, increasing the air of crisis that continues to grow, joining the repressive elements in the government in continuing to denounce citizens of Communistic inclinations, without any proof of wrongdoing beyond rumor and innuendo. Westbrook Pegler still has the greatest hue and cry in print, but others are taking up the hue and cry. That opportunist Hoover and his agents have extended their assault on our Constitutional rights, claiming that to protect the country, certain measures are necessary in the face of the subtle and dangerous enemy—Communism. He has pledged to be rid of Communists, root, trunk, and branch. Lowell Thomas is preparing a television show on "run-away" Lefties, planning to show us as cowardly and treasonous, claiming that America is better off without any one of us. Be warned that he will try to persuade your families and friends back home to denounce you. Some of you may wish to write to your closest friends and family members, but keep in mind that the letters are likely to be opened by the FBI or other federal agencies. If possible, leave the names of other Coven members out of anything you send or say in telephone conversations to anyone in the States.

DEAN ACHESON DOES not seem to be as determined to pursue those of us who have sought refuge in Europe as George Marshall was, or it may be President Truman is responsible for the change; he has decided to focus on the Soviet Union rather than Western Europe as the biggest threat, and has been disinclined to pursue those like us unless there is extensive proof of true espionage. It appears that the President is actually concerned about the number of academics who have left the United States for other places in the world, and would like some of us to come back. We will have to keep an eye on his progress. Since President Truman has indicated that he plans to put more emphasis on science and education for the "underprivileged," he could rein in Hoover and the HUAC without too much effort. Perhaps the North Atlantic Treaty Organization will make it more difficult to persist in the process of Red-baiting and paranoia we have encountered in the last two years. This reporter suspects it all hinges on the newly-divided Germany. Who knows—if the Geneva Convention is ratified, some clever jurist could decide that its protections for necessary foodstuffs, clothing, and other basics can apply to displaced persons and ex-pats as well as soldiers during wartime, and restore our pensions.

COLONEL TBT HAS sent word to our group's attorney that there may be some problems renewing passports, and providing an acceptable proof of vaccinations over the next couple years. Most of us have no plans to return to the States any time soon, but the passport is essential for any foreign travel, so if any of us need to do that, the Colonel recommends doing it now, before the new rules are put in place. By the first of the year, some American Embassies will not be able to provide renewals without a security check, which most of us cannot assume we would pass. The Colonel believes that this may be a ploy to disenfranchise many of us while we seek redress of wrongs.

THE ATTEMPT TO restore to the Central Intelligence Agency its original name, the Central Intelligence Group, has been soundly defeated in committee, much to the dismay of the CIA, where the move is seen to be spearheaded by Hoover's supporters. The CIA has complained that CIA and FBI sound like two divisions of the same agency, which is precisely what Hoover is hoping it will do, which will lead the public to accept a blending of the two, under Hoover's command.

WE ARE EXPECTING news from HAW in Boston regarding the policy on foreign lecturers at Boston College; the Catholic Church is opposed to allowing anyone from a Communist country to address the student body on any topic, political or not, claiming that such an appearance would appear to be an endorsement of Communism itself. Of course, anyone seeking to appear at a US university would have to have some guarantee of safety from the CIA and the FBI, which may render the situation moot. In regard to the policy of the Catholic Church, some among the faculties of such institutions have expressed opposition to this proposed policy, but the College's administration is inclined to go along with the Church, which should not surprise any of us. A final decision in this matter is expected by year's end, as the witch-hunt goes on.

OUR NEWLY ARRIVED Coven member from the great city of New Orleans informed this reporter that she may have found a publisher in Copenhagen who could be willing to publish works that we have had canceled or turned down out of hand in the States; if this proves to be the case, it could provide a chance for a better living for some of us, as well as a way to keep our work alive while we wait for better times. She is planning to make an appointment with him while she is in Copenhagen next month, and will telephone if she has encouraging news for us. This reporter is hopeful that she may have a positive response for a number of us. If anything is to come of this opportunity, we must be prepared to make the most of it. Thus far, we have had no doors opening to us but those in Eastern Europe, which, given the spirit of the times, would only serve to confirm the belief back home that we are dangerous radicals supporting the Communist agenda. Much as a few of our members have placed completed works with Oxford and Cambridge Presses, it would be folly to expect the English university presses to take on all our manuscripts: England has become careful about the Reds since the end of the war, and may one day try to cut back on such ventures as we have produced. CT may provide us all a second market.

OUR FRIEND WHO moved to Barcelona has written to offer his new home, a Gaudi house no less, as a place to meet after the first of the coming year. He has said he will be happy to provide bedrooms and meals for up to a week. His home has extensive grounds, all paid for by the shipping company that now employs him. His one caution is that he is fairly certain that his bosses are engaging in some kind of illegal activities, and he does not know what they are, nor does he want to find out. For any of our group who would consider that troubling, he would recommend arranging another place to meet, on the French side of the mountains: safer, but without the Gaudi house. For those of you wishing to contact Barcelona, give your letters to this editor, and he will pass on all letters that may contain questions about this proposition.

OUR MEMBER FROM Helena has departed on her self-appointed mission. She is presently in Switzerland, hoping to find a place where she can teach astronomy without any interference from the government, no matter what government it may be. She plans to give her venture about six months of travel. If she finds a place to work, she will have her belongings in storage here sent on to her new location, and she will put her house in Helena up for sale.

IF ANY COVEN members know of a job that our only member from Nebraska might fill until he leaves for Australia in April, please contact him directly. The bookstore where he has been working has been visited by someone from the US Department of State, encouraging the bookstore owner to dismiss our Nebraskan as being bad for business. That would leave him without earnings for half a year. His last day at the bookstore will be the end of next month. Trick or treat.

IN NOVEMBER THE Coven will meet on the usual holiday at the usual place at five-thirty in the afternoon for a meeting, dinner to follow for those who wish to remain: send your acceptance or regrets to this publication, no later than five days before the holiday. If we have no response from you, we will assume you will not be attending our celebration. Prices for the meal will be sent to those of you who plan to attend, though we may have to settle for duck instead of turkey.

WE ARE SADDENED to learn that Thelma Jefferson Gregg, Professor of Physics at UCLA, has resigned her post and retired to Albuquerque, New Mexico, citing poor health for her decision to leave teaching. Her husband, Henry Gregg, will be teaching statistics at the university there.

A publication for and by the victims of witch-hunts

❖ 1 ❖

IT WAS one of those *probably nothing* noises, a sound that was part scrape, part yowl, a bit sneaky, and it brought Charis Treat abruptly awake, her pulse racing, words whispering out of her at machine-gun speed. "It was a tree branch, or an angry cat, or something at the docks, or—" Or anything but the CIA bugging her Copenhagen hotel room. She sat up in bed, holding the pillow in front of her like a shield. Striving to separate herself from the fear that made her hands shake, she used her most reasonable lecture voice: "You're in . . ." It took her a couple of seconds to remember. "You're in Denmark, not Louisiana. You don't have to worry about the Committee, not here." Her voice was louder now, and she was breathing more normally. She forced herself to yawn, not very successfully, then she got up and went to the cramped bathroom, where she took a second phenobarbital and an aspirin, used the toilet, and went back to bed. Her alarm clock on the night-stand told her it was four-thirty-seven. "Damn," she muttered. She would need to get back to sleep quickly if she were going to have sufficient rest when her breakfast tray arrived at six-forty-five. If only she did not have to be off for her interview by seven-thirty. She sighed and got slowly back into bed, ordering herself not to stare at the ceiling, trying to imagine what Harold and the kids were doing; that was something she would find out later. It would be a mistake, she thought, to go to her interview overcome by melancholy. "Be sensible. They're fast asleep," she told herself aloud. "Just as you should be, Charis." She often lectured herself sternly in the waning hours of the night, had done so since she was in grammar school. Now she leaned back and rested her head on the goose-down pillow, willing herself to sleep.

After nearly an hour of watching the shadow-pattern of the birches' falling leaves in the hotel garden dancing and sliding on the wall, she sighed, reached out, and turned on the bedside lamp; its yellow glow created a cone of light that allowed her to resume reading Paton's *Cry, the Beloved Country*. She managed to get through another twenty pages before the first signs of the advancing dawn suffused the room with thin, limpid light. Marking her page with a brass paper clip, she set the book down, turned off the light, and did her best to get at least enough of a doze to restore her to the semblance of alertness.

"Breakfast, Madame," said the waiter in acceptable English as he rapped twice on her door.

"Coming. Thank you," she said, dragging on her bathrobe as she got out of bed and into the chilly morning; she made her way to the door. "Put it on the table," she said, thinking it was absurd to tell the young man that, since there was no other surface in the room that would reasonably accommodate the tray.

The waiter offered her a neat little bow and set the tray down, and handed Charis the bill on a kind of clip-board.

Charis went to pull her purse out from under the pillow, opened up her wallet, and removed four coins—the same amount she had paid every breakfast for the last four mornings—and went to close and lock her door as he left. "Eggs, toast, herring, tea," she said as she lifted the lids on three plates, stacking them together on the remaining wedge of empty tabletop. The first day she had asked for orange juice as well, but was amazed at the cost, and had dropped it from her subsequent breakfasts. The eggs were soft-poached, just the way she liked them, and there was a little ramekin of fresh butter next to the two slices of toast. The herring was broiled. Not what she would have back home, but not too foreign, either. She fit the strainer on top of her cup and poured out the dark, leafy tea through the fine wire mesh, concentrating on not overfilling her cup, as she had done yesterday. There was so much to get used to! "Book your call for six this evening," she reminded herself aloud as she pulled up the overstuffed chair from next to the bed and began to eat, keeping an eye on the clock.

The noise that wakened her returned, and this time she realized it was the squeak of brakes on the delivery van that had just unloaded the day's produce at the hotel's kitchen door. She made herself chuckle at her fears, saying, "Next you'll be jumping at phone calls."

When she was finished with her meal, she went into the bathroom to wash and put herself in order. At thirty-six, she was still passably attractive, especially for an academic, she thought wryly, but she knew enough to be careful with her make-up and hairstyle, to put the emphasis on her best features, which were her large, smoky-blue eyes and her teak-colored hair. She wished she had a shower, but made the most of a quick turn in the tub. The towel she had been provided was a pale blue, a bit threadbare, and scratchy. She rubbed herself down quickly and then took a minute to stare at herself in the mirror. She patted the dark smudges under her eyes and decided to use her Elizabeth Arden foundation—it gave the best coverage. She took a moment to pluck a few stray hairs from her dark, angled brows, and sighed. "I'll have to rely on charm, I guess. Looks aren't going to do it today." She applied her make-up with care, hoping to conceal the anxiety that had taken hold of her; it would be foolish to reveal how desperate her situation was becoming.

She left her room a few minutes ahead of schedule, her fawn-colored wool jacket long and princess-cut over an ecru blouse an understated version of Dior's New Look. Her skirt was not quite the right length for sticklers, but its deep Prussian blue matched her gloves, her shoes, and her hat. Her purse was a simple dark-blue clutch—shoulder bags had vanished from American stores when Hoover had declared that Communist sympathizers carried them—and her briefcase was a darker version of her jacket. All in all, she was pleased with the impression she could make.

The expression on the face of the clerk at the front desk confirmed her good opinion; he took her order for an eighteen-hundred-hours call to America, saying, "Will you take it in your room or in the telephone lounge?"

"I think my room would be better, thank you," she said, wondering if she should tip him.

He recognized her predicament. "Gratuities are offered when the service is complete."

She could feel her face grow warm. "Thank you," she said again, and added, "Your English is very good."

The clerk smiled. "My parents sent my brothers and me to our aunt in Canada during the war years."

"Probably sensible," she said, missing her own sons, and turned toward the entrance. Stepping out of the hotel, she asked the door-man to hail a cab and gave the driver the address she had memo-rized the night before. "I understand we should need about twenty minutes to thirty minutes, perhaps a little longer. The roads won't be crowded yet. In half an hour, they will be." He swooped into the street and lit a cigarette. "I will have you there shortly after zero-eight-hundred. I know a shortcut." He grinned around the cigarette and signaled to turn left, making a rude gesture with his hand.

The morning was nippy—not quite cold, but chilly enough to make her think she had been wrong not to wear a coat. She settled back in the cab and watched the traffic around her, but gradually anticipation of the morning's meeting claimed her thoughts: she tried to decide what she would say to this Ragoczy Ferenz, Grof Szent-Germain; how should she address him? In what language? Did he speak English? French? She knew a little Italian, but not enough to discuss her book in it. She suspected he was Hungarian: the *sz* looked Hungarian, but it might be Polish or Czech. Proba-bly not Russian: Russians weren't supposed to use titles like Grof any longer, unless he was one of the Old Regime, whose family fled before the Revolution. Certainly not Bulgarian or Croatian or Serbian or Montenegron, and probably not any other Jugoslavian ethnic group; for a while she mentally ran through the list of na-tionalities that Grof Szent-Germain might be but probably wasn't. She resisted the urge to bite the end of her little fingernail, telling herself it would smear her lipstick. The cab took an energetic turn to the left, and she grabbed the loop hanging down between the front and rear seats.

"Sorry; there was an obstacle in the road," said the driver, who was on his third cigarette.

"So I gather," said Charis, adjusting her hat and sitting back once more.

The driver double-clutched down into second gear and climbed up a small rise; the street was very narrow, with ancient cobbles and the narrowest of walkways along the edge of the stones. The buildings here were old—most a couple of centuries at least—Charis realized, and wondered why a publishing house should be in this older part of the city. She was more startled when the driver turned into an even smaller side-street, barely wide enough for the cab to negotiate, and drew up in front of an elegant four-story building that looked to be about three hundred years old. "Number 32, Madame," said the driver as he flipped up his trip-flag, and told her the price. "It's zero-eight-hundred-twelve."

She worked out the fare in American dollars: one-twenty-eight, more or less, yet another reminder of how the war had driven up the price of fuel and of operating a car. She handed over the appropriate coins, which still seemed dreadfully unfamiliar to her. "Thank you," she said, letting herself out with care onto the narrow strip of brick sidewalk, her purse in one hand, her briefcase in the other; the cab was put into reverse and backed away from Charis' destination.

It was in beautiful repair, she thought as she climbed up to the front door, pausing to look at the various ornaments above the windows: most of it was scroll-work in a subdued Baroque style. Reaching the broad top step, she saw the modest bronze plaque above the knocker:

ECLIPSE PUBLISHERS

AND

TRANSLATION SERVICES

and above that was another one, saying, she assumed, the same thing in Danish.

Charis hesitated, her confidence faltering, then remembered that Harold had not sent her the full hundred and fifty dollars he had promised her; she grabbed the knocker and swung it down on its strike plate twice and waited for someone to answer.

Roughly a minute later, a man who looked to be about fifty, with sandy hair touched with white and eyes the color of old, much-washed blue jeans, opened the door. He nodded to Charis. "Professor Treat?" he asked in English; his accent was almost flawless.

"I am," she said, trying to conceal her sudden return of nervousness with a smile. "I'm a little early, but I don't know the city and didn't want to be late."

"Please come in; I'm Rogers, the Grof's personal assistant," he said, stepping back and opening the door wider into a two-story entry hall with a single, broad staircase leading to the gallery circling the hexagonal room one floor up. He indicated a comfortable drawing room on Charis' right. "If you'll be seated, I'll tell the Grof that you've arrived."

"Thank you," she said, and glanced in at the muted blue-green walls and several large, oaken bookcases filled with hard-bound editions of all kinds, some looking to be almost as old as the building. Two sofas and a coffee-table stood in front of a handsome fireplace; the whole room was alight with watery sunshine.

"May I bring you some coffee or tea while you wait?"

"Will that be long?"

"Well, as you say, you are early, and the Grof is in a meeting."

She hesitated, worried that her appointment might be cut short because of her early arrival, which might be seen as American pushiness; she knew Europeans disliked it. "Coffee," she said when she realized that Rogers wanted an answer. "With milk, no sugar."

"Very good." He nodded again and left her to inspect the shelves, hoping to learn more about what Eclipse published.

She had removed her gloves and was perusing a volume on the archeology of the Peruvian Andes, translated from the French; the date of publication was 1948, and the book was printed on coated stock with wonderful photographs, many in color. This was most encouraging, she decided, and turned around to find Rogers returned with a tray holding a large cup-and-saucer, a plunger coffee-maker, and a jug of milk. "Oh. Good."

"Shall I set it down, Professor Treat?"

"Yes, please," she said, putting the book back on the shelf. "It's quite fascinating, isn't it?"

"Professor de Montalia's work? Yes, it is," Rogers agreed as he placed the tray on the coffee-table. "The Grof will be with you shortly. He has been in a meeting with his printing staff, and they're going to run over—something about the new presses. He apologizes for the delay."

"Thank him for informing me," she said as she went to the nearer sofa and sat down, reaching for the small lacquer-work tray as she did.

Rogers nodded toward the fireplace. "Would you like me to light the kindling?"

The room was a little cool, and without a coat she was growing uncomfortable; she did not know how much longer she would be here, she reminded herself as she depressed the plunger on the coffee-pot. "If it isn't inconvenient for you, that would be nice."

"No inconvenience at all." Rogers went to a small, antique secretary and removed a box of fireplace matches, then moved the fire-screen and lit the kindling under the quartered logs. He remained where he was until he was satisfied that the logs were starting to burn. "If you need anything more, please press the button by the door," he said, putting the fire-screen back in place, and going away.

"Thank you," Charis called after him, then added milk to her coffee and tasted it, knowing it was still very hot. She set the cup down and rubbed her tongue on the roof of her mouth, feeling the first onset of interview-jitters take hold. Somewhere in the house, a clock sonorously rang the half-hour. It was the time appointed for her interview; in spite of all her good intentions, Charis began to fret. She drank her coffee and added more from the pot.

Some five minutes later, she heard crisp footsteps approaching through the entry hall, and thinking this was Rogers coming to fetch her, she reached for her briefcase, preparing to rise.

A moment later, a man of slightly less than average height, graceful yet sturdily built, came through the door. He appeared to be in his middle forties, had well-cut dark hair with a slight feathering of gray at the temples, and an angled arch to his brows; his face was more attractive than handsome, with a broad forehead and a slightly askew nose, his eyes an arresting, strange blue-black. He was dressed in a black suit of understated elegance. His shirt was off-white and obviously silk, as was his dark-red damask tie. His waistcoat had a subtle pattern of what looked like wings in its fine black wool. "Professor Treat. Thank you for waiting," he said in English with a faint accent she was unable to identify. "And I apologize for the early hour, but I will be leaving Copenhagen tomorrow and wanted to see you before I left, which is why I suggested an eight-thirty appointment." His voice was low and musical, and his manner, though formal, was welcoming.

"Grof Szent-Germain," she said, recovering herself, and, starting to rise, held out her hand, while struggling to get out of the deep sofa cushions.

He came closer and took it, bowing slightly. "A pleasure, Professor Treat. Welcome to Eclipse Publishing. I trust your journey was a pleasant one."

"Thank you," she said, standing up a bit awkwardly. "The cab-driver smoked a great deal."

"And your journey from America?" he asked.

"When is a long flight ever comfortable?" she asked, wanting to seem more broadly traveled than she was.

He offered a wry half-smile, saying, "I concur, especially over water," then motioned to her to be seated, and took his place on the sofa opposite hers. "Before we begin, let me assure you that I am aware of the lamentable developments in the United States. It is a difficult time for academics in your country, is it not?"

"America has always had a streak of anti-intellectualism in its make-up," she said, using her lecture tone. "When the people are frightened, they often seek refuge in religion and reject science. Science is not often comforting."

"They reject knowledge out of fear," he added.

"Out of fear," she agreed.

He shook his head. "I hope you are finding a better reception here in Denmark. And in Paris, for that matter."

"I hope so; most everyone has been polite, but I don't speak

Danish, and that is a problem for me," she said, and reached for her coffee-cup to finish what was left in it, wanting her throat to be less dry. "I have pretty good French."

"The French will appreciate that," Szent-Germain said with a sardonic lift of one eyebrow.

Charis managed an uneasy chuckle.

"I've noticed you have the name Lundquist in your query-letter," he went on in the same easy manner.

"My maiden name," she said, and felt herself blush. "With my situation being what it is, I don't want my . . . political difficulties to reflect poorly on my husband or my sons. By my using my maiden name, Harold can protect his place at Tulane."

"I thought it might be something of the sort," Szent-Germain told her in a deliberately neutral tone. "If you will be kind enough to tell me what I may do to help you achieve what you are seeking?"

"That's why I'm here," she said, and then tried to explain herself. "Not that I want to impose upon you, but I would like to find a publisher who can produce my work without being in danger from the government. As I told you when I first wrote to you and mentioned my work, I'm aware that many publishers are . . . chary about what topics they consider. Your reply was encouraging, and so I'm hoping you don't feel constrained to follow the example of American university presses. I'd be grateful if you would consider my work for that reason alone, but I have learned that Eclipse Publishing has an enviable reputation, and that adds to my hope that your company will want my book." She patted her briefcase. "I have a copy of my current manuscript here, which I would like to submit to your Editorial Board. I was hoping to discuss that with you, as well as what other sorts of books you are seeking."

"You have more projects in mind?" The flicker of amusement in his dark eyes took the sting out of his question.

"Yes," she admitted. "Several."

"Very wise. It's always useful to have new works in progress. It keeps thoughts fresh." He offered another brief smile. "Will you leave that copy with me? I'll take care to get it to the Board. If it's accepted, we will discuss further works." He got up from the sofa but only to ring for Rogers. "Would you like more coffee, Professor Treat? Or would you prefer Lundquist?"

"Treat will be fine." She was about to say no to the offer of coffee, but changed her mind. "Yes, please." She suddenly felt very vulnerable; she gathered up her courage and went on. "I am in contact with other American academicians who are seeking publication abroad, since they cannot find any editor at home willing to—" She broke off. "May I tell them how to submit manuscripts to your Editorial Board and peer review? For the most part, they're in a similar predicament to mine: trying to do work while improvising a living here in Europe."

His enigmatic gaze rested on her for almost a minute before he said, "I have an information packet that Rogers will give you when you leave. Another pot of coffee for Professor Treat, and more milk." This last was to Rogers, who had come to the open door. "And a copy of our submissions protocol," he added.

"It will be ready when she departs," said Rogers, and went away.

The Grof turned back to her. "Now, if you will tell me a little about your book? Just the barest outlines, if you will—and some idea of its level of scholarship. Do you intend it for university students, or a more general readership?"

"For university level students of history or anthropology," she said. "And perhaps some of the general public with such interests—history buffs and the like."

"And how do you present your material? How academic is your style? Might a well-informed layman be able to read it without difficulty?" He sat back and propped one ankle on his opposite knee; she saw that the soles of his shoes were unfashionably thick, and was diverted by this little vanity; so many short men, she thought, wanted to be tall.

"I hardly know where to start," she said, his inquiry having taken her by surprise.

"Then please begin with the title."

She took a deep breath. "*Social Structures of Communes and Communards in Medieval Europe.* I'm primarily interested in social structures as they relate to folklore and cosmologies of the past, but the difference between Western Medieval societies before the Black Plague and afterward was so compelling that I used this for my work." She paused, then added, "Europe had to reinvent its social structure."

"Compelling," Szent-Germain repeated, recalling the terrible years that began with the first epidemic and the chaos he saw everywhere he went; the Plague continued on for more than a generation through two additional, less catastrophic epidemics, and in the end he had gone to Delhi to avoid the ruin in Europe. "The Black Plague was . . . harrowing," he added. "So few survived."

"But I touch only a little on the Plague itself," she said, a bit defensively.

Szent-Germain's laughter was more sad than mirthful. "But focusing on the communes: no wonder you couldn't find a publisher in America for such a book in these times."

"Exactly," she said, relaxing a bit when he said nothing more. "The Dean of the History Department advised me to burn the master copy and my notes, then refused to consider any paper I submitted for his opinion. The Dean of the Anthropology Department refused to look at it at all. Tulane has been pressured about what they teach, and it isn't the only university to discontinue research if the subject of the research displeases men in high places."

"A prudent notion on the part of the two deans, under the circumstances, but certainly against all the principles of scholarship. I am honored that you decided to approach Eclipse with your work." He held out his hands for the manuscript. "I trust you have other copies, and that they are protected."

"Yes," she told him, a touch of defiance in her posture; she removed the manuscript in its heavy cardstock file from her briefcase and passed it to him. "I have them in the safe at the hotel."

"Very wise. Take care to keep them under lock and key throughout your travels." He got up again and went to put the manuscript in the second drawer of a tall, old-fashioned wooden file cabinet. "As I will here."

She had to fight down a rush of fear as the lock clicked audibly. "Can you let me know how long it will take your Editorial Board to reach a decision? I'm returning to Paris shortly, and I want to know what information you will need to reach me."

"I would say between two and three months for the Board to decide, all things being equal, assuming there is no delay in getting my new presses installed and working. Two of the old ones were reduced to scrap during the war. If there is going to be any delay, Rogers will contact you as soon as possible." He came back to the sofa just as Rogers brought another small tray into the room, set it down and removed the one that was there, then left silently.

"Will you have some, Grof?" she asked, more from good manners than desire to share.

"Alas, no. Coffee does not agree with me." He resumed his place on the sofa. "How long have you been in Europe?"

"Not very long; a little over four weeks," she said, her hand shaking a little as she depressed the plunger.

"You have come alone? Or have you someone waiting for you in Paris?"

There was such gentleness and sympathy in his question that she felt the welling of tears in her eyes; she looked away to conceal them, coughing a little before she answered. "My husband and sons are still in New Orleans. For now, we agree that it is wise for him to remain there. Arthur, my older son, has polio and neither his father nor I believes that his treatment should be interrupted."

He nodded. "How unfortunate for you, Professor Treat. For all of you," he added.

"That's very kind of you." She poured the coffee into the new cup Rogers had left, and added milk from another little jug.

"I do not mean to pry, but I have seen a number of Americans— not all academics—in similar circumstances," he said. "I take it your husband does not teach."

"Most of his work is research, but he does have grad students; he is a soil chemist taking part in a governmental series of experiments; the project is in its fourth year. Had I remained with him, he would most likely have had to leave his job, and might not find work easily." She swallowed hard and lifted her chin. "I've scheduled a call to him this evening."

"Very good," he approved.

She picked up her cup and sipped. "I want to give him some encouragement," she said before she could stop herself.

"About the book? You may certainly tell him that it is under consideration, and that you will have a response by mid-February if all goes well," he said to her. "The Editorial Board will meet just after the new year. I will send a copy to each of the members in a week."

"That should relieve him," she said, and wondered what form that relief might take.

"I cannot yet promise you a contract, for I haven't read your manuscript—oh, yes, I do read what I publish—but your topic is intriguing. I, myself, have some knowledge of those times, and I'm inclined to believe that it is an area of study that has been neglected. Your work will receive close attention: believe this."

"Oh," she said, feeling less nervous with this revelation. "Any location or period in particular? that you have studied?"

"Praha—Prague—during Otakar the Great's reign, and Padova in the decade before the Black Plague, among others," he said. "Would you like to discuss these periods when I return to Paris, if you will still be here?"

"I would be delighted," she said with enthusiasm. "How long will you be gone?"

"Ten to fourteen days, or that is presently my plan," he said, and saw her face fall. "I'll be in Amsterdam for a week; Eclipse Publishing Amsterdam is also getting new presses installed, and I expect to be there for the event; beyond that, I cannot anticipate how long I will need to remain with the various branches of my company. After Amsterdam, I have business in Venice, including a branch of Eclipse Publishing. I'll be in Paris after that, and keep you abreast of any changes in my plans." He watched her more closely than she knew, and saw the little moue of disappointment touch her mouth. "I will have to be in Paris for three weeks in November. Perhaps we might meet then?"

She restored her calm. "I'd like that very much." Then she chuckled at her own confusion. "I'm sorry, I shouldn't have put you on the spot like that," she said, and took another, longer sip of milky coffee. "Be good enough to chalk it up to my American ways."

"Hardly on the spot," he said, and continued genially, "I've been to your country, you know, and have some understanding of American ways. I was there shortly before war broke out. I drove from Chicago to San Francisco. It's quite a remarkable place."

Mentally chastising herself, she said, "Which crossing did you use? Forty? Sixty-six?"

"Forty," he answered.

"Then you haven't seen the Gulf Coast," she said.

"No, which is unfortunate," he confessed, and, after a brief pause, remarked, "You will pardon me for saying it, but your accent does not seem to be of the American South. I would have supposed you came from Illinois, perhaps, or Michigan."

"Neither. I was born in Colorado, but grew up in Madison, Wisconsin. My dad taught at the University of Wisconsin. I did my doctoral studies at Chicago, and taught at Wake Forest in North Carolina for two years. Someone in the southern academic grapevine recommended me to Tulane. I've been on the faculty there for nearly a decade." She coughed once, afraid she might sob instead, and resolutely went on, "As a Coloradan, I have to know what you thought of the Rockies."

"Even an old Transylvanian like me must be impressed with the Rockies, and the Pacific Ocean."

"Transylvanian?"

"Romanian, if you like. In the east end of the central plateau of the Carpathian Mountains, to be more specific," he said.

"The USSR holds that territory, don't they?" she asked, then put her hand to her mouth, finally saying, "I'm sorry. I didn't mean—"

"For now, the Russians are in charge. The Hungarians have been several times before, and the Ottomans. The Romans gave the country its name, but the Daci were there before them, as were many others." He met her eyes with his own steady gaze. "These things change, with time."

"You're an"—she tried to choose a more polite term, but could not—"exile?"

"For most of my life," he said.

"I'm so sorry," she responded. "No wonder you understand my situation." As soon as she said it, she flushed with embarrassment. "I wish I could say something more comforting."

"You need not," he answered. "I'm used to it." He shrugged and changed the subject. "Shall I let you know when I plan to arrive in Paris?"

She nodded. "If you would, please."

"If you will provide an address to Rogers before you leave? Thank you." He rose. "It has been a pleasure to meet you, Professor Treat. I must thank you for coming to Eclipse Press before seeking out another publisher." He saw the astonished look in her eyes. "Well, you have not been in Europe very long, so what should I think than that Eclipse was your first choice?" With a half-bow, he took a step away. "I am sorry, but I must leave. Do finish your coffee. Zoltan will drive you back to your hotel whenever you like."

She watched him cross the entry-hall and vanish down a corridor on the far side of it. She sighed, trying to decide if she had succeeded or failed in this most perplexing interview. She wished she knew what to make of Grof Szent-Germain, and almost at once frowned as she strove to come up with a description she could offer to Harold when they spoke that evening. Twenty minutes later, as she left Eclipse Publishing, she had convinced herself that the less she said, the better it would be.

October 19, 1949

Dear Cousin Moira,

Uncle Howard asked me to send you news of the family, so I'm doing it. He's afraid his mail's being opened, and he doesn't want to expose you and Tim to any more trouble than you're already in. We've heard that the CIA is after you. Uncle Howard told me to ask you again if you wanted to send Regina to him and Aunt Clarise. He's worried about her schooling, you know, and says that he will be glad to act as her guardian as long as you and Tim are away. Uncle Howard says he's still trying to find a lawyer who'll take your case for something less than a ten-thousand-dollar fee. Who has ten thousand dollars they can spare? No luck so far, but he's going to keep looking. He wants the family to kick in something to help you and your family out. It doesn't seem fair that you have to stay in Europe just because you can't get a good lawyer. If criminals can do it, you should be able to, shouldn't you? It's not like you robbed a bank.

The Thanksgiving's going to be at Uncle Frederick's this year, in Raleigh. He remarried last August as you should know, and he's eager to have the family meet Alexis, get to know her. Mom tells me that she doesn't know if we should attend, given the uproar there's been about their marriage, Alexis being a Catholic and all. I think she's being too fussy, but several of the family members share her feelings. Uncle Clay has already said he and Doreen can't make it, and Uncle Frederick thinks this means *that Uncle Clay doesn't approve of his new wife. There's an uproar in the making. I'll tell you how it turns out.*

I made the swim-team at last; I'll be competing in the butterfly. They're starting girls' swim meets with some of the other high schools in the district, and I volunteered for them. They took me! Ward Springer High School has had a new pool built and they're upgrading the main building and adding a real auditorium, which means for now, half our classes are in trailers. The new buildings should be ready by the time I graduate. Everyone says it's worth it, but it feels strange to go to school in a trailer. I'm taking Math and English and American History and Home Economics and French. PE is swimming, of course. And there's a study hall every day. Next year we get Science instead of American History. Principal Houghton is very excited about Science, saying it is the wave of the future, and half of the Board of Education agrees with him. In my junior year, we'll have a choice of Biology or Chemistry.

Grandfather Larkin has been doing poorly. He's having heart trouble, and his doctor says he's not going to be around much longer. Mom and Uncle Clay have hired a housekeeper for him, and there's a nurse who checks on him once a week. He's almost 64, and that's a respectably long life—everyone says so, even Grandfather Larkin. Mom's upset, but he is her father after all, so what else would she be. She says she may go spend some time with him while she can.

Henry Lee is in fourth grade now, and being rascally. Mom has tried to get him to mind his manners, but no luck so far. The neighbors said that he killed a cat out in the woods behind our houses, but Henry Lee says he didn't, and you know Mom will stand by her son come rain or shine. Daddy is a little less certain, but he isn't about to take the neighbors' side against his own flesh and blood. I don't know what's going on with him, but you could probably figure it out. You're a psychologist, aren't you? You'd know what to do to make him behave. I know you can't come back right now, but it would sure be helpful if you could.

I went to see The Red Shoes, *and thought of you the whole time, and not just because of Moira Shearer. Daddy said it's not possible to film ballet well, but I think he's wrong about that. You should go see it if you get the chance. I also saw* The Third Man *and I can't understand what the fuss is all about. I don't suppose spies are really like that, not even in Europe. I like Orson Welles, though. He's not a dreamboat like Clark Gable, but he's got something about him. Maybe it's his reputation for getting into trouble, or maybe it's his voice. You have to look at him, and hear him. Daddy says he's arrogant and irresponsible—there was that* War of the Worlds *broadcast—but maybe he's a genius, too.*

I'm not supposed to ask what you've been doing to keep body and soul together, but if you want to tell me, I'd like to know. I can't imagine what it must be like for you and Cousin Tim. I won't tell any of the family—or anyone else.

We've been to the VA hospital to see Dennis Crowder; he's got a prosthetic leg and hand, and they've done more operations on his face, but he still looks like something out of a bad movie. He puts on a good front, but it's obvious that he is really down in the dumps about his injuries, and his prospects. He told me he doesn't know what he'll do with himself for the rest of his life. No one's going to hire him, he's certain of that.

Cousin Emily is going to have her baby next month, or so her doctor says. She may be having twins. Claude is pleased as punch, but Emily only wants it to be over. She waddles like a duck and her feet and ankles look like rising dough most of the time. After four years of marriage, everyone was beginning to wonder, but the way things look now, they're making up for lost time. Emily says she likes it in Florida except for the bugs. Claude got a promotion when they moved, so he's pleased.

Anyway, this should catch you up. Daddy's tucked in a note to you, as you can see. I hope you have a happy Thanksgiving and a Merry Christmas. We're all looking forward to the day you can come home again all of you.

Love,
Your cousin, Betty-Ann

❖ 2 ❖

By mid-morning, a squall came whipping up the Adriatic, the sea churning and frothing as it swept into the lagoon, stirring up the canals that made Venezia famous; boats of all sizes and purposes rocked in the surging water, a few of them banging against their narrow berths or the walls of houses as an accompaniment to the bluster of the wind. In his palazzo, Szent-Germain closed and shuttered his windows, then turned on the lamps over the extensive trestle table where he was working; the generator behind his laboratory in what had been a dovecote made a steady purr. It had been a demanding few days for Szent-Germain, for he wanted to keep his work from dragging on another week, forcing him to delay his departure once again: just now he was grateful for an hour or two dedicated to alchemy instead of the installation of an additional press at the Venezian branch of Eclipse Publishing, or devoting himself to the intricacies of Venezian business law. There had been too many things demanding his attention, and now he needed some privacy. The day had turned cold and damp, and although he was not often troubled by temperature, he had donned a black wool roll-top pullover and a fashionably cut Milanese sport-coat of black alpaca; the fabric had been a gift from Madelaine de Montalia when she returned from Cuzco, and the tailor who made it had waxed lyrical over the soft, light, warm cloth. His black slacks were the handiwork of his British tailor of a wool-and-Angora blend; his thick-soled shoes were made in Firenze of black leather, and fitted more like gloves than shoes.

"My master?" Rogers called from outside the door; he spoke in the dialect of northern Italy. "I am sorry to interrupt you, but you have a visitor."

"Who is it?" Szent-Germain asked as he set his box of newly made gold in the safe beneath the table. He could still feel some residual warmth through the bronze-and-brass box. "I gather this is a stranger."

"Someone from the American Department of State," Rogers replied. "His card says William C. Bereston, United States of America Department of State, Undersecretary for International Film and Publication for Western Europe. He said he's hoping to regularize dealings with American and European copyright conventions."

Szent-Germain stood up, dusted off the fine residual powder from the gold, and went to open the door. "Film and Publication—that's a new approach," he mused, turning out the overhead light. "Where did you put this William C. Bereston?"

"In the library, as usual," Rogers said.

"From your manner, you would seem to doubt Mister Bereston's credentials, old friend," Szent-Germain remarked as he stepped out of his laboratory to join Rogers in the corridor; he closed and locked the door.

"Not his credentials so much as his purpose for coming to you; he's too open and genial by half," said Rogers. "There is something *off* about him; it's not obvious, but it's there—you'll see what I mean. It's not that he smiles a great deal—Americans do that—it's something else."

Szent-Germain gave a single nod. "You have a keen sense for deception, and if you perceive it here, as I gather you do, what makes you think that William Bereston is not what he claims to be?"

Rogers, who had been speaking English, continued in Byzantine Greek. "There is a . . . quality of furtiveness about him. He insisted on hanging up his own hat and overcoat. He looks about as if he were planning to rob the fine things you have. They're little things, but they don't ring true." He shook his head. "Oh, I have no doubt that he serves his country in some capacity—he may even be functioning through the Department of State—but in an ancillary fashion."

"A spy, then?" Szent-Germain suggested in the same language.

"Or some other sort of clandestine operative," Rogers said as they went toward the front staircase to descend to the main floor.

"What other sort is there?" Szent-Germain asked, an ironic note in his voice.

"Think of Telemachus Batsho," Rogers reminded him.

"Why would an American bureaucrat seek me out? What does he think I can do for him?" Szent-Germain sounded weary; there had been so many times when people had come looking for him, with good or ill intentions, and most of those instances had been disruptive in one way or another. "Unless it is as you say, and he is some manner of operative and has a specific assignment to fulfill, which is another matter entirely." He thought briefly of the early part of the century when he himself was given a clandestine mission by Czar Nicholas of Russia; in spite of his best efforts, the assignment had failed.

"He may have questions about your time in America," Rogers warned.

"Why?" As he asked, a number of troublesome possibilities rose in his mind, and recollections of Srau, of Rhea, of Gennaro Emerenzio, of Colombius of Malta, of—he made himself stop; he gave his attention to Rogers.

"He may want to discover your vulnerabilities," Rogers said.

"That could be a problem for Rowena; I'll book a phone-call with the exchange, and let her know, so she can decide how to proceed," Szent-Germain said, casting his thoughts back to his pleasant reunion with the artist in San Francisco shortly before the outbreak of World War II, and more than twenty-five years after their first affaire in Amsterdam in the years before World War II.

"Among others," Rogers said. "Oscar King should be told as well, for the Pietragnellis as well as the properties in San Francisco. We don't know who is keeping an eye on any of them, and that is worrisome. Possibly sending letters from a name unknown, so that there will be no alerts among the watchers, to protect your associates and other Americans who have dealings with you."

"You're right; and perhaps letters to the Canadian branches of Eclipse as well," Szent-Germain said thoughtfully. "They're bound to feel the pressure from the United States. It's a shame that it should come to this, whatever *this* may be."

"It is," Rogers said, his austere features revealing little of his thoughts.

Szent-Germain stared into the distance for a long moment, then said in English, "There's no use to borrow trouble. I'd best find out what the man wants."

Rogers nodded. "It is unfortunate," he said in Italian, then went on in English, "He may have questions about the current state of Eclipse Publishing, and little more than that."

"He may, but neither you nor I believes that," said Szent-Germain in a tone that revealed his doubt; he went on in Byzantine Greek. "Have you ordered Arrigo to prepare some hors d'oeuvres for this William C. Bereston? Or perhaps breakfast would be more appropriate, hearty enough to assure him of his welcome, but not too overwhelming. Best set up the morning room for our discussion: there's bound to be one, by the sound of it." They were halfway down the stairs, on the broad landing that looked down on the loggia, and the canal beyond. The floor was inlaid marble in a complex pattern of Baroque swirls, and the walls glowed with gold-leaf murals of Venezian history.

"No reason to keep it secret," Rogers said in English. "It is taken care of. I have Arrigo readying something suitable, and sent Ettore to open a bottle of Burgundy from your larger French vineyard." He smiled briefly.

"I needn't have asked; accept my apologies," said Szent-Germain, slipping his ring of keys into an inner pocket of his jacket. "Is there any reason to think that Mister Bereston will refuse our hospitality?"

"He may refuse the wine." Rogers took a moment to consider this. "You know how Americans are about abstaining while working."

"None better," Szent-Germain said in English, and resumed his descent. "Geyserville showed us what Prohibition had done to those making beer and wine and stronger liquors, and many of the citizens approved the idea if not the reality."

"And that is seen in more than what had become of the wineries," said Rogers. "Shall I have a fire lit in the morning room? There's one already laid."

"If you would. It's going to be clammy in there if there's no fire."

He and Rogers parted company at the foot of the stairs, and Szent-Germain went along to his library. He opened the door and found a tawny-brown-haired man in his late twenties, in an American-cut suit of navy blue looking over his shelves, his brows drawn down in distress. "Mister Bereston? I am Ragoczy Ferenz, Grof Szent-Germain. What may I do for you?"

Bereston rounded on him, his open face and boyish smile concealing any hint of mendacious or sinister purpose, or the reason for his disapproval of the library. "Grof. A pleasure." He held out his hand, and shook Szent-Germain's heartily, all the while displaying an eager smile that did not reach his eyes. "Thank you for seeing me. I know this visit is unexpected, but you have been on the move these last ten days."

"And I will be again shortly; I leave for Paris the day after tomorrow," Szent-Germain said, wondering if it had been a slip of the tongue or a disguised threat for Bereston to admit that he had been tracing Szent-Germain's travels. "Restoring my publishing company's branches is turning out to be a demanding task, and it will not happen without me. I'm sorry if this disaccommodates you, but such is the nature of business."

"Yes," said Bereston, the smile vanishing as quickly as a magician's silk scarf. "That's one of the things I wish to speak with you about: your publishing companies. We have some questions for you, and better to ask them now than later." His sunny face clouded, and the corners of his mouth twitched downward for an instant.

"My publishing companies?" he echoed with an urbane smile. "Now why?"

"Among other things, I said. I understand you have a shipping business as well." His face was once again as guileless as a puppy's.

Szent-Germain regarded Bereston levelly. "Yes, I have. I have five offices in your country, and two dozen or so around the rest of the world. I'm still learning if a few of the more remote ones survived the war." That was an underestimation, but he knew the actual figure would have Bereston on the alert, and that could lead to problems for all his agents and factors. "A few of the branches I used to have are now in the hands of foreign governments which incline to be unfriendly to some of the recent alliances that are emerging from the war. When all of these new treaties are ratified, we'll proceed as best we can." *As you are probably aware,* he added to himself.

"An unfortunate turn of events, no doubt, though you are far from the only businessman to find himself in such a position. This is particularly true of men like you, engaged in international enterprises. There was so much subterfuge during the war that for many it is now a custom. You have much to contend with. I understand that: it's why I'm here. Communists are grabbing all the fruits of international finance they can reach, in spite of their endorsement of Marxist ideology and the philosophy it proposes," said Bereston, "to say nothing of how rapidly they are hoping to extend their sphere of influence."

"As the Fascists and Nazis did before them," Szent-Germain said.

"In some parts of the world more so than others. We can certainly agree on that. It is another development for us to discuss." There was an eagerness to his agreement that was subtly wrong.

"And the US is paying them back tit . . . for tat," Szent-Germain observed with a wry smile that was at odds with his dismayed eyes.

"Nothing so capricious, I assure you." He looked around the library, all signs of disapproval gone from his countenance. "An enviable collection, Grof, if you don't mind my saying so," he exclaimed, glancing over the line of spines along the west wall. "You have some treasures here."

"Not at all; I am pleased with it myself," Szent-Germain told him, starting toward the door. "My chef is laying out a small meal in the morning room, if you would like something to eat, or drink."

"That's very kind of you," said Bereston, following half-a-step behind Szent-Germain. "You don't have to."

"But I do; as a sign of good fellowship," Szent-Germain said, a sardonic glint in his eyes. "A light meal, a glass of wine to mark this meeting—"

Bereston scowled, then smiled. "As to drink, I don't touch alcohol when I am working."

"If you'd rather not have wine, so be it," he said, as if he himself planned such a libation. "Coffee or tea or hot chocolate are available if you would prefer—" Szent-Germain saw Bereston nod. "Coffee or—"

"Coffee will do, thanks. No need to make a fuss," he said, an underlying testiness to his words.

"Breakfast is hardly a fuss."

Bereston's reticence vanished as if by the flip of a switch; he offered another of his open smiles. "Now that's most generous of you, Grof. I'd be most grateful. I admit I'm peckish. It's nice of you to think of it."

"One way or another, everyone must eat, Mister Bereston," said Szent-Germain, the ironic note in his voice unrecognized by Bereston.

"True enough, Grof. Thanks. I'll take you up on it." He walked a short way in silence, then stopped, looking at a painting hanging near the entrance to the withdrawing room. "Very handsome," he approved. "Renaissance, isn't it?"

"The *Semele*? Yes, it is. It has been in my family for roughly five centuries." He recalled the dreadful day when Alessandro di Mariano dei Filipepi had burned his own paintings in the full view of all Fiorenzani; San Germanno, as he was known then, had pleaded with the painter not to do this, but Botticelli—his commonly used nick-name—had refused to listen, so San Germanno had stolen it from among the stack of his friend's work, and kept it in Venezia, out of sight, for two hundred years, and even now hung it inconspicuously.

"So you collect art as well as books?" Bereston's sudden frown lasted a short while, then faded away.

"Musical instruments, some furniture, ceramics, small sculptures, old scientific supplies, you know how it is when you've been through difficulties," he said, opening the door to the morning room and motioning to Bereston to enter.

The chamber faced northeast. It contained a rosewood table with room for six, eight chairs, a small sideboard, a hanging lantern as well as three floor-lamps; four tall windows opened on the Campo

San Luca, revealing the Romanesque church that gave the campo its name, the narrow bridge at the end of the campo that arched over an old, narrow canal to a broad walkway along the edge of the canal and the rear wall of the Ca' Tedeschi Viaggiator', and the roof of the small Crusaders' chapel, Santissimi Evangelisti, now empty and rumored to be for sale. The campo was almost constantly in shadow, and was so now, even with a faint trace of sunlight angling in the morning-room windows; two hours ago the room had been full of misty Venezian light; just at present, the reflection of the waters of the canal on the walls of the chapel looked like charcoal sketches.

"Very handsome; you're a real connoisseur, aren't you, Grof? How did you manage to get through the war without losing it all? Or is that something you'd rather not talk about?" Bereston prompted as he took a quick turn around the room. "Classical and Baroque, or I miss my guess."

"For the most part," Szent-Germain told him, going to pull the velvet draperies across the windows to keep the distraction of the storm from becoming more disruptive. "In half an hour, the worst of the storm should be over. We may even have a little sunlight."

"If there is any more sun today, this squall will keep the sky dark for hours, once it gets down to business. It's just warming up, " said Bereston with an uneasy glance at the windows. He went to the newly lit fire and studied the mantel and frame of the fireplace. "Another antique?"

"It was already in place when I bought the palazzo, so I assume it must be," said Szent-Germain as he drew out a chair for Bereston that faced a place-setting of fine porcelain china and grand French silverware; he went around the table and drew out the opposite chair for himself. "If you will, have a seat at the table, Mister Bereston. Arrigo should bring a breakfast for you soon."

Doing his utmost to conceal his impatience, Bereston sat down at the table and nodded his approval. "I gather many of your forefathers have gone in for collecting?"

Szent-Germain smiled. "It's in the blood," he said, and turned to ask Arrigo to come in. "In buon' punto, Arrigo."

The chef carried a tray with two covered dishes upon it, and a pot of coffee. He placed the smaller of the two dishes directly in front of Bereston, the larger across the top of his place-setting as if constructing a barricade for the food. Lastly, he tugged the artfully rolled napkin from the water-glass, gave it an expert shake, and dropped it into Bereston's lap. He bowed respectfully to Szent-Germain's guest before doing the same to the Grof.

"Grazie," Szent-Germain said to the chef as he left the room.

"Well, what have we here?" Bereston asked, lifting the lid on the smaller bowl and inhaling the aroma that rose with the released steam.

"Unless I miss my guess, you have two eggs coddled and served in fish-broth," said Szent-Germain. "And there is probably fruit compote on chopped smoked ham in polenta in the second dish."

"Um," said Bereston, not at all sure how to proceed.

"You'll want to eat the eggs first, before they become hard—that is, unless you like hard-coddled eggs?"

Bereston removed the lid and stared at the two eggs floating in amber-colored liquid. "The ideas you Europeans have about break-fast."

Szent-Germain leaned back in his chair. "If you would rather have oatmeal and bacon-and-eggs with toast and coffee, Arrigo will make it for you."

"Not necessary, Grof." Warily, Bereston took the soup-spoon provided for this dish and pushed one of the eggs to the bottom of the bowl to cut it open. "Smells good." He tried a spoonful, looked a bit surprised, and had more. "This is really quite tasty," he said. "The bacon-and-eggs can wait this time." He grinned and went back to the eggs-in-broth. "Aren't you having any?"

"I've broken my fast already," said Szent-Germain, who had spent most of the previous night with the widow of an engineer in an apartment that overlooked San Gregorio. "Buon appetito."

"Then you won't mind if I don't wait for you," said Bereston, giving attention to his food.

Szent-Germain watched him for a short while, and when Beres-ton had finished his poached eggs, he said, "I believe you want to enlist me in your work because of my branches in America. As I am sure you know, I have branches of Eclipse Press in your country: three of them, in Boston, in St. Louis, and in San Francisco. Eventually I would like to have one in New Orleans. I have a branch in Toronto, as well."

"Yes, I have that information." His chuckle had an angry note in it, although he went on as if he wanted only to seek Szent-Germain's endorsement of his work. "I must admit I wasn't sure you'd be direct with me. I've dealt with Europeans who refused to disclose or confirm any of what I know of them, but you are forthright; I appreciate your candor about your presses. It saves us all kinds of awkwardness." Bereston put the bowl aside and reached for the larger dish, setting the lid on its back with care. "And that you have branches in many other cities, both in Europe and the Orient. Another one of your grandfathers' projects, I imagine. Your ancestors seem most fortunate in their investing."

"Most provident," Szent-Germain murmured, thinking of the many times this had not been the case. He gazed toward the window. "We had to close our press in what they now call Leningrad some years before the last war began."

"I have a memo about that. It must have been a difficult loss." He picked up his fork, tested the firmness of the polenta, then took a first small bite. "Was this fried?"

"Baked," Szent-Germain told him. "The ham, herbs, and polenta are mixed while the polenta is still soft, then put in a ceramic baking dish and finished in the oven at medium-low heat, and the compote added when the dish is taken out of the oven. There is a peppermill on the sideboard, if you—"

Bereston looked startled. "You know a lot about cooking. There's no end to your information."

"It helps to be familiar with the workings of one's household, Mister Bereston." Szent-Germain regarded his guest with polite curiosity.

"Golly, I should think so," Bereston concurred. "You're not here a lot of the time, are you? You need to have a very trustworthy staff."

"It's advantageous, then, that I have one," Szent-Germain said.

"Been with you long?" Bereston asked this innocently enough, but there was something in his eyes that reminded Szent-Germain of Rogers' warning: something was *off* about William C. Bereston, something illusive, but unmistakable. The man was dangerous.

"Some of them have served my blood for generations," said Szent-Germain with perfect honesty.

"That European thing again." Bereston tried his coffee, added cream, tasted it again, and smiled. "Not that I mean any disrespect."

"You're right: it is that European thing, as you call it. Such arrangements take generations to put in place."

"Ever regretted trusting your servants?"

Thinking back over more than two millennia, Szent-Germain said, "Not often, and not recently."

Whatever it was that Bereston was fishing for, he apparently had the answer now; he took some of the polenta onto his fork. "With a breakfast like this, I can skip lunch."

Szent-Germain once again waited while Bereston ate; only when he laid down his fork and napkin did Szent-Germain ask, "What is it that you want to discuss, specifically? Since you have called here without arranging to visit, I think it must need urgent attention. You said something about copyrights?"

"Well, yes." He took a deep breath and began, "As you saw from my card—I assume your man gave it to you—I'm with the Department of State, doing some initial spadework on forming a more comprehensive international copyright convention, one that can apply parity to all countries signatory to it, and enforceable throughout those countries signing the convention. There are countries in the world which have endured real damage to all of their financial institutions because of the war, all of which organizations need to be rebuilt, along with the industries that will support the economic goals of the countries; one of the tasks assigned to the Department of State is to encourage the publishing and film businesses in countries where such institutions have been greatly damaged. Those who are not inclined to join with us can anticipate difficulties getting their publications into American markets. We will work to restore print and film as quickly as possible, and you, with your business still largely intact, can provide us the support that should lend us the prestige that many countries feel we lack. We have, for example, excused the Japanese from observing copyright restrictions with American publications until such time as their publishing industry is once again fully functional."

"How do your allies see this gesture?" Szent-Germain asked as if he lacked interest in the answer, and were unaware of the threat Bereston's explanations contained.

"Well, we have hopes that you might be able to explain our position to your associates in Europe. There is some dissatisfaction, as you might expect. The Czechs, for example, want to put education before any other considerations, and are pushing for full access to textbooks."

"You're supposing that I am held in high regard among my fellow-publishers, and that my opinion would make a difference," said Szent-Germain.

"As to that, we know you are; even those who envy you speak well of you." He paused to empty the last of his coffee into his cup. "This gives us an opportunity to regularize problems that are the result of various conditions for and lengths of copyrights. It could simplify the publishing business in a large part of the world." He sighed and drank the last of his creamy coffee.

"I think that would be useful for all of us," said Szent-Germain in a carefully neutral voice.

"That's what I hoped you'd say." Leaning forward and planting his elbows on either side of his empty plate, he launched into what sounded like a rehearsed speech. "We—the Allies who won the war—have a responsibility to do what we can to get the world back on its feet; it's part of the price of victory. Publishing and motion pictures are an important part of that push to restoration. It also encourages the exchange of expression and ideas, which in turn can bring about opportunities for intercultural goodwill through communications and art. We believe that publishing and motion pictures can play a crucial role in this project."

"They can," Szent-Germain said without inflection.

Bereston looked nonplussed. "How can you doubt it?"

"I only wonder how other governments will view your efforts." He held up his hand and went on without permitting Bereston to interject anything. "Many may think that your intentions are more political than cultural, and reject your project out of hand for that reason."

"The same could be true of those who participate in our attempts." There was an obstinate set to his jaw and his eyes narrowed.

"That brings us to the heart of the matter: do you plan to accept propaganda as part of arts and letters, or are you planning to impose conditions on these contrivances? And how are you to identify what is literature and what is propaganda? That will need to be defined to all parties' satisfaction if you are truly concerned about that. Not all countries have your admirable First Amendment to protect unpopular opinion, and without such a check on the degree to which a government can control the information accessible to its citizens, the more likely it is that information will become propaganda, and stifle innovation in thought. It has happened many times before and it is likely to happen again." He nodded once. "You know, I admire your Constitution, which I made a point of studying while I was visiting your country shortly before the war."

"That's interesting," said Bereston, making a quick recovery from his surprise. "What do you think of our notion, a man in your position, titled and all?"

"I am also an exile, Mister Bereston; my title is merely a courtesy now. It is useful in getting good seats at the opera and prompt attention at the bank." This was not quite accurate but near enough to the truth to make his answer acceptable. "I think your Constitution is a laudable document, and I hope many of its principles are embraced by other countries, but I also know that not all countries seek that manner of order among their own peoples," said Szent-Germain. "Writers and publishers need the protection your First Amendment provides, but it must apply to all to have any lasting impact, wouldn't you say?"

"We like to think so, though we are careful about what we decide to publish. With all the turmoil in the world, we have a responsibility not to add to it," said Bereston, his demeanor more tense, his eyes hard upon his host. "But it takes time to prepare to offer such protections."

Now Szent-Germain was being very watchful, although little changed in his outward manner. "How could that be? What preparation is there needed?"

Bereston gave a small cough. "There are subjects that, even with freedom of speech, need to be approached with utmost caution, especially in times like these, when, as you say, much propaganda is presented to the public in the guise of art. You must be aware, Grof, that the irresponsible distribution of social theories and financial schemes can only bring about dissension and unrest; this is a ticklish time in our dealings with Europe, and we must proceed with care. We're aware of that. Such material as might contribute to social turmoil must be handled circumspectly, some tracts and analyses delayed, and a few rejected for the good of the people. For everyone's benefit."

"I don't see that," said Szent-Germain, still speaking affably. "Nothing in the language of the First Amendment suggests that such standards can be imposed on original thought and its distribution. Such restrictions obviate all the guarantees of the Constitution." He reached out and picked up a small brass bell which he rang.

"It's not in the specific language, but it is *implied* by other provisions in the Constitution, and it is the policy of the United States to adhere to decisions that support the public good rather than encouraging—"

"—irresponsibility, yes, I heard you." He looked up as Rogers came into the room. "Be good enough to bring our guest another pot of coffee, if you would."

"With cream?" Rogers inquired.

"Yes." He turned back to Bereston. "I'm sorry you aren't interested in something stronger, but I surmise that the purpose of your visit makes it unwise to risk the slightest clouding of your intellect."

"It is an important issue, and deserves the whole of my concentration," Bereston said curtly. "I don't know how to explain it to you, Grof, but if you have any hope of working with American publishers—as I and others trust you do—then we must determine the sorts of work you are planning to introduce to our people." He sighed and sat more stiffly in his chair. "It isn't easy for those of you who are devoted to the European way of life to comprehend how we Americans understand the limits of freedom."

"The limits of freedom," Szent-Germain repeated. "An . . . interesting concept."

There was a blustery gust of wind that set the shutters to rattling.

"You understand the reasons for it, surely?" Bereston said, his face a mask of goodwill. "Precarious governments will need to protect their populations from—"

"I'm afraid I don't—understand the reasons," said Szent-Germain. "Perhaps I have not grasped your purpose in all this?" He spoke mildly, but he was aware of Bereston's antagonism behind his smile.

"If you can spare me an hour, I'll be more than happy to explain it to you in detail," Bereston offered.

"Alas, I think not," said Szent-Germain, as courteously as if he approved. "Since I have plans to go to Amsterdam, then to Copenhagen, and Paris in the next two weeks, I haven't the time to give your venture the close attention it deserves. When I return here, we can set up an appointment for a proper discussion."

"If that's all you're willing to do, why didn't you refuse to see me?" Bereston demanded, then visibly calmed himself.

"I had insufficient information to know whether or not to hear you out; you will agree that your business card provides very little about your work beyond the most elementary outline. I am not a credulous man, Mister Bereston, and I would need much more than your assurances to support this plan you are planning to impose upon the world. It *is* the world you're aiming for, isn't it." He rose. "If you will let Rogers know when you will be available for a meeting after I return, then I will have a better idea of your undertaking, and will be more prepared to respond to your plans appropriately."

Bereston glowered briefly, then forced his face into yet another smile. "If that's the best you can—" He stopped, and when he spoke again it was calmly, with what might have been a touch of self-deprecating humor. "I made a mess of this, didn't I? And you've been so courteous. Okay. We'll talk later, when you return from Paris and I'm back from Washington."

"Very good." He held out his hand. "I have to bid you good-bye for now. Rogers will see you out when you're ready to go. If you want to remain where you are until you have had the last of your coffee, my staff will be pleased to accommodate you." He inclined his head, then left the morning room.

Rogers was waiting for him at the edge of the loggia. "What have you learned?" he asked in Egyptian Coptic.

Szent-Germain answered in the same language. "He's up to something; you're right about that."

"What would you like me to do?"

After the greater part of a minute in thought, Szent-Germain said, "I don't know yet. Let me think about it."

October 27, 1949

D. *Philetus Rothcoe*
Hotel Saint-Sulpice
Room 34
17, Rue de Saule
Liege, Belgium

Dear Phil,
    This is my preliminary assessment on the group known as the Ex-Pats' Coven, operating out of Paris, with members in France, England, the Netherlands, Belgium, Spain, and Switzerland whom we have positively identified. I send this to you now so that you may inform me of what you would like me to pursue before I submit my year-end evaluation of their activities and their capacity to do our diplomacy harm.
    You have already asked me to help identify any members of this group who have business and personal connections to any European doing business in the United States. I have enclosed a list for your perusal. Let me draw your attention to Boris King, who has a number of relatives in Belgium and France, who is rumored to have fled the Russian Revolution at the end of W W I; I personally doubt the story—it's too pat, but in case you run into one of Broadstreet's crowd, bear this in mind; they think spying ought to be like the movies. Also, you may be interested in the meeting between Grof Szent-Germain and Charis Treat in Copen-

hagen earlier this month. As far as I can determine, Doctor Treat has submitted a manuscript to Eclipse Press for publication, and that would seem to be the extent of her ventures there. A few of the rest of the so-called Coven are looking into the possibility of publication with Eclipse, even though Professor Treat has received no response in regard to her manuscript so far, but it is generally acknowledged that Eclipse takes an average of four months to decide on any title, according to their own catalogues. Others in the Ex-Pats' Coven may follow her example, but again, there appears to be no political or philosophical connection, only a simple attempt to have a work published. Given the group's circumstances, you cannot be surprised that they seek publishers. What the work may contain, and how it is to be distributed if it is contracted for, I cannot say, and it may be a moot point if the manuscript is rejected. The same goes for the rest of the Coven.

I have a copy of Paul Blount's report on the Ex-Pats' Coven based on the two months he was allowed to participate in their Parisian meetings. I would advise you to bear in mind that Paul is very annoyed that he was so quickly identified as a spy in their midst, and is blaming others for his failings; I wouldn't put much credence in his assertions that the Coven gets its orders from Moscow, though most of the Coven are in favor of socialism as a way of providing economic parity for all those participating in it. Blount's ticked off because he isn't going out on a win, and this is his way of pouting.

Is there any way you could get our department to extend my assignment here until May, or longer? I don't want to be posted back to Washington quite yet, not while we have so many unresolved cases before us. I am certain I am making some headway with Tolliver Bethune, and that should gain us valuable intelligence. Bethune, aside from being part of the Ex-Pats' Coven, has other connections as well that are most promising. Give me six more months—eight if you can manage it—and I know you won't regret it. I, too, would like to leave on a win, and as you may not be aware, I'll be retiring on the 1ˢᵗ of January, 1951. I don't like the feeling that I've spent the last five years spinning my wheels with intra-agency cat-fights. The war felt worthwhile, bloody yet the right thing to do, but so much of what we're dealing with now is petty—like changing the Central Intelligence Group to the Central Intelligence Agency? Please tell me when have better use we can make of our time. I wonder what Wild Bill Donovan thought of that little fracas.

From this end, the bomb that blew up that bus in Grenoble was confirmed as Jimmy Riggs' work. He's left Europe by now, of course, and is back lounging on a beach in Mexico. That man truly loves to blow things up, doesn't he?

Wishing you a happy Thanksgiving, although we're far from home, and the joys of Christmas and the New Year,

Sincerely,
Nate
(Nathan S. Waters)

NSW/js
enclosures

❖ 3 ❖

A pair of barges were dredging at the far end of the canal, pulling up the broken remains of shallow-draft attack boats that had lain on the bottom of the canal for a decade, and were now being removed as a traffic hazard. Amsterdam looked like a sepia print in the veils of fog that shrouded the city, blending with the water, still as a whisper. In his office on the ground floor of his canal-side house, Szent-Germain was gazing out the window at the barges, his thoughts on the comments on Charis Treat's manuscript that he had received from three of his five reviewers. So far the reports were generally favorable, which pleased him for several reasons, not the least of which was that the accuracy of her depictions of communes brought back many memories of Padova and Saunt-Cyr and Montaubine. He took a sheet of cream-laid writing paper with the Eclipse Press letterhead from his desk drawer, removed his Mont Blanc pen from his waistcoat-pocket, unscrewed its cap, and began to write in his small, flowing, precise script:

2 November, 1949

Professor Charis Treat
Hotel Louis XII
23 Rue d'Ete Blanche
Paris, France

My dear Professor Treat,
  Despite my delays, for which I apologize, I am at last bound for Paris. I would appreciate it if you would be willing to join me at dinner on November 10th at eight o'clock to discuss your manuscript. If this is not convenient, will you advise me on when and where you would prefer to meet? If you have a favorite restaurant, I would be pleased to reserve a table for us on the date of your

choosing at the hour you select. I plan to be in Paris through the New Year, and at present have few engagements on my calendar.

Whichever arrangement is satisfactory to you, please reply to me at Eclipse Press in Amsterdam, which I have on my enclosed business card; your letter or telephone call will reach me promptly.

I look forward to our meeting.

> Most sincerely.
> Ragoczy Ferenz,
> Publisher, Eclipse Press
> Grof Szent-Germain

He read over the letter, then took an Eclipse Press envelope and copied her address onto it, slid one of his cards into it, then sealed it. Setting this aside, he got up from his chair and paced his room, pausing at the bookcases that held the publications of Eclipse Press through the last five hundred years. He regarded most of them with an affectionate pride, a few with dismay. So many books had been damaged or destroyed over those centuries, and the twentieth was no exception. Books, like art, he reminded himself in a language that no one but himself and Rogers spoke anymore, were vulnerable and defenseless but for the esthetics and curiosity of living human beings. What was this obsession about destroying books? Or paintings, scrolls, tapestries, or musical scores? The question nagged at him as it had done over more than three millennia; his long memories stirred and he again recalled the lessons of the priests at the Temple of Imhotep, who had unknowingly reawakened his humanity in his long centuries of service there.

The bleat of a tugboat jarred him out of his contemplations, and he shook himself out of his perplexity. He glanced once at the fading photograph of a girl on the edge of puberty in garments of about twenty years ago, and felt her loss almost as keenly as he had that unspeakable day in Munchen when she had been killed during a riot; he had not been able to look at any image of Laisha, his ward, for more than a decade after the event.

There was a knock at the door. "Grof? May I come in?" Rogers asked.

Szent-Germain moved to the middle of the room. "Of course, old friend," he said, setting the letter aside.

Rogers entered the room, a leather-covered notebook in his hand. He was dressed for traveling, in a gray, three-piece suit of Scottish wool and English tailoring. "I believe I have a workable schedule for my tour," he said in eighth-century Polish.

"That's excellent. You're going to travel by rail?" Szent-Germain indicated a chair as he sat down on the small couch set at right angles to it.

"Most of the way. I may have to hire a car in a few places, not all railways are fully rebuilt," Rogers replied, and changed to modern Turkish. "I need a broader vocabulary. Combining a *rail* with *road/ path* is clumsy."

"True enough," said Szent-Germain in the same tongue. "This way we don't have to invent words in an old language that had no use for present ideas. But it is good to keep in practice."

Rogers nodded. "And my Wendish is rusty." He neither smiled nor laughed, but there was a glint in his faded-blue eyes that indicated amusement.

"A problem for the long-lived—languages come and go," Szent-Germain agreed; he once again looked out the window. "I know I've been a bit . . . distracted lately."

"You've been withdrawn," Rogers concurred.

Szent-Germain shrugged. "There are so many things needing my attention."

Fifteen hundred years ago, Rogers might have spoken more bluntly; as it was, he bit back the retort that rose to his lips. "I know you have not found a willing partner in four years, and being a pleasant dream is not as sustaining for you as acknowledged contact with someone who comprehends what takes place between you."

"True enough," Szent-Germain said, all emotion carefully banked. "And since that cannot be changed at present, we had better discuss your travels. How have you set up your journey?"

"With as little back-tracking as possible," Rogers said with his usual quiet calm, accepting Szent-Germain's reticence for the time being. "Since you will be in Paris and Genova, I have not included those places in my itinerary," he went on, opening his notebook and the closely written pages. "Tonight I will board a train to Bremen—I am assured that the way is clear and delays are unlikely. From there, I take a ship bound for Norway. I will begin my inspections in Oslo, starting with Eclipse Trading offices and going then to your warehouses—you have been in Copenhagen recently and there is no reason I should return there—then go on to Scotland and England. I've already written to Sunbury Draughton Hollis Carnford and Bingley, telling them when I will arrive there, and what portion of your business they may continue to handle, which will disappoint them. They're expecting me."

"I fear we may want to engage new attorneys in London to handle a good portion of my international dealings, and who will stay abreast of changes in international law; I've had too much of my representation in Sunburys' hands, fathers and sons, for far too long. I know young Alfred has been curious about me and, now that Miles has retired, is examining the various matters they have handled for me in the past, not in the way that reassures me as to his fiduciary responsibilities or his probity. His recent letter to me hinted at changes to come."

"Blackmail?" Rogers inquired.

"Or something very like it, so it would be prudent to find barristers and solicitors with an emphasis on international legal expertise, with offices in more countries than England. That should be an acceptable reason for the change. I would not want to give them any sense that I've uncovered Alfred's game." Szent-Germain made a gesture of resignation.

"Will Sunbury protest this, do you think?" Rogers showed no sign of distress, though he was upset by this development.

"On what grounds?" Szent-Germain countered. "He can't appeal to the courts to be allowed to fleece me, unless he's willing to confess his wrong-doings. No; I'll send out a notification to them before I leave for Paris; perhaps you can make some preliminary inquiries while you're in London. A new firm with international offices; see what you can find out about three or four of them. I'll

keep some of my British business with Sunbury, but nothing beyond the island."

"Wouldn't you rather I carry your letter and deliver it for you?"
Rogers asked, surprised that Szent-Germain had come to this decision so quickly.

"No; that could be awkward for you. A special delivery letter
should be sufficient, as I would send under ordinary circumstances.
I think it best that you and I not visit their chambers, for the same
reason. For the time being, everything between Sunbury and Eclipse
has to be on paper, more's the pity." He rubbed his eyes with his
hand. "I'll let you know how Alfred Sunbury responds."

"I would appreciate that. Is there anything you want me to arrange about your new representation?"

"Not until I have settled on a firm," said Szent-Germain.

Rogers waited for half a minute, then said, "I'll send you reports
from each Eclipse Trading office I visit. Do you want the reports in
code?"

"No; it would only raise suspicions if the reports are intercepted,
which may indeed happen. How tedious it is, to have to anticipate
deception at every turn. It's as bad as Byzantium." He shook his
head, his dark eyes remote. "Write your reports in French or
Romanian—both are easily explained." He paused again. "By all
the forgotten gods, trying to extricate Eclipse from skullduggery,
we're becoming more enmeshed in it."

"Do I provide curious officials with your address here or one of
your other addresses?" The question was without any unease, as if
he had never encountered such problems on similar missions in the
past, and was not appetent to have the problem behind them.

"It would be wise, I think," said Szent-Germain.

"You're probably right," Rogers agreed.

"You will have to excuse my reticence: Constantinople—and
Lima, and Lo-Yang, and Damascus, for that matter—have made me
cautious."

"With good reason," said Rogers, who had memories of his own.

Szent-Germain gave a short sigh. "Hardly surprising," he said, and patted the top of his desk lightly, signaling a change in subject. "So: Norway to Britain—then where?"

"Rotterdam, Calais, and Le Havre. South to Bordeaux and Bilbao, west to Oporto and south to Lisboa, inland to Madrid and Sevilla. Cadiz, Valencia—"

"Be careful in Spain; it's not so long since we lived there, and we did not leave in the best of circumstances."

Rogers chuckled briefly. "With the Generals nipping at our heels."

Szent-Germain's smile lacked humor. "That was a near thing; I wouldn't like to see another departure like that one."

"Nor I," Rogers admitted. "Perhaps I'll skip Valencia and make my time at Barcelona brief."

"Keep your schedule flexible and send me information daily. If you think it urgent, telephone me." Szent-Germain's expression was carefully unrevealing. "Be discerning when you book your trains— check the stops and the connection times, reserve first-class accommodations all the way, or hire a car and a driver. I'll supply you with a letter of credit for three or four different currencies, in case you should need more money than you're taking with you: you won't have to wait for confirmation on travelers' cheques, as well as such authorizations as you may need for taking any necessary legal actions."

"Thank you, master." He studied the page open before him. "Marseilles, perhaps Nice, inland to Milano, down to Pisa, then Roma, Napoli, Brindisi, unless it looks as if it would be prudent to visit Massina before going on to Brindisi. I will arrive in Venezia the third week in February, if all goes well."

"Keep me apprised of any changes, especially if you go to Sicilia."

"Certainly." Rogers handed over a typed itinerary that covered three pages. "This is what I am planning to do. I have most of the reservations I need for the first half of my tour. I'll purchase the rest as I go along, depending on circumstances and the weather, and will wire you in Paris about any changes I may need to make." He closed his notebook and stood up.

"Do you ever wonder," Szent-Germain asked, a touch of surprise in his voice, "why we make such a ritual of travel review?"

"We've done it for centuries," said Rogers as if this were explanation enough. Then he stood very still, saying, "Perhaps because those times when we didn't, things didn't go so well. Think of Tunis, or Leosan Fortress."

"No doubt you're right. Very good; I believe you may have hit upon it," said Szent-Germain, and got to his feet. "So to continue our ritual: I'll plan to be in Venezia the second week in February. Eclipse Press should be ready to get back to business by then. I'll know where we stand with the press, and you should know whether or not Eclipse Trading is doing well."

Rogers cleared his throat. "I've gone over the household particulars with Willemyn; she has written instructions describing her duties. I'll see if she has anything she wants to know more about. I'm planning to do that as soon as I may."

"Considering you are leaving shortly, I should think so," said Szent-Germain wryly, then added more seriously, "I thank you for undertaking this tour. We need our work coordinated; though I realize that winter is not the best time for such a journey, it provides you the element of surprise which you might not have in spring. Also, more Eclipse Trading ships should be at winter anchorage and you will have the opportunity to inspect them. There is much to prepare for."

"You still believe there has been smuggling and other unfortunate acts continuing since the war," said Rogers.

"Well, it has happened before. Think of Alexandria. It is an easy life to fall into: you don't mean to continue to smuggle or steal or carry unpapered passengers now that the war's over, but somehow, you have grown used to doing it. You can always use the money it brings, and it is useful for maintaining contacts with criminals who will not make you a target of their crimes if you are willing to be useful to them." Szent-Germain shook his head. "I'd rather I find out about such shenanigans and correct the problems with as little fuss as possible than have the local authorities arrest my employees as malefactors in the full glare of the press and the law." He held out his hand to Rogers. "There are ways to handle refugees and displaced persons that put neither they nor you and I outside the law, but it takes careful arrangements. You know how best to handle any miscreants you find: you've done so before."

Rogers shook Szent-Germain's hand. "I'll do my best to resolve any problems privately. I'll inform you if I can't."

"I have no doubt."

"I talked to Jourdain earlier today; he knows what he is to do while I'm away. He's a good steward. You may rely on him to look afer your Paris properties." He opened the door. "Do you remember the time we returned to Danzig and found the staff gone, and all the furniture—every stick of it—and all the supplies stolen or sold?" He shook his head. "The officials all claimed to know nothing, and the only servant we could ever find was the laundress, and she was adamant that she hadn't been part of it."

"It could happen again; we lost everything when Timur-i came to Delhi."

"That was war," Rogers pointed out.

"Danzig was greed," Szent-Germain said quietly. "You're right; there is a difference. And on this trip, you will have to deal with them both."

Rogers suddenly said, "Do you miss America, the United States? No detritus of war to deal with, no ruined cities."

For the greater part of a minute, Szent-Germain contemplated something in the distance, then mused aloud, "Not as such, no. Certainly not as it is now, filled with suspicions and dread under a veneer of progress." He pressed his lips together, then added, "There's too much of it to contain it all in a word like *miss*. There are people and places I would like to see again, but for all its spectacular variations, it is not my native earth. No doubt we'll travel there again, North and South. Why do you want to know?"

"Europe is marked with the scars of battle; I thought, perhaps, you'd prefer a place with fewer reminders of what has happened." Rogers saw Szent-Germain's blue-black eyes become veiled.

"For now, my responsibilities are here," the Grof said remotely. "But I thank you for your concern."

Rogers studied Szent-Germain's unrevealing countenance, aware that he would get no further information from the Grof for now. "I'll leave for the station shortly."

"I wish you a swift, pleasant journey, old friend."

Rogers ducked his head. "And you as well, master. Paris is nearer than most of my destinations, but you still have to get there." He glanced at the old photograph of Laisha and then back at him, sympathy in his faded-blue eyes. "If you can manage it, I ask that you don't fall to brooding again. This detachment of yours is hard enough."

Szent-Germain's slight shake of his head was hardly enough to see, but Rogers knew what was bothering him. "I won't."

"Nor any of the others: not Csimenae, not Estasia, not Acana Tupac," Rogers warned. "This is not a good time to take unhappy risks."

"It never is."

"Then for all . . . all your forgotten gods, stop pretending you don't grieve for her, and all the others." Rogers' faded-blue eyes revealed his concern far more than his choice of words.

"You're wrong to put Laisha with the others, you know," Szent-Germain corrected gently. "Laisha wasn't like them—she was my child, not my lover, and I failed to protect her." This was a remarkable admission for Szent-Germain to make, and though neither he nor Rogers mentioned it, there was a subtle change in the office.

"Still," said Rogers.

"Yes; you're right. It is never a good time to take unhappy risks," Szent-Germain reiterated. "Do not fear: I have too many matters to attend to; I cannot permit myself to give in to grief. It would not honor Laisha's memory if I did."

Rogers nodded, but continued to harbor concerns as he stepped out of the Grof's office. After a few seconds' reflection, he closed the door; it was never a good sign when Szent-Germain dwelled on his losses. He squared his shoulders and went along to the rear of the house, where he found Willemyn Cooznetz in the pantry, checking her inventory against what was on the shelves. "Willemyn," he said directly to avoid startling her.

She turned around, her face rosy with heat from the newly in-stalled Swedish stove where two chickens were boiling with celery, vinegar, and chopped carrots to make broth. "Heer Rogers," she said; a widow of thirty-nine, she was accustoming herself to her advancement in the household. "You're leaving, then?"

"In about twenty minutes. I'll have Arnestus drive me to the station. He's in the garage, I suppose?" He had found it difficult to call the old coach-house the garage, but in time he knew it would be as natural to call it that as coach-house had been. "Thank you," he added in his overly formal Dutch.

"Yes. He's entranced by the XK120," said Willemyn, adjusting the hang of her kitchen smock. "You'd think it was a girl and not an English auto."

"How am I to say as much to him?" Rogers made a sound that might have been a stifled laugh, then said, "You have your instruc-tions to the bank and the Grof's authorization to draw on household accounts, and you have the list of provisions you will need to stock and at what time. If you have questions, you may call me, or the Grof, who will be in Paris for a time; the number will be provided to you. The same for Venezia. You already have my current sched-ule; I will inform you of any changes. You have the address of Szent-Germain's attorneys in Den Hague and Lisboa; do not be afraid to use them if you deem it necessary. Szent-Germain would expect it of you, and if you worry for your post, failure to act will be seen as more disturbing than making the contact. I am sure you will do well. Have you any questions?"

"I don't think so," she replied. "It is all very clear."

"Good," he said, and went along past the mud-room to the nar-row, cobbled courtyard at the back of the house that gave onto the alley that led to the canal-side street.

The coach-house entrance was at right angles to the alley, and just now, it was standing open, the maroon Jaguar XK120 sitting just inside. Arnestus was lying under the Jaguar, his oily work-trousers and new boots marking his presence.

"Arnestus?" Rogers asked. "When you said you'd be working on an auto, I thought you meant the Peugeot, not this."

"Oh." The shaggy-haired young man wriggled out from under the handsome vehicle, pausing to wipe his fingerprints off the lustrous maroon paint before he got to his feet. "Is it time already?"

"Coming up to it," said Rogers. "If you'll load my bags into the boot, and raise the top, you will have time for a bite to eat before we leave." He took a step back, then asked, "Why were you under the XK120?"

"I thought there was an odd sound in the brakes, but it's probably some loose cobblestones that made the noise as I drove over them when I went to get petrol."

"A good thing to be certain of, brakes," said Rogers, and went back into the house as the first spatters of rain began to fall.

Rogers' departure was not quite half an hour later, unobserved by anyone in the household but Arnestus, who sat in the driver's seat, grinning. "Do not drive rapidly, the streets are narrow and crowded," Rogers said as he ducked under the drooping canvas top, removing his dove-grey hat as he slid into the seat.

"It is a shame not to drive an auto like this one as fast as it will go," the young man said petulantly as he started the engine and then the windshield wipers.

"It may be, but if you damage it, you will have to bear the cost of repairs," said Rogers, and closed the door.

Arnestus glared, but put the Jaguar in motion at a sober pace as he started off toward the train station. He hummed as he drove, dodging bicycles and pedestrians with balletic ease. Only when they were within sight of the station and the work going on around it did he speak to Rogers again. "Do I have the Grof's permission to drive this during his absence?"

"No, you do not," said Rogers. "You may drive the Lea-Francis, or the Peugeot, if you like, but while the Grof is away, put the cover over the XK120 and park it in the last stall on the left. You may start it once a week, and back it up and repark it, for the tires, but otherwise, leave it alone."

With an exasperated sigh, Arnestus slowed as he pulled up to the station. "All right. He's the boss."

"The Lea-Francis isn't a shabby vehicle," Rogers pointed out as he opened the door, swung his legs around so his feet were on the pavement, stood up, and donned his hat. He signaled for a porter and set about unloading his trunk and suitcases, fully aware that Arnestus wanted to argue with him about the XK120. "The Grof will explain it to you, if you insist," Rogers added as he lowered the lid of the boot now that all his things were on the porter's hand-trolley.

"Be damned to him," muttered Arnestus, preparing to drive away from the station. "He's going to be away, and I'll be here."

"If you want to remain in the Grof's employ, I suggest you change your manner," Rogers said as Arnestus leaned over and rolled up the window.

The Jaguar's tires stirred up a slurry of mud and small pebbles which sprayed over Rogers and his luggage as it pulled out into traffic, Arnestus hunched over the steering wheel with a wolfish smile on his young face.

Rogers watched him go and tried to make up his mind if he should mention this behavior to Szent-Germain or send Arnestus a letter explaining what could happen to him if he continued in his present manner. He did not want to do either, but he realized that this could lead to greater problems as time went on. Perhaps, he thought, Szent-Germain could take the XK120 to Paris, or have it delivered there.

"What train, sir?" the porter asked as he shoved his hand-trolley through the crowd toward the platform and piers and the trains.

"Oh. Bremen." He looked at the line of ticket booths. "Which one?"

"Third from the end," said the porter, and waited while Rogers went to purchase his first-class ticket.

While Rogers stood in line at the ticket-booth, Szent-Germain was upstairs in his laboratory, removing a tray of jewels from his athanor. He placed the tray on a small shelf in a protected corner of his large trestle-table, and made sure that no breeze through the room could reach it, for air, cooler or warmer than the newly made stones, could cause fine cracks in them that sometimes reduced them to powder. He walked the length of the room and looked out over the canal, now freckled with rain. His gaze was preoccupied, and he asked himself if Rogers had not hit upon something when he had asked Szent-Germain if he missed America. It was Charis Treat and the prospect of dealing with other academics from the United States that had brought back memories of his short, hectic stay in that country that began fifteen years ago. He had kept his property in San Francisco as well as his partnership in the Geyserville winery, and received regular reports on both, as well as from Eclipse Trading. He found that his businesses were subject to unusual scrutiny just now, which somewhat blighted his view of the United States; the countryside was quite lovely, but it all still seemed to be far away from him now, and from those Americans taking refuge in Europe. He sighed. That had always been the way of the world: those with intelligence pressed into service by those serving the priests and generals unless the priests and generals were suspicious, at which time, those with well-trained intelligence had to flee for safety. Over the centuries he found himself in accord with the intellectuals, the teachers, and the innovators, and never more so than now.

There was a tap on the door and Trinka, the maid, called out, "The afternoon post has come. There is a large packet of papers for you, Grof."

"Put it in the 'tiring room, on the chest-of-drawers. I'll come to get it shortly."

"Yes, Grof," said Trinka, and left him to his contemplation.

Szent-Germain scowled out at the weepy day. There was not much demanding his attention just now, and that left him prone to frustration and irritation. The packet of papers was waiting for him, but he was not ready to examine them. He went to a large chest standing in the corner and worked the combination on the lock that held it closed. Once the lid was open, he took out a small scale and a set of weights, set them down, and next removed a little measuring-spoon and a heavily stoppered jar, which he opened with care. "Might as well do something useful," he said in his native tongue, and busied himself combining the ingredients for treating irritations of the intestines, allowing himself a brief, ironic smile, aware that he had none of his own since his execution, over forty centuries ago.

**Eisley Butterthorn & Hawsmede
#4-7 Upper Beresford Walk
Greenwich, Britain**

11 November, 1949

*Ragoczy Ferenz, Grof Szent-Germain
President & Owner, Eclipse Trading Company
49, Rue des Freres Gries
Paris, France*

My dear Grof,
*Having spent two meetings with your secretary, C. Rogers, I follow
his advice and write to you.*
*First let me assure you that we are not planning to remain in Green-
wich, but will establish our chambers in offices that are even now being
built not far from Pall Mall; it is not the traditional home of solicitors
and barristers, but as our practice is almost wholly devoted to international contracts and the enforcement of same, we believe we need not
position ourselves in proximity to the Courts of Law, but to the seat of
shipping. Our previous location was damaged during the Blitz, and returning to it would add another three or four years to our displacement
here which we would prefer to avoid.*
*International law is complex, as I am sure you know. We have made
it a goal for our firm to strive for clarity and concision in all we do, so*

that no client need fear being drawn into dealings that are obfuscatory or are represented deceptively. We will always seek to combine accuracy with lucidity; I assure you that you may rely on us to make all terms and conditions clear to you before entering into any contractual agreements.

Mister Rogers has told us of the widespread nature of your trading company, and we agree that with so many offices in such a far-flung business, careful attention to your various ventures would prove beneficial as well as making it possible for you to maintain your dealings on sound legal grounds. We have the list of your various legal representatives in several countries, and I am pleased to inform you that we have dealt with Oscar King in San Francisco most gratifyingly on two occasions: assuming the other firms listed are as competent and ethical as King, we should be able to provide satisfactory representation for you.

There are a great many changes taking place in international trade, as you must know; I believe that the range of legal services we can offer will surely prove worthwhile to you and all your undertaking. We also have translators available for contractual negotiations as well as all such correspondence as may be needed in your trading. I am taking advantage of this initial communication to include some examples of our work—all names and particulars deleted, of course—for your perusal. If you find our work to your standard, I will await your visit for the purpose of finalizing our representation of Eclipse Trading, and Eclipse Publishing.

Most sincerely at your service,
Everett Hawsmede

EH/psj

4

CHEZ ROSALIE was on a side-street not far from the Sorbonne, an unpretentious place with a large dining room in the front of a seventeenth-century house that catered to graduate students and young faculty, and a meeting room that had long ago been a card room was reserved for private groups seeking a pleasant, private location with more to provide than the excellent food offered here by Rosalie's son Dudon; it was set up more like a small, exclusive club that provided little beyond coffee and wine for those using it. This evening the meeting room was the gathering-place for the Ex-Pats' Coven, which had their monthly meetings at Chez Rosalie. It being a chilly evening, there was a fire burning in the tile-fronted fireplace; the flame-shaped light-bulbs in the two brass chandeliers were augmented by five floor-lamps so that the room was bright and pleasant. At five-thirty, the usual beginning of the Coven's gathering, only eight of its members had arrived and had selected the most comfortable of the upholstered chairs and love-seats, and were filling the time by sharing desultory bits of news and small-talk while they waited for the rest to arrive.

"What's keeping them?" asked Julia Bjornson, an attractive, fair-haired woman on the verge of forty; she was staring at her husband Axel—a studious fellow who had been teaching city planning at Columbia until some of his theories were interpreted as being of a collectivistic nature; tonight he was in a tweed jacket over a turtleneck sweater and wearing horn-rim glasses—as if to pry the answer out of him. Tardiness always made her worry, and although it was not uncommon among the Coven members, she could not stop complaining when anyone was late. "Don't they know when we meet?" She stared at her wristwatch as if she expected her dissatisfaction to animate the watch; after a few seconds, she clicked her tongue and sighed.

"Don't fret, Julia. They'll be here," he answered. They were sit-

ting near the fire in overstuffed chairs, a small writing-table between them.

Winston Pomeroy was sitting near the French doors that served
as windows; the curtains were drawn across them, shutting out the
high walls of the next house and the path that ran through the gap
between the business-street in front of the restaurant and the
service-alley behind it. "I wouldn't worry. It's pretty cold, so cabs will
be hard to get. They'll be along." He was thirty-three, had been a
professor of horticulture at Cal Davis, and just now was smoking
one of those strong French cigarettes most of the Coven avoided;
the smoke wreathed his head like a ghostly halo.

Russell McCall, sitting near the door in an old-fashioned grandfather's chair, had been reading the newly arrived *New York Times*—
which, as a journalist, he followed devoutly—now folded the paper
and slipped it into the small valise he carried. He wore an anorak
over a turtleneck sweater, and multi-pocketed trousers. "Two-day-
old news isn't." And when this complaint was met with blank stares,
he added, "News. It isn't news."

"There's not much American news on the radio, either," Mary
Anne Triding observed soothingly. She was a self-possessed widow
in her early forties, as neat and tidy in a wool suit over a lace blouse
as a Doctor of Library Sciences was expected to be; Indiana State
University had been her home until the HUAC took exception to
her attitude toward leftist writings and the meaning of the First
Amendment.

At the far end of the room, Tolliver Bethune, feline-slick in a
well-tailored three-piece suit of navy-blue wool, was in deep conversation with Hapgood Nugent, who, with his wrinkled shirt,
shabby jacket, and unpressed trousers, was as rumpled and thrown-
together as Bethune was polished. The lawyer was listening to the
disheveled mathematician describing the harassment of his sister
Meredith and her family. Near them, Stephen diMaggio, a twenty-
nine-year-old electrical engineer from MIT wearing bottle-bottom
glasses and a heavy wool duster over a turtleneck sweater and slacks,
was writing a note, rushing to finish it before the meeting began.

"The weather's probably slowing them down," Mary Anne

remarked. "It slowed *me* down, and I left for this meeting with time to spare."

The group fell silent for a few minutes, then the door opened and a cheerful greeting was called out: Boris and Willhelmina King had arrived. He was a blocky man of fifty-two, more used to smiling than frowning, dressed in English worsted and a long, heavy, knit cardigan under a grey trench-coat, which he shrugged out of as he and his wife came into the room; he had been a musicologist at the University of Virginia for twenty-two years, and she, a comfortable figure of a woman of forty-eight, in a long, dark-gray jacket over a funnel-necked sweater and women's trousers, who, until sixteen months ago, had taught high school science.

"And Washington will be along in a moment; he came in with us," Willhelmina announced, smiling eagerly. "Good evening, everybody."

Before there could be much of a response to her friendly greeting, the door opened again to admit Jesse Praeger; he had taught political science at Northwestern, and his wife Elvira, who returned the greetings from the group in an unenthusiastic manner, but at least they smiled. They were among the younger members of the Coven, both of them in their late twenties. Each was in conspicuously American clothes, for both of them wore blue-denim jeans under winter sweaters, like grown-up versions of Raggedy Ann and Andy dolls.

Once again the door swung back, but it was not Washington Young who opened it: Moira Frost held the door so that her husband Tim could maneuver his wheelchair into the room. "Good to see you all," said Moira. She shoved the chair over toward the fire, for Tim was often cold, which was revealed in his clothing; he was looking more as if he intended to go for a sleigh-ride than a car-ride; Moira wore a frock-coat jacket in mauve wool over a silk, high-necked blouse, and a straight skirt with a deep pleat in the center of the front.

"It's like parking a bus," Tim said by way of apology to Julia Bjornson, who had moved her chair over to accommodate Tim's wheeled one.

Washington Young was the next into the room—a tall, square-shouldered, clever-eyed black man of forty-seven, a printer by trade and a Wobbly by conviction, he produced *The Grimoire* quarterly for the Coven. He offered a lackadaisical wave to the group, and half a smile as he made for the chair on the far side of the fireplace, where he always sat. His overcoat showed wear at the collar that had been neatly repaired. As he hung his coat on the rack, he revealed his jersey beneath was topped by a leather vest, and his ink-stained trousers were made of grey canvas. He wore serviceable boots. "Where's Allanby?" he asked of no one in particular.

"Not here," said McCall, getting up to go to add another cut length of wood to the fire.

"A lot of us are running late tonight," Mary Anne remarked.

The late arrivals jockeyed for seats, and gave orders to Dudon for wine and coffee, then took out their notebooks and pens, preparing to begin.

"I know we're late; sorry. There's a good reason," said Charis as she came through the door, Szent-Germain close behind her. "Someone was following us, and we had to approach this place by an indirect route."

"Are you certain?" Nugent asked.

Before Charis could answer, Szent-Germain said, "I'm certain. A man in a dark-blue Renault."

The assembled Coven stared at them, their expressions running the gamut from curiosity to consternation.

Charis stood still while Szent-Germain helped her out of her coat, saying as soon as she selected a chair for herself, "You don't have to worry about him: this is Ragoczy Ferenz, Grof Szent-Germain, and the publisher of Eclipse Press. Some of you have already seen the Eclipse submission protocols. He's on our side, as I told you last meeting. He'd like to talk to you tonight. And I think some of *you* will want to talk to *him* after you hear him out." She could not help but smile at the relief that went through the Coven.

Russell McCall spoke up, his journalistic sense engaged. "Any idea who was following you, or why?"

"Not actually, but I intend to find out," said Szent-Germain. "I'm not even sure that he was following Professor Treat or me, but he stuck to us like a burr. I was finally able to lose him about a mile from here, and I parked two blocks away, in case he goes looking for my car. He'll find a tobacconist's shop, a cafe, and a shop selling hats, all but the cafe closing up for the night in the next hour."

"Clever," Pomeroy approved.

"We walked the last couple of blocks," Charis said, "on the Rue Tranquille." She cocked her head toward the rear of Chez Rosalie, indicating the access-alley that ran behind the restaurant and the rear of houses for more than half a mile.

"So you're not new to the game, then?" asked Tolliver Bethune, prepared to continue questioning the stranger in their midst.

Szent-Germain's answer was composed. "I am an exile, not unlike all of you, and so yes, I'm not new to the game, and I do not play it for entertainment." He did not add that his familiarity with clandestine dealings went back more than three millennia.

The door opened again and Joseph Allanby bustled in, his expression more than usually sad. A somber man in his mid-forties, he had been the mainstay of the biological sciences at Cornell; the son of Professor Emeritus Vercingetotrix Allanby, the foremost theorist on meteorology at Yale, Joseph Allanby had assumed he was academically bullet-proof until he found himself bluntly dismissed *for the good of the students.* He had been advised to leave the US until—as his father put it—*this current hysteria blows over.* Joseph's wife Norma moved in with her brother and his family in Cambridge while Allanby was away in Europe. As the unofficial leader of the Coven, he was rarely late, and when he was, it boded ill. He looked around, staring at Szent-Germain for several seconds before he said, "Sorry, everybody. I had a call from my brother-in-law, family matters. From Edward. Does Medieval studies at Harvard, you recall. I must have mentioned it. He's the one who took in my wife and youngest child. I've told you about him, haven't I? The one who was working as a code-breaker during the war? He's been planning to join us here; the Committee is breathing down his neck." This nervous repetition indicated to all the Coven that

Allanby was badly upset. He took off his raincoat, and as he went to hang it on the brass coat-rack, his heavily lidded eyes filled with tears. "Norma is in the hospital. It's serious."

"What hospital?" asked Boris King.

"Massachusetts General." This was met by concerned silence; Allanby added the worst part. "She took sleeping pills."

"Norma's his wife," Charis whispered to Szent-Germain. "She's from Cambridge, like most of her family."

Moira Frost spoke for most of them. "That's dreadful, Joe."

Allanby just nodded; took out his handkerchief and blew his nose.

"Do they know if she'll pull through?" Pomeroy asked impulsively, then changed his tone. "Sorry to put it that way."

"Edward didn't say," Allanby replied, and reached for his handkerchief to wipe his eyes. "I don't think the doctors have said anything yet. Waiting for tests, and all. Edward said he'd let me know as soon as he hears."

"Could be too soon to tell," Willhelmina said consolingly.

"Probably; yes, you're probably right," Allanby muttered, wadded up his handkerchief, and thrust it back into his pocket. "Edward will call again day after tomorrow, after he sees her doctor; I'll have to telegraph a next-of-kin transfer to him in the morning. I don't know how to word something like that."

"I'll give you a hand with it, Joe," said Tolliver Bethune.

"Do you think that's going to be necessary?" Mary Anne asked.

"Better safe than sorry. I don't want Norma to suffer if nothing can be done, but I want everything done that can be should it turn out she can recover," said Allanby, taking his place in front of the fire. "Well. Enough of that." He smoothed back his disordered hair, then looked over the gathering and cleared his throat. "Thank you all for being here. Now then, let's get down to it. Who has the—"

Before anyone else could raise a hand, Charis leaped up from her chair. "I think we should have Grof Szent-Germain speak first; then, if you like, he can leave us until the meeting is done. I know you'll all be interested in what he has to say, and a few of you don't like to talk in front of strangers." Then she blushed and sat down.

Moira seconded the idea, then offered, "I'll ask Dudon to bring some cognac. Give yourself a little time to compose yourself, Joe."

"And order some pastries while you're at it," McCall requested.

"Only if you'll pay for them," said Julia.

Allanby thought for a moment, then nodded. "All right. Unless someone objects, let him talk. Moira, do you mind if we start while you're—"

"Yes. Go ahead," she said, leaving her husband's side and opening the door. "I won't be more than a couple of minutes."

"All right," Allanby said. "The floor's all yours, Szent-Germain. I'll wait on the cognac; Pomeroy, you can take over for me." He relinquished his place in front of the fire.

"Okay," said Pomeroy, trying to hide his anxiety at having an outsider address the Coven.

Szent-Germain nodded to Allanby as he passed him, seeing anguish in his face. "I wish I could help you," he said quietly, and saw a startled look in Allanby's eyes. As Szent-Germain turned to face the room, he saw several closed expressions on the faces of his audience; in spite of doubts, his presence was undeniable; dressed in a black suit of a wool-and-silk blend, his dark-red tie standing out against the white of his shirt, he had an air of capability and self-containment that held the attention of everyone in the room. "Thank you for this opportunity." He wanted to be both thorough and brief, and set out to put the Coven at their ease. "I'll try not to take up much of your time; you have more to deal with than me and my publishing company," he said, and saw the surprise felt by some of his audience. "First let me say that I am sympathetic with your situation here, I understand how being an exile feels, being one myself. It is no easy thing to restart a life in a new place, away from your families and colleagues and friends." He did not allow himself to think of the hundreds of times he had done that—although none of his family remained, and he had lost more friends and colleagues than he could number—and the wrench it was to him, every time. "Exiles and orphans lose their contexts, and that is . . . profoundly discomposing." He felt the skepticism that greeted his statements. "Since I left my country, one of the things I have done to make my way in the world is my publishing company; it has proven to be a durable investment as well as giving me a way to sustain my ties to what I have left behind. Eclipse has branches in several cities in a number of countries, and distributes widely where it is permitted."

Moira, who had been standing by the door, turned to take a snifter from their host, then closed the door before she took the cognac to Joseph Allanby. "Pardon me, Grof. Please go on."

Unflustered by this interruption, Szent-Germain continued. "My contracts include translation rights for a dozen languages which are handled by Eclipse, and appropriate advances paid for all such translations. The translators consult closely with authors so that the translation accurately reflects the original text."

Russell McCall raised his hand. "You mention advances. Tell us more."

"God, McCall." Julia made his name a curse.

"I pay generous advances, and report royalties quarterly." Szent-Germain saw a startled look in Young's eyes. "It's customary to pay bi-annually, I know, but the accountants submit figures for taxes quarterly in several countries, including the US, so it's not a problem to pay the authors then, as well."

McCall shook his head. "How long have you been at this?"

"Long enough to know it works very well this way; Eclipse Press is quite well-established with a long history of publishing innovative work," said Szent-Germain. "You needn't worry that the company is an experiment, over-committed and inexperienced. Our advances start at twenty-five hundred dollars, and grow larger by increments of five hundred dollars. This amount is not lavish, but it will allow an author enough to work without haste, an arrangement that has been the policy of Eclipse Press since its inception." To be precise, the Press had existed for more than five centuries, he thought before he went on, and had originally paid advances in ducats. "We are generally an academic publisher but we have a very broad definition of academia, and we occasionally take on popular works, including fiction and art books. One of our most recent art books is a retrospective on the oil and watercolor works of Rowena

Saxon, an American artist from San Francisco. Five-color repro-
duction, coated stock, three essays on her work by respected critics.
One hundred ninety-seven pictures in it." Rowena had died during
the war and was now living in Wellington, New Zealand, accustoming herself to Szent-Germain's undead life and the demands it
imposed upon her. "If you would like to see a copy of it, or any of
our titles, please let me know and I'll make sure you have it."

"Aren't you generous," said Julia Bjornson at her most caustic.

"Julia," her husband snapped. "Let him talk."

"Hey, Julia, I'm interested," Young said.

"Why? So he can trot out more malarkey? What kind of publisher acts like that? Pays like that?" She twisted around in her seat
as if rallying support. "It's all a ploy of some sort. Mark my words.
He'll get money out of the group and then disappear."

Russell McCall cut this burgeoning dispute short, saying, "Let
me have a week and I'll let you know if he's telling the truth, and
what kind of record his company has." His smile was vulpine, anticipating a vigorous hunt.

"Ever the reporter," Julia sniped at him.

"Good thing, too," McCall said, unfazed by Julia's rancor.
"You'll be able to rely on what I tell you about him. I'll write out a
report and send a mimeo of it to all of you. We can discuss it at the
next meeting, if you like."

"What about those of us who want to talk to him about our
work?" Praeger spoke up, a defensive edge in his tone.

"Do it at your own peril," said Pomeroy.

"How do we know you won't sell information about our work
to . . . to anyone interested?" asked Moira.

Szent-Germain stared at her. "Because I give you my Word I will
not," he said quietly.

"His Word," said Praeger sardonically. "That's got a lock on it."

Allanby held up his hands. "Please, everyone. Let him finish.
We'll know soon enough what is and isn't true."

"I've seen Eclipse Press books before," Hapgood Nugent announced. "They put out a very good historical atlas just as the war
was getting started. We found them most useful in our work with

Naval Intelligence. They even had a lot of material on South America and Africa that isn't generally available. It had a very informative text, as well. A fine publication, in my opinion."

"Thank you," said Szent-Germain.

"If Eclipse takes your work, you'll have nothing to be ashamed of," said Charis, a bit too loudly. Color suffused her face as she made herself lean back in her chair.

"You say that because he's made an offer on your book?" Mary Anne asked as she might ask someone to pass the salt.

Charis bristled. "That's not why I said it."

Julia laughed unpleasantly.

"But they have made an offer," Young said. "Seeding the mine?"

Szent-Germain chuckled. "You mean I made the offer to Professor Treat to lure you in, thinking Eclipse is more profitable than it is? That would be doubly foolish of me, don't you think? What would be the point of it?" He shook his head. "I'd create more trouble for myself than I would gain from fleecing a few of you."

"It depends on what game you're playing," said McCall. "These days, we have to think about the CIA, and all the rest of them."

"I don't want to feel dire every time there's a knock on my door," said Mary Anne.

"I'm with you," said Moira.

"What have you got to say to that, Mister Grof?" McCall challenged.

"Great Lord Harry, Russell," Boris exclaimed, his deep voice rumbling like an approaching subway train. "Let him talk. You can search out evidence of chicanery later. Some of us are curious about what he's saying."

Nugent grinned. "Save the fight for later. Right now, most of us are enjoying ourselves."

McCall gave an ill-used sigh, and made a show of opening his notebook in order to record the salient points of Szent-Germain's remarks. "I'll make some inquiries and let you know what I find out."

"Thank you," said Szent-Germain, and went on. "I have an office here in Paris. I'll give anyone who would like to talk to me a business card, and I'll instruct my secretary that any member of this group be given timely appointments. I want you to know this: I share your distress at the current American preoccupation with oppression in the name of security. The Soviets are still reeling from the war and are in no position to launch an all-out assault on all things American, and certainly not the American presence in Europe." He shook his head. "To have intellectual inquiry stifled in the name of political exigency is—"

"We know what it is," said Tim Frost, moving his wheelchair forward by a few inches.

"Yes," said Szent-Germain. "You do."

Allanby came up to the front of the room once more. "I think we'll wait until Mister McCall sends out his report on what he learns about you and your company, Grof, before we continue this, if you don't mind." He managed a friendly nod that was also a dismissal.

"Very good," said Szent-Germain. "Those of you who would like to make an appointment to discuss your works, feel free to do so. I'll leave a dozen or so business cards with Professor Allanby." As he spoke, he drew out a small card-case from his inner pocket and removed a number of them that he handed to Allanby. "Thank you for listening to me." He nodded to the Coven, then went to retrieve his coat from the rack. "Professor Treat, would you rather stay or leave?"

She glanced at him uncertainly. "I think I should stay, if you don't mind."

"This is your organization—I am here only on your cachet," he said calmly. "Can you get home safely from here, or would you like me to return in an hour or two?"

"I'll get you home, Charis," said McCall.

"And pump me with questions all the way? No thank you," Charis declared.

"I'll be back in two hours," said Szent-Germain as he pulled on his coat and went toward the door. "Twenty—eight: ten hours I make it."

"It's six-ten now, so yes, that will do," said Charis after glancing at her wristwatch and adjusting for military time. "I'll be in the vestibule."

"Until then," he told her as if there were no others to hear him, then he stepped out into the corridor, and made for the rear of the house. As he passed the kitchen, he saw Dudon enveloped in fragrant steam, watching him, and said, "It all smells delicious; I'm sorry I won't have the chance to enjoy it tonight," which was true enough in a somewhat skewed way: he had not eaten since his execution some four thousand years ago.

"Another time," said Dudon, returning his attention to his pots and pans.

The Rue Tranquille was poorly lit, and the old paving stones were wet, but neither of these hazards was a problem to Szent-Germain's night-seeing eyes; he noticed the two young men in heavy leather jackets in the shelter of the eaves of the house down the street and on the opposite side. Szent-Germain lengthened his stride and soon reached the two young men, aware as he neared them that both of them carried knives. He uttered an obscenity in Byzantine Greek and steeled himself for a nasty encounter, even as he realized that he and Charis had not escaped their pursuers after all, that they had been waiting for the two of them to leave. "At least there's just the one of me," he muttered in Provencal Medieval French.

As predictably as the appearance of thugs in a gangster film, the two young men stepped out of the shadows and into the drizzle, slouching as much to keep dry as to seem threatening. The taller of the two stood half a head taller than Szent-Germain, and he projected an air of menace. "Stop where you are," he muttered in an accent that came from the south of France, not Paris. "Keep quiet, hand over your money, and we won't hurt you."

"I doubt that," said Szent-Germain without a hint of fear. "So if you will step aside, I won't have to disable either of you."

The second young man, only slightly taller than Szent-Germain, but heavier and more conspicuously muscular, moved to block him. "Stay right where you are." To emphasize his intent, he drew a knife with a thick handle like a boning knife but a long, sturdy blade like a skinner. Suddenly his right hand lunged out, the knife moving swiftly toward Szent-Germain's eyes. The man laughed once, a sound combined of rage and triumph.

Szent-Germain took a half-step back and reached for the man's right wrist and tugged it, all but casting the man to the ground. Keeping hold of the man's wrist, the Grof pulled the would-be robber around and into the side of his companion.

His companion cursed and tried to get hold of Szent-Germain, but failed as he turned around in a tight circle, hauling the robber he held around with him. Taking hold of the knife, Szent-Germain stomped on the man's arch and let him go. "What the fuck—?" the man said as he tried to step back only to fall as he put his weight on his injured foot.

The taller man bellowed with rage and attempted to rush at Szent-Germain, fists up at the ready. Szent-Germain made a quarter-turn away from him and kicked out at the robber's knee; the man's fist, augmented with brass knuckles, grazed the side of the Grof's face as he wobbled in an attempt to remain standing. Szent-Germain gave him a shove in his shoulder. The man howled and fell, clutching his disjointed knee.

"You'll need a doctor to look at your injuries, sooner rather than later," Szent-Germain told them as he neatened his coat, then threw the knife over a tall fence into what was probably a small garden.

The taller man uttered an obscenity; the shorter man attempted to stand, his arms flailing in his effort to keep his balance.

Szent-Germain studied the two men. "Whatever your purpose was this evening, I advise you to abandon it. And get yourselves to a clinic." He inclined his head in a perfunctory bow, then went on along the Rue Tranquille, being careful about the various dark places that connected with the street. Little as he liked to contemplate the possibility, he admitted to himself that this might have been something more than a robbery, at the same time chiding himself for indulging in paranoia. This was not Berlin, and von Wolgast was dead. Other men who had sought Szent-Germain's death had themselves been dead for more than two or three decades, or centuries. He walked quickly, making an effort to walk lightly so that he might hear any untoward sound along the way. Aside from a duet of yowls from a pair of tomcats, only the sound of a lorry on the street the other side of the Rue Tranquille caught his attention, so that by the time he reached his car, he was more at ease than he had been since before the Coven's meeting had begun. He removed the key from his suit-pocket, and while he opened the door, he studied the activities of the night. Satisfied that he was not observed, he got into his 1949 Delahaye, its roof raised against the worsening drizzle, and prepared to drive off, but hesitated, to see if any other threatening figures might emerge from the narrow passageways that emptied onto the Rue Tranquille. This was not a dangerous part of Paris, but there were other criminals abroad throughout the city, so he waited. No one came forth, and he turned the key, adjusted the choke, engaged the reverse gear, and backed out of his parking place, heading in the direction of the Seine at moderate speed, wondering if he had time enough to visit the Boutique Musique before he would have to return to Chez Rosalie to take Charis back to her apartment. While stopped at an intersection, he felt his face, trying to determine if there were any marks on it from the bout, and found himself wishing he had a reflection so he could use the rear-view mirror to remove any blood or scrapes; the taller man had landed a couple of blows that might produce bruises. He sighed, thinking he needed Rogers to take care of his appearance, wiped his face with his handkerchief, put both his hands on the steering wheel, and drove on.

When he reached Chez Rosalie he saw Charis talking to Joe Allanby and Washington Young as they stood in the shelter of the entryway to the restaurant. He drew up to the curb, stopped the engine, and got out of the glossy white Delahaye.

Young whistled at the car; Allanby raised his bushy eyebrows that lay like well-mannered caterpillars over his troubled, deep-set eyes.

"Gracious!" Charis exclaimed as he stepped into the light. "What happened to you? Your hand is bleeding."

He decided to give a direct, if not entirely accurate, answer. "A pair of young toughs tried to rob me." He looked at Allanby. "Have any of your Coven members had trouble with—"

"Not that I know of," said Allanby, frowning. "We should warn the Coven," he said to Young.

"I'll put something in *The Grimoire*. But no one's ever mentioned it before." He studied Szent-Germain. "You put up a fight."

"As best I could," the Grof said without offering particulars.

"There's a bad scrape on your jaw," Charis said. "You'll want to put some iodine on it, and a bandage."

"I will," Szent-Germain promised. "But after I take you to your residence. I'm not incapacitated." He had a quick recollection of lying on the edge of the levee on the edge of Sankt Pitersburgh, barely conscious, his broken leg aching fiercely. "I'll be over any injury shortly."

"Yes," said Allanby. "But what a dreadful thing to have happen."

"Are you going to inform the police?" Young asked.

Szent-Germain considered this. "I'll probably call to report the incident. They didn't get anything from me other than a broken foot and a dislocated knee." Young chuckled, Allanby looked startled, and Charis gave a little gasp. "The gendarmes can look for them in a hospital or clinic."

"Good on you, Grof," Young said, making the thumbs-up sign.

"Oh, for heaven's sake!" Charis burst out. "Get in the car and take me home. Then you can get your injuries looked at."

Allanby nodded. "Thanks for letting us know about the thugs. We'll make sure that everyone is alerted." With that, he opened the inner door and went into the restaurant, going toward the front room.

"He's having dinner here," Young explained, holding out his hand to Szent-Germain. As they shook, he added, "I'm more curious than ever to find out what McCall learns." He gave a kind of salute, then followed Allanby.

"Come *on*, Grof," Charis said, slipping her arm past his elbow and nudging him in the direction of his Delahaye.

Szent-Germain opened the passenger door for her, then went

around to the driver's side. Sliding into the white-leather seat, he noticed a few small drops of blood had dropped onto the pristine leather. Something more to be attended to, he thought as he settled into his seat and turned the key in the ignition, then switched on the headlights before he signaled to the light traffic passing in front of the restaurant. His jaw was starting to ache. "Better roll up your window all the way; it looks like we'll have some splashes along the way."

"Sure," she said, and twisted the handle to crank the window up the last few inches.

The engine purred as Szent-Germain drove off into the shining night.

137 Ashtree Lane
Alexandria 4, Virginia
Nov. 16th, 1949

Russell McCall
7, Rue des Cinq Jardins
Paris, France

Dear Russ,

Good to hear from you. I was beginning to think you'd gone underground and were making it your business to keep away from your friends back home. This isn't going out on the paper's letterhead; I'll drop it in a box here in Alexandria. So far none of the HUAC's minions have done any snooping around me, or most of the reporters, so I'll assume this will reach you safely without causing more difficulties for you, or any for me.

Ragoczy Ferenz, Grof Szent-Germain is unknown to me, and as much as I want to say that I have records of him in the morgue, so far as I can tell, I don't, at least nothing current. There is something about a visiting Hungarian with a similar name who was taken for a lot of money, but that was a century ago, and in London. Whoever this guy is, he either has done nothing criminal or clandestine, or he's flying well under the radar—way under—which is a smart thing to do. Maybe he's just looking out for himself and who can blame him? I can tell you that his shipping company is doing fairly well, all things considered, and his publishing company has been able to keep going for a couple of decades here in the US. Judging from the Szent, he's Hungarian, like the guy a hundred years ago; could be a relative of some sort, which might explain his exile, given how the Russians are acting these days—not that I trust Army Intelligence or the CIA to be wholly candid with the press; both of those groups have too much to gain from keeping secrets. There is a lot of speculation going around about how HUAC chooses its subjects for investigation, not all of it too reassuring. I've assumed all along that they went for you because of your opinions, and to scare the bejesus out of any journalist who is inclined to cover the Leftist point of view honestly. I'll keep my eyes and ears open about this Szent-Germain, and I'll drop you a line if I find out anything that looks important. For the time being, figure he's legit, but keep an eye out for anything cloak-and-dagger; some of those Eastern Europeans have strange commitments and alliances.

Thanks for asking about the family. Randy started high school last September, and is getting his sea-legs. Nina and I have arranged for him to continue his music lessons with a teacher from the local orchestral society. Randy tells us he loves the French horn and is thinking of it as a career. It's true that many orchestras were short of musicians during the war, but that seems to be changing, and Nina and I want him to have every chance, but we're telling him not to put too much into it until he finds out what kind of life he would have to lead if that becomes his career. His grandfather—Nina's father—isn't in favor of him playing the French horn professionally, and that's led to some clashes. Linda takes her brother's side, and I try to stay neutral. Nina's been volunteering at the local VA physical therapy facility three days a week. She wants to do her part, she says.

The paper is sending me on assignment to Hawaii next week, so it's a good thing you wrote when you did. I won't be back for ten days, and you said you needed to hear from me ASAP. This is the best I can do, and I'm sorry I can't be more helpful.

Sincerely,
Gene

❖ 5 ❖

BALTIMORE WAS coming out of the last of a blustery winter; the weather was doing its part to confuse everything: temperatures had been almost balmy the day before, with occasional flocks of woolly white clouds grazing through the cerulean sky. But there was a nip in the frisky wind today that promised winter had not quite left. On the streets, overcoats and jackets were standard dress still; a few pedestrians were wearing fur hats instead of felt, and had mufflers wrapped around their necks. The women out on errands had on shawl-collar coats with the collars turned up, and hats that were warm as well as fashionable; almost everyone wore gloves.

From his handsome office around the corner from the Coast Guard Central Atlantic Administration Building, Lydell Gerold Broadstreet watched the street out the tall windows for a short while, then switched his attention to the oversized green blotter on his rosewood desk and the morning's workload; he opened the latest file of international cables, arranged the way he liked them—not by operative but by country of origin—put on his glasses, smoothed his fine, butter-blond hair, set his foolscap notebook open at his elbow, placed his fountain-pen above it, picked up the top cable, and began to read, breaking the codes as he went, one of the few advantages of his photographic memory. Bishop in Dublin stated that he needed to get a replacement soon; the Free Irish Army were becoming suspicious of him, and although they were a small group, they were expert in making bombs, and were known for blowing up suspected informers. He scribbled a note to himself, shuffled the cables, and took up the cable from Fletcher, who sent his travel plans that would bring him to Alaska on a British ship in ten days and would need a covert pick-up; then from Vane in Istanbul where he had managed to get his network going without incident and would need a local contact to handle encoded communications. Nothing much new in any of them, Broadstreet told himself with a sigh. The self-congratulations from some of his station-chiefs were becoming oppressive: the war had been over long enough for vast numbers of uniforms to disappear from the general population, but not so long that the celebrations were completely over, particularly for those who had worked in the shadows—and still ought to do so, he told himself.

He picked up a fourth cable, this one from D. Philetus Rothcoe, who asked for permission to put an agent or two on the Grof Szent-Germain, a fellow known to be an exile, but with a great deal of money, and a number of international businesses; rumor said he had spent the war in southern France, possibly aiding the Resistance, or one of the covert groups operating in Savoie and the Piedmont. But there was no confirmation of this to be found. Rothcoe said there was something fishy about the Grof, who ran a number of publishing houses and had been in contact with some of the American academics in Paris, but there were no provable connections to either the Reds or the Nazis. *Letter of particulars to follow in diplomatic pouch* was appended to the coded message. Broadstreet tapped the page with his index finger, wondering what would be best to do; Rothcoe was a dedicated coordinator, but inclined to get overzealous with present and former aristocrats, a group the CIA was not inclined to antagonize. He wanted to get through his morning work so he could reward himself with a pipe of rum-soaked tobacco and a cup of coffee. But this business with Rothcoe needed to be resolved shortly if the surveillance of the self-proclaimed Ex-Pats' Coven was to continue, undetected this time or so he hoped. Thus far, those assigned to infiltrate the group had been discovered, and there were hints that another approach was needed to gain the intelligence sought. Perhaps a decoy of some sort would work; someone they would accept without having to admit him—or her—to their numbers. Maybe there was a way for this Grof Szent-Germain to be useful.

His ruminations were halted when the intercom on his desk clicked into life. "Mister Broadstreet?" said the voice of his secretary, Florence Wentworth.

"What is it, Florence." He made it a statement instead of a question; Florence did not often interrupt his work.

"There's a gentleman in the office. He says you'll want to speak to him. I don't know why he's come; he refuses to tell me. He says only that it is essential to see you, and that he is unwilling to disclose his identity." She stood expectantly and uncomfortably, waiting for Broadstreet's decision.

"That makes it all suspicious," said Broadstreet a long minute later, with slight fatigue at this interruption. Probably someone from the red press, or the yellow press, which was almost as bad, he thought, looking to get a lead on a story. Or one of Hoover's boys, snooping. That was more likely.

"It might be worth talking to him," Florence suggested a bit tentatively.

"Why is that?" Broadstreet grumbled.

"He has a pin on his lapel, a veteran's pin," she said, and waited, then added, "Thunderbirds."

Broadstreet clicked his tongue, then said, "Oh, very well. Show him in."

The man who came into Broadstreet's office was in his late twenties, of medium height, wearing a dark-brown suit with a white shirt, a sharkskin tie patterned in dark turquoise and dull gold. His pocket-handkerchief was also dull gold; he was carrying a tan fedora: certainly not FBI with a tie and a hat like that, Broadstreet thought. The newcomer smiled. "Mister Broadstreet. Thank you for seeing me." He held out his hand with a nice combination of bravado and humility. "I know you're a busy man, but this is—"

"—important, you say. My secretary informed me." He could see the shine of sweat on his visitor's forehead, and slightly relented. "Convince me you won't waste my time if I hear you out," said Broadstreet, taking up his fountain-pen after he managed a hint of a handshake. "Begin by telling me how you decided to come to me."

"I was told that you were in charge of the investigations of runaway university instructors," the man said.

"And who told you that?" Broadstreet's manner stiffened.

"Major Allen Korlles is a good friend. He suggested I deal with you." The man faltered, looking slightly dismayed.

"I see." Broadstreet decided he would have to have a word with Major Korlles—Army Intelligence shouldn't be so loose-lipped. "Did you tell him what you want to tell me, or was it all lucky happenstance?" He sighed once, not loudly, but enough to make it apparent that he was feeling put-upon. How providential this all seemed: Rothcoe's cable and this informer coming to see him— perhaps too providential.

"No, I didn't tell him, and I don't plan to; he doesn't want to know." He pulled up a straight-backed chair and sat down, and found himself facing a wall of degrees and recognitions Broadstreet had earned; he did his best not to be impressed. "To begin with, I should tell you I'm related to Hapgood Nugent. I'm sure you must know who he is. He's from the brainy side of the family, I'm in the commercial side." He paused to breathe. "You can call me Grant Nugent, if you like."

"Because it isn't your name," Broadstreet interjected, and saw his visitor flinch, showing that he was new to deceptive techniques.

The man nodded, making a quick recovery. "Bingo! You got that right." He took a cigarette from a gold case, tamped it, and lit it, blowing out a thick stream of smoke. Belatedly he offered Broadstreet a cigarette and snapped the case closed when Broadstreet waved it away. "A year ago, before he left for Europe, Hapgood entrusted a couple of filing cabinets to my wife; against my better judgment, we stored them in the garage. I had a look through them some weeks ago and found out that there's a lot of correspondence in them talking about economics—"

"Hardly unusual for a professor of economics," said Broadstreet in a tone that made the other man speak faster.

"But some of them talk about Communism, and not always the way most of us would like. Sure, the Commies were our allies in the war, but not any longer, no matter what the professors like to think, and that goes for Hapgood as well as the rest of them. The professors he was writing to had a lot to say about Communism, most of it favorable to the Communists. Not the kind of things I'd want my kids to be looking into—especially not now. They could stir up all kinds of trouble, these letters. I was startled at how blatant

Hapgood was about his theories. I had photostats made of the letters, of the most outspoken ones, and thought I should make them
available to you. I found out you handle the investigations of those
professors who have left America. Hapgood Nugent is in France just
now, and three of his colleagues are also overseas. I thought maybe
you can use these letters to find out where they have gone."

"And who are these professors?" Broadstreet's pen was poised
over his notebook.

"Maynard Lundkin, D. G. Atkins, and Weston Teague."

Broadstreet wrote down all three names, though he knew where
two of the three were and had men assigned to watch them. He
circled D. G. Atkins, the one unaccounted for. "And why do you
tell me this?"

"My wife sends Happy money. She thinks I don't know about it,
but I do, and it troubles me for several reasons. She says Happy
hasn't done anything wrong, and that it's all a witch-hunt." His face
grew flushed. "She says we owe him the same kind of loyalty we
owe the country."

So, thought Broadstreet, this man isn't a Nugent, his wife is;
there might be some jealousy here to use. He cleared his throat.
"And what do you think? Is Professor Nugent being hounded without cause?"

"I don't know and I don't care. That's not my business. But the
way things stand, the family's embarrassed, and the people Happy's
been dealing with are known to be working with the enemies of
this country." He stared at Broadstreet while stubbing out his cigarette in the hammered copper ashtray on the edge of the desk. "If
turning over the letters will help put an end to all this, then I want
you to have them."

"Have you brought the photostats with you?"

The younger man shook his head. "I didn't know if you'd want
them, or if they'd be safer here than in the filing cabinets in our
garage. We keep them locked, but there are three windows with
just latches. If someone broke in, and knew where to look . . ." He
made a gesture of distress.

"An attic or a basement might be better, and a lock on the door," said Broadstreet, trying to keep from chuckling at this man's idea of security. He took a chance and added, "You haven't mentioned where you live."

"No, I haven't. It's not in Baltimore, I'll tell you that much."

Broadstreet achieved a self-deprecatory smile. "You can't blame a man for trying." He cleared his throat and went on in a more authoritative manner, "And if I am interested, what do you expect for them? Money? A contract for government business? Some other advantage?"

"I expect the badgering to stop. I want my family to be left alone. You know what I'm talking about. No more letters to the principals at my kids' schools. They're six and nine, they don't know anything. They come home crying because the other kids call them Commies. Not that they know what that means. Whoever's in charge of our case—and I assume there is a case—I want him instructed to keep away from my kids. I want it known by the FBI and police that I'm helping the government. I'm losing customers because of Happy, and I can't afford that, not with my wife sending money to France." His indignation had an undercurrent of fear.

Broadstreet studied the man's face. "I would like to examine the letters you mentioned. If you will send the photostats to me by registered mail, I will mention your assistance in my next report, and provide you with a copy of that report, in case you encounter any more difficulties. I can't do much more than that without going higher up the chain of command. But I'll see what I can do." He would order more subtle surveillance, since this blatant approach was not working as they wanted, and Hoover would crow to the press about the CIA operating within the US. "If you'll get your photostats in tomorrow's mail, I'll thank you for your help the best way I can." He reminded himself that he had information on Nugent, as well as Lundkin and Teague. But Atkins had disappeared, and that worried Broadstreet more than anything he had learned about any of the other two. He held out his hand, signaling the interview was over. "Thank you, sir; I know this must have cost you a lot of thought," he said, feeling the strong grip his informant offered.

"You're welcome. Assuming you come through for me." He smiled widely and insincerely as he went toward the door. "Thanks for seeing me."

Broadstreet said nothing as he watched the door close, then picked up his receiver. As soon as he heard the dial tone, he twisted the number and listened for the ring on the other end of the line. The phone was answered before the third ring. "Broadstreet here."

The man on the other end of the line asked, "What is it?"

"I may have a lead on Atkins."

"How much of a lead?"

Broadstreet struggled to contain his nervousness; there was something about Channing—whose name he was not supposed to know—that made his skin crawl. "I'll know by tomorrow evening, or the day after."

"That's reassuring," said the voice without any hint of confidence. "It would be useful to find him."

"In order to bring him back home?" Broadstreet asked boldly.

"That depends on where he is," the voice said.

Broadstreet realized that he had asked one question too many. "Of course, of course," he said quickly, staring at the telephone dial as if to read a message in its numbers and letters.

"We'll know by Thursday, if your information turns out to be right," said the voice, in a tone there was no disputing. "Let me know when you have something to report," he ordered and hung up abruptly.

This was not quite the way Broadstreet had hoped this exchange might be, but he jotted a note on his foolscap pad before picking up his pipe and opening his tobacco pouch; he always thought more clearly when he smoked. Little as he liked to admit it, Broadstreet believed in omens, and when he saw one as obvious as this one, he gave it his careful consideration. There was something going on here, some kind of convergence, and he was determined to make the most of it.

By noon, he had the beginning of a plan for how he could employ his visitor, one that could help locate Professor Atkins, and then he would be able to come up with a way to neutralize whatever it was that the good professor was doing. Atkins had been a thorn in his side for six years, and it was time to show him who was boss. He sucked on his pipe, realized it was finished; he took a pipe-cleaner from his center desk drawer and set about cleaning the burnt tobacco from the bowl, then working on the stem and mouthpiece. After a couple of minutes, he set the pipe down, ready for use. He looked at the clock on the wall, watching the pendulum swing for a little more than thirty seconds, then pressed the button on his intercom. "Florence?"

"I'm here, Mister Broadstreet," she responded promptly.

"I think I'll go out to lunch today; will you inform the dining room? I should be back at thirteen-thirty." He waited for her to respond.

"That's one-thirty," she said. "I'll make a note. Where are you going?"

"O'Doul's, I think, but perhaps some place less crowded." He took a strange pleasure in defying the rules to this extent. "If anyone needs to speak to me, get his name and number and tell him I'll call back by sixteen hundred . . . four P.M." Before she could confirm this, he clicked off and went to fetch his overcoat; he saw the windows spattered with rain and knew it would get heavier as evening came on. He crossed the street and turned right; there were three blocks to go to reach O'Doul's, a bar and grill that was known to cater to the men who worked the classy part of the waterfront, and served Irish beer that came by ship from the Emerald Isle. Often crowded and smoky, O'Doul's was a perfect place to watch the life of the harbor.

Before he reached O'Doul's, he changed his mind, and held up his arm to flag a cab. "The Helmsman," he said as he got in.

The cabby blinked. "Out on Merrimont Road? That's almost an hour away."

"Yes, that's the one," said Broadstreet as he settled into the dusty cushions.

"You got it," the cabby said as he started his clock running and swung around in a U-turn, paying no heed to honks of complaint. "Weepy weather, yeah."

"It's the time of year," said Broadstreet in his most discouraging tone.

The cabby kept on. "Place for sportsmen, the Helmsman." It had, as everyone in the region knew, been a speakeasy with a small harbor where smugglers could tie up their boats all through the years of Prohibition. Now it was a rod-and-gun club with a private yacht facility, a toney place with a rustic exterior. It lent prestige to its members without the high expenses of country clubs and private golf courses.

"Among others," said Broadstreet, then wanted to bite his tongue for taking the bait.

"You one of those others, then? You gotta be a member to go there." The cabby laughed as if this were the punch-line of a joke. "Cause you sure don't look like a sportsman."

"I'm not a yachtsman, if that's what you mean, but I know my way around Chesapeake, and I am a member, not that it's any of your business," said Broadstreet; he had a small powerboat he sometimes used for fishing the estuaries and creek around Old Road Bay and the edge of Chesapeake Bay. He winced a little at his answer, but said nothing as the taxi rattled along the road in the steadily thickening rain.

By the time the Helmsman was in sight, Broadstreet was regretting his impulsive decision; he knew he would have to call the office and explain why he was going to be so late returning. He needed a reason that was not unbelievable, but impossible to check out closely. It would have to be related to his work, but vague enough to be seen as a testing-the-waters meeting. He'd have to come up with a contact who wouldn't come to his office. Yes, he thought as the cab turned onto Merrimont; he was going to meet a possible informant who failed to show up. A man named . . . something innocuous. Baker. That had a good, ordinary feel to it. No, Baxter. That was better, Mister Baxter had contacted him indirectly and this was the place he had recommended for their first meeting. He began to work on a legend for Baxter, trying to keep it vague enough that he could discard portions of it as needed. "Thus," he mused aloud: the potential informant was in a union, and the union

was being pressured by Communists. He grinned as the cabby cut
his speed by more than half as he drove along the muddy road, approaching an unassuming wooden building of respectable size. Nine
or ten expensive cars had drawn up in front of this structure, near
the concrete steps that led to a double-door of dark oak. In the
distance, beyond the trees, the masts of a number of boats rocked
on the choppy waters of Old Road Bay.

"That'll be nine dollars, seventy cents. If you want me to come
back and pick you up, tell me now, or fend for yourself. Pay me five
bucks and I'll guarantee you a ride home."

Broadstreet handed the cabby eleven dollars. "Keep the change.
I'll find my own way home." He had to hold his hat on his head, for
the wind was gusting vigorously now, and the rain was steady. He
squinted as the cab backed away from him, wondering what he
would do if anyone in the restaurant recognized him. That would
surely have happened at O'Doul's. But if he had lunched at O'Doul's,
he reminded himself, he wouldn't need a story to account for his
lateness. He removed his wallet and pulled out his Helmsman
membership card.

A young man in a dull-red jacket and black slacks opened the
door for Broadstreet. "Good afternoon. Will you be wanting a table
or bar-space?"

"A table. For two. I'm expecting a Mister Baxter. He isn't here
ahead of me, is he?"

"Would you like to look in the dining room?" the waiter offered.

"It wouldn't do any good. I've never met the man face to face."
Broadstreet knew he was saying too much. "I need to call my office." That at least was true, something that could be traced and
included in making the so-called meeting appear authentic.

"Down the hall on the—"

"Left. Yes. I know." He took a couple of steps in that direction,
then added, "I'd like a brass monkey when you decide where to
seat me."

"Yes, sir," said the waiter.

It cost him more than forty cents to make the call, for he had to
tell Florence enough of the story to explain where he was. As he

hung up and heard the coins he had deposited drop into the base of the instrument, he sighed, then walked back to the maitre d'.

"Your table is ready, sir," that worthy told Broadstreet, and signaled to the same young waiter who had opened the door for Broadstreet to escort him to a table with a good line of sight to the door. "For when your party arrives."

"Thanks," said Broadstreet, and followed the waiter through the sparsely populated dining room—nine of the thirty-two tables were occupied, most by no more than two people—to a table that not only had a direct line of sight to the door, but was next to the picture window that looked out on the lawn and boathouse on the far side of the building. "Much appreciated." He handed the waiter a dollar.

The waiter nodded and went to get leather-bound menus with the luncheon selections, returning with two of them, offering one to Broadstreet and putting one on top of the charger at the place opposite his. "Will you want your brass monkey now?"

"I've changed my mind. I'll have a hot buttered rum, light on the butte— No, make it an Irish coffee." A day like today called for Irish coffee, Broadstreet decided, and gazed out the window, trying to piece together a story of the fictitious informant he would use to explain his unusual behavior, and perhaps be reimbursed for the taxi fare and the lunch.

There were eight members who arrived together some twenty minutes later, and boisterously took over two tables pushed together; they seemed to be celebrating something. By listening to their excited conversation, Broadstreet gleaned the information that they worked for a marine engineering firm and had just secured a contract from the Navy for a device that would monitor all kinds of marine traffic along the coast from Norfolk to Charleston. The eight men ordered two bottles of Tattinger's and drank a toast to Bateman & McNally. Making no apology for their merriment.

"I think I'd better order even if my guest hasn't arrived," Broadstreet said to the waiter as he came by the table. "I don't want to have to spend all afternoon waiting."

"Have you decided yet, sir?" The waiter gave a sign of acquiescence.

Broadstreet had barely opened the menu but he said, "Sirloin steak, medium."

"Mashed or baked potato, sir?"

"Baked, with butter and spring onions, and a side of creamed spinach." He handed the menu to the waiter.

"Another Irish coffee, sir?" The young man had not written anything down, but he offered a confident-yet-diffident smile.

"Not just now," said Broadstreet. "But a cup of strong regular coffee would be welcome."

"Right away, sir," said the waiter.

All through his solitary lunch, Broadstreet continued to formulate his explanation for his atypical behavior, and by the time he had his dessert—a slice of cheesecake with whipped cream on top—he had a scenario that he was certain would prove sufficient to gain the approval of Channing: someone associated with the marine engineering firm had been leaking the design for these new monitors, and because of that, the effectiveness of the devices might be compromised. He would have to work out how his contact was associated with Bateman & McNally. Something tangential. Maybe he worked for the blueprint company Bateman & McNally used. Broadstreet thought this over for a good ten minutes, then decided that might be too easily checked. He needed something more clandestine, more daring yet secret. He signaled the waiter for more coffee and the check. "And will you bring me some note-paper? I need to leave something for Mister Baxter. If he should happen to show up."

"Will do," said the waiter, and came to retrieve Broadstreet's large coffee-cup.

The bill was over fifteen dollars and Broadstreet decided to leave a generous two-dollar tip, which he handed over along with the note he had composed to Mister Baxter. He took a last sip of his coffee, pushed back from the table, gave a last glance at the eight men from Bateman & McNally, and glanced at the window to see the wet, darkening afternoon. It would be dark by the time he got back into Baltimore. As he got up, he caught sight of his watch and was shocked to see that it was nearing four. He went to the front desk and asked if they would call a cab for him, and was assured that they would.

By the time the cab arrived it was almost four-thirty. Broadstreet hurried out to the cab, got in, and gave the address of his office rather than the nearest intersection, as he had been trained to do.

"Traffic's thickening up," the cabby said as Broadstreet got into the rear seat and slammed the door.

"Not unusual for this hour," said Broadstreet, and lit up a cigarette, letting his mind turn its attention to the problem of Mister Baxter, hoping to have this invention fully realized by the time he got back to his office. He would begin by informing Channing that he had a lead on D. G. Atkins, and use that to reveal that he was following up on a tip he had received a few days ago, one that might or might not be worth pursuing. In order to make such a tip credible, Baxter would have to be someone who could listen to Bateman & McNally employees talking and know that what they said had value. He would have to be someone of little importance, someone who had years of experience to draw upon in listening, someone who could—

Broadstreet sat up straight so quickly that he nearly dropped his cigarette. A cab driver! Now that could be a workable part of the legend. Bateman & McNally must surely use taxis from time to time, probably called the same company for most jobs. He grinned. The cabby could be a failed engineer, a man with bitterness in his heart, a grudge. Average in appearance, the kind of person no one would notice, or remember. It was true that the cabby had to post his chauffeur's license on his sun-visor, but who bothered to look at the name, unless the picture didn't match the driver. He told himself he should have thought of this before. It even gave him a plausible explanation why Baxter did not show up for lunch—he had a fare going some distance. That would do it, if he needed it for the right touch. He reminded himself that he couldn't reveal too much about Baxter in his first report; he would have to draw out his revelations, and be at pains to seek out this contact. The party from Bateman & McNally was an omen, he realized, giving him the chance to turn his work to advantage. He could show his value to Channing, pursuing the nefarious cab-driver and investigating Bateman & McNally in the process, perhaps finally get the promotion he had been denied for six years.

The taxi turned onto Madison Road, and almost at once braked for a stoplight ahead. "Told you about the traffic," the cabby said. "This is gonna add ten minutes to the time."

"Get there as best you can," said Broadstreet, feeling quite benign now that he had the framework of his plan in place. "Safety over speed." He was enjoying the afterglow of a good meal and the satisfactory beginning of a new operation that could do much to advance his career. He reminded himself to keep that admonition to the cabby in mind, for considering what he was embarked upon, he would do well to take safety to heart.

December 9ᵗʰ, 1949

Dear Charis,

 Christmas will soon be upon us, but it doesn't feel very Christmasy without you here to share it with the three of us. Mom and Dad have asked us to come to Raleigh for Christmas and New Year's, and I'm inclined to go, for the boys' sake. They miss you almost as much as I do, and they don't understand why you can't be with us. Arthur is especially fretful, fearing that you are gone because of his polio. I've done my best to reassure him on this point, but so far he is unconvinced. David wanted you here for his birthday—turning five is such a milestone—and pouted when you weren't. I read them every letter you send, but there are times that makes it worse.

 I'm going to get them a dog for Christmas. I think having a pet will help them through your absence. I've asked Jake Parmutter to recommend a breed; his brother's a vet and knows what will be best for Arthur. Nothing too large or too frisky, but enough to keep them engaged. Not a cocker spaniel: Mother can't abide the breed, and since she'll have to keep the dog in the house during our visit, I think we'll manage better if I find something that might make things easier for her as well as the boys.

 Henry Eisley resigned last week. He's been offered a job with Standard Oil, and will be moving out to California next week just like that. Milly put their house on the market today, and she's packing up a storm. Bill's been helping her, and is planning to add UCLA to his list of potential universities he'll apply to. The pay Henry will be getting is a lot more than anything the university can pay, or a grant. As much as I love my work, that kind of money would tempt me, not just for what it could do for how we live, but it might be possible for you to return without having to jump though hoops or spend weeks answering questions from the HUAC. Standard Oil needs a good geologist, apparently, and Henry doesn't want to have to spend his time struggling to get grants, especially now that there have been questions asked about him. He was into some pretty Leftist causes while he was a grad student, and it's coming back to haunt him. So I think he's being smart about taking the job for a lot of reasons. We had a going-away party for him night before last. Milly came for part of it, said good-bye to all of us, and invited us all to visit them in Los Angeles.

I'm thinking of taking out the old magnolia tree in the back, and putting in something else, maybe a palm of some sort. The magnolia dropped two limbs last month, and will probably drop more this winter. I'll ask Mother what she'd recommend—you know how well she keeps up her own garden—and I'll arrange to have it put in come spring. And I want to trim back some of the honeysuckle; it keeps trying to get into the pantry through the loose window-frame.

Dr. Nolan says that Arthur is showing some improvement; not a lot, but enough to be encouraging. He's given me the name of a physical therapist who works with polio patients. He thinks that she may be able to get Arthur to build up his strength a bit, and that could help him do more in spite of his braces. I'm checking up on this woman and what she charges for her services, and I'll let you know the next time we talk. I don't want you to get your hopes up too high, but this may be the way to make the best of this bad situation.

By the way, I fired Priscilla. I caught her taking food—a ham and three jars of pickles—just before Thanksgiving. I'm going to hire Dahlia Crawford to handle the housekeeping while I'm at work. She's no-nonsense and the boys like her. I've arranged a three-month trial period, to be sure that the terms I'm offering are good ones. Since her own kids are in high school, Dahlia has far more flexible time than Priscilla had, which I trust will make things easier around the house. With you gone, I have to take a more active role in the household, and Dahlia is willing to pick the boys up at school once David is in kindergarten, and to sit with him all day if necessary. She's a tolerable cook, as well, and that will be an improvement on Priscilla.

I've got a project meeting tomorrow morning, so I'll end this now. Remember that we all miss you and love you, and that we're praying for your return as soon as your situation is resolved.

Your adoring husband,
Harold Treat

❖ 6 ❖

"I'D INVITE you in, but there isn't much room," Charis said as Szent-Germain held the door to her apartment open for her to step out of it. "This outward-opening door is just the beginning. The sitting room—you can see a little of it—is about the size of a couple of those red English phone-booths, and the bedroom can barely accommodate the bed and a chest-of-drawers. The closet is a little bit bigger than my spice cabinet back home. And don't let me get started on the so-called bathroom and kitchen. All six light-bulbs are low wattage, too." Little as she wanted to admit it, she was embarrassed by the apartment she had found, and was reluctant to invite anyone inside to see how shabbily she was living. She had already promised herself to find something better as soon as she could afford it, for all of this place had an air of dreariness about it, a sadness left over from the war; she was glad to have a chance to get out of it for a while in spite of the cold day. After closing and locking the door, she bundled herself into her leather coat with a fox collar, nodding her thanks to him for helping her. "Looks pretty chilly," she said as she started down the stairs, two treads behind him. She buttoned the top two buttons of her leather coat—a knee-length country style with a deep pleat in the back to allow her to ride without having to open the coat—and was pleased with herself that she had decided to wear slacks and her sensible gardening shoes; her turtleneck sweater alone now seemed inadequate to the day's outing, no matter how shattery-bright the sky was, and, she realized, she had not left her building, so the bluster of the wind was still to come.

"As you like; the Delahaye is parked outside," he said, keeping his eye on the twist of the staircase. "Does your landlady approve of single men visiting you?" He, too, was dressed for the country in a black hacking-jacket over a cream-colored roll-top pullover, heavy twill hunter's-slacks tucked into glossy field-boots. He had gloves in his coat-pocket, but no hat.

"I doubt she approves of anyone visiting me; she complains if any of her tenants brings home company," Charis said, but quietly and in English, in case Madame Gouffre was listening at her door, as she did from time to time.

"Have you told her I'm your publisher?" he asked, seeing a slight gap between door and frame on the landing below.

"No. I don't think she'd believe me." She was surprised to hear how angry she sounded; she realized she was tired of being thought a liar. "She likes to think the worst of people."

"Is it your lack of a husband that bothers her, or that you're foreign? Or is it something else?" He spoke without stress, and waited for her answer with interest.

"I have no idea, though I wouldn't be surprised if she's against me on general principles," she said brusquely. "She doesn't say much to me, other than to inform me of what I'm not to do. She claims she doesn't understand my French; if that's so, she's the only person I've met in Paris who had so much trouble with my accent."

"Has this caused problems?"

She shook her head. "Not really; more like inconveniences. My better command of the language wouldn't change her mind about me. She isn't very fond of Americans. Her other tenants are Europeans of one stripe or another. The couple above me are from Czechoslovakia, and the old man below me and across from Madame is Lithuanian—probably not unusual for Paris, or any other big city in France right now, but nevertheless, I feel a bias from her. The couple across the landing from me came from Holland; they said their whole house was ruined in the war; we can't open our doors, they and I, at the same time." She stepped aside to give him the room to reach the head of the stairs. "The landlady has fourteen tenants. She says that she is having to be selective about renting out her rooms, so as not to turn away someone worthy—that's her word: *merite*. Apparently I haven't enough of it."

"What is she looking for: has she told you?" He took a step down the coiling iron staircase. "Does she know what she's trying to discover, or is she just rooting around in the hope of coming upon—?"

"A truffle of information?" Charis shook her head. "Nothing so cold-blooded. She's looking for displaced Europeans, or so I think, though she doesn't put it that way. She claims that they have suffered the most, but I don't think that actually means much to her. She usually says that she wants to help those who have nothing to go back to, those who have suffered. She's told me twice that I am too well-off to need to stay here."

"It sounds like she's trying to find an excuse to evict you, or to pressure you into leaving."

"I've been afraid of something like that. The last time she asked me to have tea with her, she warned me about my associates, but didn't mention any names."

"Whom do you think she meant?" he asked, and stepped off the narrow landing onto the lowest twisting flight of stairs.

"I think she means the Coven," Charis said. "I don't have any other so-called associates. Madame Gouffre was annoyed that I brought a typewriter with me when I moved in, and she says I'm not to use it, or play the radio after ten. I've been thinking about moving, but I don't know if I can afford anything much better than this, not if Harold doesn't continue to send along the money he promised." She put her hand to her mouth. "Oh, Lord. I sound like one of those dreadful women in Tennessee Williams, don't I? I shouldn't have said that. I'm sorry." The steps clanged as they made their way down to the tiny reception area.

"Is he having difficulties? Your husband, that is." He paused, then went on, "I don't mean to intrude. If you'd rather not answer such questions, tell me."

She made a quick gesture, her fingers wiggling to show that she was not concerned that he should know. "We talked five days ago—our regular schedule—and he didn't mention anything like that—nothing about finances, but . . . how can I find out if he won't tell me anything? I asked him if everything was all right, but he said it was nothing for me to fret over. My dad always said that to my mom, and I could see it drove her nuts. Now I know why."

"The lack of useful information, perhaps?" Szent-Germain surmised.

"I had the feeling he was dodging the whole issue. When I left to come here . . . he—Harold—promised me that he'd provide me a hundred and fifty dollars per month, in case I found it difficult to get a job. Which I have, thanks to you, though it's not as Harold envisioned. I have a second book to write, and that would not have happened had you not bought the first one. In fact, without your second contract, I'd still be in over my head, rather than treading water." She looked at Szent-Germain, trying to decide if she had revealed too much; she saw no sign that she had affronted him, so went on, "I said something about this to Harold after I'd been here a month, and he told me that I might have to accept a low salary, that I shouldn't set my sights too high—nothing like Tulane, or even teaching. He reminded me that Arthur's treatments were expensive, and that upset us both because he's right: lots of people manage on less than a hundred and fifty dollars a month. I thanked him, really thanked him, and the most he's sent at any one time since I arrived is a hundred and twenty, and that was in the first month. It's been a hundred even since then. When we talked on the phone a few days ago, he said he'd have to wait until mid-month to send me my money."

"Did he tell you why?"

"I didn't ask. We've been married nearly ten years, and I know when he doesn't want to discuss something. He keeps telling me to take advantage of any opportunities coming my way. You'd think I were on sabbatical, not fleeing persecution. He wants me to send fewer letters to the kids; the FBI or someone keeps opening them, and Harold is worried that it is upsetting the boys—I think it's Harold who's upset. And it was his idea that I come to Europe. He said he wanted to spare the boys pain and me frustration." Her tone made it clear that she would not venture any opinion against her family's interests. "At least he let me know I wouldn't have the money until next week, and I'm grateful."

"It seems to me that your husband owes *you* an apology, not that you owe *me* one." He had reached the ground floor and now stood

beside the registration desk. "It's bad enough that you were constrained to leave your home."

"Well, neither of us wanted what was likely to happen if I stayed,"
she said quietly. "And there are the boys to consider. Can we talk
about something else, please?"

"Certainly. How are you coming with your new book?"

"Well, it's not something I could have tackled from the US,
that's a fact; I think I have to be in Europe to do the research and
have a look at what's left, so in a way, this self-exile is a good thing:
Harold certainly thought so when I told him about it, " she said
with a hint of a relieved giggle. "We have so few Dark Ages convents and monasteries in the US, you know."

He offered an answering smile. "And that lack makes being here
an advantage. I agree. There are times you must see the place, taste
the air, feel its earth beneath your shoes, to have any sense of it."

"Yes. I hadn't realized how much of one until I began to study the
history in detail. It's really a much more complex system than I
thought at first. I'm hardly the first to think that, but I didn't comprehend it until I came here and could see how they were organized." She tried to show her interest by speaking faster. "Some of
those institutions were more like towns and cities than the towns
and cities were."

"Quite true," said Szent-Germain, remembering the monasteries in Poland before Karl-lo-Magne summoned him to Franks-
land, and established Szent-Germain on an estate in what was
now Belgium.

"It's hard, not having someone to talk to. The Coven is a great
help, but so often I need to speak to someone who isn't interested
in my field of study, to see if I can create some flicker of curiosity
in them—you know, as you do with students. I've even talked to
Madame Gouffre about it, but she showed no sign of interest in
Dark Ages monasteries."

"How much have you told your landlady?" he asked as he reached
for the door to tug it open; street noises flooded in with the cold
morning air. "Not just about Dark Ages convents and monasteries?"

"In my incomprehensible French? A fair amount. When I first

moved in, she asked me to tea a couple of times and spent most of the time plying me with questions about my background. The FBI couldn't have done better. I wanted to be sure she watched my mail and notified me if anyone came to speak to me here. I think that worried her."

"And has she . . . told you about anyone calling here?" He stood, waiting for her.

"I don't know," she admitted. "I think she suspects I'm some kind of spy, just like the Committee does back home—they see spies and Communist sympathizers everywhere. I've told her that it is a matter of politics that brought me here."

"You've given her a lot to think about. She may be worried about you doing something that could redound to her discredit."

"I'm a little old for prostitution," said Charis wryly. "What else could discredit her if I live in her building?"

"Smuggling, perhaps, or some association with Nazis." He softened this remark with a quick smile that crinkled the skin at the corners of his eyes; in that instant there was something in his face that was ancient, like the texture of parchment in books many centuries old. His smile vanished and he was Szent-Germain again; he offered her his arm once more as she stepped onto the narrow sidewalk next to him. "If that's the case, and she believes you have a secondary motive for being in her building, you're being prudent not to offend her. She may start looking for confirmation of her suspicions." The hard sunlight struck his face, making him wince, thinking he would need his dark glasses before they set out. His jaw was still discolored from his fight with the two potential robbers.

"My dorm monitor didn't place those kinds of restrictions on me, and I was nineteen at the time. You think she'd like a note from my mother?" She stopped, raising the collar of her coat. "Where did this wind come from?"

"Greenland would be my guess," he said lightly, moving a little ahead of her to open the door to the passenger side of the Delahaye. "There's a lap-rug folded up on the floor, if you want it. There's a heater in the auto, but this wind might need something more substantial to keep you warm."

"I probably will use it. Thank you," she said, suddenly feeling shy. "How long will it take us to get to Sainte-Thecla of Iconium?"

"Not more than an hour, I should think," he said, waiting until she had gathered her coat inside the car before he closed the door and went around to his side. By the time he slid in behind the steering wheel, Charis had the lap-rug half-open and was spreading it across her legs.

"I want to thank you for doing this for me," she said, a bit stiffly. "I don't want to—"

He took his dark glasses from the glove-box. "You will be able to begin work on your new book as soon as this and a few similar expeditions are done," he interjected, and started the engine. "Oh, there's a camera in a case behind you, in case you want photographs of the ruins. You may take as many photos as you like; I have four more rolls of film in the camera's case."

She blinked at him, and managed to say something that sounded like *thank you* as they pulled away from the apartment house, realizing as they did that the camera would come in handy once they reached their destination. "That's thoughtful of you, Grof."

Traffic was moving fairly well, and they made their way toward the southeastern part of the city in good time, on their way to the remains of a sixth-century convent that was now little more than a pile of old, weathered stone. Szent-Germain had seen it during his time at the court of Karl-lo-Magne, and a few times since then, and thought that the ruins would help Charis to get a better sense of convent life from visiting what was left of the place, seeing the lay of the land and its relative emptiness even now. It was more than a matter of layout and scale; it was also a reminder of the isolation of such places that could be conveyed there.

"Do you know what Order of nuns the women were at the convent?" Charis asked after a long silence.

"I don't think they had that level of formality, being part of an Order as such; that came later: in the seventh and eighth centuries, many religious communities were self-defined, and so long as they heard Mass daily and they prayed the Hours, the Church recognized them. This was more true of women's establishments than men's. The nuns usually called themselves the Sister of Sainte and added their patron's name, so I would suppose they were the Sisters of Sainte Thecla," said Szent-Germain, easing into a busy roundabout, and setting himself to exit its merry-go-round chaos at a good clip, his recollections more than a millennium away. "They followed a Rule of sorts developed by them from Boniface of Crediton, or so some of the local people say. There's no proof either way about that, but it is a reasonable guess, given some of the other old religious houses in the area. I don't know how zealously the nuns pursued their religious obligations at Sainte-Thecla." This was true enough, for he had only visited the convent twice when it was active, and both times he was bound for Roma, without more than a night to spare for the convent. He maneuvered the Delahaye through a street crowded with lorries and a few horse-drawn vans, then slipped past the remains of an ancient gate and out into the suburbs and the countryside beyond. The road was not made for speed, and there were notices of improvements being made ahead. "We'll turn before we reach the work-crews," Szent-Germain said as he noticed Charis' gaze light on another announcement of repairs ahead.

"Thanks. By the way, who was this Sainte Thecla the convent was dedicated to? I don't recognize her name, do I?" Charis asked. "Why her?"

"Now that, I can tell you: she was one of those early Christian martyrs, or so her legend says. It is pretty standard fare: a young noblewoman betrothed to a young nobleman coverts to Christianity, repudiates the engagement in favor of perpetual virginity for Jesus' sake, is punished by her non-Christian family but remains adamant, so is persecuted and tortured by the warlord or king or pagan priests, still remains Christian, and at last is martyred. And as a result of her piety, her former affianced husband, her family, and those who abused her are converted to Christianity, et cetera, et cetera, et cetera. She had a substantial following in the . . . Dark

Ages. A fair number of girls preferred the convent to marriage in those times."

"Was she real, do you think, this Sainte Thecla?"

"I doubt it," he said, slowing to pass a woman herding a gaggle of geese along the side of the road, her birds making sounds like a choir of rusty hinges. "But the story appealed to the people of the times, or there wouldn't have been so many versions of it."

Charis nodded thoughtfully. "Um-hum." Then she fell into a silence that lasted nearly five minutes.

They went by a section of new fence, with an elderly tractor plowing the field beyond. "He'll try to get it done before it rains," Szent-Germain said conversationally.

"You drive very well," Charis remarked as they reached the first small group of farms after the Parisian suburbs.

"Thank you," said Szent-Germain as if her long stretches of silence did not concern him. "It helps when you know the way."

"That's one of the things that surprises me," she told him. "That you actually know the way, and aren't just meandering about the countryside. I was afraid that might happen." She took a second or two to realize how this had sounded, and began to apologize.

"Why should I not know the way?" he asked, cutting short her abashment. "I have a few small holdings in this part of France that have been in my family for centuries; I should have mentioned them to you. One is near the convent. As soon as the war was over, I went to see what had become of my properties, to assert my claim to them, and to reacquaint myself with the people." It was near enough to the truth that he felt no qualms in revealing it. "And there are records in the muniment room at my holding that go back quite a long time; the convent is mentioned in them." The records went back to the time when Karl-lo-Magne had bestowed it upon him for his service to his court scholars, before he fell from favor, but he made no mention of this.

Charis' eyes brightened. "Do those records still exist?"

"A few do: not very many, and some of them are suspect, as is the case of so many things from that era. You may have a look at the ones I have, if you like." He reached a crossroad and chose a narrow lane marked by a row of poplars. "We should be at the convent ruins in twenty minutes."

The road was graveled, not quite wide enough for two cars to pass on it. It was flanked on either side by fields of blighted sun-flowers that still stood up straight, reaching for the sun, their husks rattling in the wind. In the distance there was a pasture filled with thick-wooled sheep; even on so cold a day, there was something lovely about its isolation in the clutches of late autumn.

"You wouldn't think something like this would be located so near Paris," Charis remarked as they approached a hamlet consist-ing of eleven houses, a general store, a travelers' inn where locals gathered to gossip, and a granary. "Talk about a wide spot in the road."

"A very apt description," said Szent-Germain. "Bear in mind that Paris has grown since the convent was built, and that horses travel more slowly than automobiles." He paused. "Most of this was forest interspersed with farmsteads—if the old maps are to be believed."

"So that would make going from Paris what?—a day-long ex-cursion?"

"Two days, more likely; the only good roads then were the Roman ones, and half of them were in disrepair." He stopped at the first of two single-lane cross-streets. "If you are hungry later, you can get a lunch-basket at the store."

"We're going farther?"

"Not much more than two miles." He slowed to a stop for a man with a curly-coated bull on a lead coming along the road.

Charis stared in surprise. "Nothing more than a lead in a nose-ring for that behemoth?"

"That's a prize bull; he makes an appearance at every fair and festival around here. He's used to people and traffic and was taught when he was just a calf to mind his manners. His name is Frisé, and he's almost six," said Szent-Germain, waving at the farmer, who gave a desultory wave in return.

"Are you making this up?" she demanded while laughing.

"It's all true," he assured her. "If you like, we can stop and you can ask Giraud if I'm telling tales."

"I wouldn't dream of it," she said, although she was suddenly very curious about what the farmer would say.

"As you wish," Szent-Germain said, and continued on as soon as Frisé was across the road. "Giraud—"

"Is that really his name or are you inventing things?" she challenged him, not quite laughing.

"It is really his name: would you like to roll down your window and ask him?"

"Is Frisé really his name?"

"Yes it is. Look at the curls in his coat," Szent-Germain replied with a genial chuckle. "He is one of the leaders here in Sainte-Thecla, as the place is called now, and the convent is nothing more than an untidy pile of stone. Giraud is a very careful fellow. He worked with the Resistance throughout the war even while he sold meat and grain to the Germans in Paris. If you ask about Frisé, he'll probably assume you'd like to buy him or want to ask about stud fees. Frisé has done much to make his owner a very successful man. During the war, Giraud kept his sheep and goats with him here, but had to hide his family and his cattle—too many hungry soldiers roaming about, taking livestock for food."

"Only Germans?" Charis asked.

"Germans, Americans, Canadians, Britons, Poles, French, the Resistance forces, and displaced farmers, as the tides of war swept over the country; almost all the soldiers were hungry, and no farmer could count himself safe." He thought of the war years when he had remained at Montalia, Madelaine's estate near the Italian border, and how she had sent her horses off into Switzerland, and her sheep into the Pyrenees in the care of distant relatives, leaving only the lands, a few crops, and the Medieval manor for him to look after.

"You were here for the war?" She was astonished to hear him speak so calmly about it.

"Not here, but in the mountains in the south of France, for most of it. I was at a manor near the town of Saint-Jacques-sur-Crete; it's not much bigger than Sainte-Thecla. But nine years ago, I had some dealings with the Resistance, too, and met Giraud then." He clutched down and slowed into an old lane that led off to the east, the middle of the road overgrown and the two ruts flanking it so rough that the Delahaye moved no faster than a jog-trot. "There's a little bridge up ahead, over the stream. It's very old, and could use some repair, but it's safe enough for us to cross." He flinched in anticipation of the enervation the running water would visit upon him.

She looked at him, surprised that he would mention the bridge. "Did the convent use it?"

"They diverted its course once they were established, and that gave them fresh water almost all the time. There was a problem in the fourteenth century, but the convent was well into decline by then, and most of it was in poor repair." He remembered seeing the clumsy dam that had been built a little below the convent, resulting in a marsh that spread over the lower pasture. He had been going from Orgon in the south to Hainault in the north, trying to keep ahead of the Black Plague, with only a shaggy donkey for a companion, Rogers having gone to Olivia, at her small villa near Trieste. He recalled how desolate the whole place appeared at the time, and how the water had been choked with debris and bodies; the stench had been appalling. "The Plague hit hard in this region."

"It appears to have hit hard everywhere." She thought of the war and how destructive it had been, and wondered if the Plague was as bad as World War II.

Szent-Germain braked for a bend in the road that led to the bridge. "As you see, very old, but serviceable enough for our purposes." He moved ahead, the Delahaye going at a walking pace. The shoulder of the road was sloped and fallen away in a few places, nothing too broad or potentially dangerous but sufficient to require an even slower advance.

"Are you sure it will hold up?" Charis asked, her smoky-blue eyes worried.

"I believe so; it did in October," he said as the Delahaye rolled off the bridge onto a little track that wound its way around a stand of berry-vines. "If you can see that thick pediment at the edge of the vines, that was the main gate to the convent. It was made of thick slabs of wood and heavy iron banding." He thought back to his time with the Khazars, aware that they would have called these ruins orphans of memory.

"Is the rest of the gate pediment in the thicket?" Charis asked, trying to imagine it.

"No, it went the other direction. This gate was in the curtain-wall, and was reinforced. The inner door was a bit smaller and lacked the iron. The inner part of the convent was more like the usual Medieval design, but between the inner wall and the curtain wall there was an apple orchard and a long line of coops and hutches for chickens and ducks and rabbits." He set the brake and turned off the engine; the sound of the wind rose up around them, its chill no longer playful. "The village may have snow tonight."

Charis sat, perplexed. "How many nuns lived here?"

"At its height, possibly a hundred-fifty or -sixty, not counting slaves." He saw her give him a startled look as he was opening the door to get out. "Oh, yes, those Dark Age nuns had slaves, as did many of the clergy but anchorite monks, and so did what passed for upper classes then; most of the slaves came from Eastern Europe, but others from Africa through Spain, and from the Greek islands. The last century the convent was active it had forty or so. The local Bishops ignored the place, and the nuns were left to fend for themselves. By eighteen hundred, they had sold off much of their livestock and their geese, but they continued to labor in the traditions of their Order. Such as they were, in time all of them died, and there were no novices to take their places." He had come around the back of the car and now went to open the door for Charis, then reached into the back for the camera-case. "Come, Professor Treat."

"Are you making those figures up? or have you some basis in fact to account for them?" As she spoke, she realized how remote from the rest of the world she felt here. Why had she come so far from what little she knew of Paris with this smooth-mannered foreigner who might, in truth, be anyone, or anything? She put her hand on the door-release and made herself conceal the first quivers of panic that had taken hold of her. He held out the camera-bag to her; she took it. "Thank you, Grof Szent-Germain," she said, taking care not to slip on the swath of dry grass that encroached on the road.

"Professor, let me—" He held out his hand to her, and was non-plused by the jolt of sexual need he felt from her as her hand took his wrist; he had sensed loneliness in her from the first time he met her, and occasionally a twinge of erotic longing, remembering Rosza of Borsod at Otakar the Great's Court, and Melidulci when Heliogabalus reigned in Roma; Rosza had been as demanding as what he sensed now; Melidulci was unabashedly hedonistic, but nothing like this, nothing that was as potent a mix as desire, yearning, and despair. He recovered himself almost instantly, and guided her onto safer footing. "Be careful where you walk," he advised her. "There are stones and tumbled stairs all over the old convent. The people of Sainte-Thecla don't often come here, they say the convent lands are unsafe. It's one of the reasons no one's farming it—too much labor for too little return." He glanced at her, then pointed with his free hand to a tumble-down stone tower about half a kilometer away. "That's the north-east limit of what's left of the convent's property."

"Is it?" she asked with an assumption of innocence; she was finding it difficult to talk at all. "Unsafe?"

"No; overused perhaps, and the Church occasionally tries to re-claim it, but nothing more."

She let go of him. "Thanks," she said, smoothing her leather coat. There was heat mounting in her face which she hoped in vain that he would interpret as the work of the cold wind. "I'll be careful." She moved a few steps away. "Okay. Tell me where everything was." As she spoke, she thought of her mother's firm but kind rebuke not to be vulgar or to tell men what to do; her jaw clenched.

"The curtain-wall went from that low tower to about where those willows are standing," he said, pointing the trees out and di-recting her attention to the crossroad shrine. "And another seventy degrees or so to the north, you can see the hayward's guard-post—they grew hay here for a few centuries . . ." For the next two hours, he led the way around the wreckage of the convent, explaining each building's function as well as its location while she photographed the places he indicated. They had made a circuit of the field and were approaching the place they had begun. "Are you getting tired?" he asked, and held up his hand to add, "Because I am." The sun and the near-by water had done their worst, and now that it was midday, he was finding it increasingly difficult to keep up the pace he had set for himself.

Charis could not bring herself to admit that she was exhausted, so she said, "Maybe another half-hour?"

He nodded. "Of course." He turned and lifted his arm to point at a heap of berry-vines with a portion of a squat broken column emerging from it. "We can go through where the old gate was, and that would put us in the nuns' part of the convent." He indicated some broken stones that had once been stairs. "That was the entrance to the refectory. There were three rooms in it: a kitchen, a dining room for travelers, and the nuns' dining room. There were fireplaces in the dining rooms where meat was cooked on spits, and the kitchens, where there was a kind of stove where the rest of the meal preparation was done. The bakery was just beyond it—it's all gone now, but in the part of the plan for the convent, it's clearly shown."

"Will you let me photograph that plan?" She had not expected to ask such a favor, but once she had spoken, she all but held her breath waiting for his answer. "If it's not inconvenient," she added.

"If you'll let me bring it to you, yes. The house I have in this part of the countryside lacks electricity, and you will need a good, strong light to bring out the ink; it's quite pale now." He was a few steps ahead of her, his fatigue starting to give him a headache while he did his best to recall the original buildings.

She was not paying much attention to where she was walking until she felt him seize her shoulder an instant before she turned her ankle; sharp hurt from the sprain warred with intense sexual desire that erupted with his touch. She pulled away from him, and very nearly fell again, and the camera slipped out of her hands, falling through the brush onto the convent's stones below. She shrieked softly as she heard the clatter of falling metal and breaking glass. "Oh, Grof. I am so sorry," she exclaimed, then fell, entangling herself in berry-vines and weeds while cutting herself on some of the glass.

This time he did not bother to ask for her permission; he bent down to lift her from the ground. "If you try to walk you'll only make it worse."

His nearness made it difficult for her to breathe. "But you're tired. I can make it to the car."

"Perhaps," he said, moving a bit more quickly, his muscles straining against the weariness that would enervate him until the annealing arrival of nightfall. "But I would prefer you don't fall down again." He slogged onward, and although it took him a little more than five minutes to reach the Delahaye, by the time he set her down in the passenger seat he felt her passionateness as if it had been on the road to Damascus once more. Closing the door, he leaned on the boot for a long moment, doing his utmost to ignore the sunlight that gnawed at him, using the time to think and to marshal what little stamina remained in him. How had this happened? He removed his glasses and wiped his eyes with his fingers, getting rid of the fine dust that blew off the fields; he buffed his dark lenses with the lining of his jacket and put the glasses back on. How to go on from here? They were doing well as colleagues, and, he had hoped, might have arranged a brief affaire during her stay in Europe, something that would allow each of them a glimpse of the soul of the other and relieve the burden of loneliness for a short while; he knew now that would not be possible: she was married and had not recognized her degree of attraction to him. She was lonely and would endure it as part of her exile, at odds with the emotions now stirring in her. There was also, he acknowledged, his esurience responding to her unidentified desire. He felt her conflict wearing at her, and wanted to offer sympathy, but was aware that would make her discomfort all the greater. For now, he would have to be careful during his time with her or risk summoning up as much demoniacal hatred in her as the concupiscence he had awakened. He got into the auto and saw her head turn toward him, her gaze avoiding his eyes.

"I'm sorry about the camera. Really." The contrition in her voice was for something more than the camera.

"I have others, Professor. You didn't plan to have such a fall, or to break the camera. No apology is needed," he said calmly; he could feel her frenzy diminishing, as well as the effort it cost her. Starting the engine, he said, "Try to rest as we go back. I'll call a doctor to have a look at you when we get there." With that, he turned the auto around and started for the bridge; he found himself trying to decide how he should deal with Charis Lundquist Treat.

General Delivery
Paris, France
December 5ᵗʰ, 1949

592 Sinclair Way
St. Louis, Missouri
USA

Dear Mimi,
  Apologies for not writing sooner but it's been one hell of a time here. Good news first: I finally got a job, not teaching math or anything rational like it, but working four hours a day at a tourist kiosk, helping the lost and bewildered who speak English find their way around the city. There's a Spanish guy who does the same for Spanish-speakers, and he says he can do some Portuguese. We have another American who handles the Italians, and a guy from Hamburg to help the few Germans who venture to Paris. The pay isn't very good, yet better than nothing at all. You can tell Jim that you won't be sending your pin-money to me for now. I know you say it's no problem, but Jim isn't an idealistic academic like me, he's an ambitious entrepreneur with cars to sell, and I'm not his brother, I'm his brother-in-law: you can't expect him to share your inclination to help me. Anyway, for now, I'll be busy explaining to baffled American and English tourists how to find their hotel, or the Louvre, or the Left Bank. It's not hard to do, and it leaves me some time for working on my own.
  Believe it or not, there is more good news. A fellow I met through the

Coven runs a publishing company, and he's interested in a book on the applications of calculating machines that are neither military nor governmental. He agrees with me that such machines—once they have become smaller and need less constant attention—have a place in commerce and travel and archiving of all manner of information. He has offered me two thousand dollars for such a manuscript, paid in two installments. That should keep the wolf from the door, at least for a little while. Once I've finished the book, I'll discuss other topics with him, including my theories on how mathematics should be taught in schools as a language, not a code. I won't bore you with another harangue on the subject.

Speaking of the Coven, there is sad news there. Joe Allanby's wife died, having never truly responding to attempts to revive her from the overdose of sleeping pills she took. That happened about a week ago. Joe didn't come to our unofficial Thanksgiving dinner we had at Chez Rosalie, and we all understood why, or thought we did. His housekeeper found him the following Sunday, dead of a self-inflicted gunshot wound. He left a note, blaming the Committee and J. Edgar for Norma's death and saying he couldn't think of any reason to stay alive any longer. He was sorry he hadn't arranged for a successor for the Coven. I think it's just as well that we, the Coven, get a little time to debate among ourselves to resolve that problem. His brother arrived yesterday to arrange for transportation of the body back to the US. We've asked his brother if he would join us for a private memorial service here before he leaves, and we're waiting for his answer.

On the subject of brothers, how is Corwin doing? Sorry I missed his graduation, for all manner of reasons. You said he might try for Cambridge for a year, to get a good start on his Masters with someone like Ronkowski or Haste. How's that coming along? His work so far should open many doors for him. And what is he doing in the meantime? Don't tell me he's still playing brass with that jazz-band. All right, tell me if he is doing it, but let him know that he ought to be concentrating on studying; blasting away at Eubie Blake and Scott Joplin may be fun but it doesn't support the assumptions of his devotion to math. Given Mama's opinion of jazz, I must suppose he isn't living at home now, in which case, where is he staying? He's the most aggravating fellow I know, and I miss him like stink.

There. I've had my spasm for the month now, and I won't cry on your shoulder any longer, at least not until January. Keep in touch as much as you can, give my love to the family, including Jim, and let me know how things are going for all our family. I don't like to be away, especially not for the reason I'm away; hearing from you, and from Aunt Jenny, makes it a little less awful. So even when I growl, never doubt that I am almost pathetically glad to hear from you.

Your loving brother,
Happy (who isn't)

P. S. I had a note from George last week—he says he's been traveling. The note came from Ceylon—and he asked me to tell you that India is really beautiful and recommended you—and I quote—"bone up on it." There. I have done it. Mission accomplished. I told him to write to you directly next time, but he probably won't.

❖ 7 ❖

"COME IN, Broadstreet," said the voice Lydell Gerold Broadstreet had heard often, one of those attention-demanding announcements that were unfamiliar to a quiet, sonorous voice that oozed with the power of the man, beneficent and sinister at once, making an omen that was hard to understand. "It's about time we have a face-to-face, don't you agree? Sorry I had to ask you on such short notice, but you got here in good time." The invitation had come to Broadstreet in Baltimore yesterday afternoon at four, and was fairly sternly worded: he would be expected at one of the CIA satellite offices in Washington, DC, where he would meet with the Deputy Director for Clandestine Services at ten A.M.

Broadstreet had dressed for the occasion in the same three-piece pin-stripe suit he had worn to testify before the Congressional Subcommittee on International Intelligence, his ivory shirt and foulard tie proper to the nth degree. Knowing he was presentable enough, he summoned up all the courage he could and opened the rosewood door, stepping into a surprisingly small, ascetical room: simple, paneled walls bare of ornamentation, two windows looking out on the rear entrance to a hotel, draperies without valances, three chairs, an old-fashioned oaken desk, a glassed-in bookcase, and a pair of filing cabinets—pretty meager for a man of Channing's position. Broadstreet held out his hand, not daring to come too close to the desk, and saw then that Channing was in a wheelchair and that his left hand ended in a hand-like prosthesis. How the devil, Broadstreet wondered, had Channing come by such private calamities? Channing moved the wheelchair near enough that he could reach across the desk. Broadstreet remained utterly still until Channing raised his right hand to take Broadstreet's, who gripped it heartily, inwardly grateful that he did not have to touch the artificial hand.

Channing held up the artificial hand. "Jimmy Riggs' work. Some eight years ago."

"His heyday, I've heard," said Broadstreet with as much savoir-faire as he could muster, hoping to show his knowledge effectively.

"Sit down, Dell, and thanks for driving into DC; it's a bit of an inconvenience for me to travel," said Channing. He, too, was in a three-piece suit—his was of charcoal wool, his shirt was chalk-white, and his Prussian-blue tie had university colors worked into it just below the perfect Windsor knot. "That's what your friends call you, isn't it? Dell for Lydell?" Channing tried to lighten Broadstreet's demeanor. "I'm assuming you've discovered who I am. I would have done so were I in your position."

"You're Channing. I believe your first name is Alfred." He shivered a little, and he decided that the room was chilly—not surprising on this sleety day.

"Manfred, actually, but like Alfred, known as Fred," Channing said, indicating a comfortable wing-back chair. "I'll have some coffee brought in a bit later. You take yours with one sugar and a little cream." Channing slipped his chair behind the desk more fully, and leaned forward, his elbows on his blotter-pad. "You're here about that luncheon you had some weeks ago—that contact you went to meet before Thanksgiving . . . anything ever come of that? Or did it fizzle? Or was it a way to distract your attention from something else?" He gave Broadstreet no chance to answer as he laid his hand on the report that lay on his desk. "By the looks of it, you washed out there, but it might not have been a total debacle. I've gone over your report and your contact's failure to present himself. Most disappointing. But if there's hope of something developing, then it's in our best interests to be patient. Anything more about D. G. Atkins from your more accessible informant?"

"Nothing solid; I want to get more information before I authorize Rothcoe or Leeland to put one of their men on it. You know how it is, and far better than I, when you have odd bits of facts but no notion on how to put them together." He saw Channing's brows draw together, portentous as storm clouds; he hurried on. "I don't want to chase wild geese if we can help it, but I don't want a Communist sympathizer running loose in the world with a head full of our secrets, so Atkins is my first concern. But Baxter seems to know something useful, as well, and it behooves my department to investigate thoroughly." Broadstreet nodded stiffly, then sat down, feeling as if the well-padded chair were made of concrete. "I want to give the case preferential attention for the next couple of months."

Channing was not convinced. "And how do things stand with your mysterious visitor? Have you found out who he is yet?"

"I don't have solid confirmation yet, but I'm convinced that the man who came to my office was James Rutherford, Nugent's brother-in-law. Isling in surveillance promised me a photo of him by the end of the week. That's a bit tricky, since we aren't supposed to be operating in St. Louis—or anywhere else in the US—but there's going to be an opening of another car dealership, and the press will be there in force. If Grant Nugent is really James Rutherford—and I am reasonably sure he is—then we'll know soon enough." He paused, aware that he had lost Channing's attention. "That's what Rutherford does: he sells cars, new ones, used ones. He started out as a Pontiac salesman, then branched out. Now he owns three dealerships and a pair of used-car lots. He's doing quite well for himself. He brings in about twenty thousand a year, Rutherford does."

"And you say Nugent's sister is in contact with him? Nugent, that is. Do they exchange letters frequently? I assume she and her husband see each other quite regularly." This attempt at levity was not successful. Channing cocked his head like a perplexed hound in search of a scent.

"Yes, at least enough to send him—Nugent—money on what appears to be a regular basis," said Broadstreet with a moue of distaste. "It's always difficult when a brother has to ask for help from a sister, isn't it? It seems less than manly to impose on a female that way."

"Is this sister older or younger?" Channing's lips were turned toward smiling rather than his more habitual frown.

"I don't know. I'd guess she's older, but I can't confirm it. Does it matter? I can find out if you think I should. Her name is Meredith, by the way, but Nugent calls her Mimi."

"Older sisters often take good care of younger brothers," said Channing with a look that was very like nostalgia. The intercom buzzed; Channing tapped it on, all traces of nostalgia vanished from him. "Yes?"

"There's a call from Miller at State," said Channing's secretary. "Do you want to take it now?"

"Not now. Tell him I'll call back in an hour." He clicked the intercom off and stared at Broadstreet; this was an improvement on the interview's first omens. "About the age of the sister."

Broadstreet neither knew nor cared, but he did his level best to agree. "I hadn't looked at it that way, sir. I'll find out who's older, and get back to you."

"What else do you know about her?" Channing inquired. "She may be more important to this than we thought."

"She may be," he said at once, not believing for an instant that her importance was anything more than minimal. "I'll send Wehkind to St. Louis and ask him to find out as much as he can about the family. We have all the basic material on Hapgood Nugent, and from what we can tell, it all shows that there is strong support for examining the possible ramifications that everyone is aware of, but there has been no reason at this point to look further into the family. Well, it didn't seem that important, did it? since we've assumed from the start that—" He realized he was babbling, and stopped.

"Any other siblings, or don't you know?" Channing asked, and Broadstreet knew this was not just an idle question.

"There's a younger brother, one of those surprise babies: the mother was almost forty when she had him. He's just graduating from college. He took honors in mathematics—I guess it must run in the family." This attempt at mild jocularity brought only a glower from Channing. "He's settling on a graduate school now. He is considering Stanford and Cornell."

"I'll want all the family particulars by tomorrow. Vital statistics, school records, financial statements, the lot. We need to know how Hapgood gets along with all of them, and to target some pressure on them that way."

"From what Grant Nugent told me, that's been done already. His children—Grant Nugent's children; Hapgood Nugent doesn't have any that I'm aware of—have been watched and the schools they attend have been informed of the possibility of anti-American activities on the part of the family. Nugent wanted it stopped in return for his cooperation. I've sent a notice to the schools in question, informing them that the family is no longer of interest to the government and that the children and their parents are no longer regarded as possible wrong-doers." He could feel his pulse racing, hoping he had done what Channing would approve.

"Which means we can continue our observation, but clandestinely." Channing nodded. "Much the better way. We'll have fewer chances to be caught off our reservation. It saves us the tedium of having to winnow out the gossip and rumors from useful intelligence, or at least we can minimize the extent of the damage such idle speculation can do to our case." He leaned back in his chair as much as it would allow. "Oh, these civilian zealots! Certain that if there are Communists, they must be coming after them, as the good capitalistic patriots they are. They have no idea how our enemies target us, or why, and they want to think that of all this country has, the Communists want to control its sum; the crux of the matter is their city, their town, their institutions." He rubbed his hand through his short-cut hair. "It's a kind of civic pride, thinking the Commies are after you."

"I'm still going to send Wehkind," Broadstreet said tentatively. "He comes from St. Louis and can use his contacts advantageously."

"Oh, yes, of course. Best to put him on it today. Have him pack up and take a plane. Rent a car in St. Louis. You don't want DC plates to draw attention to him, do you?"

"Of course not," said Broadstreet a little too quickly. "I'll give Wehkind his orders as soon as I leave here."

"I'll arrange for hazard pay for him. That should stop any reluctance to travel so near to Christmas." He chuckled, contemplating the windows. "The weather is really turning nasty. If there are delays in flights or road closures, I'll extend your deadline appropriately, but don't try to make it an excuse if you cannot complete your assignment in the time allowed."

"My Aunt Mildred says a storm is coming, and she's rarely wrong," Broadstreet said, in order to show he was listening. "I always call her before I travel." This was not quite the truth, but it was enough to get Channing's attention.

"Is she more reliable than the weather service?"

Broadstreet hitched up one shoulder. "The family thinks so."

"How fortunate for her, and your family," said Channing.

"I don't think she sees it that way," said Broadstreet. This mention of Aunt Mildred made him think for a few seconds that he really ought to call upon her before Christmas Eve, and do something nice for her. She lived only twenty minutes away from him and was his father's last living sibling. But the thought of her relentless cheerfulness and Bible-quoting seemed more than he could endure, and the impulse faded as rapidly as it had come. "What would you like me to do about Baxter? I am prepared to wait, and I think it would be a wise idea." He was beginning to hope that he could get a trip to Europe as part of the investigation, if only he could keep the story believable. He would have to make up his mind about Baxter over Christmas, find some way to make him more crucial to what was happening than he had imagined at the start of all this.

"I have assumed that," said Broadstreet, sounding testy now. "We need to show that his presence has claimed the attention of—"

"The meeting at the Helmsman was one of those cobbled-together arrangements. You know he didn't come to our meeting after all, but that did not surprise me when I thought it over. There was no acknowledgment that the meeting had not taken place. No explanation, nothing. But there was a note in my mail-slot at home three days later. Unsigned, of course, but I'm fairly sure it was from my contact, Baxter. It said *Better luck neXt time*. No salutation, no farewell. Not even an address, which means he brought it himself. The paper on which it was written could be found in any stationery, and it was typed on a Royal with a new ribbon."

"Someone who knows about our line of work, then," said Channing. "Any notion of who he might work for?"

Broadstreet shook his head. "Nothing solid, and no reliable confirmation about him. I have reason to believe the man's name is

Baxter, though it may be an alias, but I haven't been able to make sure of that one way or another, and so I continue to think of him as such. I have begun to wonder if the appointment wasn't a serious meeting at all, but actually some kind of test." He spoke steadily, as if from a memorized text, which it was, for he had spent more than a week getting his story ready for this conversation.

"Baxter," mused Channing. "Nothing in the name to help, is there? Why bother with an alias when you have such an anonymous name to begin with. Assuming it is his name: it may not be." He sighed, looking toward the bookcase at the far end of the room. "Why can't conspirators have unusual, one-of-a-kind names? Papadapolis, or Brinquedo, or something obviously Russian. Ouspensky would be a good one." He slapped his right hand on his blotter-pad. "Baxter. Ha. Why not Smith, or Jones? His first name is probably John." He tapped his fingers on the desk.

"I have saved the note, and if you like I can send it to our laboratory for fingerprint tests, but they may only find mine: I didn't realize what it was until I opened it and read it." He knew it was folly to reveal too much too soon, so he only added, "I'm planning to look into any connections that may exist between this Baxter and Bateman & McNally, for it has occurred to me that the men from that company may have known Baxter, which would explain his being missing from the Helmsman, where men from Bateman & McNally were having a celebratory lunch. Whatever they were celebrating, I might have compromised Baxter."

Channing sighed again. "It may be that you're right and this was a test, that your Baxter was among the men celebrating, and he was trying to determine if you were truly alone and not part of a trap." He drummed his fingers some more. "This bears more attention than I thought at first. You'll need to find out the names of the men from Bateman & McNally and try to determine if there are any connections with Atkins. I wish we didn't have to think about that lot in Paris being in the middle of all this—it complicates matters. But since Nugent appears to know where Atkins is, his is a lead worth following. There are good reasons to think Atkins is helping the Commies in places in Malaysia and French Indo-China, or even in Indonesia, for it appears that he's hoping to gain the favor of the Chinese."

"How do you figure that, if you'll pardon me asking, sir?"

"Because of the linking of Atkins with Hapgood Nugent, whom we know to be in France. Nugent's brother-in-law appears to believe that Nugent and Atkins are in regular communication, or so I gathered when he called upon me. Our best intelligence out of Pei-King suggests that Atkins has offered the Chinese leaders information that could not have been available to Atkins at the time he left the US, but is part of a project Nugent has been involved with. There could be something more going on with that ridiculous Coven in Paris, but there would be clearer signs of it by now if that were the case. It's an ex-pats' shared-interest club, I'm sure of it, from our agent in it, and the reports say that there's nothing more dangerous going on among the Coven than in the board room at Montgomery Ward."

"You have an agent in place with the Coven?" Broadstreet asked, astonished to hear this news. "Who is it?"

"The best kind of agent; one who doesn't know about being an agent." Channing's smile was small and wicked. "All you need do is ask a favor—some minor information your unaware agent might have—and thank him when he provides answers."

"You mean an amateur, or he doesn't know he's spying on the group?" He wanted to know everything, but doubted he would be told today.

Channing shrugged. "The latter. The Coven's found out all the professionals. I think this may be the only way to keep an eye on them." He reached over to his intercom and placed coffee orders for them both. "This is more of a coil than I had expected. What other cases are you working on at this time?"

Broadstreet was fairly certain that Channing knew everything he had been assigned, and so he enumerated the eight other investigations going on under his supervision. "Two should wind up by the end of the month"—Bishop should be out of Ireland by then and the new team ought to be in place in Turkey by about the same time, and that would mean much more time for Atkins and Nugent—"which will free up some time."

"Not enough, and not soon enough," Channing grumbled. "I'll need to see you busy on this Atkins matter by the first of next week, which means that we need to settle the Nugent/Rutherford question as soon as possible. I'll lighten your load by three cases before Thursday, so you can concentrate on Atkins. We don't want him slipping through our fingers once we locate, or at least identify, him." He dropped his head, chin on his chest, in deep thought; Broadstreet sat still, watching Channing in a growing rapture of fear, becoming so entranced that he visibly jumped when one of the serving staff arrived with a wheeled cart laden with coffee-pots, -cups, creamers, sugar-bowls, and three covered dishes of appropriate food for a ten-thirty A.M. break.

The waiter who brought the cart laid out the various dishes and comestibles—two bear-claws, two raisin muffins, and two large glazed doughnuts and a covered butter-plate—then poured coffee into two large mugs, handing the first one to Channing and the second one to Broadstreet. "Is there anything else, sir?" the waiter inquired.

"No, Walters. This will do us very well." Channing waved a dismissal in Walters' direction. "You can pick up the cart in an hour."

Walters went toward the door, then stopped, his demeanor showing how willing he was to relay crucial orders. "Oh, sir: they're closing the building at one today. They want everyone out after lunch, on account of the weather. There's supposed to be a blizzard coming this way, and the Mayor wants to keep the streets as clear of cars as possible."

"Does that include Baltimore, or is it just DC?" Broadstreet asked.

Channing looked up from his mug. "Thank you for the information, Walters. I'll endeavor to be away by noon."

With a nod, Walters let himself out of Channing's office.

"He's very good at his job," Channing muttered once they were alone.

"I suppose so," said Broadstreet, reaching for the creamer, only mildly curious about the waiter.

Channing reached for a muffin. "He's an FBI agent, sent to keep an eye on us for Hoover, just to make sure we don't do anything domestic." He opened the butter-plate, removed the small knife, and cut off three pats of softened butter. "I think he's foolish to waste such a good operative in our dining room, but that's Hoover's way. He wants all security agencies in the US under his thumb. He's after Truman to make the CIA part of the FBI."

"You're sure of this?" Broadstreet asked, almost choking as he bit into the side of the nearer doughnut.

"Of course I am. And I suppose Walters realizes that, though he's not said 'boo' about it." He buttered the top half of his muffin and took a bite, chewing thoroughly, his face showing he was lost in thought. After he took a long sip of coffee, he said, "I have a feeling he keeps a lot to himself, Walters does."

"Holding something in reserve?" Broadstreet asked, taking another bite of his doughnut. "For bargaining?"

"Nothing so crass as that," said Channing. "He is making sure he has options. If he wants something from me, he has information to trade, information he can withhold or deliver to the FBI."

"Surely you could fire him, for some reason other than spying," Broadstreet exclaimed.

"Why would I want to do that? He is showing himself to be reliable and he's an excellent waiter. Whomever Hoover sends next, I imagine he won't be quite so useful. No, I'll keep Walters and see what I can gain from him."

"Do you think he's aware you're onto him?" Broadstreet asked, then realized that he had asked the question badly and made another run at it. "Why would he think you were onto him?"

"He's in the business to know such things," said Channing, finishing his muffin and reaching for a bear-claw.

"But if you're both aware of the other's knowing, why bother? Surely both of you have more important things to do?"

"Gamesmanship, my lad, gamesmanship. Never underestimate the power of gamesmanship. Why did you go to so unlikely a meeting as the one at the Helmsman? Same sort of thing. Practice is as important as performance where intrigue is involved. We both have the opportunity to keep our skills sharp, to keep on our toes. We need to have these games or, when our opponents are Russians or Bulgarians or native rebels in Latin America or Indo-China, we won't end up compromised and cut loose for it." He began on the bear-claw. "Make sure you have yours. They're very good today."

Broadstreet finished his doughnut, then reached for the second bear-claw; his mind was racing, and finally he dared to say, "Then if Baxter comes to nothing, you won't mind?"

"Oh, I'd mind, all right, but I wouldn't do anything foolish. You've been behind your desk too long; you're turning into a bureaucrat, and we have far too many of them in DC than we need already. No, you need to get your feet wet, and this seems as good a way to do that as anything." He chewed in reflective silence.

"Um," said Broadstreet—the bear-claws *were* very good today, if his was any example.

Finally Channing spoke up again. "That doesn't mean you're free to do whatever you like. You have your orders and I expect you to follow them. No dawdling, no getting sidetracked. If you want to think of this as a test, or an audition, go ahead and do so." He poured more coffee into his mug and held the pot out to Broadstreet. "Top up?" He clearly expected to have his offer accepted.

After a brief hesitation, Broadstreet extended his mug. "Thank you." It was the least he could say, yet it would show that he was aware of the potentialities of his immediate commitment to the case he was going to pursue. "I'll try not to disappoint you, sir. I'm grateful for this opportunity."

"Keep in mind that Atkins is really up to no good. Don't waste sympathy on him. What he's doing is not an intellectual ploy or a trick he's playing: he is deliberately giving our enemies—our *enemies*—information on rocket fuels and load-thrust ratios as well as the formulae for them to do similar calculations. If there are intercontinental ballistic missiles involved, those formulae could spell real trouble for the US for years to come." Channing shook his head. "He has to be found and he has to be stopped, and everyone who aided him has to be checked out, and dealt with appropriately, or it's possible that the work will continue even after we eliminate Atkins from the picture."

The word *eliminate* made Broadstreet uneasy, but he made sure his discomfiture was unnoticed. "Do you expect any trouble with him? Extradition, and so forth? Or do you think the Commies have got him already?"

"I don't believe we will bother to ask. Nor should you. We can't bring Atkins into public view until we know how much damage he has done." Channing spoke softly, which convinced Broadstreet of the sincerity of Channing's threat.

"Understood," said Broadstreet, and bit more bear-claw off than he had intended. He could feel a bit of the filling cling to his cheek. He grabbed his napkin and rubbed it away.

"I'm looking forward to seeing what you can accomplish in the next few days. We need to be diligent as well as accountable in everything we do." Channing took the nearer of two folded napkins and wiped his fingers. "You have most of the afternoon to get all your ducks in a row, and tomorrow, I want to see results. Give me a call around mid-day to apprise me of your progress. I want to see you get a promotion out of this." He bared his teeth in imitation of a smile. "This way, you'll be prepared to deal with Baxter, if he ever shows up."

Realizing that his audience with Channing was almost over, Broadstreet returned the half-eaten bear-claw to the plate on the serving-cart, picked up the second napkin to get the sugar-glaze off his hands, and brushed down the front of his jacket and vest, working out how to end this audience on an appropriate note. "Thank you. I'm glad to have something useful to do for the . . . company. I will do all I can to perform to your expectations."

"Yes, yes," Channing said, sounding a bit bored.

Standing in the doorway, Broadstreet asked, "Is it true that Atkins' first name really is Daedalus?"

Channing blinked, somewhat surprised. "Yes. Daedalus George Atkins."

"I supposed that he gave himself the first name," Broadstreet said. "In a gesture of self-aggrandizement."

"No. His parents had big plans for him from the first. They called his brother Pythagoras William. He died in a prisoner-of-war camp in 'forty-two." He laughed once. "Can you imagine getting through grammar school with a name like Daedalus? Or worse, Pythagoras?"

"Must have been rough," said Broadstreet, who knew it was expected of him.

"Not half so rough as I require you to be in dealing with him. Keep in mind that he is working against US interests. Persevere, Broadstreet. Do not hesitate to do all you must to end Nugent's spying, with or without the help of Baxter. We need to get a good result on Atkins, and soon. He cannot be allowed to escape. Hoover's men should have kept him from leaving the country, but since they didn't . . . So long as I see results, you can keep your position, but if you become lax, someone else will take over for you, and you'll be in the archives for the rest of your career."

"Don't worry." Broadstreet drank most of the coffee remaining in his mug, and rose to his feet, not needing an omen to make it clear what he would have to do. "It's an honor to be—"

Channing waved him in the general direction of the door. "Tomorrow, Broadstreet. We'll talk tomorrow."

"Yes, sir," he said, just barely resisting the urge to salute. He bent to pick up his briefcase, then started for the door. He paused as he put his hand on the doorknob. "I know this is a real opportunity, sir. I'm most grateful." Confident that he had said enough, he let himself out of the small room and made his way down a long corridor to the elevator. He pushed the buzzer and the mechanism sprang to life, the dial over the door marking the progress of the cab, all the while thinking he had found the meeting much more encouraging than he had expected. He could tell that there were complexities here that needed a lot of attention, and he would have to be careful how he presented whatever he learned from Baxter.

The uniformed elevator operator opened the door into the elevator cab. "Sir?" he asked when Broadstreet hardly moved.

"Oh. Yes." He walked into the cab, wondering as he looked at the middle-aged black man running the elevator, if he were some kind of agent as Walters the waiter was. He sighed, reminding himself that no matter how he looked at it, this was more than sport: he would have to watch himself closely, and be at pains to make sure everything he reported on Baxter was consistent, which meant establishing his own file on the man, so he could keep track of what he revealed. Under other circumstances, he would have told Channing about his deception, but he was convinced that Channing would not give any approval to the scheme Broadstreet was putting together in the cab-ride back to his office. He left the cab with a preoccupied air, but as he started toward the door into the building, he noticed a man in a navy-blue raincoat standing by the newsstand, who glanced up as Broadstreet went by. Broadstreet made an abrupt change of plan, and veered off toward the parking lot; he increased the speed of his walk as he made for the staircase to retrieve his Frazer. He glanced back once and thought he saw the fellow keeping pace with him some twenty feet behind him. He sighed. He would have to be doubly careful if he were to be under surveillance, if the man behind him was actually following him, and not just going to the parking lot. This possibility did not reassure him, and he lengthened his stride, but did not look back as he made for his car with unusual swiftness, trusting that his speed would be seen as diligence by anyone observing him.

7B Avenida de Santo Alonzo
Havana, Cuba
18 December, 1949

Le Comte de Saint-Germain
108 Rue Currie
Paris, France

My most dear Saint-Germain,
*Peru, Ecuador, and Venezuela are all withholding dig permits. I've
used every academic contact I have that might convince the various ministries that I have nothing nefarious in mind, but just at present, there is
a fear that any European seeking to venture into the back country of
South America must be an escaping Nazi, looking for a remote place to
start the Fourth Reich. Rumor has it that there is a small but steady
stream of Nazis leaving Germany through Genova and Marseilles for
South American ports. Argentina and Paraguay are said to be the most
popular destinations.*
*Since I haven't been able to secure permits for a dig in South America,
I have accepted my friend Hugo Gemelo's invitation to join his dig in the
Yucatan Peninsula, unearthing Mayan cities. It's not what I would ordinarily want to do, but it's preferable to remaining here in Cuba watching the tourists gamble and whore their way through Havana as a
preparation for Christmas. So I will be off tomorrow for Mexico City,
which means hours in a plane over water; you understand what that can*

be like among those of our blood. I will be met by a guide and an escort next Thursday, and will go from Ciudad de Mexico by road to the Yucatan and prepare to spend months digging and cataloguing racks of stone skulls and stone glyphs. I'll try again in a year or so to see if Peru at least will consider letting me look for Incan cities. There is so much I have left undone, and that I want to explore. I confess I didn't understand what you called the advantage of long life—perhaps because I hadn't lived long enough to gain the perspective one can gain—but since I'm well past my two hundredth birthday, I do begin to appreciate what I can do with so many years to come.

All this means, of course, that I shall miss seeing you for another decade, which is one aspect of this vampire longevity that I do not enjoy. I must also admit that I am becoming accustomed to dealing with people who assume I am the age I appear to be, which is one of the reasons I am so glad to see you, and James, whenever our paths can cross. James, I understand, is in Canada now, still writing adventure books for boys as J. T. Emmers. When I have sent this to you, I'll write to him so you will both know where I am. When I have an address in the Yucatan, I'll send you the particulars.

Repairs at Monbussy are proceeding well; work starts on Montalia once winter is over. In three years I should be able to return to completed homes and electrical wiring in both places, remodeled kitchens, new windows, and improved plumbing. There was trouble with the gaslights at Monbussy during the Allies' advance, and the German soldiers who had occupied it left it in a disgraceful state. All that will be taken care of, and I have Jean-Marie de Camp, to supervise both. He has been a great support to me even though he has decided not to take that final, sixth step and come to our lives when he dies. I have found him most dependable, especially since he is a former lover and is now a married man with two children.

Would you mind very much if I gave him your address so he can consult you if he cannot reach me? I know you will get on with him. No doubt you will be interested in the other changes being made at Monbussy and Montalia, and Jean-Marie will know all the details. He's not a man to intrude, so do not worry that he will consult you on every detail of the decisions; I left him comprehensive written instructions that will no doubt prove valuable to him during my absence. I will remind him not to approach you unless there is a real problem, or a legal complication. You may rely on him to be discreet. He's aware how important it is that anything to do with me be kept utterly confidential.

Saint-Germain, I miss you. I would like to be in your company from now until the end comes, whenever that may be, but I know that would be unwise in many ways. Being apart is difficult but it is preferable to being found out for what we are, and were we together we would be at risk. Think of what modern science would make of actual vampires! I know what academia is like, and I don't like to imagine what they would want to find out about us. All this does not change my love for you. The Blood Bond has sustained us at great distance since I came to your life in 1744, and it will be there until the True Death, as steady and dependable as the Evening Star. What dreadful sentimentality, when I hoped to express myself with concision and profundity, in a manner befitting a tenured professor. So before this becomes too cloying, I will close with

> *My eternal love,*
> *Madelaine*

Part Two

THE EX-PATS' COVEN

January 3rd, 1950

My dear Charis,

If only you had been with us, Christmas and New Year would have been perfect, but as it was, I think having my parents come to New Orleans rather than the boys and me going to them was a fine solution to the weather problem. The boys were thrilled, and it made your absence a bit easier, having Mom and Dad here. In fact, it turned out so well that they'll be staying on, at least to the end of the month, and perhaps longer. This means that I needn't pay for a housekeeper since Mom is taking that job over and is a much better cook than Priscilla. Dad says they might consider moving out of Raleigh and coming here until such time as you return; Dad is planning to fix the back porch and put in new plumbing in the upstairs bathroom, which needs it badly. They've bought one of those home movie cameras—Mom plans to take movies of the boys and send them to you so you can see how they're doing. You should be able to find a projector somewhere. My parents and I have asked the boys about the possibility of Mom and Dad making the move, and both of them are pleased at the prospect of having them living with us. I can see improvement in Arthur's behavior already—he's not so timorous anymore, and he has fewer crochets. David is happy to have the attention they will provide. With you gone from the house, he has gone around it like a little ghost.

I realize this is a sudden development, and I won't blame you if you aren't too much in favor with the arrangement. You've mentioned feeling isolated, and said you were worried about the boys. But it appears that you're going to be away for at least another year, if the news is to be believed, and for kids that's a long time. Your letters have helped; I read them to the boys as soon as they arrive, and your copy of The Grimoire *was a real hit with them. Even Mom and Dad liked it; they had been worried that you were being pressured to work with strangers. I know they worry that your unresolved difficulties here make you something of a target in Europe. I think Mom and Dad have a better understanding as to why you haven't come back. I hope you'll keep those coming, the letters and the* Grimoire *issues. It is a relief to see that you are in good company and that you have not had to resort to less distinguished associates. We discussed that before you left, including how it might impact us here at home, and it is gratifying to see that you took your situation to heart. When you return, you will have publications to bolster your position, which should make it easier for you to find a respectable position at a good university, but perhaps something smaller than Tulane. Of course, please send us a copy of your book as soon as it's available. I'll be happy to show all your colleagues that despite being under a cloud, you continue your studies.*

How is work coming on your second book? Have you solved the problem of dealing with slavery in Europe during the Dark Ages? You told me when we spoke the last time that you plan to work on it all through the spring and possibly the summer. I must say, your dedication to your writing is a surprise to me, but it reminds me that you are truly a gifted academic, and when your reputation is restored and it is safe for the family, you should have no difficulty in returning to teaching in the US with the regard of the faculty intact because of your continuing scholarship. It is just like you to turn a difficulty into an opportunity. You have good reason to be proud of yourself for your enterprise.

You told me your sprained ankle was better, but I am worried that you may yet have problems with it if you use it too much, so let me ask you to curtail your jaunts into the countryside to see old convents and monasteries as part of your research. You said that the French physician who took care of you was very experienced and dealt with you in a most capable way. No doubt he was the best of the lot for you to work with, but I would feel more secure if you could find an American doctor to ex-

amine the sprain, to be sure that it is healing as it should. There must be an American military base near Paris, and as a citizen of the US, you ought to be able to command the attention of one of their physicians. Let me know what he has to say once you have consulted him, and what his prognosis is for your recovery. There are many risks that come from sprains, as you know, and it troubles me that you may have to cope with some of them because of your misfortune.

Speaking of prognosis, Arthur is going in for an evaluation next week; Doctor Sutherland has said that it is time to have a comprehensive look at him, and to determine how great the muscle-wasting is. Arthur is deeply worried, but Mom has promised to go with him to the hospital and to stay with him the entire time. This has calmed him somewhat, and that is encouraging in itself. Whatever Sutherland finds, I'm certain he will be candid with me in terms of its implications. I'll send you a letter as soon as I have something to report, and I will tell you more when we have our next conversation.

Things are running along well at the lab. Our corporate patron is increasing the amount of our grant for 1950, which will allow us to expand our testing into three new regions of the state, which should make our comparisons much more useful. If all goes well with this, we may be in a position to apply for a five-year grant with options for increasing our areas of operation by this time next year. There are several states I would like to include in our studies for the purpose of comparison if nothing else, and that is what we will have if all our requests are accepted, which is all the more reason I'm sorry that Marcus Sylvester will be leaving the team in May—he has the offer of a position at Texas A & M, which is what he has been hoping for. I don't like the thought of losing him, but for his own sake, I have to support his ambitions. I am going to spend the spring looking for someone to take his place, though a geologist as capable as Marcus will be hard to find. I have another soil chemist who would like the position, but we need a geologist more than we need another soil chemist. If I can't find a competent geologist, I may have to take on the soil chemist, just to fill out the roster. Next September, the government will review our work, along with Geological Services, Inc., which might lead to an even broader application for the techniques we are developing.

I tell you all this because it will probably mean that I will not be able to get free from my work this summer—like you, I have too many obligations to contend with. There is too much riding on our current project, and as leader of the team, I will have to supervise all our work in the field. I've asked Mom and Dad if they would be willing to accompany the boys to Paris to visit you, but Mom is worried about Dad's heart and a long flight might be too great a strain on him; she is understandably disinclined to make the trip without him. It is a disappointment, I know, but you can see how crucial this year will be for me, and it would be a disservice to out patron, the university, the Department of the Interior, and my team for me to interrupt our efforts for what would appear as a vacation in Europe, especially in light of the suspicions that linger about you. I know you'll weather this disappointment with your usual aplomb, as you always have.

I'm attending a reception in Chicago next week, returning late on Sunday, if weather allows us to fly at all: the weather report calls for high winds and snow, and ordinarily I would stay home, but the reception is part of a conference on natural resources, and there will be over six hundred attendees for the reception, discussing our natural resources. I will take the plane up on Thursday, so that I may make the most of the opportunity to talk to all those attending. I'll be having meetings with Wilkins, Berryman, Clauster, and Szpondiski: when am I likely to get those four within five hundred miles of one another within the year? The featured speaker will be Professor Teller, who is going to deliver a talk on the necessity of building up a nuclear arsenal and preparing for nuclear war. He may be right about the Russians, but I need to hear more before I start telling everyone to build a bomb-shelter in the basement. Don't worry—I won't say anything about you to that crowd. I know you understand the need for my attendance at this conference. So I will have to postpone our next-weekend conversation; you would have to stay up after midnight to make the call, and from what you tell me of your landlady, she is likely to refuse your request to book such a late call, let alone put through any call I might make. I'll plan on talking to you the weekend after, if that suits you. I know you understand, and I thank you for it.

I have arranged the wire of $120 to you for January. You should be able to access it in five days. Spend it wisely: I know you will. If all goes *well, I will be able to provide a little more in February, and possibly for March as well. Keep your spirits up, continue working, make the most of being abroad, and rest assured that all is being taken care of back home.*

Your devoted husband,
Harold

❖ 1 ❖

SUNSET WAS fading over Venezia, and a slight, chilly haze had begun to glow an intense, deep blue, rising from the water and drifting along the canals large and small, making the whole of the city seem to be floating on dark clouds; it would not last long, but for now, the entire city seemed touched by magic. Traffic on the Gran' Canale was moving a little slower than usual, as if taken with the dream-like atmosphere of the place. The boats in the canals and the ships at the Basino di San Marco were battling with the occasional gusts of wind that snapped along the buildings as if to scatter the blue mist like annoying water-sprites. One gondoliere swung his boat away from the Gran' Canale toward the small, elegant palazzo that fronted on the Campo San Luca but backed onto a small canal; the steps leading up from the Rivi San Luca to the loggia of the palazzo were newly scrubbed and shone white as teeth in the swath of illumination from the electric lamps at either end of the landing.

"Ca' San-Germanno," said the gondoliere at his most laconic, pointing out the small jewel of a palazzo that was the second landing in from the Gran' Canale.

"I see that," said Szent-Germain, starting gingerly to rise as the gondoliere nuzzled his boat up to the stairs. He fought down a sudden onslaught of queasiness, reached out to grab the nearest ring on the side of the palazzo, installed two centuries ago to aid those leaving boats in reaching the steps without mishap. It bothered him more than he liked to admit that for those few seconds when he was between the gondola with its special, shallow keel lined with his native earth and the instant he was on the stairs of his palazzo, with his native earth in the foundation, distributed over the cluster of ancient logs, he was hard-put not to succumb to the nausea that water brought on. His exhaustion was taking a toll on him, and he knew he needed to strengthen himself in order to accomplish all he had set out to do in the next three days. He would have to ask Rogers to refill the soles of his shoes with his native earth to avoid another episode of discomfort. He steadied himself, watching the gondoliere hovering at the edge of the landing. "You can put the gondola away for now, Biagio, and have something to eat." He flipped an old coin to Biagio.

"Grazie, Signor' Conte," said Biagio, who knew the worth of an authentic ducat. "Is the gate open, or will you send someone down to open it?"

"It should be open: we're expected. Tie up in the boathouse and come inside. There should be food in the staff's room; if not, go to the kitchen and ask for a meal." He looked up at the darkening sky. "The wind's picking up and you will want to be secured for the night. The tide is starting to rise, and that will mean more water in the boathouse." His arrangements made, Szent-Germain went up the stairs rapidly, wanting to be free of the disorientation water engendered in him; vertigo swam at the edge of his vision, and he swallowed twice against it. As he entered the magnificent loggia, he allowed himself a sigh of relief as his native earth in the foundation worked its annealing magic on him.

"I will bring your bags up to you," Biagio called out, for he had seen that the Grof was exhausted from travel.

"That is good of you, Biagio," Szent-Germain replied, glancing through the pillars up at the scudding clouds sweeping across the sky, chasing away the last of the afterglow; with most of the color gone from the evening, the luminous, sapphire-blue mists were becoming little more than low-lying fog.

"A hard trip, my master?" Rogers asked him from the gallery in front of the main reception room on the floor above; he spoke in Byzantine Greek. "It's worse because you're tired." He faltered, trying to decide what more he should say that would not cause the Conte to withdraw into himself, with only bad memories for company.

"Hectic," said Szent-Germain in the same tongue. "More so than I'd like. The weather made for delays, and a lot of crowding on the trains when they finally ran. A day ago, there was talk at Bern of closing the tracks until the storm blows through—they decided to keep the tracks open for five hours—though when I reached Verona, they claimed it was a miracle that we got through, and prepared to close the tracks again, but that hasn't happened yet, so far as I know. The station in Verona was a madhouse. The train to Milano and Genova left an hour late."

"You have never liked things hectic, not in all the years I've known you." There was a glint of amusement in his faded-blue eyes—the years they had known one another numbered almost two thousand.

"A fault of mine," Szent-Germain conceded, his tone of voice lowered a little to indicate he would not discuss it yet. "How have your travels been?"

"Some good, some not," Rogers answered, his glance around the loggia alerting Szent-Germain to the likelihood of being over-heard. "Winter is always hard on traveling."

"Meaning there is some trouble," said Szent-Germain in a re-signed voice. "Why do I suspect that the trouble was not about trains?" he added in the language of Visigothic Spain.

Rogers gave a tactful cough. "You might be more comfortable in the withdrawing room; there's a fire lit in there, and the carpet on the floor helps keep it warm." He, too, continued in Visigothic Spanish. "We can be more private."

"Very good," said Szent-Germain, and made for the broad stair-case that had replaced the old steep, narrow one two centuries ago. Despite his fatigue he climbed steadily; with the night drawing in around them, and being over his native earth, much of his strength was returning. He glanced over his shoulder toward Rogers, who was coming to the head of the staircase. "You mentioned in your report before last that there is some trouble in Barcelona and in Genova," he remarked as he took off his overcoat and handed it up to Rogers.

"There are problems, and in more places than those two ports, although the trouble is most obvious in those places," said Rogers. "Not all of them small."

"I suppose it was to be expected. After all the black market dealings in the war, it is hard to give up the trade, " Szent-Germain said as he reached the top stair. "Should we be prepared for legal action?"

"It wouldn't hurt to inform the attorneys." He lowered his eyes, and said in English, "Better safe—"

"—than sorry," Szent-Germain finished for him, and went on in the same tongue. "True enough. Will there be any action taken, by police or other agencies?"

"Possibly," said Rogers carefully, turning back toward the reception-room door. "You will probably want to ask a few of your factors to . . . retire, or take them to court."

"Retirement is a far better solution," said Szent-Germain. "How badly are we . . . dipped?" His choice of this old-fashioned word earned a wan smile from Rogers.

"Millions of lire," said Rogers. "And franks, and reales. The Genova office particularly has been secreting money in plenty, and gambling on not being noticed." He gave a single shake to his head. "I don't know that anyone gambles the way Gennaro Emerenzio did, but Signore Bastone in Genova appears to be working in that direction." Emerenzio had nearly bankrupted Eclipse Trading and Eclipse Press in Venezia four centuries ago, having misappropriated most of the money Szent-Germain then had in Venezia to support his gambling fever. Leonardo Bastone had established a money-laundering business with ties to the remaining Nazis still at large in Europe, and was backing his work with Szent-Germain's money. "That is something to be thankful for, isn't it? Think what greater damage he could have done if you hadn't been warned?"

"This is not much different, though by the sound of it, less single-minded. Is there any indication how the money was acquired? Smuggling, or black market dealings." He was thoughtfully silent for several seconds, then said, "Millions of lire are not worrisome, but franks are another matter. Reales must be considered as well." He looked around, taking stock of the room. "At least nothing has been initiated yet. I don't remember matters being this complicated after World War One."

"They weren't, not for your businesses, in any case." Rogers waited for Szent-Germain to say something, and when he did not, he added, "The level of destruction was less after the First World War. This Second War has been more than a continuation of the hostilities of the First, it has dragged in countries that played no part in the First, or had not yet existed. Also, there were no atomic bombs in the First."

"There was the 'Flu, though," said Szent-Germain, his face for an instant showing his age. "In many ways it was deadlier than the war." He studied Rogers' posture. "You think there is another one coming, don't you: another war."

"As you do," Rogers said.

"I hope it will not, but there are so many temptations that accompany wars, they are difficult to avoid at the start." Szent-Germain paused. "About these problems you've encountered. Have you completed your assessment?"

"Not yet; I have only a few preliminary notes for your businesses here; I had intended to do more before you arrived, but, as it turns out, I was also delayed in getting here," Rogers told him. "I have a summary for your attention of the state in the French and Spanish offices, if you would like to see it now."

"Is it that urgent that I must undertake to study it tonight?" It was an atypical question for Szent-Germain to ask, and it ignited Rogers' curiosity.

"Urgent, but not desperate, at least not yet," said Rogers. "No doubt, one night won't make much of a difference."

Szent-Germain nodded. "Will this summary of problems take long to discuss?"

Rogers studied him as he hung the overcoat on a brass rack near the door. "Why do you ask?"

"Because I will be going out later this evening, after I have a bath and change clothes. On foot—no reason to use the gondola for this." He wanted no one to know where he was going, or why, as much as he wanted to avoid another journey over running water; he removed his muffler and dropped it onto his overcoat.

Rogers made no attempt to conceal his relief. "You will visit a woman? Long overdue, my master. Have you decided whom it will be, or will you decide later, after you have seen who might welcome you?"

"It is my intention to visit a specific woman; her name is Evangelista Bonuomo. I shared a compartment with her on the train; a widow from Milano, personable, well-mannered, not quite forty would be my guess, and missing her husband profoundly. She told me a great deal about him. He was fortunate to have her high opinion. I believe she would be glad of a dream that brings her pleasure." He went to the brocade-upholstered sofa and dropped onto it. "The war was hard on her, particularly after her husband died."

"Does she have children?"

"Two, she said, in what the Americans call boarding schools, an odd term for them; it almost sounds like a stable for horses. The older one is in Switzerland, the younger one in Firenze. She misses them, but she has to work—her words, not mine—and not for money, for a sense of worth. She teaches the blind."

"Is she expecting you?" Rogers asked as neutrally as he could, realizing that too much interest could cause Szent-Germain to become more reserved in his answers.

"I think not. She only talked to me because there was no one else to listen; we were the only occupants of the compartment. As it is, I don't plan to arrive until after midnight. Have you any plans for tonight, old friend?"

"Nothing very exciting. I had thought I might listen to some music on the radio. There's a concert of early music being played in Padova and it's being broadcast." He looked to the windows behind Szent-Germain. "There's going to be snow in the mountains tonight. The wind will be cold."

"Early music," Szent-Germain mused. "Medieval or Renaissance?"

"Some of both," said Rogers. "Ancient music." He gave a solitary laugh. "Historic might be a more appropriate term. There was music well before you restored me to life, most of which is lost." He resisted the urge to sigh. "I wish I could hear some of the songs from Nero's reign, including some of his own. He came up with a few good songs before he angered the Senate. The one he wrote for the Legions was a fine march."

"*Wherever the*—no, that's not right, it's *As far as any eagle flies, the might of Rome will go/From out of steaming Africa to Hyperboric snow,*" Szent-Germain sang quietly. "Is that the one you mean, with the octave jumps in the refrain?"

"That one, and *Jupiter, the Biggest and Best,*" said Rogers, surprised at how these memories stirred him.

"Oh, yes. But you need a hydrolic organ and a crowd of fifty thousand voices singing to do it justice," Szent-Germain said with a touch of nostalgia. He ran one hand through his hair. "Best to get this trimmed tomorrow—after I see the press-men."

"Is there anything you'd like me to do before then?" Rogers inquired, his demeanor as inscrutable as a cat's.

"If you would, have Duracoprir draw me a warm bath, and, if you would, set out my black suit I bought in Chicago, and a black roll-top pullover. Foreign but not obviously so; not easily remembered."

"Certainly. Should I plan to shave you, as well?"

Szent-Germain rubbed his chin. "Probably. I don't want to scratch her. I should have had the barber tend to it before I left Paris, but time was short."

"I'll ask for the razor, and the lather-mug." Rogers let himself smile as he went to the door and motioned to the servant in the loggia to come up. When the young man arrived, Rogers said, "Tell Duracoprir to draw a bath for the Conte, and fetch the razor, mug, and shaving basin."

The young servant nodded twice. "Now?"

"Within fifteen minutes; they'll be wanted in the Conte's bathroom," said Rogers, then stepped back into the reception room. "You've selected your clothes, and your bath is arranged. Is there anything else?"

"Keep the fires lit until two hundred hours, if you would," he said, "and banked for heat after that."

Rogers pretended to be shocked. "Feeling cold? You?" He answered his own question. "Or it is for the staff?"

"The staff, of course." He sighed. "Tomorrow I'll need to go to the press. Ogniosso has been fairly insistent that we discuss the problems with the press-men. He, being their foreman, is determined to address the issues as soon as possible."

"They want raises now that the war is over and Italy is rebuilding?" Rogers said, accepting the change of subject without annoyance.

"Among other things. They want greater participation in the decisions about what we publish. And want to have a board or committee oversee our publishing program." Szent-Germain made a gesture of helplessness. "Most of them don't understand the books we publish and those who do don't know why we bother, so that is unlikely to work out to anyone's satisfaction if some changes aren't made. They need something they can call theirs, or we're apt to lose them."

"Have you anything in mind?" Rogers asked, knowing it was expected of him.

"I thought perhaps a secondary line of books, more popular, would please them, something they could point to at a bookshop and give as presents. Nothing too slick or obviously commercial, but attractive and stylish. Perhaps a series of illustrated travel books that could be updated regularly, or perhaps something for children. Or both." He shook his head. "We'll have to see."

"Most of the press-men are Communists, aren't they," said Rogers. "Will that be a problem?"

"Why should it be? If the Americans object to books typeset and printed by Communists, we needn't sell our books there. Those Americans who want them can order them from England." He got up. "Any word from the Coven?"

"Are you expecting something?" Rogers asked.

"Not specifically, no," said Szent-Germain. "When I left, McCall told me he wants to talk with me when I get back, and would not tell me why, or about what. He's a very suspicious fellow: many journalists are."

"So I have discovered," said Rogers, adjusting the placement of a small occasional-table so that all four legs were on the carpet.

"You've borne up under the load very well." Szent-Germain began to pace. "What is most difficult is finding a way to work around those absurd restrictions that are regarded as protection from Marx and Lenin. The Americans are driving away many of those whose abilities they need. It's more destructive than protective—all based on innuendo and gossip, and backed up by manipulation of the facts and invention if there are no facts." He stopped moving, willing himself to be calm. "Or so it appears to me, and from a distance."

"You're satisfied that the Coven isn't a secret Communist cell, then?" Rogers asked in a sardonic tone.

"How could it be? They aren't well-enough organized or philosophically united to be Communists."

"Then you are more specific in your aggravation."

Szent-Germain nodded. "I am."

"More trouble for Professor Treat?" Rogers guessed. "She has told you something that worries her?"

"It appears so," Szent-Germain said. "Just before I left Paris, she said that she'd had an unpleasant telephone call from her husband, but was not inclined to go into details. I surmised it wasn't about her older boy, but it distressed her, which leads me to suspect that there is still trouble about her political alliances. She apologized for intruding, but wanted to ask my opinion on her situation, yet could not bring herself to say what it is, precisely, which concerns me more than knowing whatever it is that troubles her. She talked around it—what the suspicions about her are. I gather it was tied to the reason she left New Orleans in the first place. She did tell me that the HUAC is after more academics, but did not want to go into that."

"And what did you do?" Rogers asked, fairly certain he knew the answer.

"I listened."

Rogers nodded. "And then you came here."

"This journey, as you warned me, could not be postponed. I have work to do here. I gave her my Word that I would contact her as soon as I return, which should be in four days, and gave her the address of Eisley Butterthorn & Hawsmede and told her to contact them if there was any need of their services, and I sent a note to Hawsmede instructing him to bill any services she requires to me. That should help her achieve a better legal stance. At present, it's the most I can do without causing her embarrassment." He made a gesture of frustration. "Now I should go and soak. If you'll come to my rooms in an hour or so, I should be ready to put myself in order for the evening." He smoothed the front of his jacket, and glanced at Rogers. "You are so discreet, I am thrice-fortunate to have your help in these dealings."

Rogers ducked his head. "Do you want to have my report to-morrow before or after you talk with your press-men?"

"Before, I think. Between eight and nine hundred hours. I want to be prepared for what I might encounter." He left without more ado, his full attention now turned to his plans for the advancing night. He entered his private apartments a little later, aware that someone had been watching him; he had caught sight of Angelo Ruscel, the under-steward, out of the tail of his eye as he went down the corridor. This constant spying was wearing on him, and he had to stop himself from turning on the under-steward and demanding to know why Ruscel should be watching him, and for whom. A moment later, he changed his mind, and continued on toward his private apartments: it would do Szent-Germain little good to reveal his awareness of Ruscel's activities, and would demonstrate that he was looking for watchers. He had a brief memory of his last conversation with Sidney Reilly in what was no longer Saint Petersburg in Russia: the master-spy had been surprised to discover that Szent-Germain had known of Reilly's interest in him. Ruscel was much clumsier in his snooping than Reilly and his associates had been, which was little comfort to Szent-Germain.

His private apartments had a sitting room, a bedroom, a dressing room, and a bathroom, each lacking the elaborate decoration that marked most of the palazzo. Most obvious was the total lack of mirrors in any of the three rooms. The walls were painted a sub-dued green-blue with valences and frames of doors and windows done in dull gold. There were Oriental carpets in the sitting room that echoed the colors on the wall. Two floor-lamps and the small chandelier overhead provided light. Szent-Germain made his way across the room, patting the Turkish saddle-chair as he went. He poked his head into the bathroom and was pleased to see steam rising from a full tub. There was a towel and a bathrobe laid out on the bench along the wall, and a bar of Pear's soap on a washcloth next to the tub. He took the bathrobe and left the bathroom, going toward the polished rosewood door that led into his Spartan bedroom. Ten minutes later, he was undressed and soaking in the hot water, the bathrobe on the broad rim of the tub. There was more of his native earth under the bath, and that provided more comfort than the very warm water that lapped around him. He picked up the soap and washcloth and set to work ridding himself of the grime of travel.

As he had done for all his undead years, he avoided looking at the wide swath of scars that covered his torso from his ribs to his pubis, grim reminders of his execution by disemboweling. He recalled the horrified stare Rakhel had given when she had seen them, and how studiously she had avoided his company after that. Olivia had not been appalled when she had finally convinced him to show her what had been done to him, but she was distressed by the sight of them, and did not hesitate to tell him so. He could not blame anyone for being upset by them, but when the sight led to distraint, it doubled his loneliness. Despite his determination, he could not entirely shut out his disquieting speculations; his litany of anguish continued while he strove to shift his attention, but with little success. What would Hyacinthie have made of them, or Avasa Dani or Ranegonda? Madelaine had not seen them until after her death, and she had been riven with sympathy for so arduous an ending to a life. He tried to shut these memories from his mind, but they persisted in scraps and pieces, all of which left him in a somber mood as he rose from the water and wrapped himself in the towel, drying himself briskly before donning the bathrobe to wait for Rogers to come and shave him. Some five minutes later, Rogers arrived, during which time Szent-Germain managed to gather his thoughts and turn them in a more productive direction.

"I apologize for my state of mind," he told Rogers while Rogers stropped the razor.

Rogers tested the blade and set it aside as he took the brush and mug. "Not necessary. You always become a bit saturnine when you go long periods without taking sustenance," he said, knowing that Szent-Germain had gone more than six weeks without finding nourishment.

"I thank you for your understanding, old friend," Szent-Germain said before Rogers slathered his jaw, upper lip, and cheeks with soapsuds.

"Don't spend the evening chiding yourself for your nature; you taught me that after you restored me to life; consider it a lesson for yourself," Rogers said as he set to work with the razor.

Szent-Germain chuckled as the shaving began. By the time Rogers finished with him, it was past twenty hundred hours, and Szent-Germain set about dressing, vaguely aware of the sound of Rogers' radio-concert from Padova. He took a little time to listen, aware that one of the pieces was being played much too fast and that the braisel was not in the right rhythm. As he tugged his roll-top pullover on, he checked it carefully with his fingers, making sure the roll-top was properly flat on his neck, and that the garment was smoothed on his chest and back. He adjusted the cuffs, pleased that he could see what he was doing on the arms; even after more than thirty centuries of coping with his lack of reflection, he still found it awkward to deal with his limited vision. When he was fully dressed, he chose his shoes—a pair made for him in Firenze of black deerskin leather, with thick soles—liking the flexibility of the pair, and how quietly he could walk in them. As he tightened the laces, he realized that his native earth in the soles had been very recently replaced; the surge of energy this provided him also lessened the gloom that had threatened to engulf him earlier. He found that he was anticipating the coming night with pleasure. "Good riddance," he murmured to himself, and let himself out of his sitting room into the corridor. A minute later he descended to the loggia; he was feeling ready for his night-time venture.

"I have your overcoat," Rogers said as he came out of the vestibule to the side of the loggia. "Do you want a hat, as well?"

Szent-Germain gave this a brief moment of thought. "I suppose it would be wise. Most everyone out tonight will probably be wearing one." He was offered a knit watch-cap, which, after a brief hesitation, he took. "I'm going to go to Eclipse Trading Company before I seek out Evangelista's hotel. I have my keys."

"You'd better take mine," Rogers said, taking a crowded ring with a great many keys depending from it out of his trouser-pocket and removing the one with the blue dot on its bow. "You'll need it—they've changed the locks."

"Of course they have," said Szent-Germain, his voice world-weary. He took the key and slipped it into his coat-pocket. "Not a good sign."

"No, but we can discuss what you find in the morning." Rogers went to open the door that fronted on Campo San Luca. "When do you expect to return?"

"Before five hundred hours. The city becomes active soon after that hour, and I will want to be here before someone discovers I'm out." From the edge of the loggia facing San Luca, he looked around the campo, taking note of the few people about, nodded, and slipped out; he heard Rogers close the door behind him. It was a brisk ten-minute walk to Eclipse Trading, and included crossing the Rialto Bridge. He passed the rivi where Basilio Cuor had tried to kill him, all those years ago, and went along the flank of the Gambero di Mare, a fishermen's tavern where there was a rowdy night under way. Finally he took a turn down a narrow alley, and at its end were the offices and warehouse of the Eclipse Trading Company. He approached the door, bringing the key out of his pocket, and opened the door. His excellent night vision did not need the lights on to see as well as most persons would do on a cloudy day. He saw the furniture had been rearranged, and there was a new safe in the far corner of the front room. It was a new acquisition, for when Szent-Germain had visited the office on his last short stay in Venezia, there had been no safe. A line of filing cabinets stood against the west wall, at right angles to the safe. If only there were someone like John Henry Broadribb to assist him now, as Broadribb had done eighty years ago. He approached the filing cabinets and noticed they were locked. Much as Szent-Germain was tempted to break them, he realized that would give away his presence in the morning, and he had no wish to do that. He went to inspect the two desks that faced the front door, hoping to find a scrap of paper he could examine. With an impatient, whispered oath, he left the front office for the one to the rear, where the factor and his secretary worked, but this turned out to be as frustrating as the front office had been; the secretary's desk was distinguished by a typewriter and a box of twenty-pound bond paper. He tried the drawers on the factor's desk, and to his surprise, the center one opened, revealing a vast number of paper clips, a stapler and a box of staples, a stack of envelopes—one of which he removed—and two expensive fountain-pens along with an inkwell.

A nearby church-bell struck nine, and was joined by others in a ragged chorus.

There was a ragged cheer from the Gambero del Mare that echoed eerily along the buildings that crowded the limits of the alley, providing a disquieting counterpoint to the bells. Urged on by the clamor, Szent-Germain decided to jimmy the lock on the factor's two file drawers of his desk. He had a thin, pliant knife in the inside pocket of his overcoat; he drew this out and began slowly to slide the blade into the tight top of the drawer on the left, easing the knife up against the latch, and struggling to get the lock to open without obviously damaging the wood. It took him twenty minutes, but finally he heard the snick of the wards turning, and the snap of the latch releasing. He pulled the drawer open and looked through the files inside, finding little of interest. Closing the left-hand drawer, he frowned, then set to work on the right-hand drawer. When he got that drawer to open, he noticed an un-evenness in the bottom of the drawer, so he removed the files in their manila envelopes and worked the bottom of the desk until it lifted up, revealing a ledger in the space. This he lifted out and laid open on the blotter-pad, and began his close perusal of the figures it contained. The more he read, the more concerned he became, until he had to resist the urge to bear the ledger away and spend the night reading it through. But he put the ledger back where he had found it, put the files back in the proper order in the drawer, and used his thin knife to lock the drawer. He left Eclipse Trading Company with caution, taking care not to be seen, and trying to decide how he would go about what would be a very tricky meeting the following afternoon. His thoughts were preoccupied as he went toward the Rialto Bridge; there were fewer people on the streets, and most of them hurried through the cold bluster of the wind, hunched over as they moved toward their destinations.

At the Stella del Mare, he found the reception desk busy with a late-arriving group of priests from Toulouse, who kept the registration clerks busy while Szent-Germain went toward the stairs and went up them. He had seen Evangelista's reservation confirmation letter on the train, when she had asked him if he knew the hotel, and what he thought of it. He had told her what he could, and made note of the room number: B 14. Now it was simply a matter of finding it, and making sure that Evangelista was completely asleep before he entered her room and deepened her slumber so that he could impart pleasure to her and gain nutriment for himself. For the first time in two days, his mood lightened as he reached the top of the stairs, and started down the hallway that was marked "B 11–18"; in spite of the weather and the difficulties at Eclipse Trading Company, he was looking forward to sharing the ephemeral sweetness of Evangelista's dream.

Feb 14, '50

For the third time since the beginning of the year, I've swept the meeting room at Chez Rosalie, and for the third time I have found half a dozen small listening devices of what looks like American construction in clever places. I have disabled them all, and taken out all but one, so that whoever put the bugs in place will suppose that we did not locate them all, and may not resort to other methods of surveillance than listening devices. Because of this constant scrutiny, I fear we will have to find a new meeting place for the Coven, one that isn't nearly so public, or so readily accessible to outsiders; no matter where the eavesdroppers come from, their persistence makes them dangerous to us. If there is anyone in the Coven who has a possible site for our meetings, we should find out as soon as possible. Anyone willing to take us in should be made aware of our situations so that there can be real understanding among all of us.

I think also, that we should ask Young not to put any information about this in The Grimoire. *It would be foolish to provide any of our new arrangements for those watching us. We have good reason to keep our moving and the reason to ourselves. I know a good number of the Coven members pass along our news to their friends and families back in the US, and this way, we can at least postpone the hour when our pursuers once again run us to earth.*

In that regard, I would advise you to speak with Szent-Germain about our predicament. He has many reasons to assist us, for not only is he as much an exile as we are, but he has publishing contracts with six members of the Coven, one of whom is you. If any stranger might be helpful to us, I am fairly confident that he would be able to garner information that could enable us to change our meeting place with a minimal risk of exposure. Charis Treat has told me that the Grof's manservant has located a flat for her that is more conveniently located than her apartment was, in a safer building—it is a trifle old-fashioned, but not unattractive—and having more room than she had before. She will move at the end of the month, so I don't think I am betraying a confidence by telling you this in advance of our meeting. I admit that I am not at all acquainted with the man, but his conduct has been exemplary so far, and that persuades me to want to take him up on his offer to aid us wherever possible. I understand that he has returned to Paris at the end of last week, and may be found at his flat or at his publishing office.

We must be discreet in our endeavor now, and that may be difficult for some. As our leader, I think that proceeding in a covert manner is essential to our protection. I cannot emphasize this enough: we must be at pains to protect ourselves, or we will end up in just the same sort of fix that we're in now, and that would probably prove to be an unsustainable development for the Coven, necessitating our disbanding our group and seeking out other cities where we would look for havens in smaller numbers so that we would all be harder to trace.

So you have my opinion—possibly more than you were expecting. I will sweep the meeting room again an hour before our next meeting; you and I can discuss what we are to do before the rest of the Coven arrives.

Stephen diMaggio

❖ 2 ❖

LYDELL BROADSTREET sat alone in his office, nervously biting at
the cuticle on his left thumb. The morning had been passing at
glacial speed, giving him plenty of time to realize what a gamble
he was taking, and how much of his career would be destroyed if he
failed to pull it off; the omens suggested that he was in over his
head. He had made every effort to use his deception to advantage,
but was not convinced that he had achieved what he sought. He
was embarked on a new level of dissembling that worried and
excited him, ruining his concentration for the stack of files on his
desk that were filled with reports and complaints about those who
were now members of the Ex-Pats' Coven. If he succeeded in pulling off this ploy today, he would have the power he was seeking
and would enhance his reputation throughout the Agency. It was a
temptation to buzz Florence and ask her if the mail had arrived yet,
but as he never asked such a question, it would be suspicious if he
should do so now, and then the letter he had been at such pains to
make believable would be seen as false. He selected one of the files
at random and opened it, laying it next to the stack. *Axel Bjornson*
said the heading. The man had taught city planning at Columbia,
having degrees in both sociology and architecture, with three
books published as well as half a dozen papers on his subject. The
photograph showed a middle-aged fellow wearing tortoise-shell
glasses, with a neat moustache, with a slide-rule and two drafting
pencils in the pocket of his tweed jacket; he was considered one of
the top men in his field, and had been doing well until it was discovered that his grandfather, who still lived in Norway, was a fire-
brand Socialist, supporting all manner of Communistic reforms in
Scandinavia. As an outspoken critic of capitalism, he often held up
the Communist model for comparison and praise, which Broadstreet felt should vitiate all merit in his work, and gain him the
contempt of the American part of his family, but that was not the

case. The Bjornsons on both sides of the Atlantic stayed in regular contact, an assertion confirmed by photographs of intercepted mail between them all. Broadstreet read through the letters, paying less attention to their contents than he wanted to demonstrate. He was determined to have the Baxter letter in his hands as soon as possible, so he could write his report on it, have it hand-delivered to Channing, and then wait for developments.

A gentle knock on the door pulled him out of his muddled reverie, alarmed at being interrupted before the mail was distributed at eleven-thirty. He closed the file and called out, "Who is it?"

"Florence," said his secretary. "I'm going to make some tea. Would you like a cup?"

It was an unusual gesture for her to make, and that roused his misgivings. "Thank you, Florence, but I think not."

"All right. I'll be away from my desk for fifteen minutes at the most," she said, and he heard her footsteps as she left the outer office.

He sat for ten minutes, waiting for her return, all the while wondering why this day, of all days, had been chosen to make such a courteous gesture. Had she done it on her own, or was she carrying out orders from Channing and his other underlings? Had they caught him in some minor error? Was Broadstreet under suspicion, or was he seeing spies where none existed? If he were not being watched, then he could assume his machinations were undetected, and if he had to explain himself, he could fall back on claiming that he was attempting to draw Baxter out. He got up and went to the window, staring out at the remainder of winter, and recognizing the signs of a late spring: there were no pale-green frills on the trees, promising leaves; the gardens were sere and bare, edged in ice. This rain today mixed with snow was so dreary, he thought, that it made him wonder if he should use Baxter to provide himself an excuse to seek out a nicer climate for a week or so. But Channing would not approve such a request, not now that the Baxter plan was moving. He felt the morning chill take hold of him, and he decided to turn on the space-heater to raise the temperature in the room; there was a reassuring hum as he turned the knob to start the coils going. He went back to his desk and opened the Axel Bjornson file once again, seeking out the professor's correspondence with his grandfather. The tone of the exchanges between Bjornson and his grandfather was always respectful, but Axel had a different view of the Communist model than his grandfather did, that indicated that he, Axel, was in favor of the economic systems of capitalism, at least in so large a country as the US. Broadstreet weighed this assertion against all the other evidence gathered about him, and after some quiet reflection, concluded that Axel knew his mail was being read, and slanted his remarks accordingly. He also saw a note from Phil Rothcoe that indicated that Bjornson had a shrew for a wife, who was no help to him. This was something that almost amused him: did Bjornson like tyrants, and was dedicated to Communism because of it? He would have to talk to Channing about it, but not just now. He saw a note from Channing's man in the Ex-Pats' Coven that Bjornson was completing a book for Eclipse Press on the purpose of cities in the future, and the changes that was likely to bring. He closed the Bjornson file and picked up the next in the stack.

Tolliver Bethune—Broadstreet read—had been in Europe the longest of all those in the Coven, and had not run into questions about his loyalty until he began preparing cases for the War Crimes trials, when it was noticed that he regarded those Nazis who had connections to the Communists as less guilty than others, or so his colleague Jerome Kinneman claimed, who worked with Bethune. If Kinneman wanted to oust Bethune from his position in the pool of attorneys working on the War Crimes, compromising his loyalty would be an effective way to do it, but it was also possible that Kinneman had found out about Bethune, just as he claimed in his initial report, and was doing what any attorney would have to do in such circumstances. There was a note that hinted in obscure terms that Bethune might be homosexual, and therefore was ripe for blackmail, which might be the case, as well as any other possibility that could lend credibility to such an accusation as Bethune had laid against him. Broadstreet sighed and moved on through the file. The outer office door opened, and the sound of high heels announced the return of Florence. Again Broadstreet closed the file and waited.

After five minutes, Florence rapped on the door. "I'm back, Mister Broadstreet," she said. "The switchboard says there was a call for you."

This startled him, for Broadstreet was not expecting any telephone calls this morning, and it seemed strange that he should receive one so unannounced. He sat a little straighter in his chair. "Who was it from?"

"A Guidion Wallace," Florence reported, opening the door. "I checked the log: this is the first call from him."

"Did he say what this was about? Is there any record of him calling the CIA before today? If he asked for me by name, he must have something specific in mind, mustn't he? But how did he know to specify me?" Broadstreet asked, baffled by the elaborate, unfamiliar name. "Did the operator say why he would want to talk to me?"

"Not that the operator made note of; she didn't mention anything," said Florence, sounding like a chastened child. "I'm sorry; I should have asked. I'll do it right now, if you like. It won't take me but a couple of minutes." Her footsteps moved away from the door.

Broadstreet sat still, wondering why she had not used the intercom to tell him of the telephone call. It could have come when she was on her tea-break, he told himself, that would explain it. He heard the sound of Florence's voice but not the words she spoke. He considered thumbing the intercom to find out what she had learned, but could not bring himself to take that very minor action; while he wrestled with what he ought to do, he almost missed the tap of her heels as she approached the door again.

"Mister Broadstreet?"

His anxiety racheted up. "What is it, Florence?"

"I need to speak with you," she said.

Not more trouble, he thought. "If you need to, then go ahead."

After a brief silence, she asked, "May I come in?"

Broadstreet was now thoroughly flummoxed. "Yes," he said, still wondering if her unusual behavior was significant. "Is something the matter?"

Florence walked up to Broadstreet's desk, obviously trying to hold her emotions in check. "Yes, there is. I hate to tell you, but you have to know." She took a deep, shaky breath, then spoke rapidly. "Cole lost his job. I told you this was likely to happen, didn't I? He wants to sell the house and go where there's more construction going on, where they need engineers like him."

"I've been told that business is good, that there are more jobs in the offing," Broadstreet said warily, wanting to know why Cole had been fired, but he did not ask, afraid that this might lead to more revelations than he wanted.

"And so it is, but this is not the best place for a job with potentials, not in this area, anyway. The Navy and the Army Air Corps"—now the Air Force, he reminded himself—"have all the engineers they need up and down the East Coast. Cole has an offer from Titan Construction in Texas, near Houston. They build military bases, airplane hangars, that sort of thing, and Cole does that kind of work—designs bridges and hangars and airport towers. He's up on all the safety standards and the materiel being used for such work."

"Oh. Yes," said Broadstreet a bit vaguely. "So I remember. Annapolis, wasn't he?"

"Class of thirty-eight," she confirmed. "He placed in the top ten percent of his class." In spite of her tears, there was no disguising her pride. "I don't want to go away," she repeated. "But Cole needs me with him."

Broadstreet could think of nothing to say, so he patted her shoulder carefully and made what he hoped were comforting noises. Emotional displays always upset him, and he could feel a headache starting behind his eyes.

"I'll put it in writing for you, tonight, so you can have the same date on your agenda record and my resignation; otherwise someone might think this is a disguised firing, and that could turn out to be a problem. This will be my sixty days' notice. I wanted to wait a while longer, but we may have to move quickly, and I didn't want to leave you stranded." Now that she had said it, she dabbed at her eyes with her handkerchief, in a futile effort to stem the crying. "I don't want to go to Texas. I like Baltimore. I like my job. I like our house. I like my neighbors. I like my kids' schools. I like the weather, even if it's miserable. I like the way the coast squiggles in and out. I want to stay here." She started to weep in earnest. "I'm so sorry. I meant to conduct myself properly."

Truly alarmed, Broadstreet stepped back and pointed out the better of the two visitor chairs. "You ought to sit down, Florence," he said.

She nodded and backed up to the chair he had indicated. "I hate having to ask you for a recommendation, but if we have to move . . ." Her voice trailed off in sobs.

"Of course, of course," said Broadstreet, still unable to determine how much of her tale was true. Was her husband out of work, or was this a ploy to get someone else into Broadstreet's office, someone more loyal to the CIA than to Broadstreet?

"I'll have to find a new job," Florence wailed as quietly as she could. "Oh, dear. I don't know where to start. Houston sounds like a rough-and-ready place, with oil-wells everywhere. At least I have a security clearance. That should help." These practical observations helped her to rein in her weeping. "Oh, Mister Broadstreet, you've been so helpful. I'm sorry I have to go. You're a good boss, but this is not your problem—it's something Cole and I have to work out for ourselves."

"He's your husband, Florence. Your duty lies with him." He did not entirely believe her, but he did not doubt her, either.

She wadded up her handkerchief and shoved it back in the cuff of her cardigan's sleeve. "Thank you for being so understanding."

"No thanks necessary," he said, and moved more than an arm's length away from her. "I'm glad you let me know. Tomorrow I'll tell the coordinator that I'll need someone. I hope we can have a two-day overlap so you can show the new girl the ropes." He did as much as he could to give his words a genial warmth, but realized he had not succeeded.

"I'll do my best, Mister Broadstreet." She patted her hair to determine if she needed to comb it or set it to order. "I'll fix the back at lunch-break." She turned on her heel and stumbled a bit, but

managed not to fall. "I'm sorry, Mister Broadstreet. I wasn't thinking. I should have done this differently." On that self-effacing note,
she hurried out of his office and closed the door behind her.

Broadstreet stood still for about thirty seconds, his thoughts
racing in a tangle. Then he went to his desk, pulled out his agenda,
opened it to the current date, and wrote on the eleven A.M. line:
Florence Wentworth gave sixty day notice. It was another troubling
omen. He added no additional information, wanting to keep the
record as clear and factual as possible. Then he stared toward the
window, wanting to summon up the nerve to leave the building
for lunch, but the recollection of what had ended up happening
the last time he ate away from the building kept him where he was.
Besides, he told himself, he needed to be here to receive the mail
and begin the second stage of his plan. With that idea to calm him,
he put his agenda away and took the next file off the Ex-Pats' Coven stack and began to read up on Tim Frost, and his wife Moira,
who, it appeared, was the family bread-winner. She had done all
that she could to put her husband in circumstances that would improve his chance of recovery. A very committed woman, this Moira
Frost, he concluded as he read on. At eleven-thirty, he buzzed
Florence on the intercom to ask her to call the cafeteria and order him
a hot meatloaf sandwich on white bread with catsup and mustard,
one of his favorite dishes from the cafeteria, and to pick it up for
him, with a carafe of hot coffee and a small creamer. "I'll give you
the money when you bring in the mail."

"Okay," she said without vitality.

"That's one dollar, five cents, to cover the food and their preparation," he said as if this information were new to Florence.

"I'll bring my lunch back to the office, too, if you like," she offered. "And pay my own prep fee."

Not wanting a repeat of her emotional display, he said, "I think
one of us sticking to the desk is about all that's fair. Take your
forty-five minutes for lunch. But thank you." He leaned back in his
chair. "Don't rush because of me, please. Having a little time out of
the office can be very restorative. If I hadn't so much to do, I'd welcome the break myself."

Florence took on a brisker tone. "Meatloaf sandwich on white bread, catsup and mustard, and coffee with cream, coming up."

"Thank you, Florence," said Broadstreet, and toggled the intercom to *off*, and sat back to read more about the Frosts. He knew that Tim Frost had been paralyzed from the waist down after a severe concussion—at Guadalcanal, according to his file—where he was ferrying supplies to the troops on the island. Frost was recognized as a hero then, for he had saved eight other men along with himself. He had studied the tides around the island and knew where to swim to keep from being washed out to sea. Had his loyalty not been questioned, he was said to be on his way to a Congressional Medal of Honor, but his statements about the Russian successes in Germany at the end of the war earned him the condemnation of the general public; he had to pay the price for his stance. He had been on disability through the Veterans Administration, but now that he was in Paris, he no longer received benefits and, unable to continue his work as an oceanographer, was reduced to being supported by his wife. One of the agents who had briefly penetrated the Ex-Pats' Coven had summed her up as a clinical psychologist who was striving to hold her family together by seeking out clients in the ex-pats' community. Tim and Moira had a sixteen-year-old daughter, Regina, who was attending school in Paris and coaching a half-dozen of her classmates in English. Tim's parents were dead, and so was Moira's mother; her father was retired and living in the Florida Keys, on Big Pine Key, if he remembered correctly. He supposed he ought to arrange to have him checked out, just to fill in any blanks about Tim.

The next folder was Hapgood Nugent's: Broadstreet set it aside, planning to study it closely later. Too many of his plans depended on Hapgood Nugent to try to concentrate on him now. He wished he could take the file home so that he could expand his review of the material in it, but he would need Channing's written permission to do this, and he was fairly certain that was unlikely to be forthcoming. He went back to worrying his left thumb, paying no attention when the cuticle started to bleed. His aggravation was increasing, and he was losing patience with everyone, himself included. If only the mail would come!

The crackle of the intercom cut into his exasperation. He was so startled that he jumped in his chair, and looked around as if he expected to find someone lurking behind the draperies. He forced himself to answer, clearing his throat before he activated his side of the intercom. "Yes, Florence: what is it?"

"I have Guidion Wallace on the line. Shall I put him through?"

"Ask him what this is about, if you would." He fiddled with his tie, then reached for his pen and his notepad, prepared to write down anything once Florence toggled back on. He wrote down the name on the top of the notebook page. What kind of a name, he wondered, was Guidion?

"He says it's about a screen-writer in Paris, one whom the Committee has accused of pro-Communist activities. Mister Wallace says that there may be—"

Broadstreet interrupted. "Tell him, if you would, to talk to Alice Jamison; she has the lesser Hollywood run-aways. And thank him for contacting us." He saw his hand was shaking; he dropped his pen and balled his fingers into a fist, then counted to ten before he flipped the intercom to *off*, which allowed him to overhear what Florence was saying to Mister Wallace; as usual, Florence was being tactful and patient. He decided he would ask Alice about Wallace when he next saw her, and would hope that she would tell him what she learned, as a quid-pro-quo for making sure Wallace reached her. As the only woman coordinator in the CIA, she was known to be amazingly tight-lipped about her cases, fearing poaching from her male colleagues, and not without cause. Perhaps he could offer to trade information with her: academics and screen-writers could be in touch with one another. Maybe Guidion Wallace was associated with screen-writing himself. Guidion sounded like the sort of name someone in the movie industry would have. He went back to staring out the window, giving up all pretense of work while he indulged in a great deal of anticipation, imagining the heights to which he could rise if his ruse worked, and how far he would plummet if he failed.

Fifteen minutes later, Florence brought in the mail, and Broadstreet sighed his relief. "Is something the matter?" Florence asked him.

"I don't know," said Broadstreet. "There's an inconsistency in these reports"—he gestured to the stack of files—"and I don't know if that's important or not. Inconsistencies don't always mean deception, do they? But they might." He had made the answer up on the spur of the moment, but now that he had said it, he decided it was a useful tack to take in terms of pursuing information. "I should send a wire to Phil Rothcoe; he can assign one of his men to check these things out. I can't manage it from here."

"You've said before that inconsistencies are one of the hazards of field work, and this is probably just more of the same," she reminded him as if addressing a favorite teacher. "Why ask for more field work to clarify matters?"

"Yes, I understand your point," he agreed. "But it's those inconsistencies that lead to problems—that is why cases remain open when they should be closed. I want to be able to settle the cases on these professors, once and for all, and that means taking the time to find explanations for all the information that is lacking, and all the statements that are contradictory." He did not add that it would make his reputation if he did, and that he would be able to get the promotion that had eluded him for so long. He wondered how he might work Baxter into Wallace's information, once he got Alice Jamison to tell him what it was.

"I called in your lunch order," said Florence, as much to get his attention as to impart what she had done on his behalf.

"Thanks," he said a bit distractedly. Then he looked up at her. "Sorry." He reached into his trouser-pocket and pulled out a small coin purse from which he took out two half-dollars and a dime. He gave her his version of a smile. "Keep the change." He added a nickel to his offering. "Get yourself a roll to go with your salad."

She took the coins, an unreadable expression on her face. "Thank you, Mister Broadstreet," she said tonelessly before she turned and left the room, closing the door softly behind her.

In a kind of self-torment, Broadstreet waited to open his planted letter last, wanting to make the most of this moment. He ordered the various letters in a single stack, overseas letters on top, domestic letters underneath. He noticed one of the envelopes said Grant Nugent as the return addressee and was post-marked St. Louis. This he set out on the desk, wondering what Hapgood's brother-in-law had to tell him now. Last of all, he picked up the envelope addressed by a standard Royal ten-point typewriter, his first name misspelled—he thought that was a nice touch—and no return address. It was post-marked Wilmington, Delaware, two days ago; the envelope was somewhat wrinkled as if it had been carried in a pocket that was too small for it—another nice touch, he felt.

The intercom buzzed.

"Yes, Florence?" Broadstreet asked, annoyed.

"I'm going up to lunch, Mister Broadstreet. I'll be back within the hour." She clicked off, and he was distantly aware that he had offended her in some way, although he had no such intention. "Women," he muttered as he continued his inspection of the letter he had been at such pains to make look right. The lined yellow paper off a legal pad was a clever choice, and the small coffee-stain in the right-hand corner gave it the air of something written in haste. The text was a mix of script and arbitrary printed capitals, suggesting the writer was attempting to disguise his handwriting, which, of course, was true. He read it through twice, glad that he had chosen to put his brief message in the middle of the page, the ink a standard blue, bought with the lined paper at Deering Office Supplies in Philadelphia, where he had paid cash and had not kept the receipt. He noticed the few grains of beach sand that were in the envelope, hardly more than six or seven, something that anyone might ignore; he had brushed them off his sleeve after he had spent half a day in his little boat on Christmas weekend. There were no fingerprints on the paper beyond the few he had supplied when he opened the letter to read it: Broadstreet had worn thin cotton gloves when he worked on it; he had thrown the gloves into a public garbage can in Oxon Hill, Maryland. He had covered his tracks very well, he told himself. There was no way to trace all this back to him. He congratulated himself on his accomplishment.

Mr. Broadstreet,

    I have T*ried twice be*F*ore to contact you in regard to the ma*T-
T*er I approached you about, but was unable to* K*eep our appointment to discuss. Now I would like to* T*ry to see you at the same
place at twelve-thirty on this co*M*ing Thursday. Co*M*e alone.* IF
*this is con*V*enient, call* MA*dison 7-43*0 0*, in Ale*X*andria and
leave an answer for me with the recep*T*ionist con*F*irming the ap-
poin*T*ment.*

*Ba*X*ter*

He folded the letter carefully and put it back in the envelope,
trying to decide how best to approach Channing with this. He
should call him, probably within the hour, and make a case for
keeping the appointment. He would be surveilled, that much was
obvious, but he had thought of a way to turn it to his advantage. He
decided he would need to express curiosity and concern in equal
amounts so that Channing would not be tempted to turn the meeting over to one of his restless young agents who had not yet received an overseas assignment. For ten minutes he remained at his
desk, looking over his other letters, including the one from Rutherford, which informed him that Hapgood's sister had received another
letter from him, and in it he mentioned that he was going to go
into the country for a couple of weeks in May—*one of our group has
access to a place near Nice,* Nugent had written—and if she wanted to
fly over and join him, he would be glad to see her. That was something worth looking into, Broadstreet thought. He would bring that
up as well when he called Channing.

    At twelve-forty, he picked up the receiver and dialed the switch-
board; he wanted his call logged in. "Please connect me to Deputy
Director Channing, in the Washington satellite. This is Lydell
Broadstreet."

    "Just a moment, Mister Broadstreet," said a bored woman, and
there was the sound of dialing four numbers, followed by a quick
exchange between the operator and someone Broadstreet could not
hear. "I'm sorry, Mister Broadstreet. Deputy Director Channing is
out of his office. Do you want to leave a message?"

This was a worthwhile development. "Yes, if you would: tell him that I have had a note from Baxter."

"From Baxter?" the operator repeated.

"Yes. Baxter."

"Anything else?"

Broadstreet bit his lower lip to keep from laughing. "No, thank you." And he hung up before a guffaw could burst out of him and ruin his whole scheme. He continued to laugh, but more quietly, delighted that things were going so well. This was turning out to be just what he had anticipated, he told himself, so he would have to be careful not to give himself away by too much confidence.

Florence returned a few minutes later, carrying a rectangular steel tray with a one-inch brim and a white stoneware plate with his sandwich and two slightly wilted lettuce leaves on it, along with half a large pickle. The coffee-carafe, a creamer, and a white stoneware mug along with a rolled paper napkin containing a knife, fork, and spoon completed the array. "Your sandwich, Mister Broadstreet," she said as she set the tray down on his desk, on the side away from the files and envelopes.

"Thank you, Florence," said Broadstreet. "I'll let you know when I'm done."

She said nothing, giving him a long, sad look as she started for the door. "Enjoy your sandwich."

"Um-hum," he responded, to let her know he was listening; he busied himself making stacks of the files and letters, and surmounted them with paperweights before moving the tray to the immediate front of the desk. The sandwich had been cut diagonally, with red-frilled toothpicks fixed in each half. Broadstreet opened the napkin, removed the utensils, tucked the end of the napkin into his collar to save his tie from getting spotted, removed the toothpick from the nearer one, and bit down. The meatloaf had both beef and pork in it, along with breadcrumbs, minced onions, salt, chopped celery, a smidge of garlic, and some shredded cheddar cheese. Not quite like Broadstreet's mother used to make, but a good, substantial sandwich nonetheless, he decided, and took a bite of the end of the pickle.

He was on his second mug of coffee when the phone rang; the sound was so jarring that Broadstreet nearly dropped his coffee in his lap. Chiding himself for foolishness, he reached out for the receiver. "Broadstreet," he said, pleased that he did not sound nervous. He drank the last of his coffee as he waited.

"Will you hold for Deputy Director Channing?" asked a voice that Broadstreet did not recognize.

"Certainly," he said, trying not to seethe at this ritual of who-waits-upon-whom. The day would come when this would no longer be a trial for him, he reassured himself, tapping his fingers on the side of the mug.

"Dell Broadstreet, what's up?" said Channing with just enough condescension to remind Broadstreet that he, Channing, was the one in charge. "I understand you have a message for me?" He let his question be a challenge.

Broadstreet did not like the phrasing Channing used, but he curtailed the sharp reproof that rose in his throat. "Yes, sir. I have a few developments that I thought I should discuss with you before I take the next step. I'm in new waters here, you know."

"Sounds important," said Channing in a tone that implied that the developments had better be important.

"I think it may be." He took a deep breath to steady himself, then said, "I have a letter here from Baxter."

"Baxter, is it?" Channing said, his voice changing with saying the name.

"It's very brief, sir. And since it refers to the meeting that did not take place—obliquely, but clearly enough—I am pretty well convinced that it is authentic." He waited long enough for Channing to say something, and when he did not, Broadstreet went on, "The paper and envelope will have my fingerprints, but there may be something useful the lab can find."

"I'll have a messenger pick it up within the hour." He sighed. "I'll be glad when we're all under the same roof, and not spread all over the region in satellite offices. Well. For now it can't be helped."

"No, sir," said Broadstreet, taking the letter and its envelope from under the paperweight.

"What does Baxter say?" Channing asked.

"He wants to meet again, same time, same place, next Thursday." He paused a second or two, then added the risky part. "I think it might be worth another try. He's a little like pulling teeth out of ducks, but I think we may be getting some place with him."

"You think so, do you?" Channing asked.

"If he doesn't show, then that's the end of it. If he does, we might get useful information from him."

"I'll order surveillance on you on Thursday. We'll find out who this Baxter is one way or another."

"He said to come alone," Broadstreet said.

"Sure. They all do. And we promise them we will. But we know how to keep an eye on you and on him without making it obvious, as a precaution." Channing sounded energized by this development. "I'll call you tomorrow with the arrangements." He sounded ready to hang up. "Anything else?"

"Nugent's brother-in-law tells me that Hapgood has asked his sister to join him in France, near Nice in May. Could be a real opportunity."

Channing coughed once. "All right. Send me your preliminary report on both of these today before you leave the office. I'll want to study them this evening. You did the right thing in calling me," he added, as if patting Broadstreet on the head. Then his receiver went down with a bang, leaving Broadstreet alone, vexed that he had forgotten to tell Channing about Florence leaving; he would put that in his report. "Roger. Over and out," he said quietly to the sullen sky outside his window. Satisfied, he leaned back in his chair to grin as he finished the last dregs of his coffee.

Feb. 27, '50

Mr. J. Haste-Windlass
The Mirror
5-9 Fleet River Close
London, England

Dear Jonathan Haste-Windlass
    *Your request for an opportunity to interview members of our group of
ex-pats must be refused. I submitted your offer to the group and all but
one declined your invitation; the one who did not decline also did not
accept; he abstained. Most of our members have been exploited enough
already, and do not want to dredge up our problems to help you sell
papers. Surely there are other American ex-pats in Europe who might
benefit from your attention; this group seeks to remain out of the public
eye. There has been embarrassment enough to go around, and we are not
anxious to renew the kind of commentary and public disrepute that caused
us to leave our own country, in the first place, which might very well
become yet another insult to our relatives back in the US. You claim you
want to show our side of the accusations to the world, theoretically on our
behalf, or so your message implied, but that would still require the revelation of various personal experiences which the group has made a practice of keeping private. I do not want to appear ungrateful, but the group
has spoken, and I am bound to uphold the group's decision.*
    *Why not asked Dalton Trumbo or Sterling Hayden to give you infor-
mation on the witch-hunts? You may have to travel a way to find them,*

but a trip to Mexico isn't so dreadful, is it? They're a lot more famous than the members of our group are, and they have an international following, which we do not, nor are we seeking one. From what we hear, there are likely to be more actors and directors and screenwriters Black Listed before this is over. There are a number from Hollywood in Europe now, and their numbers are going to increase through this year, according to my contacts at The Washington Post. I believe your paper would get more mileage out of them than our academics.

Sincerely,
Russell McCall

❖ 3 ❖

THE BUILDING had once been a coaching-stable, but its transformation into a printing plant thirty years ago had not entirely erased the signs of the past: the largest of the offices had been stalls for the storing of large carriages and coaches, and the tack-racks in them had been kept for the hanging of ink-stained clothing. It stood a few blocks from the Baroque enthusiasm of the Opera, in a cul-de-sac that backed onto a park that had once been the private garden of the Duc de Orleans. The building stood a little apart from either of its neighbors—a company that made purses and briefcases, and a culinary supply warehouse—allowing the printers in the day, and tonight the Coven's members, to park in the alleyways between them. The windows on the old box-stalls had been enlarged and were designed to be opened at the horizontal middle during the summer months; at present, all were closed but unshuttered, revealing a molten, late-afternoon sky. The day had been attempting warm but had not achieved it, and it was clear that the night would be chilly.

"It's the Vernal Equinox next week," said Miranda Nevers, who, until a year ago, had been a professor of astronomy at the University of Montana, and who had been away from the Coven for almost six months, trying to find a position in Europe. She was forty-one, divorced, had a grown daughter living in Minneapolis, and three horses back in Helena, just now being cared for by her neighbor, Jasper Raskin; she was not sure if she missed her daughter or her horses more. "I always like the sky around the Equinoxes; day and night, light and dark, it all goes together so well." She glanced over at Szent-Germain. "Sorry. I don't know what kind of thing I'm supposed to say about printing presses."

He chuckled. "That's fine. I like skies at the Equinoxes, too."

Moira Frost maneuvered Tim's wheelchair out of the press-room, into the front reception room; she was taking care not to rush in such close quarters. Behind Tim, the Praegers came in, hand-in-hand, their pea-coats over identical turtlenecks and jeans. "Pleasant night, sorry we missed the tour," they said almost in unison; they received a number of casual greetings in return.

Tolliver Bethune, in a beautifully cut dark-gray suit over a white linen shirt and a silk foulard tie, moved fastidiously away from the press-room, glancing toward the meeting room off to the east side of the building. He looked directly at the evening's host. "Grof, you said there would be coffee? Do you mind if I help myself? No offense intended, but that room is pretty cool." He seemed almost apologetic, and that made three of the others look at him, suspicion in their eyes; Bethune rarely apologized for anything.

"Go right on in. It isn't Chez Rosalie, but I trust it's sufficient to our present needs. The coffee is at the far end of the room. There are pastries, if you want one, and if you'd like tea, there is a samovar. Rogers can help you," Szent-Germain said, noticing that the members of the Coven were beginning to mill in the smallish area at the front of the building. "In fact, why don't you all go into the meeting room? There are couches and chairs, as well as half a dozen tables. Make yourselves comfortable." He stepped aside to give Stephen diMaggio and Hapgood Nugent the chance to go past him, into the meeting room.

Axel and Julia Bjornson made for the meeting room as well, Julia brushing at her sleeve as if she feared it had been smirched with ink in the press-room; Winston Pomeroy smiled at Szent-Germain before going into the meeting room. Mary Anne Triding offered Szent-Germain an approving nod.

Charis went to Szent-Germain briefly, saying fairly loudly, "Thanks for showing them the galleys of my book." Then she lowered her voice and moved a little nearer to him, trying to pay no heed to the physical thrill that went through her. "I need to talk to you."

"I'm glad you're pleased," he said, adding, "I'll drive you home." He felt her excitement, and stepped back from her.

"No," she said too quickly. "I'll come here tomorrow to give you the list of those who will review the book, I hope. No need to hold up the meeting. But thank you for the offer. Of the ride home." Her skin tingled and she began to breathe more rapidly.

"I'll give you a second set for your own use, before you leave tonight, so you have something to send home."

She shook herself mentally. "That's kind of you, Grof," she made herself say, an odd note in her voice, not knowing what she wanted to tell him, or how, and hoping he was unaware of her tangle of emotions. Had they been alone, she wondered what would have become of her. Tomorrow, she reminded herself, there would be printers and binders working, providing her a kind of shelter from her inexplicable desire.

"Shall we say thirteen hundred hours—one P.M.," he suggested.

"Yes, that should be fine," she told him with a nod, and hurried into the meeting room.

Washington Young had lingered in the doorway to the pressroom, which had been the exercise arena for the coach horses kept here a generation ago. "Those skylights must help," he said, pointing at the ceiling, where large windows, strengthened with wire, provided wonderful illumination for most of the day, and now showed the glory of sunset.

"They do," said Szent-Germain. "And the light-tables, as well. I have a cleaner in once a week, to get ink off everything, or the light-tables would be useless." He nodded in the general direction of the drafting-tables with glass tops and shielded light-bulbs behind the glass. They had been expensive, but had proved their use as soon as they were installed.

"How many copies of books do you turn out from here?" Young asked. "Not to pry."

"You're not prying. At present, not as many as I would like. The usual print-run is three or four thousand; I'd like to double that in the next eighteen months, when the other press arrives and the bindery has been added. We're still having to build up our production and hire out the binding. Why do you ask? Are you interested in a job?"

Young blinked in surprise. "I might be. The work I do right now isn't very challenging, or very regular."

"Then have a look at what Eclipse Press does, and decide if it could be your cup of tea." He went to the shelves in the short corridor between the meeting room and the press-room, and took down a pair of books from one of the upper shelves. "This is what we're shipping this week." He held them out to Young, who paused before he took them. "Two more will go out at the middle of April."

Young touched the covers with knowing fingers, smiling as he did, then he opened the larger book and studied the frontispiece. "Thanks, Grof," he said at last.

"My pleasure." He indicated that Young should go ahead of him.

Russell McCall glanced back toward the press-room. "Pretty impressive. But why do you need a second press?"

"I had two before the war, but something happened to one of them," Szent-Germain answered. "And before you ask, no, I don't know who took it or why. It may have been for the metal itself rather than for what it could do."

"But you doubt it," McCall said, watching Szent-Germain closely.

"I don't know. I have no reliable information from which to form an opinion." His enigmatic gaze revealed nothing. "Do you know anything about it?"

"Not really." McCall gave a quick, cynical grin. "I didn't mean to prod," he said. "It's force of habit."

"Indeed," said Szent-Germain as the sound of the door-bell sounded. He shrugged, wondering who it was. "Excuse me."

"It's the Kings," said Pomeroy from just inside the meeting room. "They made it. I was worried that something had happened to keep them away."

Szent-Germain went to answer the door, taking care to be sure Pomeroy was right. There was a short pause as he disengaged the lock and swung the door open.

Boris and Wilhelmina King stood on the threshold, both looking a bit bedraggled. "Sorry," said Boris. "Couldn't be helped."

"We're just sitting down for the meeting," Szent-Germain said. "Go left at the short corridor. I'm going to close up the press-room." He waited while the Kings came inside; as they went directly to the meeting room, Szent-Germain secured the lock once more. Then he went to turn out the lights in the press-room and to bolt the door closed.

The Coven had gathered in the meeting room, and the last four of them in the room were getting their coffee and tea while the rest settled into their selected chairs. The room was painted a pale, pale blue and there were six sconces on the wall, each shedding bright light. A pair of electric heaters made the place quite comfortable.

Winston Pomeroy held out his large cup to Rogers and asked for a refill. "I always like to have something to drink when I talk," he explained.

"A very good idea," said Rogers, taking the cup and filling it for him, then handing it back. "Let me know if you need more."

"I'll do that, don't worry," said Pomeroy, then addressed the Coven. "Okay, everyone. Sit down." Those who had not chosen a seat carried their coffee and tea with them as they made their selection from the chairs that remained unoccupied. When Szent-Germain came in, only McCall had not yet sat down. The level of conversational chatting died away and the group turned toward Pomeroy, who cleared his throat and looked at the group. "I suppose we should let Miranda tell us how her job-hunt went."

There was a little murmur of commiseration; everyone knew that if Miranda had found work, she would not have returned to Paris and the Coven. The group prepared to hear bad news and to find out what gossip she had heard.

Miranda Nevers, who had taken one of the overstuffed Victorian lounge chairs, sat up straight, put her coffee on the side-table, and began, "I'd had some dealings with the university in Grenoble, so I started out there. Nothing worthwhile happened. My department has been putting out some damaging remarks about me, in part to justify firing me. If I were back home and in a good position legally, I'd consider suing my dean and the administration for what they've done, but under the circumstances, it would be futile, and if I weren't in this position, the matter would be moot." She gave a little, angry shake of her head. "But I tried other places. Padova took my inquiry seriously, but had no openings and no specific policy for taking me on as an adjunct; my Italian isn't good enough to lecture in the language, so . . ." She paused, gathering her thoughts. "I met Sam Dawson in Milano. A couple of you know him, I think. He's been doing lectures on physics—his French is good enough for that, but he doesn't do much Spanish and no Portuguese. He's working on his Italian, and he's planning to try the Swiss next; he has good German, which right now is almost as bad as knowing Russian." She went on for nearly twenty minutes, and was peppered with questions when she finished.

The Kings had a two-day-old copy of *The Washington Post*, and read three articles aloud, articles describing the work of the House Un-American Activities Committee, the FBI, and the fledgling CIA, not in glowing terms but respectfully, which led to another round of discussions within the Coven. When that was over, Axel Bjornson talked about some of the news he had had from a former colleague who wanted to inquire about a conference that was scheduled for the University of Uppsala in Sweden, seeking recommendations about attending, and asking was he—meaning Axel—planning to go; he said he doubted they would want a city-planning professor discussing the ethics of science with them, but he believed that others of the Coven might want to attend. This meant a lively debate on making an appearance at such events, and trying to determine if that would help or harm their current predicaments. Bethune discoursed on the legalities and the possibility of attracting the attention of the CIA, which was bound to have agents at the conference.

The meeting ended a little before twenty-three hundred hours; the Coven left quickly, many of them sharing rides with those who were bound for the Metro. As Charis pulled on her coat, Szent-Germain handed her a set of galleys.

"Oh. Thank you, Grof," she said, working the galleys into her briefcase. "I'm amazed that you got it to galleys so quickly."

"Well, as I said, we haven't our usual load to attend to, and you have been available to advise us, and there was only one project ahead of yours. I'd like your corrections back by April first, or before if you can manage it. I know your current book is demanding a great deal of your time." He held the door open for her, taking care not to come too close to her, but he could not keep from asking, "Have you changed your mind about the ride?"

"The Kings will drop me off; I don't want to keep them waiting," she said, almost out the door. "I'll see you tomorrow. At one."

McCall was the last Coven member to leave, saying to Szent-Germain as he went out, "It's a nice set-up here, I'll give you that. You have other presses, you say?"

"I do. The largest is in Venezia." He knew this was easily discovered, so that mentioning it would not give away anything crucial.

"Venice? There's quite a history of publishing there, I think."

"I would agree," said Szent-Germain, making no mention of how long he had had a press in that city; he watched McCall start his motorcycle, closing the door as McCall roared away into the night. As Szent-Germain went to help Rogers clear the meeting room, Szent-Germain said, "McCall isn't going to give up until he has answers to his questions." He spoke in Imperial Latin now, as he often did when he and Rogers were alone.

"Is that because he is a reporter, or because he is trying to find out about you for other reasons?" Rogers asked, in the same language, gathering up cups and mugs and stacking them in a large wash-basin. He poured soap-flakes on them and ran hot water on them.

"It could be either, or he might be a mole: we would be fools to think it is impossible for the Coven to be infiltrated. I know they have detected others and thrown them out, but does that mean that all the members have no connection to any intelligence group? I doubt it. There's so much at stake, they must have had offers."

"Do you think it's going to cause problems?" Rogers asked, bearing his load of cups and mugs into the wash-room behind the meeting room.

"I'd guess that it already has. Remember that fellow in Venezia? The one who tried to persuade me not to publish Black Listed Americans? He didn't say how he came to know I was going to do this, since it wasn't yet formally announced, but he had gained the information somehow, and where better than from someone in the

Coven? You didn't tell anyone, and I didn't tell anyone about the Coven members, but somebody had to."

"Do you mean William C. Lambeth?" Rogers asked as he filled a second basin with rinse-water, and set it in crowded proximity to the large wash-basin.

"That's the man," Szent-Germain said. "Friendly in his way, open-faced, engaging, yet with that underlying righteousness so many Americans possess. It's the Puritan in them; it makes them think in absolutes."

"Does that include the Coven?" Rogers inquired.

Szent-Germain picked up the coffee-brewer—an old-fashioned machine made along the lines of an Italian steamed-coffee-maker—and bore it into the wash-room. "I'll bring the samovar next."

"There are a few pastries left. What would you like me to do with them?"

"Cover them and put them in the bread-box. No doubt a few of the printers won't mind having slightly stale pastries in the morning. They're usually hungry, and pastries are better than bread." He looked at the tray with its few remaining pastries. "If we throw them out, we'll attract rodents." He went back to the meeting room for the samovar.

"You spoke with Young?" Rogers asked, continuing with the washing.

"I did. I think he may well decide to work here, at least for a while." He carried the samovar into the wash-room, setting it down on the table next to the sink.

"Is that what you wanted?" Rogers asked, knowing that Szent-Germain was capable of making an offer to see what the response would be.

"I believe so; des Ponts is getting tired of being master press-man; he wasn't trained for it, and it's against his nature. I don't see that Renaud is going to be ready to take over for des Ponts, not with his asthma," said Szent-Germain, and began to wipe the cups and mugs Rogers had placed on the drainboard, returning them to their place in the narrow cupboard next to the old-fashioned cooler. As soon as the tables in the meeting room had been wiped clean, and the basins stored beneath the sink, Rogers washed the zinc sink, and declared himself ready to leave. The two of them donned their coats, Szent-Germain retrieved his briefcase, turned out the lights, secured the doors and windows, and locked the front door as they left, stepping into the frosty night.

The Delahaye was the last remaining automobile in the alley; Szent-Germain unlocked it, climbed in, and opened the passenger door for Rogers. "Have you seen anything out of place?"

"There's a ragged man asleep on a bench just inside the park. Probably one of those shell-shocked soldiers, poor man," said Rogers. "I can see him in the light-spill from the streetlights."

"But you have doubts? that you have seen him before?" Szent-Germain ventured as he started the engine.

"I do."

"What are they?" He turned on the headlights and put the car in reverse, then backed out of the alley.

"They're nothing specific, except that I have seen just such a ragged man before, outside your present flat. It may be that the men look alike because they are afflicted in the same manner, but perhaps not."

"Keep alert to another such man," Szent-Germain said as he shifted into second gear and headed in the general direction of the Sorbonne, keeping with the speed of the light flow of traffic.

"You will meet Professor Treat tomorrow?"

"At one, yes," said Szent-Germain.

"About her book?" Rogers sounded curious; he did not want to reveal his concern.

"I don't know," Szent-Germain said. "I'll have to wait until she tells me."

They went on in silence until they were almost at the flat. Then Rogers said, "I'll shave you tonight, unless you plan to go out again?"

"Thank you. I would appreciate it," Szent-Germain told him as he stopped to open the garage door—a sheet of corrugated metal on a simple counterweight system.

"I hope it goes well," said Rogers as Szent-Germain drove into the garage and turned off the ignition.

"As do I," Szent-Germain said, and went to close and lock the garage door.

Rogers knew he would have to be content with this response; he got out of the car and took the short walkway toward the building where Szent-Germain's flat was, and opened the rear door so both of them could go inside.

By one in the afternoon on the following day, Szent-Germain's curiosity was piqued, and he found it difficult to concentrate. He had cut short his meeting with three of the press-men, asking them to put another set of galleys of Professor Treat's book on the desk in his office, and explained that she would arrive shortly for a conference. "Have your luncheon early, and go back to work by two-thirty; you'll still receive a day's pay."

"That's generous of you," said des Ponts.

"I hope you will turn your extra time to good use," said Szent-Germain, getting to his feet and preparing to leave the room. "I have a few things to attend to in my office."

"We'll leave within ten minutes, out the back way; I'll lock the door," said des Ponts, motioning to the rest of the men. "Come on. Let's get our things and leave."

Szent-Germain crossed the reception area and entered his office, where he opened the shutters, and was looking for an ashtray when he heard the summons of the knocker; he left the office to answer it.

Charis had not slept well, and it showed in her eyes. Despite her fawn-colored Bonnie Cashin suit, Hermes gloves, and Italian high heels, she seemed neither buoyed up by her fashions nor ready to buckle down to a discussion on her books. "Thank you for seeing me, Grof. I have that list of reviewers you wanted." Reaching into her large, square purse she pulled out two pages paper-clipped together, which she handed to him.

"Professor Treat," Szent-Germain said as he held the door open to admit her. "My office is the second door on the right."

"Fine," said Charis, sounding distracted; she faltered as if she were uncertain that she should proceed. "I probably shouldn't have asked you to see me, but I'm relying on you not to be too condemning. I really didn't think it would come to this." Her smile crumpled and she looked away from him.

"Why on earth should I condemn you?" he asked, genuinely puzzled. "You are an Eclipse Press author; you may command my attention as you wish, and to the limits of my capacity, I will try to accommodate any request you have."

She gave an unhappy, uneven laugh. "You make it sound so easy. And I know it's not."

"What's the matter, Professor?" he asked as he followed her into his office. "Please sit down—the chair or the sofa, as you prefer."

She looked from one to the other, and to the chair behind the desk. "I'll take this," she said, sitting down in the chair, where she sat stiffly; to occupy herself, she removed her gloves, tucking them into her purse. "Do you mind if I smoke?" she asked, and before he could answer, she took a pack of Chesterfields from her purse and pulled out a cigarette, holding it up defiantly as if she expected him to deny her.

He went to the desk to get his lighter, holding it out with its little flame already burning. "What's wrong, Professor? I can see something is bothering you. Why not tell me at once, and be done with it?"

"I'm trying to work up the nerve," she admitted. She inhaled, buying herself a second or two to gather up her courage; she plunged into her crisis. "My husband wants to divorce me," she said in a rush, and began to cry. "Oh, damn," she muttered as she put her cigarette in the nearest ashtray and wiped her eyes with the rumpled handkerchief from her jacket-pocket.

"Are you sure? Did he offer any explanation?" He was startled by this announcement; he had expected other problems. "Why would he want to do that?" he asked levelly as he hitched his leg over the edge of his desk so that he was nearly touching her.

"For his work, or that's what he claimed," she said. "He's afraid his corporate sponsor will discontinue funding his work if I'm still in the picture, being a known Communist sympathizer, which I am not—or not the way the Committee means it. Harold told me he wouldn't ask this if it weren't so necessary to his research. He tells me he's sorry, but he's got so much riding on his project, he's afraid he won't be able to find another backer, and without corporate money, the university won't support his work, either with lab-space or grad students to assist him." She started to tremble. "If I refuse, he'll despise me for ruining his career, so we'll end up apart, no matter what. It's bad enough that my career is in ruins."

He reached out and took her hand; he felt her quiver again, but for different reasons than she had before. "Your career is not in ruins. You may be sure of that. It has changed direction but it hasn't ended."

"Harold doesn't see it that way. He's in a panic."

Szent-Germain was aware that Charis was trying to hold her agitation at bay. "If he truly needs corporate backing, I can proba-bly arrange something. I have . . . business associates who some-times invest in academic projects." That most of these *associates* were various aliases he had used over the centuries, he did not bother to tell her.

"I'm too indebted to you already." She wadded up her handker-chief and pushed it back into her pocket.

"Do you mean you want to keep this between you and your husband?" he guessed, knowing the answer.

She nodded. "Un-huh," she said.

"Even though it may end your marriage?" He said it bluntly, knowing she did not want to be treated like a weak-willed female.

"If I'm not worth more to him than five years' funding, it's better to learn it sooner than later," she said with a forlorn attempt at bravery. "He's got his parents living with him now, and they're taking care of the boys, and that leaves me cut out of the family. I don't like the thought of losing Arthur and David, but"—her voice broke and she clung fiercely to his hand—"I don't know if he'll al-low me to see them."

He studied her while she fought back tears. "Can he do that? Won't the courts make some provision for access?"

"They m-might," she allowed as she stifled a sob. "In some states, but not Louisiana. He could claim I deserted the family, or that I w-was indoctrinating my sons in un-American Activities, and he could probably get an Order of P-protection to keep me away from them." She seemed not to hear her childhood stutter.

"Are you certain?" He knew of far more draconian measures taken against unwanted wives, but not in the US, at least not this century. "Did he say so?"

"Not in so many w-words, no, but I know H-harold, and I know when he's g-giving me a warning. He has a style h-he uses, and he was using it w-when he phoned me." She pressed her lips firmly together, then went on more steadily. "If I agree to let him divorce me, without contesting it, he'll be willing to arrange some kind of visitation with the kids."

"Do you think he will?" He spoke gently; he could feel her anguish triggering her need of him, and he chose his words carefully. "Do you have friends in New Orleans who would be willing to work as your intermediary in this?"

She looked away. "I don't know. I used to think I had friends who would stand by me, but when push came to shove, no one did. And I ended up here." She shook her head. "Good lord, I sound like such a *ninny*!"

"Not a ninny," he said, standing up and holding his hand out to her. "You sound alone. There's a difference."

Taking his hand, she rose into the haven of his arms, resting her head on his shoulder, and finally giving way to tears that were drawn as much from anger as they were from pain and frustration. It took almost five minutes to cry herself out, and even after her tears were gone, she remained standing in his embrace, her heart pounding so loudly that she could not hear his pulse at all. When she finally took a step back, he released her, though he did not move away from her. She retrieved her handkerchief and was about to use it when he offered her a square of black silk; she took it, whispering, "Thank you."

"Not necessary, but you're welcome—I believe that's what they say in the States," he told her, at last knowing what she needed most from him.

She nodded. "It is," she said, and gave an awkward laugh. "I don't know what to say."

"You don't have to say anything," he assured her.

"I thought . . . I thought I wasn't so overwrought."

"You needn't apologize; I'm not offended."

"Still . . ." she said, offering him his handkerchief; he waved it away. "We're doing business together, and it's not appropriate to . . . to mix personal and professional."

"Under ordinary circumstances, an excellent rule, but these are not ordinary circumstances for you, are they?" As he watched, she shook her head, unwilling to look at him. "What you need now isn't a publisher, it's an ally."

This caught her attention; she stared at him. "An ally," she echoed.

"You have one, if you want one."

"An ally," she repeated, this time as if testing the word for intent and sincerity.

"If that is what you want," he said again.

"I might be here for a long time, if Harold has his way," she cautioned him. "It could be long and drawn out."

"I'll be your ally as long as you want one," he told her. "What you decide about your husband is up to you." He extended his hand.

She took it with both of hers. "You're on."

EYES ONLY

March 7, 1950

Deputy Director Channing,

Baxter did not appear for our second scheduled meeting, not even in the unusual way in which he presented himself to me at our first encounter; I still want to know how he got into my car and was able to remain hidden for as long as he was. Your men must have looked in the back windows to see if there were any potential problems with the car. Baxter said he crouched on the floor of the backseat for well over two hours I should think your men would have spotted something, though I must admit, I saw nothing amiss as I came up to my Packard after lunch. I wish he had not been so diligent in keeping his face partially concealed. He has rather heavy brows, fairly dark, and hazel eyes. His accent is Midwestern, perhaps Chicago, and he used technical terms correctly and with ease. At least the information he provided as I drove back from the Helmsman made the journey worth the time it took away from the office. All those fomulae for wiring systems can help us to detect piggy-back coding on radio signals. Baxter left a note for me under my windshield wiper; he put it in a Traffic Authority envelope, so that it appeared I had received a parking ticket, but who would be ticketing a restaurant parking lot baffles me.

The note informed me that he fears being observed, so he has suggested another place that he and I might meet: Branco's Oyster Beds. It is not quite as remote as the Helmsman, and it is much louder and busier. Even now, when there is an "R" in the month, Branco's does a great deal of business. Baxter's note informs me that there is a potential difficulty with the Helmsman: its very remoteness makes individuals more likely to be remembered. Branco's has a significant turn-over, and single individuals don't stand out unless they are unruly or loud. I see the advantage of his recommendation: after due consideration, I believe Baxter is right, and so I'm applying to you for a voucher for two meals at Branco's on the 14th. Baxter has assured me in his note that he will make an appearance or notify me in the morning that he will be delayed.

I am, of course, continuing my efforts to discover the identity of Baxter. I remain convinced that he is an engineer of some sort—those capital letters interspersed throughout his first and second note are often encountered in the handwriting styles of engineers. It would also explain the information that Baxter has provided us. I see a number of advantages in using Baxter as a resource as long as his information is useful to us, not the least of which is that he came to us, which demonstrates his patriotism and his own loyalty. If his employer is indeed mixed up with questionable persons, this way we can be sure that we are not in the hands of a double-agent. Engineering cannot easily be faked, which makes me fairly confident that we are getting straight goods, as my mother used to say.

If you are willing to give me a free hand in dealing with Baxter, I know I can establish rapport with him, and perhaps I can find out how Baxter and D. G. Atkins intersect, and where Atkins has gone. A few more lunches is a small price to pay for such necessary information. Let me know when you have decided how much leeway I am to have with Baxter.

Submitted
Lydell Broadstreet

❖ 4 ❖

CHARIS' NEW flat took up the whole of the top floor in a handsome building in the now-passe but very beautiful Art Nouveau style; each window overlooking the street had a balcony with railings ornamented with carved trailing vines. There were stairs up the front and back—the front stairs were interior, the rear were not—and there was an elevator that required a key to reach the top level, which was a large, well-laid-out flat: it had a modern kitchen with a dumbwaiter that connected to the building's kitchen on the ground floor as well as a chute that led to the dustbin at the back of the building on the alley that gave access to the garage. There were two bedrooms, a living and a dining room, one full bathroom and one guest bathroom, a study, and even a terrace outside the master bedroom, with a number of potted plants providing shade and shelter. The bedrooms and the living room as well as the study had rolled carpets standing up against the wall, and some very simple furniture on the bare floors.

"I'm waiting for the furniture to be delivered," she said to Szent-Germain as she held the door to the small elevator lobby open, beckoning him to come in. "I hope you won't mind sitting on wooden benches. I've put pillows on them, to make them easier to sit on." She was in a simple house-dress, her hair wrapped in a long, peach-colored scarf; she wore no make-up. "As my ally, you won't be put off by all that needs doing, will you?"

"Not at all; it is part of an ally's work to assist when needed in such situations," said Szent-Germain. "Is there anything you would like me to do while I am here?"

"If I think of something, I'll tell you," she said, touching the scarf holding her hair in place.

"I trust you to do so," he said, handing her a medium-sized package wrapped in colored paper and tied with shiny silver ribbon. "Something for a house-warming," he added as she took it. "If it isn't to your taste, let me know and I'll replace it."

"I have no doubt it will be fine," she said, but made no move to admit him.

"I hope it will," he said, his dark eyes fixed on hers.

In order to cover her emotion—it could not possibly be lust, she thought, not the way she felt in his presence; it had to be something cleaner, something untainted—she began to talk about the first thing to come into her mind. "I still can't believe that Lord Weldon is willing to let me have this place for such a small rent. You didn't talk him into it, did you?" she asked, holding the package with both hands. Looking down at it, she realized that just touching what he had touched exercised a disquieting flare in sexual need; she took several deep breaths to regain her composure.

"No; he was glad to have someone reliable living here, who would take good care of the place. An academic appealed to him. The Germans had it while they occupied Paris; they took almost all the carpets and furniture they didn't ruin, and Lord Weldon would prefer that wouldn't happen again, or that it not become an attraction for what you would call squatters. He is pleased to get some of his furniture out of storage—he's found evidence of mice in the upholstery."

"That's . . . upsetting," she said, at last giving him room to enter the foyer. "Do you think I'll have to look out for mice?"

"Possibly, but not from the stored furniture; everything coming to you is in good repair, he's explained to me; he had furniture for two other houses among his stored goods, so there is ample for your use," Szent-Germain told her as he entered the foyer, recalling the time, a quarter century ago, when he had provided the flat to Irina Ohchenova and her new husband, Phillippe Timbres, to occupy until such time as they found a house to their liking; they had lived here for almost three years. This memory brought back a remembrance of Laisha, his ward, whose death still left him shaken; he gave Charis his full attention.

"But to furnish the flat for only a token additional charge . . ."

She shook her head. "Is he a bit eccentric? So many lords are, aren't they?" As soon as she realized what she had said, her cheeks reddened. "I didn't mean that the way it sounded, Grof."

"I'm sure there are those who know Lord Weldon who find him eccentric; he'd take no offense at that description," he said, for he had cultivated a certain well-educated dottiness as part of the Weldon persona. "Sometimes great wealth has that effect."

She studied him, trying to decide how much of what he was saying she believed. After a second or two, she asked, "Should I open this now?"

"Well, it's not set to explode, but—"

"Great!" She hugged the package. "It's been a long time since I had a real present. This is a real present, isn't it?"

"I'd like to think so," he answered.

She sighed a little. "Thank you, then." She sat down on the largest of the benches in the living room, and began to remove the paper with meticulous care, folding it carefully once she had all of it, then rolled the silver ribbon on her fingers as if it were embroidery floss. "I hope to have some place to put this in a few days. It's not fragile, is it?" Inside the paper was a cardboard box; she lifted the lid.

"I wouldn't recommend dropping it, but it's sturdy enough," he said, though she barely heard him.

"Oh, good gracious," she said quietly as she put the box lid aside, then reverently removed the century-old clock from its bed of tissue paper, smiling as she looked over its superb craftsmanship. "How did you know I needed a clock?" She studied the clock. "It's a coachman's clock, isn't it? I'm so glad to have it. Thank you, Grof. Thank you."

"I didn't actually know you needed one, but most people like them, and you may have more than one without appearing vainglorious." His demeanor softened in response to her obvious pleasure. "I hope you enjoy it."

"It's wonderful," she said, flushing slightly. "I haven't had . . . oh, anything like this since I got here. Every gift since I came to

Europe has been *useful—practical;* I feel like a scullery maid. Harold and the boys sent me what they called a CARE package for Christmas—Halo shampoo, Dr. Lyon's tooth powder, scouring pads, dish cloths and dish towels, four bars of castile soap, Ivory flakes for laundry, even two large bars of Hershey's chocolate with almonds. As if I couldn't get things like that in Paris, and better shampoo and chocolate. They did it to remind me of home, I guess. I didn't know about Harold's problems with me then. Now I understand his gifts better." She got up from the bench and took her new, elegant clock and put it on the mantelpiece. "There. Now it's a proper living room."

"Lord Weldon told me that the telephone should be working by tomorrow, and that he will not require you change the number; he hasn't used it for himself in more than twenty years, but he's paid to keep it active."

"Tell him thank you, for me. Or I'll write him a note and you can send it to him, if you would; I gather you know how to reach him." She stepped back to admire the clock on the mantel. "Where on earth did you find it?"

"In Switzerland, of course. Where else does one get clocks?" He smiled to let her know he was being amusing.

"And so nearby, hardly more than a day away," she marveled in an exaggerated way, while still gazing at the clock. After a dozen seconds, she went on in a more ordinary manner, "If I get my furniture by the end of this week, I'm hoping to give a party a week later, once the place is fitted out. Most of the Coven is going to help me get the furniture in, and arranged. The least I can do is throw them a party. But only if you can come. I want to invite the Coven, but since I wouldn't be here without your Lord Weldon, it wouldn't be right if you weren't able to attend."

"If that is what you want, I will be here. You have only to confirm the time." He paused. "Have you decided what you want on the walls?"

"Paint or wallpaper, or do you mean art?" she asked, turning away from the clock at last. "I'll set it later, I didn't wind my watch last night—I am still getting used to my new surroundings, and it didn't occur to me until quite late at night that I hadn't—so I'm a bit fuzzy on simple things like that."

"To answer your first question, I meant art. Or"—he blinked as if to shut out a very bright light—"mirrors."

She laughed. "I can't afford art, and mirrors would only make this place look bigger than it is, and that would disappoint the Coven—it would be too much like showing off my good fortune in finding this wonderful flat."

"What is the trouble with that?" Szent-Germain asked, and held up his hand so he could answer. "You don't want to appear boastful. That would vex the Coven."

"Yes," she admitted. "And I know with the divorce looming, I have to be very careful not to make it seem that I am taking advantage of Harold. That's just the kind of thing that could ruin my position in the case, and making a great display of a place like this could be the straw that breaks the camel's back. You know as well as I that Julia Bjornson would have a lot to say about greedy women using divorce to feather their nests. And who knows what Harold would think."

"Are you so certain he would be vindictive? Mightn't he be relieved that you are in a position to care for yourself?" He asked the question gently, hearing her misgivings in her voice.

"Oh, yes. I think he would. He's already balking at the idea that the boys might visit me during summer vacation. He says it wouldn't look right, letting them visit so soon after our separation, though that's been going on since fall. He told me he would send his parents with them, but that might call the divorce into question, and that isn't acceptable to him." She went back to the bench and sat down. "I think he'll use the boys to force me to conduct myself as he sees fit, and this—this place—isn't part of his vision for me."

"Did you tell him about your apartment? How small it was, and how inconvenient?" He kept indignation and criticism out of his manner so that Charis would not feel that she had to defend her estranged husband.

"Yes, I did, but he said he couldn't afford to send me more

money, so I would have to make the best of it. I told him about the state of the plumbing, and the condition of the walls. I even sent him some photographs, but he made no comment. You'd suppose he might make allowances for my situation, because I was in it in part to help him." She put her hand to her face. "I'm beginning to think I never understood him, not really. I never thought he would put his career ahead of our marriage, because I wouldn't do that."

"I take it that one of the reasons it took you two months to decide to accept Lord Weldon's offer was that you supposed you would not be here long enough to make it worth his while to move you in," he said, kindness in his steady gaze.

"Was I so obvious? I thought I had—" She gave a little gasp. "If you guessed, the others might—"

"No, they won't, unless you decide to tell them. I haven't mentioned your . . . arrangement with Lord Weldon to anyone: why should I? At best, I am a go-between in this, and there is no reason why I should impart your dealings with Weldon to others." This was not quite the whole truth: he had discussed it in detail with his attorney in Paris, Hugues Curtise, who supervised Szent-Germain's several aliases as well as his actual name and titles. "I will give you my Word that I won't, if that would ease your concerns."

"I don't know, I'm just nervous about the whole thing," she said, sounding aggravated. "Something so unusual, you might bring it up with . . . oh, anyone."

"You may rest assured that I have not, and that I will not," he said, his voice low and musical. He took a couple of incautious steps toward her, wanting to offer her comfort but aware of her attraction to him, and the tumult it caused within her. "Don't let this dishearten you, Professor," he recommended. "Your husband may still come to his senses, and realize that you have as much right as he to see your children. If Lord Weldon's agreement with you improves your position in this regard, your husband may be trying to reduce your credibility in the eyes of the divorce court. He may be trying to blame you so that he can excuse himself for using you so unkindly. He may be embarrassed by his bad behavior, and it would not help to remind him of it, not at present." He paused. "I gather you want the boys to come here, since returning home is not an option for you, and thus far, your husband is recalcitrant."

"I miss them so much," she said barely above a whisper.

"Do you have a relative who might be willing to escort the boys here? Someone your husband would approve?" He said this lightly, not wanting to add to her dismay, but trying to provide her with the means to arrange the visit.

She swung around to look at him, her eyes wide. "I don't know," she said, much struck by his question. "I'll have to think about it."

"Someone older, perhaps? Someone who isn't immediately associated with you? If your husband is worried about turning attention on your separation, someone with a different last name, perhaps, would be appropriate."

"Why that?" She gave him a hard, perplexed stare.

"To lessen the identification with you. Someone whom your husband would not perceive as working on your behalf. If you concentrate your argument on keeping the boys from close scrutiny by the Committee because of you, then your husband would not be able to claim you're putting yourself above the welfare of your children." He watched her as she took in his suggestion.

"I don't think the Committee, arbitrary as it is, would go after two kids," said Charis. "And one of them crippled."

"They might, if they believed they could influence you through such devices," he said, recalling what Hapgood Nugent had said about the surveillance of his sister's children who were still in grammar school. "If you can provide an escort who is unexceptionable, it might be enough to convince Harold"—it was the first time he had spoken Charis' husband's name to her, and he could see surprise in her face—"to allow Arthur and David to come."

She nodded a couple of times, her thoughts moving swiftly in this more promising direction than the grim disappointment that had possessed her. "I have an aunt or two, and an older cousin who might serve well enough." She took his hand impulsively without being aware of what she had done, but hoping to find solace in this simple contact. He remained still while she held it tightly. "At least it's something to consider," she said, abruptly releasing his hand as if her fingers had been burned. "Harold says that if I do anything to disgrace him, I won't see our boys again."

"Do you know what he means by anything to disgrace him?"

"No scandal, no politics, no speculation on his work, no problems with his colleagues, nothing that would reflect badly on him—at least that covers the basics." She summoned up her nerve to go on, hearing her pulse quicken. "For example, he might not like me talking to you alone in this room."

"If you mean he assumes I would attempt to seduce a married woman in a room with nothing more than a rolled carpet and a pair of benches, he must have a very low opinion of me and those like me." He smiled quickly, his countenance ironic. "This is not the time nor the place for such . . . um . . . shenanigans. That is the word, isn't it?" He had heard it used during his stay in America twelve years ago.

"That's the word," she said, a little breathlessly.

He was aware of her disquiet, and said only, "You have enough demanding your attention; you need not fear unwanted importunities."

Charis sighed to cover her renewed confusion. "That wasn't exactly what I meant about Harold's disapproval," she said, a bit stiffly, because she realized that perhaps it was, "but if he knew I was here with you alone, he would feel that I had compromised myself."

"Isn't that a bit unrealistic?" Szent-Germain could feel her attraction diminish as he moved a few steps farther away from her. "He knows you are alone in Europe, and he knows that in your profession, you will be required to be interviewed, at the least, so prohibiting you to be alone with a man is enough to keep you from gaining employment."

"He says he is concerned for my reputation," she said, color rising in her face again.

"Then he has a curious way of ensuring your protection," he said.

Wanting to avoid any more discussion of the implications of being alone with a man, Charis remarked, "I'm having Stephen diMaggio install electronic locks on the doors and windows here, later today. I think this will reassure Harold when I send him some photos of the place, which he has insisted on seeing. He doesn't want Arthur and David to visit me if my flat isn't safe."

"He preferred your apartment for safety?" Szent-Germain shook his head incredulously.

"I can only guess, and my guesses haven't been very accurate where my husb—I really shouldn't call him that anymore, should I?—Harold is concerned," she told him, her face averted while she did her best to take on a serenity she did not feel. "As I said, I don't understand him as well as I assumed I did." An ill-at-ease silence descended between them. When she spoke again, it was in a different tone and manner. "Steve offered to do it for me, and I took him up on it."

"DiMaggio should do a good job for you—he has access to all the military electronics, I understand," said Szent-Germain, wondering as he did how many excuses Harold Treat might conjure up to refuse any visitation between Charis and her sons.

"Well, he *had* access, which is what got him into trouble," Charis told him with a touch of chagrin. "But he tells me he can set something up for me that will do the trick, and I believe him. He's one of those engineers who has the feel of their work beyond their knowledge; he could probably make a Mixmaster play the ukelele. He does better with machines than people." She made a flustered gesture with one hand. "I notified Lord Weldon about it, and apparently it's acceptable to him. His telegram in response to mine just said *Carry on*."

Three days ago, Szent-Germain had sent a telegram to the manager of Eclipse Trading Company in Madras, asking him to send that telegram for him, which Khorbin Singh did the day before yesterday. Singh was dependable and rarely said anything about the requests he received from his employer. "That doesn't astonish me."

"Can you tell me about him?" Charis asked. "What sort of man is he?"

"Old title, old money," said Szent-Germain. "Eccentric, as you guessed. Something of a wanderer."

"You've known him a while?" Charis prompted.

"Yes; quite a long time." He had created the alias in 1731, and had used that identity sporadically ever since, when he needed a name that was not in any way related to his own.

"Then it's no surprise that he would pay attention to your advice. I imagine that is how he came to provide this place for me. I can't imagine that he heard about my predicament from one of the Coven." She glanced away and then back at him. "You must be how he found out about my situation."

Szent-Germain concealed his appreciation of her astute guess, saying, "He told me, and not for the first time, he wanted someone responsible living here, and what he would expect of the tenant; I told him about you, about the books you have with Eclipse Press, and described the place you were living. He said he would look into it." He disliked having to add to the fiction he had created, but to admit to being the owner would drive a wedge between them, which he wanted to avoid.

"Did you make any other suggestions?"

"You mean did I recommend any other Coven members? No; I don't know them as well as I know you, and a few of them seem to be reasonably comfortable in where they are living. The Frosts require a very special place because of his . . . condition, so this would not have suited them, though it does well for you." He ducked his head. "Was I in error? Are you upset that I gave him your name?"

She did not answer at once, and when she did speak, it was with a rueful smile. "No, you weren't in error, though I'd bet that Tolliver Bethune would love this place. He's just the sort who would adore the . . . the Frenchness of it all." She studied him. "I wish I could figure you out, Grof."

"Why is that?"

"I'd like to know why you took me under your wing. And don't say you didn't, because it's obvious that you did." She put her hands together, left hand over right hand. "From the time you talked to me in Copenhagen, you have supported me more than I had any reason to expect. You've been helping me on my second book for you, and well beyond what an editor would do. You've driven me all over the countryside to look at ancient ruins of convents, you've taken an interest in the Coven, and now you're offering advice in regard to my husband and children. I'm more puzzled than you can imagine. Don't get me wrong—I'm flattered and grateful, but I'd like to know why you do this." She stopped talking, turning to him, waiting for what he would say.

He went to the windows, moved the filmy cotton curtains aside, and looked out on the busy street below, taking care not to address her directly. "When we first met, I liked your spirit. It takes strength to do what you have done, for whatever reason you have done it, and I admire that strength. You are also intelligent, and I admire intelligence." He was also very much aware of how she used both these qualities to keep her distance from him without obvious rejection, and although this saddened, he admired her skill; had she known of his cognizance of her desire, he wondered if her reserve might have lessened.

"Is that why you said you'd be my ally?"

"In large part, yes," he said, moving away from the window and toward the open double-doors that led to the dining room. "Is Lord Weldon including draperies for your windows?"

"I believe so, yes," she answered.

"Very good," he said. "These light curtains aren't sufficient. You need something more substantial."

"I guess that's so," she said, baffled by his change in subject.

"You'll need towels for your bathrooms, and all the rest of it," he went on, walking slowly toward the door to the kitchen. "What of cookwares? What, if anything, did Lord Weldon offer you?"

"I'm not sure. He said the furnishing would be complete, whatever that means. I suppose I'll know by this time next week." She moved around the room, taking stock of it in light of what Lord Weldon had pledged to do. "If he changes his mind, I suppose I can make do with the benches for a while, and the basics I brought from my apartment."

Szent-Germain nodded his approval. "You see? This is what I admire in you." He could sense her yearning for him, and her determination not to act upon it, so he stayed in the dining room.

"There's room enough for a good-sized dining table. You may want a buffet as well, and a china cabinet."

"There is room enough," she agreed. "And I'd like all those things, and chairs enough to make the most of this room. I should like to be able to accommodate eight or ten at table, preferably one with leaves, so that private dining won't require megaphones in order to converse."

He managed a brief chuckle. "An interesting image, indeed."

She felt an unexpected spurt of laughter escape her. "Yes, isn't it?" She continued to smile. "Do you want to see the rest of the place, or have you seen it already?"

"I have seen it, but not for some years, and then it was furnished to suit the tenants at the time. I don't know what or how much of his stored furniture he has marked for your use." He made a little bow. "If you would like to show me, I would enjoy seeing its bare bones."

"That's a good phrase for it," she said, going out of the living room and into the corridor that led toward the bedrooms. There were French windows at the beginning of the corridor, giving access to the roof-top terrace; there were two large tubs of flowering bushes that blew in the afternoon breeze, but for the most part, the potted garden was neglected. "I may do more gardening now that I have a garden of sorts."

"Flowers? Herbs? Topiary?" he inquired as he followed her.

"I don't know yet. It depends on whether or not the boys visit me." The sadness was back in her voice, and she walked slowly while she tried to restore her good mood. "The guest room is on the left, the master bedroom on the right; it has access to the terrace, and the full bath at the end of the hall. As you probably know, the guest bathroom is reached from the foyer, between the dining room and the kitchen doors. The door next to the study leads to the stairs to the lobby. The study is across the foyer from the dining room and kitchen, and looks out onto the terrace." This recitation was without enthusiasm, as if mentioning her sons had taken the joy out of moving to this location. "Sorry. I'm a . . . little tired. I think I should lie down for half an hour or so. That way I'll be refreshed when Steve arrives to install the locks." She wandered back toward the living room.

"On what?" he asked, walking a couple of paces behind him. "The bench? How can that revive you?"

"I have the mattress I purchased when I couldn't bear the lumps in the old one at my apartment. Madame Gouffre wanted to keep it because I was moving out before a year was up, but I refused, and since she wanted me gone more than she wanted the mattress, I was able to come away with it, along with her warning that I would not find as nice a place as she had. I've slept on it for the last two nights. It's a little like camping out, but without the tent, or the countryside."

"Speaking of countryside, how is your ankle?" He had noticed that she had begun to favor it; there was a slight hesitation in her walk. "How are you doing with it? I haven't seen you use a cane in the last week or two."

"Almost healed, I'd say, but still not quite where it should be. A sprain like that can take time to recover from." She was startled that he had noticed the very slight limp that had started to bother her. "That's what the nap is for."

"Ah." He would have offered his arm, but knew that would not help her to relax. "Then I won't detain you. Get your rest. I'll call back the day after tomorrow, in case you would like some help with your furniture."

"You don't have to," she told him.

"No, I don't. But what sort of ally would I be then?" He went toward the foyer, saying as he went, "I hope you will find this flat satisfactory, and that your stay here, for however long it lasts, is a pleasant one."

"Very prettily said," she told him and she pressed the button to summon the elevator. "I do like the clock; it's a lovely present. And I meant it about the party. I will arrange it on a night that is convenient for you."

"Get yourself properly moved in and then we'll talk about it," he said, hearing the elevator approaching. "If you will call my office

when you have your phone number, and leave it for me, I'd appreciate it."

"Of course," she said, and reached to open the door of the elevator cab.

He stepped inside the small cab, which would accommodate
three or four persons at most, and watched as she pulled the col-
lapsible metal gate across; he shut the interior door and heard the
buzz as she depressed the button to descend. As the elevator made
its way downward, Szent-Germain spent the length of the ride
trying to determine what it was about her desire that frightened
her so much that she was unwilling to admit it existed. For a capable, educated woman, he found Charis' obdurate blindness to the
physical passion within her as puzzling as it was troublesome. She
was not like Margrethe, who had known of her attraction to him,
but saw it as sinful, and who was willing to admit her longing;
Charis had no such compunction about her, yet she was as edgy in
his company as Margrethe had been, more than seven hundred
years ago. There was more of Tulsi Kil in Charis than there was
Margrethe, or Rakhel. As he reached the lobby, he let himself out
of the elevator, and nodded to the elderly woman who lived in the
apartment next to the building's kitchen on this ground level, then
went out toward the rear of the apartment building, where his
Delahaye was parked in the shadow of the newer apartment building next door. He caught a glimpse of a face in a second-story window as he got into his automobile, and for an instant, wondered if
he were being watched. With that perturbing thought for comfort,
he started the Delahaye, adjusted the choke, and drove away.

TEXT OF THE EX-PATS' COVEN NEWSLETTER, TYPESET
AND PRINTED BY WASHINGTON YOUNG IN PARIS, AND
DISTRIBUTED TO COVEN MEMBERS ON MARCH 9TH, 1950.

THE GRIMOIRE

newsletter for Spring 1950
Washington Young, printer and publisher
Volume 3, no. 1

AS YOU CAN see, Grof Szent-Germain has allowed me the use of his third press for the purposes of bringing out *The Grimoire*. I have decided that Bodoni is handsomer than the typeface on the typewriter I have used in the past for mimeographing. This is a much more satisfactory style. If you disagree with me, you may tell me so at our next meeting, which will be on the third Friday of the month at the new flat of our member from Louisiana. There will be a buffet of Coq a Vin, aubergine with mushrooms, Spanish rice, and asparagus in lemon-butter, with coffee, tea, and wine. You are asked to give regrets only.

WE HAVE NEWS from the US that is of interest to all the Coven, not all of it welcome: Alger Hiss has been found guilty of perjury for failing to reveal his connection to the Communist Party. He is appealing his conviction, but it does not look as if he will win an acquittal. Klaus Fuchs has also been found guilty of providing British atomic secrets to the Soviet Union. Fuchs was part of the Los Alamos team, for any of you unfamiliar with the case. Harry Gold, who worked with Fuchs, is also headed to prison by the looks of it. At the other end of the scale, President Truman has authorized the Atomic Energy Commission to develop a hydrogen bomb for the US, in large part on the possibility that the Soviet Union may already have an atom bomb of their own. There is more fuel being added to the pyres of the witch-hunt currently under way in the US. Senator Joseph McCarthy of Wisconsin has been making some waves claiming that the government needs to conduct more rigorous pursuits of suspected and known Communists occupying sensitive positions in governmental agencies; he is claiming that there are hosts of Soviet spies in the US, going about their work unhampered. He has gained the support of the members of the HUAC and Army Intelligence, but his influence may spread. This reporter thinks that any return to the US for Coven members could prove dangerous as long as the political climate remains so extreme. From this point on, I believe we must be diligent in guarding the Coven as well as our relatives back home, some of whom may be pressed into taking the brunt of our absence. We have no reason to doubt that the FBI, like the CIA, has the names and addresses of everyone who is a blood relation, and is prepared to use that information to create pressure on our families and through them, on us. HN has already seen this with his sister's children, who are in grammar school, but were harassed by the CIA, which is specifically chartered not to operate in the US. As the fear of Communism grows among the population of the US, and is encouraged by governmental action, incidents of intimidation are likely to increase.

IN OTHER PARTS of the world: Johannesburg at the end of January, the colored population protesting the new apartheid program. The King of Belgium, Leopold III, will be able to return to his country later this year; his return from exile is favored by most UN member-states, but there are some nay-sayers. The King of Sweden, Gustav V, has been ill for some weeks, not surprising in a man over ninety, but there is concern for his well-being in all of Scandinavia. Pope Pius XII is causing some excitement in Rome, claiming that he has had a number of visions regarding the Virgin Mary, and that Roman Catholics may expect a Papal Encyclical in the near future. With the war behind them, the Japanese are about to release a new tape recorder, first in Japan, and then, if sales warrant it, on a larger market. The terms of the Marshall Plan may yet permit the Germans to do the same in the near future.

IT IS RUMORED that Britain, the US, and the UN will recognize the People's Republic of China diplomatically, and that although Chiang Kai-shek is resuming the presidency of Nationalist China, with a fair amount of shoring up from the US and its allies, will continue to be a separate state. This does not bode well for south-east Asia. There is an indication that the US will recognize VietNam—until recently French Indo-China—and provide military support as a means of holding the People's Republic of China at bay, at least for a while, though it is also feared that the People's Republic of China may direct its expansion toward Tibet, not the former French colonies in the south. All of this may test the newly formed United Nations, for with so many new forms of conquest being tried out, it is not at all certain that the UN will be able to live up to its lofty ideals, and make its rulings stick.

OUR MEMBER FROM Helena has returned from a month in Barcelona ("the Gaudi house was splendid!"), which was an opportunity to rest up from her six months of job-hunting. While she is discouraged, she remains determined to find a position for herself even if it is only giving planetarium narrations in English for tourists. She would like to try some place where she can work at the science of astronomy, not just its public appeal. She has asked if anyone has contacts with astronomers in India or New Zealand, where she would not be at the disadvantage that she is now, and could continue her work on the asteroid belt beyond Mars.

OUR HELPFUL COLONEL has been transferred to Alaska, out on the Aleutian Islands, running an installation dedicated to monitoring Soviet activities in the northern

Pacific, and the various communications made in Korea, where more trouble is expected. While this is not a demotion, it is an isolation, and our helpful Colonel admits that the method is effective. He informed me that this is an unofficial punishment for the assistance he has given us for the last three years. He says the Army wants him where he is as closely watched as the Soviet Union is, and this is a way to do that, as well as using his fluency in Russian to military advantage. He apologizes for having to depart in this abrupt way, and extends his good wishes to all of us. He informs this reporter that those of you who have ordered hi-fi components from him will be able to pick them up in Le Havre after May 10th.

WE ARE SADDENED to learn of the death of Yale Professor Leonard Nye, 61, in New Haven. He suffered terrible injuries in an automobile accident in January, when his Packard was rammed by a Chevrolet delivery van which had gone into a skid on black ice; the driver of the van was killed outright at the scene. Police investigators concluded that the accident was just that: an accident, one of several that occurred on that stretch of road in a period of a week. After almost a month in a deep coma, Nye died on February 21st, and is survived by two brothers and a sister, six nephews, and four nieces. His long-time associate, Maurice Yeoman, has arranged a memorial service for March 17th , at Holy Trinity in New Haven. In lieu of flowers, Yeoman requests donations be made in Nye's name to American Red Cross, Easter Seals, or The American Humane Society.

T.B., OUR LEGAL genius, has filed an amicus curiae brief on behalf of B. and W. K. and T. and M.F., seeking to have their positions at their schools restored in good standing, and in the case of K. PhD, his tenure with compensatory pay as part of the attempts being made at many colleges and universities to fire all faculty and administration accused of having Communist connections without any proof beyond the accusation itself. He has also prepared a challenge to the Farm Security Administration's new claims that W.P.'s work on disease-resistant wheat is not sufficient to brand him a Communist sympathizer. Guilt by association is not valid evidence for prosecution, T. B. affirms, and in W.P.'s case, doubly so: the government approved his working with Soviet agronomists on this problem in 1942, and not simply because we were allies in the war, but because their research dovetailed with P.'s. Those of you who believe you might have a similar claim, speak to T.B. at our next meeting.

THERE WILL BE an extra Coven meeting on March 18th at the Sign of the Raven Bookstore on Avenue Isabeau, in the upstairs lounge, to hear a progress report from our foreign publisher friend, which will include six titles by Coven members. Bookstore owners are also being asked to attend. The meeting will begin at seventeen hundred hours or five pm, and is expected to last two hours.

ONCE AGAIN, WE find ourselves in need of a permanent meeting place, and are asking for recommendations for any location fairly centrally located. We need a location that allows us privacy to speak openly without fear of being overheard, an is not conspicuous in any sense. Pass on your locations to this reporter or to W.P., who currently leads us.

A publication for and by the victims of witch-hunts

5

By Tolliver Bethune's standards, the figure he cut was decidedly unkempt: his coat was of military design and none too clean, his hat resembled a peaked cap although it lacked an insignia and was of a color so neutral that it hardly seemed real, his sweater was olive-drab with patches at the elbow and worn over a khaki-colored shirt and slacks. He carried a postman's bag over his left shoulder, its weight pulling that side of his body down a bit, changing his clean, swift stride to more of a furtive crouch. In such garb and behavior he could easily be mistaken for a courier or a member of the US Embassy staff, which is what he intended. On this weepy morning in late March, Bethune could not summon up any enjoyment of this drizzly spring day, for the summons he had received twenty-six hours ago had been terse and demanding; he knew better than to attempt to negotiate his way out of it. He suggested a salute to the Marine guards at the gate, keeping his head down, so that the camera that took the picture of everyone entering the building would not get a clear view of his face. He flashed an ID and went into the marble-fronted building, moving at a pace that suggested that he had an urgent appointment, which was correct. He climbed to the second floor and stopped at the desk newly set up in front of the corridor leading to the office where he was expected. Another cosmetic approach to security, Bethune thought as he took out his ID card and handed it over to the pretty young WAC lieutenant who seemed to be too tired or bored to enter his name in the log-book in front of her; he could feel her sizing him up with her eyes. "Good morning," he said, but got no response to his greeting. He pulled a plastic cigarette case and a brass lighter from his overcoat-pocket, selected a cigarette, tamped it on his fingernail, and lit up, then repeated, "Good morning," and added "Lieutenant," this time.

"Good morning," she said as if overwhelmed by boredom.

The doors of the various offices along the corridor in front of Bethune were closed and the whole floor seemed almost empty, though he supposed it was not; it was coming up to the lunch hour, but was not there yet, and that meant there would be workers in a hurry to finish up the morning's business before their forty-five-minute break. Another drag on the cigarette gave him a second or two to try to locate any cameras set up to record all visitors on this floor—he saw nothing. He looked from one door to the next, trying to determine who, if anyone, was watching him, for given that these were CIA offices, he was fairly certain that someone more than the WAC lieutenant was keeping an eye on the corridor.

"Tolliver Bethune," he said, hoping to gain the WAC's attention.

"Yeah. That's what it says. I can read, mister," she told him in an annoyed tone as she handed the card back to him and tapped a line on the daily schedule; looking over his name, her curiosity was sparked and she asked, "You were one of the men assigned to the Nuremberg trials, weren't you?"

"I was." It had been demanding work, but he felt that his service was worthwhile, or he had until he was accused of passing information to the Soviets. He had not done that, but he had occasionally discussed the progress of the prosecution of the Nazis with some of the Russian advocates who were presenting evidence to the court, and that was enough to tarnish him. He had left Germany without being able to prove his alleged espionage untrue; the calumny still followed him, and left him in the awkward situation of having to assist the CIA or risk being brought up on spurious charges that were likely to ruin him completely.

"Who are you here to see?"

"Whom," he corrected her. "Whom am I here to see?"

"That's what I'm asking," she said.

"But that's not what your grammar says," he persisted, wanting to kick himself for antagonizing the WAC.

"You understood me, didn't you?" She glowered at her telephone. "Lawyers!"

He ignored her expostulation. "I understood you, yes, but not because you were right, but because English is structurally very flexible. You don't strike me as uneducated, so you should have learned this in school. The person I am here to see takes the objective—whom—since I am the subject of your question."

"If you say so," she said testily; her brightly lipsticked mouth made a moue of disgust.

"Say goodnight, Gracie," Bethune muttered, had recourse to his cigarette again, then raised his voice. "Deputy Coordinator Peter Leeland. I know where his office is."

She consulted her schedule for the day. "He's going to be in the Blue Room—three doors down on your left. He's waiting for you."

"Why isn't it in your log, then?" He had the knack of being able to read upside-down, and at moments like this, it came in handy.

"Because this meeting never happened," she said as if the answer were obvious. "It only appears on this schedule, and the visitors' schedule is destroyed every evening."

Bethune went cold, shocked by this practice that erased events and people with the lighting of a match, but did his utmost to conceal his reaction, assuming that it would be reported if he did not. "Fine." He went around the WAC's desk and made for the door in question, wondering as he went why the meeting had been rescheduled for the smaller conference room rather than Lee's office; he did not like any of the answers that raced through his head. He did his utmost to banish uneasiness from his demeanor as he raised his hand to rap on the door.

"Come in," called the familiar voice from inside.

Bethune swung the door open, and slipped inside the conference room, letting the door close itself. "Why all the secrecy?" he asked, turning to face Leeland while taking in the cobalt-blue draperies and upholstery. Only then did he see a second man at the broad oaken table. Bethune stopped still.

Peter Sinclair Leeland, who looked to be a decade younger than Bethune, though was only four years his junior, had the practiced manner of an ambitious bureaucrat, and now managed a lupine smile as he stubbed out his dark, odorous Turkish cigarette in the ashtray that was the size of a long-playing record. "Well, we are spies, aren't we? This is Philetus Rothcoe. Phil, this is Tolliver Bethune."

Knowing that he had to appear forthcoming, Bethune took a step toward Rothcoe and held out his hand. "Pleasure to meet you."

Rothcoe half-rose and shook Bethune's hand. He was in his early thirties, his navy-blue suit, white shirt, and maroon tie making him all but invisible in a place like this Embassy; he had an air of anonymity about him, an ordinariness that was so comprehensive that Bethune knew he would be hard-put to describe the man after he left the Embassy. In Rothcoe's unprepossessing appearance, the one feature that stood out was his hazel-green eyes, which had the shine of singular purpose that told Bethune that Rothcoe was a zealot, prepared to do anything for his country and his cause. "Pleasure," he said as if he had said *perfunctory.*

"I didn't realize that we were going to have . . . Mister Rothcoe with us," Bethune said to Leeland, not caring that he was being rude; he, too, put out his cigarette in the large ashtray.

"No; I didn't tell you," said Leeland smugly, relishing Bethune's discomfort.

"Is he the reason I'm here?" Bethune inquired, recognizing that Leeland was showing off for Rothcoe's benefit.

"That remains to be seen," Leeland responded, his smile becoming fixed and humorless.

"Right you are," said Bethune, trying to conceal his consternation. What was going on here? he asked himself, and took out his cigarette case, putting it on the table in front of him. "Let's get down to—"

"You're doing legal work for the group calling itself the Ex-Pats' Coven," Rothcoe said, cutting short the verbal fencing that Bethune and Leeland had started. "I have some questions that I hope you'll be able to answer for me."

All of Bethune's legal senses were now on high alert. "I am their counsel of record, so I'm not at liberty to discuss—"

"Tell him what you can, Tolliver, and remember, it could prove helpful to your clients if you can provide proof of your answers," Leeland said bluntly. "I don't want you to fail your clients, but you do understand that Rothcoe needs as much help as you're able to provide." He indicated one of the empty chairs. "Put your sack down and sit."

As a beginning this left much to be desired. Bethune hated being manipulated like this, knowing that if he did not supply at least some of what was asked, Leeland's disappointment would be taken out on the Coven and their families. That meant he would have to warn them all, no matter how this meeting turned out, which brought with it a sharp pang of chagrin. He shrugged his postman's bag off his shoulder and dropped it on the table with a solid *thunk*, then removed his coat, draping it over the back of the chair before he sat down. "Okay. What are you after? I'll answer anything that I ethically can."

"Two things are all I need from you," said Rothcoe, much too smoothly. "One is a connection to D. G. Atkins—"

"He's not a member of the group," Bethune said, cutting Rothcoe short. "That's one I can't help you with."

"We know that," Leeland interjected. "Your group isn't the enigma you seem to think it is. We know who's in it now, who was in it before, and we can make a good guess about who'll seek you out later. That Eastern European publisher isn't the only un-American in your Coven."

"Actually Szent-Germain isn't in our Coven, technically; he's associated with some of its members, but he isn't the victim of a witch-hunt so far as any of us knows," Bethune said with a diffident glance at Rothcoe.

"Can we get back to the question?" Rothcoe glowered at Bethune as if he suspected that the attorney was intending to confuse and delay with the interruption. "We suspect that at least one of your group is acquainted with Atkins, and may know where he is."

"I don't know if that's the case, but whether it is or not, anything I could report would be hear-say at best, and not much use to you." He heard a telephone ring behind one of the closed doors somewhere along the empty corridor.

"Can you confirm whether or not Hapgood Nugent is a member of the group you represent?" Rothcoe asked sharply.

"Since you've made it plain that you already know the answer, I'll say yes," said Bethune. "I'm assuming that Leeland gave you access to his files on the Coven. If not Leeland, someone in the upper levels of the CIA administration did."

"That he has; Leeland is most thorough, and helpful," Rothcoe said, looking at Leeland with an emotion very like satisfaction. "That first question isn't so hard, is it?" He cleared his throat. "Does your group have many other associates living abroad for the same reason your group does? I mean Americans who have decided to leave the country for fear of being investigated for un-American activities. You needn't mention anyone who isn't American—you've made it clear about your publisher—he's only doing business with a captive audience." His smile was an unappealing blend of obsequious and sardonic.

"I don't know," said Bethune. "They might, or they might not. I know Nugent keeps in regular contact with his sister, who lives in St. Louis, I believe." He directed his gaze to Rothcoe. "You undoubtedly know that, too."

"We know she—Nugent's sister—is coming to France in May to spend ten days with him. She has her tickets and her passport and her vaccination certificates. She flies to London and from there to Marseilles, where he will meet her." Rothcoe rested his folded arms on the table. "Her husband doesn't approve."

"You or Hoover's boys been opening mail again?" Bethune challenged sarcastically. "Tisk, tisk, tisk." He took another cigarette from his case and prepared to light up.

"That would be illegal," said Leeland.

"So it would," said Bethune, as Rothcoe waved his hand at the stream of smoke Bethune blew in his general direction. He stopped talking.

Quiet sizzled in the Blue Room; Leeland opened the notebook in front of him, picked up his pencil and wrote something down, then closed the notebook. Bethune let the silence stretch out, watching Rothcoe to see how he reacted.

Finally Leeland spoke up. "Do you think you can bring to mind anything about Nugent that would suggest that he has been aiding Atkins? Providing it doesn't compromise your integrity, of course."

"Since I don't know if they are in contact with each other, why would I have such an impression? You're jumping to conclusions with little or no support. Everyone in the Coven has associates and friends with whom they communicate from time to time, which isn't surprising; you'd probably do the same thing in their situation, don't you think?" Bethune mused aloud. "If you are trying to make it seem as if I have been suborning treason, I will tell you right now that I have not, that I resent the implication that I would do such a thing, and furthermore, I will swear to that in any court you select."

Rothcoe offered a singularly unpleasant smile. "That's a reckless promise, given your state of affairs."

"Would you care to elucidate on that?" Bethune knew he was being foolhardy, but he was beginning to dislike Philetus Rothcoe so much that he did not want to hide it. He rested his cigarette on the scalloped rim of the ashtray. "What exactly is my state of affairs, as you see it?"

Rothcoe cocked his head. "Some of your . . . social associates might prove problematic for you if you had to explain your friendships before a judge."

"Another guilt-by-association ploy?" Bethune asked, though the very notion made him feel faintly ill.

Leeland held up his hands. "Let's keep on track, fellows. No need to wrangle."

"I'm willing," Rothcoe declared reluctantly. "So long as Bethune here cooperates."

Bethune took up Rothcoe's tone as he would have done if he were conducting a cross-examination. "So long as I'm at liberty to answer questions, I will, but only about matters pertaining to your investigation, Rothcoe. I'm in no position to speculate, so if you're on a fishing trip, keep that in mind. You want to know about the Ex-Pats' Coven, in particular, anyone who knows someone named Atkins. Anything else is outside your purview, wouldn't you say? Why should I succumb to your bullying—it's all pretense, isn't it?

An attempt to bring me to heel. Well, that isn't going to happen." He reached for his mail-sack and pulled out four thick files, rubber-banded together, and half-flung, half-passed them to Leeland. "This is everything I can show you within the canon of ethics. Whatever your questions, any answer I can provide you is in there. These are copies of my originals; I have other copies on file with my family attorney in Raleigh, all notarized."

Leeland and Rothcoe exchanged glances.

"Isn't that a bit . . . paranoid?" Rothcoe suggested, goading Bethune.

"Don't you mean realistic?" Bethune asked.

"You're a damned fool, Tolliver," said Leeland with an abrupt sigh. "If you throw in your lot with those working against America, you will have to answer for it."

"Hardly—and you know it as well as I do." He paused for a heartbeat. "I'm not a novice, either. You're forgetting I'm not new to this game, gentlemen," said Bethune, once again reining in his temper, this time with more success than his previous attempt. "You want to intimidate me as many ways as you can, and then compel me to help you in unethical dealings so that your hold on me grows stronger, and I become your tool."

"That's uncalled-for," Rothcoe declared.

"Oh, really?" Bethune countered, picking up his cigarette once more. "Are you willing to sign a statement describing our current conversation, and the reason for it?"

"You seem to think we're attacking you," Rothcoe began only to be interrupted by Leeland.

"Gentlemen, please." Leeland stared at the stack of files, then lit up another of his Turkish cigarettes. "If you know that any of these people are working to destroy the United States, Tolliver, don't you have a larger ethical obligation to inform us, even if you violate attorney-client privilege? Isn't your country worth more than a handful of Communist sympathizers?"

"I am unaware that anyone in the Coven is making such an attempt," said Bethune. "And even if I did know such a thing, that would not release me from my obligation to keep the confidences of my clients. If my country wishes to defend itself through the persecution of its citizens, it isn't the country I have served for half my life." He paused as he heard a door open, accompanied by a loud clatter of typewriters. "Lunch time is almost here." He tapped his cigarette on the edge of the ashtray.

"Stay on track, Bethune," said Leeland.

"He's probably hungry," said Rothcoe, as if this were a moral failing. "I don't imagine your clients can afford to pay you very much. You'd like to get a meal out of this, wouldn't you?"

This time it was Leeland who took exception to Rothcoe's prodding. "That's enough, Phil. What he charges for his services and where he dines is none of our business." He took two serious puffs on his Turkish cigarette; Rothcoe scowled and pretended to cough a little.

"We can subpoena bank records," Rothcoe went on as if he were not listening to Leeland.

"You may try," Bethune said. "But I wouldn't recommend it. The French are a bit touchy about such matters."

"I think we have a good chance of gaining their support," Rothcoe said with a smug look. "They don't like mischief inside their borders."

"If they find out about it, I will have a fairly good notion of who is responsible for it," Bethune warned.

"But we have access to legal channels not generally used," added Leeland. "We can file our motions in one of these courts—"

"You might not get such an order through the US courts," Bethune said with a great air of confidence, making no apology for this interruption. "The Coven isn't wholly without support."

Leeland nodded. "Bethune's uncle sits on the Ninth District Court, and Winston Pomeroy, as head of the group, is a Californian, and will want to handle the matter."

"The liberal Ninth?" Rothcoe scoffed. "It figures."

"And you were aware of that when I walked in here," Bethune said firmly, stubbed out his cigarette, then addressed Leeland. "I've provided you what you asked for to the limits my profession allows, and both of you are cognizant of them. If this is your opening salvo, I'm not impressed. If all you want to do is try to aggravate me so that I tell you something out of turn, you're going against the purpose of the CIA: you bastards are supposed to be invisible." He stood up quickly, and reached for his mail-sack, handling it easily now that it was empty but for his peaked cap. Next he returned his cigarette case to the inside pocket of his overcoat.

"You're not dismissed," said Rothcoe.

"I'm also not under orders, so it hardly matters. Were you planning to fire me?" He said this last with a nasty smile.

"Don't press me," Rothcoe warned.

"Phil, shut up," said Leeland with superficial geniality. "Tolliver, get down off your high horse." He held up a hand. "Yes; Phil has been out of line. You're right about that." He smoked more Turkish tobacco. "But this is a serious investigation, and there are reasons we have to be strict in our pursuit of the truth. It involves so much more than your run-away academics. You can understand that, can't you?"

"I certainly can. But I do comprehend the difference between truth and innuendo." Bethune remained standing; he shook out his coat and began to pull it on. "Which is why I am leaving now." Without any farewells, he turned and made for the door.

"Hey, Bethune," Leeland protested.

"Another time, Peter," said Bethune, and stepped out into the corridor, which once again presented nothing but closed doors; even the WAC lieutenant was gone from her desk, whether to lunch, or to reassignment he had no idea. Descending to the lobby, he saw a few clusters of workers gathered in the large, echoing space, but none of the Embassy personnel gave any sign of noticing him. At the iron gates, he returned the Marine's salute as he left the grounds and turned right, bound for the small house where Boris and Wilhelmina King lived with Wilhelmina's aunt. He would call on them first, then the Praegers, and last of all, the Frosts; in February, they had moved into what had been a fine old hotel but was now a group of neat apartments designed for those left crippled by war or misfortune or disease. He paid little attention to the ruffles of new leaves on the branches of the trees lining the street; he was reviewing the meeting in his mind, trying to discern why it had been called. Then, he promised himself, he would find a good bistro where he could dine and try to figure out what Rothcoe had really wanted. He decided the whole ploy smelled to high heaven, and he needed to proceed with great care.

Wilhelmina opened the door, her clothes making it obvious that she was doing her housekeeping. In spite of that, she smiled and said, "Come in, Tolliver. I'm sorry, but Boris is away just now. Let me make you a cup of coffee, and you can tell me how it went at the Embassy." If she noticed his appearance, she made no mention of it.

"Thanks, Willie," Bethune said, using her nick-name as a reassurance. He entered the small, enclosed entryway,

The entry-hall that ran the length of the house was flanked by two drawing rooms at this end, one pressed into service as a library that smelled of books and Boris' pipe tobacco, the other graced with a fireplace and two, mismatched sofas and a trio of armchairs. There was a butler's table in front of the fireplace piled with books and magazines. "In here, I suppose?" he asked as he looked at the cluttered, comfortable chamber.

She waved at the sofas. "Make yourself comfortable. I'll bring the coffee." When she went down the hallway toward the kitchen in the rear of the house, a frail voice called from upstairs.

"Who's there?" came the question in French.

"Our attorney, Aunt Eugenie," said Wilhelmina in the same language. "Do you need anything?"

"Not just now," her aunt replied.

Listening to this exchange, Bethune wondered if the old woman would listen to their conversation. He had been told that she had some English, but not much beyond pleasantries. Or was he too much concerned about being under surveillance? He had been careful coming here, anticipating being under watch; Leeland always had that effect on him. Impatiently he chided himself for not applying Occam's Razor to his predicament, and letting his anxiety add to the convolution of possibilities that had taken hold of his imagination. The trouble was, he thought, he might be right about the convolutions, so he could not ignore them. He left his coat on, for the house was cool. He hung his postal sack over the arm of the sofa and sat back against the well-padded join of the back and the nearest arm. Now that he was in this house, the keyed-up nerves that had rattled him all morning began to fade, leaving him tired and a bit jittery.

From the kitchen, he heard Wilhelmina call out to him. "Did the meeting go well?"

Bethune shrugged. "That's what I'm trying to figure out," he responded. "I feel like a mouse that sneaked past a badger."

"Is that good?" Wilhelmina persisted.

"I don't know yet." This admission made him wince. "And I don't know how long it will take to find out; I wish I did."

Wilhelmina appeared in the kitchen doorway, a large tray in her hands, with coffee-service for two, and two small plates of elegant little pastries.

Seeing her with this burden, Bethune got to his feet. "Here, Willie; let me help you with that."

She stopped moving and offered him an uneasy smile. "Much appreciated. That's very nice of you, Tolliver," she said in her unflappable way. "I'm afraid I overloaded it."

"Well, if you did, since it was on my behalf, it's only right that I carry this for you," he said, thinking of how much she reminded him of his first-year biology professor in college. There was something about teachers, he decided.

"Put your hands next to mine," she recommended. "That way we won't drop it accidentally."

He went to her and took the tray from her hands as she had instructed him to do, carrying it slowly back to the butler's table, where he set it down. "It looks wonderful."

She smiled. "I bet you say that to all the girls."

There was a tiny, awkward pause before he returned her smile and told her, "You're right: I probably do. And I shouldn't." He waited until she had sat down in the lady's easy chair that faced the fireplace and the butler's table, then sank back down onto the sofa. "I'm glad you were in, Willie."

"So how did it go today?" Wilhelmina asked him.

"I don't know that, either. They want information, but it isn't the kind they were asking about, or it didn't seem so."

She got up. "The coffee won't pour itself," she remarked as she took the coffee-pot and held it up. "Milk and sugar?"

"You remembered," he approved. "Yes, if you would."

"I most certainly will," she said, and poured out a fragrant black stream into a large white cup. "It's hot," she added, putting in two small spoonfuls of sugar, and then milk from a jug, which she handed on a broad saucer to Bethune. "The cream-puffs are very nice, but so are the fig-rolls. I have a few apple turn-overs—I forget what the French call them—still in the fridge."

Bethune was sitting up very straight now. "May I have one of each?" he asked.

"Of course you may," she said as she prepared her own coffee. "On Fridays, they do something similar to a hot-cross bun, but it is an actual cross, and it has a filling of buttered crushed almonds. You must come on a Friday, when you can." She returned to her chair.

"Will there be enough left for Boris when he gets back?" Bethune asked while he waited for his coffee to cool a bit.

"Boris rarely drinks coffee; he prefers tea, that Russian tea that comes in bricks. A pianist he knows sends them to him from time to time." She made a gesture compounded of affection, resignation, and exasperation. "You'd think he were one of the lost Romanovs, wouldn't you? Nesting dolls on the mantelpiece, Orthodox crosses on the doors." She settled herself more comfortably in the chair, drawing her leg up under her. "Close, but no blue ribbon. Boris' father, who was born and raised in Poland, read that Pushkin thing about Boris Godunov, and couldn't wait to name one of his kids after it. It was because of his name that Boris got interested in Russian culture, Russian music in particular." She shook her head, at the same time steadying her cup-and-saucer on the arm of her chair. "The Committee thinks he's Russian and only claims to be Polish as a way to keep his disguise, as it were. The Committee claims to have proof of his being Russian, although how they can have, I have no idea. But I met his father when Boris and I were first married, and he was well and truly Polish. His mother was

Scandinavian—I can't recall what flavor." She took a very small sip of her coffee, and asked as if she were beginning one of her once-infamous pop quizzes, "Does any of this interest you?"

"It's good to know as much as possible about him, but why are you telling me this?" Bethune asked deferentially.

"Oh, no very clear reason," she admitted. "I think I want to know if anything occurred at your meeting at the Embassy this morning, but I don't want to have to say so directly, so this is a kind of fishing." She grinned suddenly, the unexpected expression blossoming on her features as if she had been magically transformed.

Bethune laughed, and after a half-second, so did Wilhelmina. "You must be wily in the classroom, Willie."

"Oh, I was," she said, her smile vanishing. "Athletic boys lived in terror of my random quizzes, and pretty girls with crushes on Jimmy Stewart would implore me to excuse them from any exams." Then she looked away, her eyes turned toward the window, but seeing a classroom on the other side of the Atlantic.

"How's your aunt doing?" Bethune inquired, trying to buy Wilhelmina a little time to collect herself, as he tested his coffee and found it cool enough to drink.

"As well as can be expected. She recently arranged for us to have this house for our residence as soon as she dies, no delays in court. Her attorney has already filed the papers. Aunt Eugenie has been very good to us."

"Any idea—"

"—when?" She drank more coffee. "No. Probably more than three months but less than six." She looked in the general direction of the stairs. "She's pretty much bed-ridden. Her doctor comes twice a week."

"She's in her sixties, isn't she?" Bethune asked, and took a bite of a flaky-crusted fig-roll.

"Seventy-two. She's had a good, long run, and I think she's ready for all this to be over." She got up to get a pair of cream-puffs, then sat down again. "I can tell she isn't hanging on very much. She's not eating very much, and about all she likes to do is read Victorian novels. She's clearing everything out."

Something occurred to Bethune as he listened, something that had not crossed his mind until this afternoon; he asked it while it was fresh in his mind. "When all this Red-baiting is over, are you going back home, or will you stay here?"

Wilhelmina almost tipped her large saucer off the chair arm. "You know, Tolliver, I've been thinking about that recently," she said. "I suppose it depends on how long it takes to get things straightened out. Boris and I aren't spring chickens, and if we're still here five years from now, then we may just keep on. There're a lot worse places than Paris, wouldn't you say?"

"Do you think Boris agrees?" Bethune asked, his speculations already on the rest of the Coven. How many of them thought the way the Kings did?

"I don't know specifically, but it wouldn't surprise me if he did." She drank half her coffee and picked up the first of her cream-puffs. "The trouble is, I don't know about the Frosts, or how any of the rest of them, for that matter, feel."

Bethune heard her with the intensity he usually reserved for news bulletins out of Berlin. It had not occurred to him before now that for some of the Coven, return to the US was not necessarily the desired end of his efforts on their behalf. He realized he should say something, so he looked at Wilhelmina and said, "You're right. These fig-rolls are excellent."

April 3rd, 1950

Dear Cousin Moira,

Sorry to hear that your husband is in the hospital. Tim's had a horrible five years, hasn't he? What a sad thing that is, you being in a foreign country and all. Do the doctors think he's going to have more seizures? Do you know what caused it? And in the car, too. You're lucky he didn't fall out the door. Golly, you two have been through a lot. You tell him I hope he gets well soon, even better than he was before he had the seizure. I have to tell you, I never knew a bad concussion could be so awful for so long. I don't think I could stand it, either having such a concussion or taking care of someone who had one. Is the friend you mentioned helping you out? You say Tim will be in the hospital for another week—that's a long time, isn't it? Is there anything they can do to lessen the kind of seizures he has? Some kind of medicine, maybe, or an operation to help? I can ask Dr. Ives, if you like, to see if he can suggest anything. He's just our local doc, but he's good at his job.

I don't know if anyone else has told you, but Uncle Frederick and his second wife, Alexis, are signed up to do a month-long Mediterranean cruise in June, to celebrate their first anniversary. They'll be stopping at Barcelona and Nice, and nine other cities. Dining is formal, and women must wear long skirts. They start out in Belgium and end up in Greece; Uncle Howard says that Alexis is going to want to go to every chapel, church, and cathedral they encounter along the way. The trip is costing $4,000—each! For what they're spending on this trip, they could live *pretty well for a year—not lavishly, but not pinching too many pennies. Daddy says Uncle Frederick is a fool, that he should put that money to good use so it can keep him and Alexis comfortable in their old age, not use it for gallivanting around the world. We haven't done anything with them since Christmas, which is kind of too bad, since I do like Alexis. The rest of the family doesn't agree with me, but they don't see what she's done for herself, and that she really does love Uncle Frederick. The thing is, her Daddy took a bad fall in the Crash, and she said she decided she would make money and make the most of that money having fun with it. Daddy warned Uncle Frederick that he would live to rue the day he married Alexis.*

You may have heard that Grandfather Larkin passed away last Tuesday in the evening. He had been in badly failing health for over a year, so we all knew it was coming. Sixty-four is the age he reached, not too bad, when you think about it. The last six months were really hard on him. His housekeeper did a good job. She's a retired nurse who takes on cases like his. Grandfather Larkin asked Uncle Howard to handle the Will, and to make sure that Mrs. Cassidy gets something extra for all her trouble. I don't expect we'll receive anything from him: he gave Daddy the grandfather clock two years ago. It's not like Grandfather Larkin was an extravagant man, like Uncle Frederick is. Mom told me that she thought Grandfather might make small gifts to his grandchildren, and if he did, she wants to be sure that I put mine toward my college fund. I won't count my inheritance until it's in my savings account.

Cousin Emily's twins are finally doing better; their doctor says they'll be fine, but I still think it wasn't a good idea to call them Mason and Dixon. Everyone coos and giggles over those little boys, because their names are so cute. I don't think they'll think that when the boys are in grade-school. They're like to be teased to distraction. But Cousin Emily won't hear a word against them, and her husband positively boasts about them. You probably think that's a good thing for parents to do, but keep in mind, there are all kinds of hassles that happen to kids that the parents never find out about. You know about that, too, don't you?

I'm not supposed to mention current events, but there was a long article in the paper yesterday about how the FBI hunts down Communists, and how dangerous Communists are. There was a little something about the CIA doing the same in foreign countries. There was nothing about how they coordinate their work, but that could be because they want to keep that part secret. Daddy says it's because they're rivals, but I don't see the point in that, do you? I probably shouldn't be asking you this, but I think you know more than I do, or anyone else in the family.

Swim team practice starts next week, and I'm taking ballet lessons, to improve my stretching and stamina. Mrs. Rollander, who teaches American History and Current Events, is the coach this semester. She was on her college swim team, and I think she's doing a great job. We wear regulation tank suits for our competitions, and they look awful, but Mrs. Rollander tells us that they help us swim faster. I'm not going to argue with her, but it seem like a dumb idea.

Let me know as soon as you have Tim home again, and give him my best wishes in getting well. We all miss you here—even Emilia, who thinks you guys are up to no good—and when you can come home, Uncle Frederick promises to throw you a big party. No one will want to miss that. Until then, our prayers are with you.

Your loving cousin,
Betty-Ann

❖ 6 ❖

"SORRY WE'RE late," said the Praegers as they came into the living room of Charis' flat, almost in unison. Both of them were dressed in a manner to show that they were one of those who saw themselves as a pair who can display the appropriate sartorial requirements of all those in the Coven: they would look appropriate to half the university campuses in the US, and similar to the look of students in Europe. Their arrival somewhat startled the group gathered in the eclectically furnished living room, for they had come up the stairs and had not bothered with the elevator, so that the sound of their footsteps in the foyer had sent a chill through those who had already arrived. "It's the Praegers," Jesse added, in case they were not the last to come; he and Elvira were taking off their jackets to hang in the coat-closet. "We would have been here sooner, but I had a call home booked for six, and I didn't want to lose it. My mother's birthday." In spite of his energetic way of talking, he had the air of someone wrestling with a difficult problem; Elvira seemed scared, and a little short of breath, for she huddled in her jacket as if to keep out something worse than the evening chill. They went from the foyer to the half-open double-doors, where they paused to admire the way the place had turned out. "Say—not bad. Not bad at all," Praeger decided aloud. "What do you think, honey?"

Elvira managed a rictus smile. "It's beautiful. Different. I like it."

"I'll pass your praise on to Lord Weldon, whenever he gets back from India." Charis had risen from her carved pear-wood Oriental chair, and went to the newcomers. "I think there're chairs enough. If not, Wash, would you bring one in from the dining room?"

"I'll slide over, that'll give room for one of you," Mary Anne offered from her place on one of two gondola sofas at either end of the gorgeous Chinese carpet of muted lavender woven in a pattern of chrysanthemums edged in silver. Other Oriental chairs, some deeply carved, some far more simple, were set about the living room, most with occasional tables next to them. A large brass-topped coffee-table dominated the center of the room, standing on six mahogany legs, shining in the light cast by the elaborate chandelier depending from the center of the ceiling.

"You could have let us know you'd be late." Julia Bjornson scowled at the Praegers. "We'll have to start from the top," she complained.

"I'll be glad of that," Bethune said at once, to quell the bristling around the room. "I'm still trying to compile my information, you know, keep everything up-to-date. I'm just finishing setting up my pages." He was in his usual elegant clothes, a clip-board with a number of yellow sheets of lined paper on his knee, an expensive pen poised over them. "It'll give me a chance to catch up with all of you."

"What about Miranda?" Washington Young asked as he carried in a chair from the Empire dining suite. "Will she be here? It's Tuesday—nothing much happens on Tuesday."

"No, she won't," said Charis.

"Don't tell me she has a date?" Julia Bjornson asked with a slight, derogatory laugh.

"No, she's got a job," said Charis, settling the Praegers on either side of Mary Anne. "She's had an offer from the Turks, of all people."

There was an astonished silence; finally McCall said, "The Turks. As in Turkey."

"Yes," Charis told them all.

"That was sudden, wasn't it?" Julia Bjornson asked.

"Oh, yes," said Charis. "She left as soon as she had a confirmation of the offer. She's probably reached Istanbul by now." She paused, expecting questions; when none came, she went on. "One of their archeological digs back at the eastern end of the country have turned up some clay tablets in a fairly good-sized city that may be astronomical charts—at least, that's what the antiquities people there think, but they need an astronomer to confirm this. They want her to come and work it out for them. If the tablets are star charts, it will help date the site. Miranda said it was too good an offer to turn down, even if she weren't floundering for work. They've provided a three-year study grant, an office, and a small staff. It came out of the blue. No pun intended," she added, flushing a little.

"Astronomical archeology," mused McCall.

"Don't be sarcastic," Pomeroy advised.

"Still, not bad," McCall approved for the rest of them.

"And Steve? Does anyone know where he is?" asked Axel.

"He's gone to Switzerland for a short holiday; he called me on Saturday, just before he left," said Bethune. "One of his former colleagues is going to be in Zurich for a week, and Steve wanted to see him. He'll be back on Friday."

Washington Young came from the dining room, an elegant chair in his hands, one of an Empire suite of dining table, sideboard, china cabinet, and ten chairs, all done in chestnut wood. "Where do you want this put?"

"Over there?" said Charis, waving her hand in the direction of the fireplace. "Any place the light is good. Next to the bronze floor-lamp. Thanks."

Young did as he was asked, nodded to McCall, who occupied the chair next to it, and went back to his round-backed Oriental chair, sat down, and took out his hand-rolled cigarettes—unlike the ones at his apartment, these were filled with tobacco. He lit up and reached for his secretary's notebook, where he kept his notes for *The Grimoire.*

Axel Bjornson glanced over at Winston Pomeroy, and nodded toward the grandmother clock that occupied the corner between the dining-room door and the tall windows, at present covered by draperies of light-bronze velvet. "Isn't it about time?"

"Where are the Frosts and the Kings? I know Happy is out of town, but the Frosts and the Kings are in town, aren't they? Don't they need this up-dating?" Mary Anne asked. "Shouldn't we wait for them?"

"I've already spoken with them," Bethune said, "as part of a legal matter I'm handling for both couples; I realized I hadn't enough information to manage the negotiation properly. That was true for

all of you: I need to know more. I just thought it would be faster
and more . . . useful to have a general meeting. There's nothing I
want to know that requires confidentiality, and I thought it might
clear the air for . . . some of us." He looked around and nodded
once.

"Did you learn something at the Embassy?" Axel asked, trying
not to sound too interested. "Is that what you're asking about?"

"Are we being surveilled?" Young, who had been listening with
his head down, now raised it enough to stick out his chin.

"Is the Grof going to be here?" McCall interjected his question
with a predatory smirk.

"I would like it if he were," said Bethune quickly, glancing at
McCall, and making no attempt to conceal his annoyance.

"Possibly later," said Charis. "This doesn't impact him directly,
but possibly indirectly. Eclipse Press has an interest in several of us,
and it's printing books we couldn't place with a publisher back
home. If there's going to be trouble, he'll want to know."

"Or he may just want to spy," said McCall.

"McCall, please," said Bethune.

"If he comes later, he won't be in on our discussion, which is all
to the good," said Pomeroy.

"Why?" Charis asked.

"In case McCall's right, and the Grof's watching us for some
purpose other than publishing," said Pomeroy, looking away from
her. "Not that I want to think of him that way, but we need to be
circumspect."

"Better safe than sorry," said Young.

"Please." Bethune held up his hands. "Let's get to this; we can
argue when we're done. For now, we need to confront all manner of
private issues."

"Shouldn't we do it in private consultation with you?" Axel regarded Bethune sternly. "Doesn't our speaking with everyone present end attorney-client confidentiality?"

"Since you are all in the same group, and are acting in concert,
the Coven itself is my client, and confidentiality remains in effect,"

Bethune explained. "Think of the group as a specialized union, and I am your counsel of record."

"All the more reason for the Grof to stay away," said Axel. "He isn't one of us, and his presence could obviate our privacy. Do you think we can maintain our complaints and actions without exposing ourselves?"

"Do you mean that Szent-Germain could be called to testify about what he might witness tonight?" Bethune asked. "We may have to include him in the Coven."

"But he's not an American," Jesse Praeger pointed out. "Wouldn't that change the status of the Coven?"

"Perhaps, if that's what troubles you, you may prefer to do this all by private appointment, but that could become divisive, and that wouldn't serve any of us at all well," Bethune told him. "If you don't feel comfortable answering my questions, just say so and we'll set up an appointment."

Jesse Praeger looked over at Bethune. "Does this have anything to do with your visit to the Embassy last week? Or is it a coincidence? Are you working both sides of the street?" His posture was relaxed but his face was confrontational.

"The Embassy?" Julia echoed, her face distressed; she was fishing her crocheting from her large purse. "What is this nonsense about the Embassy?"

Bethune wondered if Praeger intended to rattle him; he expected more outrage from Julia. "As a matter of fact, it does. We're getting some increasing pressure from the intelligence boys, and it's not going to let up any time soon. We need to be prepared for more surveillance and invasions of privacy. We already know that our overseas phone calls are being tapped—well, that's likely to increase. Since this interest could have importance to you, I thought it would be best if I could talk to all of you at once."

Again the group went silent. Finally Pomeroy spoke up. "Can you tell us about it? Why did you go to the Embassy? Or is it all secret?"

"Some of it is secret, yes, and some of it is confidential. But there are a number of things we can and should discuss. I'll be glad to explain as we go along. And I will explain anything you want to know as much as I can. But before I do, there are some things I need to know for my end of the legal system; I need to represent each of you according to your best interests as you see them, which means I need to clear up a few matters," he said with his usual aplomb. "I'll be able to handle things more efficaciously if I have a couple of answers. Since I was discussing the Frosts' and the Kings' case at the Embassy, I got the answers from the Kings and the Frosts when I reported to them after the meeting. Moira Frost suggested it might be a good idea to have this information from all of us. Boris King and Moira Frost are hoping to demonstrate that their dismissals were without basis, and therefore they should be restored to their positions and provided recompense for the time they have had to live here. Some of you may want to initiate similar actions if King and Frost succeed. In any case, I'll speak to Happy and Steve when they get back, but for now, we can deal with it here, while we're all together." He took a moment to smooth the ends of his tie back inside his jacket, then went on. "I know how long you've all been here, so for those of you who have been away from the US for more than twelve months, I have to find out a few things."

"I've been here eleven months," said Mary Anne. "Do you want me to stick around?"

"That's close enough for government work," said Bethune with heavy sarcasm. "Sure. We'll include you."

"I'll go make coffee while you get your answers," Charis said, standing and starting toward the dining room and the kitchen beyond. "I've got a few things to eat as well; I'll set them up for you. You don't need me here: I haven't been here long enough to participate."

"Thank you," said Julia as if she had been about to collapse of thirst, a sure sign she was nervous about the meeting.

"I'll have everything in place in twenty minutes," Charis promised, and went into the dining room, closing the door after her.

Bethune looked at the Bjornsons in their Victorian trifoil chair

next to the fireplace; the third seat around the main column unoccupied except for Axel's hat and Julia's shawl. "Why don't I start
with you?"

Julia was ready to argue, but before she could, Axel said, "Fine,"
and lit his pipe. "Ask away."

Bethune nodded, becoming more business-like as he straightened up and prepared to write on his pad of paper. "Okay. Let's
refine this a little more. Please take time to think about your answer
so I can have a sense of perspective about your position." He looked
around the room, taking stock of everyone. "Here goes: if your case
could be resolved to your advantage within the next year, would
you return to your home in the US?" He had labored to pare the
question down to something concise but without bathos. Now he
would find out if he had succeeded; he nodded to the Bjornsons,
anticipating a well-reasoned response from Axel. "Why don't we
start with you?"

Axel started to speak, but was interrupted by Julia. "Of *course* we'd
go home!" Julia exclaimed, dropping her crocheting; it lay like a small
octopus at the foot of the trifoil chair. "Wouldn't we," she added when
Axel remained silent. Gradually her face crumpled as she realized
that her husband did not share her longing for home.

Axel drew on his pipe. "I'd want to, I suppose, yes, if the case
were truly resolved advantageously, and I had my job back without
conditions or limitations, but given the tenor of the times, I doubt
such a thing could occur in a year. I'm beginning to think that we'll
need a decade to work all this out. There are too many politicians
making political hay out of Red-baiting; that's not going to stop
any time soon. So long as Joseph McCarthy is in the Senate,
Communists will be an issue—longer, if Hoover keeps on at the
FBI. He's blowing the whole question out of proportion, but it
keeps his name before the public, and gives him a strong negotiating
position with Congress. It's helping his agency, this Communists-
in-the-pantry stance, of course, but it's also silencing a lot of leftist
opinions." He hesitated, then went on, "I sometimes wonder if there
aren't financial influences at work here, making the whole matter of
Communism a device of the financial industry, in order to gain

control of the commercial interests of the US. By discrediting socialism and Communism, they create an environment that makes it possible for capitalism to establish itself as the only acceptable choice for the country."

This was the kind of discussion the Coven had regularly, and most of the members were glad to be on familiar ground. "He's got a point," said Young. "If you hanker to be rich, you're going to want to keep a lot of folks poor."

"I'd have to say I think you're right, Wash, little as any of us would like that kind of exploitation. We need to think about how many compromises we might have to make for the chance to return to our former positions, if the hold of the major business interests becomes greater than it is now. The trouble is, a lot of politicians would jump in with both feet, given so much graft as that could create. It wouldn't be good for the country, but I don't know that there is much that can be done about it. The Republicans are doing all they can to buffalo Truman, and who knows if he's up to the fight. I think that the big money institutions want the unions reined in permanently, and the government is more willing to put business interests ahead of social ones," said Jesse Praeger, getting into lecture mode, and was about to go on, but Axel interrupted him.

"Maybe in five years, if Congress stops grandstanding about Communists, it might be possible to rebuild public confidence in unions, and progress, and liberals!"—he made a dismissive gesture punctuated with a snap of his fingers—"but as things are now, I'd reckon it will be a decade before we can safely go back, and maybe not even then." He turned toward his indignant spouse. "That's what it appears to be, Jul," he said to her.

"But you'll take me home when it gets fixed," she prompted in an unusually quiet voice. "Won't you?"

"It will depend on what's happening in Europe as much as what's going on at home." He nodded to Bethune as he bent to pick up his wife's crocheting to return it to her. "Does that help, to any degree?"

"It probably does, and I thank you for your candor; I know it wasn't easy," said Bethune, scribbling as quickly as possible. "I think this is something I'll have to bring up to the Frosts and the Kings. I should have thought of these problems before now. But what if it were possible to have the scale of resolution you want— hypothetically—would you return to the US?"

"Would I return to the US if all the furor over Communism and Communist sympathizers ended?" Axel shrugged. "Since it can't happen in a year or two, no, I wouldn't. The deliberate creation of fear and anger in the general populace has led to all kinds of infringements on the Bill of Rights, and assaults on the Constitution as well. I went through it once, I don't intend to go through it twice." He stared at Bethune. "I'm sorry. I don't know what else to say."

"Well, *I would*, I would go home, and as soon as possible," Julia announced, no longer taken aback by her husband. "I'd be on the first plane that would get me to New York. *Anywhere* in New York. Poughkeepsie would do." She began to sob, her head on Axel's shoulder. "I don't care about the Committee or Hoover or all the rest of it."

"Do you want to leave Paris?" Elvira asked, sounding incredulous.

"I can't stand Paris," Julia sobbed, shoving her crocheting back into her purse.

"For God's sake," McCall exclaimed. "Axel, do something about your wife."

Winston Pomeroy held up his hand. "Come on, people, let's keep this civil. We know how to disagree if we must, don't we?"

Julia shot Pomeroy a look of loathing and prepared to excoriate them all. The slight pressure of her husband's hand on her arm stopped her. She wiped her eyes with a tissue and swallowed hard twice. "Mister McCall, I take offense at your tone."

McCall chuckled. "Just don't have another tizzy."

Axel glowered at McCall, and was about to say something cutting, but Pomeroy got in ahead of him.

"Not to belabor the point, this is difficult for all of us, and we need to be willing to hear one another out, without bickering about what each of us thinks. We may disagree, but let's give Bethune the answers he needs to help us. What do you say?"

Fortunately, Charis chose that moment to open the dining-room doors wide, indicating the buffet. "Help yourselves. There are chocolates in the pink box, fruit tarts and cheese on the trays. Simple crackers are in the basket, and pastries on the tiered tray. Help yourselves."

Julia strove to wipe her eyes and got up, standing as if daring anyone to mention or even think about her display of homesickness. "That's very nice of you, Charis," she said as grandly as Edith Evans playing Lady Bracknell. "Are you coming, Axel?"

"In a moment," he said as he set his pipe in the nearest ashtray.

Young and McCall were quick to get up, and each watched the other as they made for the dining room.

The Praegers were already on their way through the door, Elvira laughing as she claimed a linen serviette and a butter-dish for her selections. Jesse said something to her in a whisper and she gave him a roguish smile.

The Bjornsons went to the cheese-tray, Axel looking eager to sample some of the array that waited next to the basket of crackers.

McCall watched them with a cynical smile; he picked up a serviette and butter-dish, and went to the table where the foods were laid out. "Snazzy," he said to no one in particular, and reached for a small, sugar-dusted cream-puff.

Mary Anne poured her coffee first, then went to look over the delicacies offered, starting with the chocolates.

Winston Pomeroy gave a low whistle. "You didn't have to go to so much trouble, Missus Treat."

Coming in from the foyer unnoticed, Szent-Germain went up to Charis, who was still standing in the dining room doorway. "It's astonishing, watching those two," he said quietly, watching the Praegers. "I don't think I can remember being that young." He had been thirty-three when he was executed, and four millennia ago, that was an older age than Jesse was now.

She almost yelped, then turned toward him, his nearness setting off her craving for him. This no longer alarmed her as it had at first, but now there was something else in her response to his presence, something that was as disquieting as it was enticing. "Grof.

You're . . . earlier than I expected." She tried to decide whether she had heard him come up the stairs, since he clearly had not used the elevator. "I'm glad you're here," she said, resisting the urge to lean back against him as she shifted her thoughts away from his presence to the issues before the Coven. "I don't suppose you want a snack?"

"Regrettably, not just now," he said, taking a step back from her and almost hitting the door.

"No. No." She could feel her pulse going faster, but did her best to ignore it. "I'm glad you're here. This is turning out to be a . . . touchy evening. I didn't think it would be so difficult to discuss when and how we might return to the US." She nodded to Mary Anne. "I have some fruit in the kitchen, if you'd rather have that," she said to the older woman. "Or milk instead of cream. I'd offer you a croissant, but the two I have are a day old."

"That's kind of you," said the librarian. "But I'm sure some stinky soft cheese on a few of those simple crackers will do me fine."

Holding a cup-and-saucer in one hand and a small plate of raisin tarts and a couple of shavings of Tete-des-Moins cheese, Bethune nodded to acknowledge Szent-Germain's presence. "You and I should talk," he said calmly. "Sooner rather than later. Before Friday, if you can arrange it."

If this startled Szent-Germain, he gave no indication of it. "Certainly. Would tomorrow at three be convenient? I'll be at the press then."

"Tomorrow at three at the Eclipse Press offices. I'll be there," Bethune confirmed and passed on into the living room.

Half an hour later, Julia was definitely more composed, the Praegers rather less. Some were on their second cup of coffee; others had had more cheese or a chocolate. Almost all of the Coven was back in the living room; only Young and Mary Anne were still in the dining room, refilling their coffee-cups for the third time. With the exception of the Praegers, the group was more at ease, and Bethune was preparing to continue his questioning.

Winston Pomeroy put his coffee-cup aside on the occasional table at his elbow and looked around, taking stock of the Coven members. "We should get back to Bethune's questions. The sooner we do it, the sooner all this is over."

"Oh, Christ," muttered McCall, without apology.

"Let's not start again," Pomeroy said as if trying to get a classroom to go quiet. This was not as successful as he wanted it to be.

"Come on, Pomeroy," said Axel. "We can manage to do this properly."

"You hope," said McCall.

"Cut it out," said Young, who had returned to his Oriental chair. "We need to do this."

"Who'd like to answer my question?" Bethune inquired of the air, making the offer as friendly as possible. "I don't want to distress you, but it will help me act for you if I know how you feel about this."

"I would," said Mary Anne, surprising everyone. She took her place on the gondola sofa near the windows. "I've been thinking about this very issue for several days, and I believe that I'm prepared to say that I would go back if—if, mind you—I would not be under constant scrutiny, which may not be possible for some time to come. We've been stigmatized, and a superficial apology from the government won't get rid of the taint. I feel all at loose ends here, and I'm beginning to think that there may not be anything for me in Europe. I'm a capable librarian, but English-language libraries aren't plentiful here in Europe, and I've made a few overtures to private parties in England with vast private libraries, but no luck so far. I may have to try India or Rhodesia, but they aren't any more welcoming to women in my field than are libraries back home. Who knows what kind of weight a PhD from Northwestern would have there?"

"There's always Australia or New Zealand," McCall suggested snidely, and was rewarded by a glare from Charis.

Watching them unobtrusively, Szent-Germain could feel their fear, as if the air had become acidic. The Ex-Pats' Coven was under increasing strain, and it was taking a toll on all of them. The next year, he believed, would make or break the group. Which way? he wondered; which way?

"Oh, Mary Anne, it can't be that bad," Elvira said, doing her utmost to be sympathetic. "It's frustrating, and sometimes unkind, but you make it sound so . . . dire."

"Because it is dire," said Mary Anne. "Even without the Committee's interfering, it was getting hard to find a job. The war is over, so women can go back home and be a free maid to a husband coming back from the Front. But mine didn't come back. He's in an unmarked grave somewhere in Germany. And surviving on a widow's benefits is pretty austere. I like being a librarian. I do it well. I'm in no position to do it as a volunteer or a part-timer, and that's made my circumstances difficult. I did all I could to find a position that would make the most of my skills. But the best job I could find before I left the US was as a librarian at a junior high in Michigan, and that was provisional, requiring that I prove I have no affiliation to or associations with Communist organizations."

"Gracious, you sound bitter," said Elvira.

"I *am* bitter," said Mary Anne, her bluntness surprising them all.

"Sour grapes," said McCall.

Pomeroy held up his hands again. "Come on, people."

"Why don't you go next, Pomeroy?" McCall suggested sweetly, expecting a refusal.

"Okay," said Pomeroy. "Unless someone else would rather—"

"Just do it," said Young. "Then McCall can do his stint."

"All right," said Pomeroy. "If I could go back and have it the way it was, would I?" He stared at the ceiling as if he expected to see an answer appear there. "I don't know," he admitted after the greater part of a minute had passed. "Because it could never be the way it was. That's the part that bothers me. The way it was is gone. Whether it could be possible to come close to what it was like before I had to leave, I would still be changed because of what I've been through the last twenty months, and I would remember what it's been like living here, trying to find work and being watched by agents of the US government, or other governments—unless there's a way to have selective amnesia. As it is, I'll always have almost two years of sporadic employment here in Europe in my CV, and that will influence my decisions from now on. I'm not about to forget what my time here has been like, or what brought me to Paris." He sighed. "I miss Davis. I like the Valley. I like skiing in the Sierra in the winter, and going up Mount Shasta in the summer. I hope I can do those things again one of these days, but I don't know if that would be enough after all this."

"Then you wouldn't go back?" Bethune asked, wanting to be certain he understood.

"I don't think so, no; but who's to say how I will feel in five more years, or even ten. I say that because I think Axel's right: this isn't going to be over in a year or two, and when it is over, who knows what the country will look like?"

"He's got a point," Young said.

Bethune made a number of notes, then looked at McCall. "Well? What about you?"

McCall drank the last of his coffee and said, "I have no idea. Not one."

"Hey, no fair," said Jesse Praeger, trying to sound more jovial than he felt. "We've all answered the question. It's your turn now."

"But I am answering the question," McCall said, and got up. "I have nothing more to say," he said, "so I'll leave you to your discussions. Thank you all for your engaging conversation, as my mother would have said. Gentlemen. Ladies," he said, and left the living room to reclaim his jacket from the coat-closet off the foyer.

"Well!" Julia announced.

"Wash, do you want to say anything?" Pomeroy asked, determined to keep their colloquy going.

"Not yet," said Young. "My situation's a little more ticklish than yours. I'm going to have to think about it a while. I'll arrange a time to talk to you, Bethune."

"That's fine with me," said Bethune, and would have gone on but he saw Elvira Praeger go pale. "What's wrong?"

Elvira trembled and suddenly bent over. "I'm sorry," she whispered. "I'm expecting, and sometimes I have a bad response to food."

There was a general buzz of surprise, most of it delighted, a bit of it not; Szent-Germain watched Elvira with concern.

"That's wonderful news," said Mary Anne, her stiff posture giving way to something more welcoming; her enthusiasm silenced the others. "When are you due?"

"The first week in October, I'm told," Elvira answered, still hunched over.

Charis went to Elvira's side. "I have some phenobarb in the bathroom. Would you like a pill?" For the first time she felt genuine sympathy for Elvira.

"That's nice of you, Charis," said Jesse, "but I'll make sure she gets a hot brandy toddy at home."

"Yes," Elvira said, doing her best to sit up straight. "I think I'd better just go home. Jesse?"

As if this were a signal, the sound of the elevator rising in answer to McCall's electronic summons grabbed everyone's attention.

"Yes. I think I'd better go," said Pomeroy. He addressed Bethune. "Do you have what you need?"

"Almost all," said Bethune, accepting his defeat with good grace. "I'll follow up by telephone if there are any other questions that come up." He got to his feet. "Let the Praegers go down with McCall. There's not much room for more. They can send the elevator back up, and we'll figure out who goes next. I think I'll take the stairs."

Mary Anne got up and looked around the room. "Do you want some help clearing up?" she asked Charis.

"Thanks, but I can manage. I'll soak the dishes over night and wash them up in the morning. There's enough room in the fridge for the left-overs." She resisted the urge to gather up the abandoned coffee-cups, recalling her mother's strictures on taking care of guests.

Young got up, and spoke to Pomeroy. "I'll walk down with you. I have some thoughts about *The Grimoire* I'd like to talk over with you."

"Yeah," said Pomeroy, standing aside so Jesse Praeger could help his wife to stand. "Okay."

"I'll wait in the foyer," said Young, nodding to Charis as he left the living room. "A fine evening, Professor."

"Thank you, Wash," she responded, unaware that she had taken

Szent-Germain's hand until she was shaken with another jolt of desire, when she let go of his hand with unusual haste.

"Better hurry, Praegers," McCall cried out from the foyer. "The elevator's almost here."

"We're coming," Jesse barked, anxiety making his voice gruff. "Can someone get our jackets from the coat-closet?"

"I'll do it," Szent-Germain offered, and went to fetch them. He took the two almost-matching garments from their hooks and stepped back into the lobby to hand them over to the Praegers.

"Thanks," said Jesse, taking care in helping Elvira with her jacket.

"Is this an uncommon problem for her?" Szent-Germain asked, and quickly added, "I hope you do not mind my asking."

A bit nonplused, Jesse answered, "Elvira's been having a rough time. Her doctor's not worried, but I am."

"Episodes like this one should not last much longer," Szent-Germain said, and, seeing Jesse's startled expression, he went on, "My brothers' wives were often afflicted with similar discomforts." It was the truth, as far as it went; Szent-Germain did not mention that those events had taken place more than four thousand years ago.

"I didn't know you had brothers," Jesse said as he pulled on his own jacket.

"I don't, anymore," Szent-Germain replied.

"Oh. I'm sorry," said Jesse, then helped Elvira toward the elevator, where McCall was waiting.

Julia Bjornson came into the foyer as the elevator began its descent. "Axel and I will ride down with Mary Anne and Mister Bethune," she decided aloud. "Axel, my coat, please."

Watching the Coven leaving, Szent-Germain turned to Charis. "What about you? Would you go back if you had the chance and the circumstances were right?"

She lowered her voice a little. "A month ago, I probably would have said yes." She finally dared to meet his gaze. "Now, I don't know. Pomeroy's right; it wouldn't be like before, no matter how hard we tried to make it so." She attempted a smile, then gave it up as a useless effort. "What about you? Would you go back?"

"To the US?" He saw her shake her head. "You mean to my native earth in the Carpathians? I do go there from time to time, but it's nothing like it was when I was a young man, and never will be again."

"I'm sorry," she said in a rush of confusion. "I shouldn't have asked."

This time his fleeting smile was kindly. "Well, I started it, as you Americans say."

His response surprised her, and she stood very still, her attraction to him growing more insistent, fed by his nearness and his obvious concern for her. "Not really," she made herself say, and moved away from him as more of the Coven gathered in the foyer, ready to depart.

April 18th, 1950

Dear Coordinator Broadstreet,

Let me extend my heartiest congratulations on your promotion, and express my confidence in your enhanced leadership.

Now that I am back home, I have augmented my report on my meeting in Paris with Tolliver Bethune, attached to this memo, along with copies of the amended filings Bethune has made in regard to the attempts of his clients to recover back-pay and professional damages for wrongful termination of employment. He appears to support the decisions of some of the group he represents who are disinclined to return to the US, but still believe they are entitled to remuneration from their various colleges and universities. I must tell you that from what I have learned, the members of this group are sincere in their claims—these are not nuisance suits—and may therefore require the attention of the courts, which would shine a light on their plight, and that would not benefit us or the HUAC.

There is also more information on the so-called Grof Szent-Germain being sent to me, and which I will provide you as soon as I have the photostats of the report in hand. There is reason to suspect that some of his shipping company has been engaged in smuggling, a continuation of activities left over from the war. If that is all there is to it, the Europeans will remedy it in their own way, but if it goes beyond tolerable limits, then I will be prepared to act to guarantee that this "Grof" cannot continue to profit from his criminality.

I am scheduled to return to Europe on April 24th, and before that time I believe we should meet and review any developments that have been brought to your attention or to mine so that I might make the best use of my scheduled ten days abroad.

Sincerely,
Phil Rothcoe

Part Three

Lydell Gerold Broadstreet

May 10th, 1950

My dear Charis,

Awkward though it may be, I want to thank you for returning the divorce papers so quickly, fully executed and notarized, with only the most minor of alterations to the matters in dispute. I'm glad you see the wisdom of not drawing this out any longer than necessary. Your attorney, Mister Bethune, has been the soul of reason in his concerns, and has not sought to drag out our negotiations with needless haggling and recriminations. There is no reason for either of us to create unnecessary impediments to a sensible concession to all portions of this settlement, especially in regard to the welfare of our boys. We can come to an agreement about alimony without too much difficulty, I'm sure. Mister Bethune can advise you regarding what would be reasonable, just as he can in matters touching on your contact with the boys. You may tell Mister Bethune that I said so, if you are willing to bring up the matter.

Speaking of the boys, I will provide you my usual report on them and their activities, as is my custom: David took a fall from the neighbors' tree, and had the good fortune to land in some garden-trimmings; he is bruised, but nothing worse. I'm afraid to admit it, but my mother is spoiling him shamelessly, which he laps up like chocolate milk; he's becoming very good at getting his own way. Arthur has recently taken an interest in chess, and my father is teaching him the fundamentals of the game, so it would appear he has an aptitude for it, and a good head for the strategies for the conduct of the game, as well, which is most promising.

As he gets older, he can turn this interest to good use if he decides to pursue it, and it will decrease his distress at not being able to participate in sports. David has no interest in chess thus far, though that may change in time. At present, sports are beginning to hold his interest. He saw a movie last week that took place in Hawaii, and he was fascinated with surf-board riding. As much as I look forward to his participating in sports, surf-boarding is not one I'm inclined to encourage. Baseball, or football, if he develops the size for it, would be the games I would think he would most enjoy. He may choose tennis, but that lacks the camaraderie that I am convinced he would like. He's too young to make any final decision in this regard, but I am looking forward to discovering at what sport he will excel; these next five years are going to be crucial in that regard. Maybe I should take him golfing the next time I have time for a round. It's not the kind of game most boys like, but he's his father's son, as you used to say.

My parents are going to take the boys on a road-trip this summer, to give them something nice—a Treat, you might call it—to make up for not being able to bring them to Europe for a visit with you. They will be going up the Mississippi and over into the Dakotas, North and South. The weather will be hot, but not so severe that they will not be able to enjoy what they see. David has said he wants to see Old Faithful in Yellowstone, and Arthur is eager to visit the Museum of Natural History in Chicago on their way back: you probably remember his fascination with dinosaurs, which has increased of late. They plan to be gone a month. My parents are very pleased to be able to help their grandsons, and so when they heard that Dr. Feldon—you don't know him; he has been supervising Arthur's physical therapy—had vetoed a long airplane flight, they came up with this alternative, which has the added advantage that it gives me a good block of time for fieldwork. If this trip goes well, we can discuss the possibility of a trip to France in '51 or '52. I realize this is a disappointment to you, but I'm convinced that you have no desire to do Arthur any harm by requiring him to undertake something that is inherently dangerous to him. Don't worry: in time we will work out something that will be less cumbersome for all of us.

II don't know if I should tell you this, but it redounds to you, so I think I should: I've had a request to make myself available to discuss the current state of our marriage with an agent of the CIA, here in New Orleans, which has distressed me more than I can say. You'd think I were a common criminal by the way this Broadstreet framed his questions. We are divorcing so that I can avoid this sort of thing, which is another in-dication of your good sense now, although it doesn't make up for your folly of speaking out in support of the Soviets during the war; that was unfortunate, though at the time, you were hardly the only American doing so, and I have no wish to be harassed governmental lackeys. My attorney—Douglas Pond; you may remember him from the Neilsons' Fourth of July party—advises me to comply with the request as soon as I can, so that I will not appear to be dragging my feet. Apparently this Broadstreet is a way up the ladder, and known to be as determined a Red-hunter as that Nixon fellow from California is. Doug is also en-couraging me to provide them with photostats of our divorce papers, for as ironic as it may seem, the records of our terms of divorce can serve as a good faith demonstration that you and I are not planning to con-tinue our marriage any longer, and that our estrangement is more than a response to physical separation. In this case, in fact, the distance between us is advantageous to me when questions arise, including the very rea-sonable terms we are using. He recommends that I provide you with living expenses for the year it will take us to have the case before a judge, and possibly to continue for the year that will be required for my claim of abandonment to be verified. You, being the mother of my children, will not be seen to be without means in a foreign country, which will show that although you have left the country and our marriage, I am not cut-ting you off. Since I am claiming abandonment as the reason for the divorce, I'm going to have to reveal the reason you have left and are unlikely to return for some years. It is a tricky maneuver, but one that can speed our final resolution of our commitment. Doug is sure that this will work out well so long as neither of us does anything foolish, such as becoming entangled with another person, whose presence could be inter-preted as a motivation for the divorce, and not your fleeing the inquiries of the law. If we can present a legal demeanor of making-the-best-of-a-bad-situation, so much the better: polite but not cordial is the posture we should both seek to maintain. If we both keep our heads, our boys will not be beleaguered at school, either by their classmates or their teachers, and I can continue with all my grants and my fellowship assured until we have a final decree, when the matter will be settled. I am glad that this will be a clean break, as you must be, too. Doug has a good friend at the US Embassy in Paris—I gather he's in the CIA or some similar organization—and Doug has asked this friend to pass on any information that may be pertinent to our case, confidentially, of course, and nothing considered really secret. You needn't think that this will reflect badly on you. Nothing about his search will show up on your records. This can show the due diligence the courts require, and spares me the inconvenience of having to engage a private detective in France, or similar investigator, which I am persuaded neither you nor I would like such a development.

You have asked me not to inform you of any events taking place here that you would be sad to have missed, so I will only mention that there is a series of summer concerts of New Orleans jazz planned for the end of July into August. It's in the newspapers and there are posters everywhere, and I have assumed you are aware of this series of events. I will miss half of it, for it will overlap with my fieldwork. I had dinner with the Swansons last Thursday; Muriel asked to be remembered to you. Their oldest daughter—Penny—is starting her senior year at James Buchanan High School and is planning to go to college; she may even qualify for a National Merit Scholarship. She's got an ear for languages, it turns out, and a skill at translating. Too bad she isn't prettier, but under the circumstances, it might be just as well. She'll look better when the braces come off, but there is no sign that she will be other than plain. Muriel wanted me to thank you for encouraging Penny to apply at colleges and universities two years ago. Susan isn't inclined to go on past high school; she says she wants to get a job and catch a husband, not end up a teacher or a nurse or a fancy secretary for the rest of her life. Susan is afraid, with all the men killed in the war, there won't be enough of them to go around. Susan is a very useful kind of girl, as you probably recall. She'll turn sixteen in July, and is beginning to look pretty: fair, curly-haired, and sunny, and unlike many girls her age, she has her feet on the ground, and is realistic about her future. No mooning around about movie stars, and no expectations beyond her reach. I believe she has made a good decision. Not all women are cut out for the scholarly life.

Sean Pettigrew has been having some of the same kind of problems

you did about this time last year, and he is planning to follow your ex-
ample and leave the country, for he does not want to find himself in Al-
ger Hiss' situation, which he is convinced he will be if he is detained by
the FBI. By leaving at the end of semester, he can spare himself a great
deal of trouble. He's had better luck with finding work than you have,
for he'll be going to Newfoundland on the Monday after the end of the
semester, St. John's offered him a position in their geology department.
Jennine is going with him, and the kids. He's already looking for a house:
there's a realtor who handles out-of-country clients and often works with
academics. There's a rumor that part of his salary in Newfoundland will
be picked up by Shell, and that his father will pay his moving expenses.
Leave it to the Dutch to cover all their bases: Shell Oil. At least he and
Jennine won't have to follow our example, and divorce for Jeannine and
the kids to be rid of the taint of Communism.

I'll send this off to you tomorrow morning on my way into the lab.
Your signature will confirm that you have it, as you know, and at pres-
ent, it will be helpful to us both. I'll write again in two weeks, or maybe
a bit more. You can answer this, but don't write again until I write to
you. Doug says we've been communicating too often, and now that we
have agreed to our divorce, I should write less frequently, since we have
worked out all our problems and you have accepted my settlement terms;
the FBI will be suspicious if we write frequently. Same thing with phon-
ing. It will be at least a month until I call you: I'll book the call from
here. If there's an emergency, of course I'll let you know promptly, but
otherwise, it's best if we keep our distance, as it were.

Until next time,
Your soon-to-be-ex, Harold Treat

P. S.
Don't hesitate to send the boys a copy of your book as soon as it's pub-
lished. They will be thrilled to see what you've been doing. But it's best
not to send one to me, or to pass along any announcement—that could be
enough for real trouble.

❖ 1 ❖

A LIGHT spring mizzle was falling, looking like a dusting of minute diamonds in the shine of the streetlamp. Across the Seine and a short way ahead of them, the Louvre appeared to be a painted backdrop, its image flattened by the mist and the night. There was almost no wind on this cool, late evening, though the damp was adding a chill to the air; sidewalks and streets shone black, and the river glinted silver where the spill of lamplight struck it; a barge headed upriver was leaving a frothy, spangled wake behind. It was almost midnight and the streets were nearly empty of traffic; only the two-toned whoop of an ambulance a block away gave any reminder that this was a large, active city, not a forgotten, abandoned relic of a metropolis.

Szent-Germain and Charis had been walking for more than two hours, the sound of their footsteps seeming preternaturally loud, like nearby gunfire. When they had first set out they had indulged in desultory conversation now and again, but for the most part, their nearness created a private dialogue that was welcome to them both; they had covered the last kilometer in companionable silence.

"I gave Harold's letter to Bethune—well, I put it in an envelope with his room number on it and left it at his hotel," Charis said as if continuing a discussion rather than beginning one; she stopped walking to pull a scarf from her coat-pocket and tie it over her head; her desire for Szent-Germain was banked within her, but its heat remained powerful and strangely comforting. "I wanted to destroy it—burn it or tear it to pieces—but I knew that wouldn't be smart. So I did what I was supposed to do and left it for Bethune."

"The better choice of the two," he agreed, and waited for her to continue; he could feel her exasperation with her estranged husband and had no wish to add to it; he was aware that if he said anything derogatory about Harold Treat, she would feel the need to defend him, so he only asked, "Have you spoken with Bethune yet? Has he made any recommendations to you? You needn't tell me if you'd rather not."

"No, I haven't spoken to him, but I already have an appointment with him—Bethune—on the eighteenth. I guess two days isn't too long to wait. It may even be a good thing; I don't think I want to talk about Harold's letter with Bethune just yet. I'm too . . . muddled about it all. I want to be sensible, rational, make considered decisions, but my impulse is to demolish the letter and find some way to upset Harold as much as he has upset me."

"And yet, you're ambivalent about his eagerness for the divorce. Do you want to remain with him?"

She shook her head several times. "But the letter confuses me: is Harold being spiteful, or is he really trying to protect our boys? I can't decide. He may find it difficult to be forthcoming with me, but he may also want to keep me at a distance. He knows the letter is likely to be read by one of the intelligence organizations, so he may be reticent on that account. And maybe he's got some other intention I can't figure out. Bethune might be able to explain it all. Or you." She stifled a sigh. "He seems so . . . self-righteous when I read what he wrote. I mean Harold, not Bethune."

"Do you think he is being encouraged to be autocratic with you?" It was a possibility that had first occurred to him when Charis had telephoned him, nearly in tears from fury and despair.

"I don't know. He doesn't say much about his parents, or what they think about the divorce. And it could be that his attorney, Douglas Pond, might have something to do with it, but my guess is that it's Harold, wanting to keep me off-balance and cooperative."

"Has he always been that way?" Szent-Germain asked calmly, suiting his tone to her mood.

"A little. He's a big cheese in his field, and he knows it, so he . . ." She shook her head again and pressed her lips together as if to keep any critical words from escaping. When she was certain she had succeeded, she went on, "And he could get pompous when he wanted to have his way. He'd take an attitude that was indignant and . . . petulant rather than yell and scream. Why do I speak of him in the past tense?" She frowned, then went on, "Sometimes when he gave formal lectures, he ended up sounding like Sydney Greenstreet—portentous, orotund, and gravelly—but with a bit of a Loosianna drawl. I never realized how much that annoyed me until recently." She gave a self-deprecating laugh. "Or maybe I didn't let myself notice it before."

"Which is it, do you think?" He took a step to the side so that he could see her face more clearly.

"That's the problem," she said, her frustration making her abrupt. "My thoughts are like jackrabbits, bouncing about in all directions. I can't keep my attention on anything for very long, not even my work," she said, as if admitting to a failing of character. "I can't sustain my concentration."

"Hardly surprising, considering everything he's thrown at you," said Szent-Germain.

"I'd like to think so," she said, and could not meet his kindly gaze. "I feel so *lacking*, that I should be bowled over like this: I knew it was coming. As soon as I discovered that I wouldn't be able to return this year or next, I anticipated something like this, and made myself prepare for it. But I was bonked on the noggin, all the same," she burst out, more loudly than she intended, and pinched the bridge of her nose to try to keep from crying.

"Why do you try to trivialize your feelings? *Bonked on the noggin* turns your outrage into a fit of peevishness." He waited until she looked at him. "You don't have to do that for me. Rail at him, swear, cry, shriek, weep, whatever you want."

She tried to keep her tears at bay and very nearly succeeded. "Maybe I do it because . . . because if I don't let this get to me, I can salvage something at the end of it—something with the kids." This time when she wiped her eyes, there was a smudge of face-powder on the handkerchief he had handed to her.

He gave her a little time to compose herself again. "Why do you think your husband is being so peremptory about your divorce? other than to badger you into compliance?" There was no condemnation in his tone, but no approval, either.

"That's what's been driving me nuts. I wish I could figure that out," she said, sounding tired. "When I tried earlier, I couldn't get a handle on it. I wanted to scream." She announced this last in a burst of self-condemnation.

"But you didn't?"

"No. But I smoked almost a whole pack of Luckies. I haven't done that since the night before I sat for my orals." She ran her tongue over her teeth. "My mouth still tastes awful."

He had smelled tobacco smoke on her clothes when he had come to her flat in answer to her summons. "Did it help?"

"Smoking? It gave me something to do with my hands." She shrugged. "Not really." She went half a block without speaking.

"If you want to talk about any of this, I'll listen," he offered. "Sometimes talking helps."

"Are you trying to analyze me, Doctor Freud?" she challenged playfully, but with a hint of feeling affronted behind her too-ready smile.

"I don't believe so, no; I'm not qualified for one thing, and I'm too much concerned for your welfare to have the therapeutic removal from your perceptions that is necessary for the analytic process," he answered directly, with a suggestion of humor lurking in his eyes. "Attempting to psychoanalyze you would be intrusive as well as condescending, and you do not need either of those right now."

"Then what do I need?" she asked, and suddenly flushed, the return of her sexual desire taking her by surprise.

"I've told you before: an ally." He took her hand and settled it in the bend of his elbow, then resumed his ambling pace. "I'm doing what allies do."

"An ally," she echoed, as if she had never heard the word. It was unnerving to touch him, but she strove to conceal her emotions.

"Isn't that why you called me? Weren't you looking for a kind of shock-absorber? Allies are supposed to do that, aren't they?" he asked as if he were inquiring about the thickening mist or the lack of taxis on the street. "You told me you wanted to talk about what Harold said in his letter. Is that still what you want?"

She looked over the low wall at the river. "I don't know why I called you, to be honest. I felt I was in a bad situation that was getting worse, and I could do nothing about it. I didn't want to bother you, but I was sick of thrashing about the flat like a caged tiger, and I didn't want to dump this on any of the Coven. I don't want to add to what they're already dealing with." The last sounded a bit too uncertain, so she added, "You don't want to compare scars, the way the rest often do."

"No," he agreed, "I don't like comparing scars." He wondered what she would make of the broad swath of striated, whitened tissue that covered his torso from sternum to genitals, a continuing reminder of his execution over four thousand years ago. Roman matron though she was, Olivia had been squeamish about his scars, Tecla had been condemnatory, Gynethe Mehaut had flinched when she touched them, and even sensible Rowena Saxon had been put off by them; he worried that Charis might share their repellence if she ever saw them, a notion he dismissed because it reminded him of how much he wanted that to happen.

She glanced at him; she was slightly shorter than he, and in her high heels, they were about even. "And you won't tell me to buck up, or take it on the chin, the way Happy would if he were still in Paris. His sister is worse than he is that way. Relentlessly optimistic and . . . confident."

"Sounds like you know them both," said Szent-Germain, trying to draw her out.

"In a way. I don't know Mimi, not as well as Happy." She used his handkerchief to blot her face and to conceal her expression from him. "Mimi's what the family calls her: her name is Meredith."

"You're close to Professor Nugent?" Szent-Germain asked with mild surprise.

"You mean theoretical math and cultural history make an odd combination?" she asked sharply, folding his handkerchief carefully.

"No, I mean I'm curious how your paths came to cross. Academia is like most professions are becoming in this century: essentially small towns spread all over the world, where almost everyone in the profession knows the hierarchical position and the gossip about everyone else." He could feel her welling defensiveness keenly, and went on, "Isn't his sister in France just now?"

"She was; she left a couple of days ago," said Charis, wanting to appear unconcerned. "I'm not surprised that she wanted to stay away from the Coven—she doesn't want to make her own situation more awkward than her visit to Happy is already, and she probably doesn't want to make any trouble for her husband and kids. You can bet the CIA kept an eye on the two of them for the whole of their visit." In spite of her efforts to remain calm, she shuddered at the thought of surveillance.

"But you know you're being followed," he said, his voice gentle. "All the members of the Coven are."

"I don't like it. Happy has the most trouble with it, because there's some kind of connection he has with someone whom the CIA and the Committee consider to be much more dangerous than what most of us have seemed to the powers-that-be, or what the Committee or the FBI or the CIA thinks we might be part of. Happy doesn't talk about it, but he is touchy, knowing that he's got more strikes against him with the government than any of the rest of us, except for Win Pomeroy." She did not look directly at him, worried that she might see distrust or something worse in his eyes.

"And why is his case more troublesome than yours, or the Kings'?" He was conscious of this difference but had not been able to find out why it should be so.

"I thought you knew all about us. Pomeroy worked on improving strains of wheat with the Soviets, from the late Thirties until the end of the war, poor guy."

"I see," he said.

"The Committee is doubly wary about people who've had direct contact with the Soviets. Look at Washington Young: he's a Wobbly, and he used to print pamphlets for them for free. He might have it easier if he weren't colored." She was relieved to have something to talk about that did not involve Harold. "It's tricky for me because I knew Happy and Mimi before."

"And that might make your position more precarious?" he suggested. "Because you know both the brother and sister?"

"Sort of. The Coven is wary about having members who have any kind of personal history, and if anyone does have such a connection, we're asked to deny it outside of the group." She made an impatient gesture. "I don't mean that the way it sounds. His sister and I were in grad school together for a couple of semesters, and shared an apartment the size of a rabbit hutch. I met Happy then. He was a bright kid, very ambitious about his theories, and blithely unaware of his ambitions." She managed a partial smile that lacked the brittleness that her previous attempts had possessed. "I liked him more than her."

"Ah," he said.

"Not that kind of like," she amended. "He's a lot more accessible than Meredith wants to be. She had the idea to be a free spirit back then, but somehow, that didn't really suit her. She and Happy are very close."

"Her name is Meredith?" Szent-Germain asked. "The family calls her Mim—"

"Meredith Isadora. They called her Mimi; at least they did then. Happy told me she'd gone back to Meredith when she got married." She lowered her head. "We didn't part on good terms, I'm sorry to say. Among other things, Mimi didn't think the war would come, so she dropped out of her PhD program, and went on some kind of extended travel, about a year or so before the war broke out in Europe. She had trouble getting home. Happy told me she married a car dealer about ten years ago, and that she has a couple of kids, now. She isn't as much a free spirit as she used to be." She felt a strange pang of jealousy, and wondered if it were because Mimi had settled down, or because she, herself, had been deprived of her own security.

"Did Nugent offer to bring you and Meredith together during her visit?" Szent-Germain asked, encouraging her to talk.

"No." She stopped again. "Aside from Happy, we don't have anything in common, Mimi and I."

"You have children," he pointed out.

"Not that that's anything remarkable," she answered darkly.

They had reached one of the flights of stairs leading down to the river; they paused under the light that marked the spot. "The clocks will strike midnight in two or three minutes," he remarked, looking down the street. "I should probably get you home." He spoke reluctantly but with a pragmatic half-bow.

"Have we really been walking for almost three hours? My ankles will be the size of softballs tomorrow," she lamented.

"In that case, I should definitely see you home." Night and his native earth in his soles provided him with increased strength and stamina, and he knew he could easily carry her back to her flat if she required it, but he only added, "Don't wear yourself out; you have enough to deal with. If you like, I can try to find a taxi."

"It's nice . . . no, it's kind of you to say that, but I'll walk," she told him, staring at him with an air of discovery that she did not realize was apparent to him; her attraction to him had modified during their walk to something more comprehensive than it had been; seeming to hasten them on, a chorus of pleasantly discordant bells began to ring from nearby churches. They increased their speed from an amble to a more rapid clip; she felt her desire become yearning, and she started to consider what she might do to express that yearning. When she realized what she was seeking, she had a brief, internal scuffle with herself, appalled that she should consider making their alliance physical as well as affectionate, then decided that if he wanted the same thing, she would take him up on it, and wrestle with her conscience afterward. They would have to keep their lapse quiet, she knew, and that one consideration jangled at the back of her mind like an out-of-tune piano. She wondered if he were as discreet as she had assumed.

They spoke little, but as they turned into the rear alleyway behind the building where her flat was located, she brought her keys out of her purse, mentally chiding herself for the risk she was taking.

"Do you see anyone?" she whispered as she hurried with the lock.

"No; but then, I'm not supposed to," he said, ironic amusement softening his observation; no one had been posted at the mouth of the alley, and the windows looking out on the cobbled narrow street were covered with draperies and shutters; there might be observers behind the dustbins, but he thought it unlikely. He listened intently but heard nothing more sinister than the hum of a new refrigerator in the rear apartment beneath Charis' flat; Charis' pulse was rapid.

She could not keep from glancing around, but she, too, saw nothing. "You'll come upstairs?"

"If that would please you," he said, perceiving the fluctuations of need and expectation and desire that were creating such foment within her.

"I think it would," she said, and opened the rear door to the private staircase to her flat. "Go on, Grof. You know the way."

"If you take your shoes off here . . ." he recommended, stopping to remove his own.

"Oh, what a good idea," she said in an undervoice, then bent to unbuckle the ankle-straps so that she could kick them off; then she carried them by the straps in her left hand with her purse as they went up the stairs quickly and quietly.

When they entered the foyer, Charis spoke again, but softly. "Steve diMaggio checked it out yesterday. He's a real wonder. We should be safe." A single wall-sconce was shining, casting the room into a glowing half-light that made everything glisten. She pulled her damp scarf off her head and shoved it into her coat-pocket.

He closed the staircase door and set the substantial latch in place. "What now, Charis?" he asked, his question mellifluous.

She did not say anything while she studied him: short, stockily trim, with a deep chest, beautiful small hands, and arresting eyes. Not handsome, but mesmerizingly compelling, she decided. Tonight he was dressed in an Italian roll-top pullover of silk the dark color of aged iron, and a suit, also of Italian cut, in ash-black Turkish wool. His black loafers were from an expert bootmaker in London. The air of culture hung about him, and she had a moment of panic that he might be a practiced seducer, a man attuned to—She could find no word that described the predatory sort of behavior she feared. To cover her hesitation, she asked, "May I ask you something?"

"Certainly," he said.

"How old are you?"

If this were unexpected, he gave no indication of it. "If I told you, you wouldn't believe me," he said.

"No, really; how old are you?" she persisted.

"What do I appear to be to you?"

"Other than coy?" She cocked her head. "Somewhere between forty and forty-five," she said at last. "Maybe a well-preserved fifty, but I doubt it."

"I'm older than you think," he said. "Does that make a difference?" It had on a few previous occasions with other curious women.

"I doubt it," she said, taking off her coat and going to the coat-closet to hang it up. As she emerged, she said uncertainly. "What am I getting into?"

"Whatever you want," he said, still standing near the door to the stairway. "So long as it brings you joy."

"You see," she said suddenly, "I never thought I'd do this—commit adultery. I didn't imagine I'd ever consider doing what I'm probably doing now. I always thought I wasn't that kind of girl. I meant my marriage vows when I gave them. It never occurred to me that Harold and I would get a divorce, either. And so now, I can't decide what I should do. You attract me. Well, you know that." She took two steps toward him, then stopped still. "I can't . . . you'll have to come to me."

Unhurried he went to stand directly in front of her, less than a hand's-breadth between them. "I'm here."

"Would you leave if I tell you to go? Considering what I've said?"

"Of course," he responded without heavy emphasis. "I can't imagine anything worse than a reluctant lover. It would benefit neither of us." He had known that kind of futile encounter three millennia ago, when he had been confined to an oubliette for being a demon, and had been given a living sacrifice every full moon; those hapless women had provided him the blood he required, but beyond that, all he gained was the impact of their fear; throughout his long life, he had often encountered a resistance at the core of desire: he remembered the elusive gratification of Tulsi Kil, the unremitting need for sensation from Estasia, and the perplexing air of performance that had infused Photine d'Auville's passion.

None of them had been reluctant, but none of them had sought or wanted the intimacy he craved.

"You'd better kiss me, so I can make up my mind," she said.

"Now?"

"Yes; now," she said.

He took her hands in his, holding them at her sides, and leaned forward a little, his mouth touching hers gently, exploring. It was a long kiss, a slow kiss, developing as it went along, one that grew more intense as seconds faded into a minute and more, their kiss becoming deeper and more exciting than any other Charis could recall. She told herself that it was because of her long celibacy, but knew it was not: she had remained faithful and content to be so for two years during the war. This had been little more than six months, and this one kiss was running riot through her in a way she had never experienced. She pulled his hands around behind her, then reached around his neck to draw him nearer to her. Still neither of them broke from the other. Finally she sighed and turned her head a little; he continued to hold her. When she was still for a short while, he said, "Well?"

She started as if interrupted in a critical point in her ruminations. "Oh. I'm sorry. Yes. You'd better stay. I think I'd like it if you would." She seemed unable to let go of him. "You know where my bedroom—yes, of course you do," she added, then went on as if resuming a recitation. "I want you to stay with me, all night if you can."

"If that is what would please you," he answered.

"Oh, please, Grof!" she exclaimed, moving a few steps away from him, afraid that if she remained near him, she would seek out another kiss, and then more. "Will you stop being so infernally *reasonable*? I want you to stay. In my bed. With me." She took a deep breath. "So? Do you want to stay?"

"I thought I'd made myself clear," he said, smiling as he spoke. "Yes, Charis. I want to stay the night with you."

"And if I change my mind?" This was asked more tentatively.

"Then I won't inflict myself on you. My Word on it." He lowered his voice but remained focused on her. "Believe this."

There was a look in her eyes that he could not read. "Do you mean that? If you don't, it's quite a pick-up line." She made no apology for the skepticism in her tone and demeanor.

"Of course I mean it," he said with a single chuckle.

She continued to watch him as if she were prepared to bolt from the room. "So what would you do?"

"If you changed your mind?" he asked easily. "I would rather you not change your mind, but if you do, be benevolent enough to tell me." He did not add that he would know in any case, for that admission would be likely to daunt her present desire.

She hovered where she stood, unable to make herself move. "You'd better come and kiss me again," she told him.

He closed the distance between them, and this time caught her up in an embrace as their lips met. This was a more tempestuous kiss than the first, which was a question asked and now was answered. Gradually, without apparent effort, he lifted her into his arms, his mouth never leaving hers, and carried her down the corridor to her bedroom, where he set her down and took a step away. "Will you let me undress you?"

She looked around, her features pleasantly dazed. "Did you really do that? Carry me?"

"Yes," he said as if it were nothing unusual.

"How?" She took his hand. "Why?"

"To spare your nylons," he said.

"Really, why?"

He knew better than to try to answer her question, so he put his hands on her shoulders and asked, "Where do you want me to put this?"

"What?"

"This," he said. "Your jacket."

"In . . ." She pointed to the closet. "No. Just put it over the back of the chair. Put it all over the back of the chair."

He began to unbutton her rumpled linen jacket, working steadily, serenely. "All right." He moved behind her and slid her jacket off her, then laid it carefully on the back of the wing-back chair. "How do you manage to get into this? It's designed for a contortionist."

He was unbuttoning her blouse that closed down the back; it was silk crepe, simple in line, ecru in color, with small mother-of-pearl buttons.

She laughed, a little breathlessly. "I button the lower ones before I put it on, and then only have to fasten the top six," she said, surprised that he should think of such a thing.

"One day, you must show me how you do it," he told her, a suggestion of amusement in his voice. "For now—" He freed the last button and eased the blouse off her arms, the backs of his fingers lightly brushing her skin. She shivered, but not because her bedroom was cool; she was entranced by the time he took to rid her of her clothes. Nothing was done in haste: her silk blouse was draped over the chair's wing to minimize wrinkles, and now she had only her bra above her waist. Then she felt her bra tighten, and almost at once a release as he undid the hooks and eyes at the back. For a second she felt exposed, defenseless; she had to fight the impulse to keep hold of the bra, to use it as a shield. No one but Harold and her doctor had seen her without clothing for more than a decade, and suddenly it seemed that she had forgotten herself entirely, that she was giving in to impulses that no decent woman would indulge, but she could not bring herself to say the words to stop him.

He set her bra on the seat of the chair, then removed his jacket, hanging it on the far wing. "Would you rather remove your own hose? I can't promise I won't run them."

There was something so wonderfully ordinary in what he said, that she dared to respond, "No; you do it. My garter-belt is elastic."

He reached around her to briefly cup her breasts in his hands, caressing the luxurious swell of them and fingering her nipples deftly, then unbuttoned and unzipped her skirt from the back, and instead of dropping it down so she could step out of it, he lifted it over her head, folded it lengthwise to preserve its pleats, and set it over her jacket on the chair. "Would you rather sit down?"

The question was so unexpected that she did not quite understand it. "I don't know. Why should I?"

"If you're sitting, you won't have to worry about your balance—

standing might be otherwise," he said, sensing she was again feeling out of her depth. "Sitting is easier. Which would you prefer?"

She blushed a little—and at my age, she thought—and said, "Yes. You're right. I will sit on the end of the bed."

He sank down on one knee before her to unhook her hose from her garter-belt, taking care to handle the nylons carefully. He then pulled her garter-belt down from her hips over her thighs and legs; he gathered it up with the rolled hose and put them on the chair-seat with the bra. "Why don't you get under the covers? You're chilled."

"About my panties?" She felt like a schoolgirl, calling them *panties,* but no other word came to mind.

"No reason to rush," he replied.

Now thoroughly perplexed, she faltered, staring at him in consternation. "Do you want me to undress you?"

He gave her a smile that was nearly a kiss. "No. I'd rather you get comfortable."

"Oh." She turned around and grabbed the corner of her duvet and flung it back, leaving a triangle of sheet. She half-stretched, half-crawled onto it and reached for the duvet again. "There. All snug." She tried to imagine what he was going to do that was different from what she expected.

"That's good," he said, and sat on the side of the bed across from her in order to remove his shoes and socks; he set them next to the night-stand as he stretched out beside her on the top of the duvet.

Once again she was surprised. "Don't you plan to undress?" She was troubled as soon as she said it. "How are you going to—you know."

"I'm not going to, not tonight," he answered, making a few adjustments to the duvet. "Tonight is for you."

"But if you don't . . ." She felt herself lost again, unsure of how to say what she thought she should.

"If you are satisfied, then I will be as well," he whispered as he lay on his side as he reached out to her, the duvet rising between them, and curving around her shoulder like a fine fur stole. "For now, close your eyes and let me awaken your desires." He fitted himself to her back, lying spoon-style, his hand moving a bit of the duvet aside to give him access to her body.

The thought of closing her eyes was a bit unnerving, for if she could not see him, he might do . . . anything. But she had come this far, and she decided that she would do her best to trust him. "All right," she said, and closed her eyes as he turned the front of her body away from him. "What now?"

"This gives you freedom to move as you wish, even if it is to leave where you are," he said, and moved his shoulder so he could turn her face in order to kiss her, and had both hands free to touch her. While their mouths were joined, she felt his hands move toward her breasts; she had a moment of panic, but she fought against it, trying to decide how she would kick herself free of the covers if that became necessary. Gradually she relaxed as he stroked her body, starting at the base of her neck and going down to her panties, then caressing her along her sides, doing nothing in haste. When he finally fingered her breasts again, her body was already becoming excited, her nipples were stiffening, and she started to approve of this unorthodox approach to love-making; it did give her a freedom she never realized until now that she lacked. His touch was light and deft, rousing her nipples as if they were precious ornaments for an heirloom, for although his ministrations were thoughtful, they were also playful.

With her eyes closed, Charis said, "Give me a sec," and reached to wriggle out of her panties; she tossed them in the direction of the chair. "Now go on," she whispered eagerly.

"As you wish," he said, and extended his unhurried exploration of her flesh. From her breasts and flanks he shifted his position enough so that he could reach the apex of her thighs. Conscious of every nuance of her increasing passion, he began to awaken her deepest concupiscence, stimulating her already swollen clitoris with soft, expert caresses, taking all the time she needed to feel the full range of her desire. His own esurience was increasing as well, and he tantalized her to draw out her carnality, so that they would both have the full enjoyment of their awakened passion.

Charis had never known such transcendent excitation as what possessed her now. Her entire body quivered with the release that gathered within her. As her first orgasm overcame her she hardly noticed his lips on her throat, nor would she care if she had. Some incaluable time later, as the rapture started to diminish, she found herself hoping that the next time she spent the night with Szent-Germain, it would be for this ecstatic fulfillment and not for revenge on her husband.

Avignon, France
May 19, 1950

D-D Broadstreet,

In response to your inquiries related to my preliminary report:

No, I did not notice anyone accompanying Hapgood and Meredith Nugent any time during their visit beyond a local guide in Nice, who was at least fifty; she remained with them for the greater part of the day, showing them the usual points of interest as well as providing for tours of buildings not generally open to public viewing. At the end of the day, Hapgood took her recommendation for a restaurant, paid her, and there was no other communication between them.

Brother and sister appeared to be in good health, and spent a little time at the public beaches for which the Riviera is famous during their drive westward. Meredith is the stronger swimmer of the two. After their time at the shore, they ventured inland, into the Central Massif, where they visited a number of hill-towns before arriving at the small villa that Hapgood had rented for eight days. I could detect no pattern to their travels beyond that they would end up at Sainte-Clairmonde. They spent most of their time at the villa, the greatest part of their time in the vineyard attached to it, and in the village securing food for their meals; the villa has no electricity.

No, no contact was made with those outside the village. There is no telephone in the villa, so I can state confidently that the only calls they made were from the post office in Sainte-Clairmonde, most of them to members of the group called the Ex-Pats' Coven in Paris. There was one telephone call logged in for them, from Russell McCall, also a member of the Coven; Hapgood did not return it, and the call was not renewed. Hapgood received three letters at the post office, collected each in turn, but sent none himself.

As I described in my preliminary report: at the end of their visit, Hapgood drove Meredith to Avignon, and she took the train to Brussels, where, according to the passport officer there, she was met by a man from the University. She spent the night with him and his family, and in the morning spent two hours and twenty minutes with her host at the University, then took a taxi to the airport and was on the afternoon airplane bound for New York. Thus far, there have been no reports of questionable activities in Brussels.

Hapgood returned to Paris on the seventeenth, as I mentioned before, and aside from having dinner with the Praegers and Mary Anne Triding, has had no formal contact with any Coven member but Steven diMaggio, who searches for bugs for the Coven—usually finds them, too. There has been nothing remarkable in Hapgood's routine.

Aside from a meeting at Eclipse Press, Paris, there has been no contact between Hapgood Nugent and Grof Szent-Germain. Incidentally, the title appears to be genuine: the man actually does own a family estate in the Romanian Carpathians, and the family has been there well back into the Middle Ages, or so my affiliate in the region informs me. Unlikely as it may be, the man appears to be what he claims to be.

I will prepare a follow-up report next week.
Philetus Rothcoe

❖ 2 ❖

SZENT-GERMAIN'S FLAT was quiet; even the new hi-fi set was turned down to a hush, so that only a whispered thread of Bach's *Brandenburg Concerto No. 3* could be heard. A library lamp stood guard over the main desk, on the lowest of three settings. "Probably just as well," the Grof said to Rogers with an ironic smile. He had risen from his wing-back chair, the one with his native earth enclosed in the upholstery; as Rogers came through the door Szent-Germain sat back down again. "Parisians still dislike almost all things German, including Bach. The light-bulbs are the Italian ones." They were speaking in Imperial Latin, aware that they might be overheard, in spite of it being four in the morning.

Rogers, still dressed for traveling, was looking somewhat rumpled as he sat down on the small sofa in Szent-Germain's study, a room of good size that opened onto the corridor on the east wall, and onto the extensive library on the north wall. He dropped his briefcase onto the floor next to the sofa. "That's unfortunate, for them as well as for the Germans. Though you can't blame them, after the war."

"That's been a frequent excuse through the centuries—one of them does something the other cannot tolerate, and so they begin another war, claiming it is justified and necessary. It made some kind of sense back in the Middle Ages, or so everyone thought. The demands of honor take curious forms, and open aggression requires an active defense. This last war most certainly was needed, but for reasons of fashion or custom, as some of the others have not been," Szent-Germain reminded him with little heat, but with sorrow in his dark eyes.

"It's become a matter of character and style for both cultures, which is unfortunate." He bent to open his briefcase and pulled out a manila envelope straining to hold the report it contained. "You would have thought that the Revolution could have changed that, given all their humanitarian posturing," said Rogers, falling into the subject with the ease of long practice, aware that the Grof did not want to discuss his findings now. "Their intentions were admirable, those Revolutionaries. The French were on a course to have better . . . diplomatic relations with their neighbors."

"With the ones they were already inclined to like, yes, they were," Szent-Germain said, sounding melancholy. "They have trouble even now with those they actively dislike."

"They have justified their goals before their first shots were fired," said Rogers. "It wasn't their decision in the last war."

"No, and not for all of their neighbors," the Grof stated. "The French have a different relationship with the Dutch, but that may be changing, too. The weapons are too powerful now. No country can afford the risks of war, not with the bombs and guided, long-range missiles—" He had trouble finding Latin terms for these, and broke off.

"And the character of the first large encounter defines the hostilities from first to last—at least it does often." Rogers stretched, yawning. "Harking back to the Revolution."

"The Revolution, perhaps; the Terror, never," Szent-Germain said, thinking back to the hectic days in Lyon, trying to get Madelaine de Montalia out of the country before the Guillotine claimed her head and delivered the True Death.

Rogers sensed some of the Grof's troublesome memories, and said, "Do you think there will be a way to end their animosity?"

Szent-Germain shrugged. "It may happen, eventually. It cannot be forced."

"Do you mean that they cannot resolve their differences without battles? at least for now?" Rogers rubbed his eyes. "I hadn't realized I am as tired as . . . this."

"Bear with me a little while. I doubt a military contest will serve the cause of peace; it certainly hasn't in the past. The Great War was supposed to end all wars, and yet it has just been fought again. The French and the Germans haven't got on since Karl-lo-Magne ruled, and France wasn't even a country then," said Szent-Germain. "Neither you nor I can change them; it would be folly to try. It is up to them to change themselves." He took the sixteenth-century atlas off his desk and put it back on the shelf in its usual place. After a couple minutes of silence, he said, "You were telling me about your journey before we got sidetracked." He said the last word in English, since it was difficult to express *sidetracked* in Latin.

Rogers rubbed his eyes and stretched out his legs, crossing his ankles, very nearly yawning. "I spent most of the time on the train from Milano typing out my notes, which will make matters easier for you to assess, I think. There is a real tangle in Genova, and possibly one in Athens." He was still speaking Imperial Latin.

"Where did you get the typewriter?" Szent-Germain inquired.

"I borrowed the Olympic in the Athens office, the little portable, and I took a ream of paper from the Eclipse Publishing branch there. The notes are in Greek, not surprisingly, but I thought it would be wise to have a record not everyone can read. Border-guards can be too curious." He picked up the manila envelope and handed it to Szent-Germain, who received it with a single nod.

"No doubt, as can others," said Szent-Germain, and sat a little straighter in his chair as he reached out to put the manila envelope on his desk. "What slowed your journey? I expected you at twenty-two hundred hours. I had Fabert call the train station about half an hour before midnight; they said there had been a delay."

"Don't tell me he was worried too? Fabert?" He did not laugh or make any display of humor, but there was something in his faded-blue eyes that indicated that he was amused that Szent-Germain's houseman would be concerned for Rogers, of whom Fabert was deeply jealous. "I thought it best to leave from somewhere other than Genova, considering all the things that have been going on there. You'll have to arrange something with your factors there. I didn't want to have to explain anything to the police, so I went to Milano. It was a clamber, getting to the station in time, but I'm here now. We were delayed twice, once at Varese, once near Montargis. An old bomb went off and damaged the track."

"I'm relieved you got here safely. Those old bombs are a serious matter for everyone. Not even you and I could survive a direct hit . . ." His voice faded out as he shaded his eyes, contemplating the library lamp. "How provident that you should anticipate a need for a typewriter in Athens." He started to rise, leaning a little forward and moving his arms on the chair. "I suppose you're hungry," said Szent-Germain in his most cordial tone. "There's a fresh-killed capon in the refrigerator . . . I put it there when I learned you'd be late, though it is much later than I supposed it would be." This was usually a suggestion that they postpone any more discussion until morning, but for once Rogers did not respond as Szent-Germain expected.

"Not as hungry as I thought I might be; I'll have it tomorrow, when I'll probably be famished. I'm sure it will keep that long," Rogers told him, draping one arm along the back of the sofa. "And I'm convinced you're right; I should go and spend a week or so in Copenhagen. That could serve to throw some of the hounds looking for any crime that we might be accused of off the scent."

"You mean the Italians, the Dutch, or the French—or the Americans?" Szent-Germain's countenance was wry as he sat back down again. "For now, we needn't bother about the Germans. And we needn't consider the Danes. They're pleased about Eclipse, both shipping and publishing, and they're trying to keep from being dragged into the post-war scramble. I'm glad you changed your mind. But I imagine caution would be a wise course for both of us."

"You are being as paranoid as some of the Coven members; I don't think we've attracted the scrutiny you believe we have, though I don't rule out the possibilities, especially since this last trip. There are all sorts of refugees and exiles in Europe. You and I are just another two," said Rogers, and was about to apologize when Szent-Germain waved him to silence.

"You may be right—indeed, I hope you are," he declared as loudly as he had said anything since Rogers' arrival. "Please go on," he said in English.

"You suspect we may be overheard?" Rogers asked, a touch of aggravation in his tone; he was still speaking in Latin.

"Perhaps," Szent-Germain said as if it were of little interest.

"It seems . . . unusual," said Rogers. "Even at this hour? Who would be up now, and not cause suspicion for it?"

"When we go to the press, I'll explain as much as I know." This was once again in Latin. "I've had diMaggio look for bugs there, but he didn't find any."

Rogers looked askance for an instant. "You mean that you have found electronic bugs here? In this flat?"

"No, I didn't. Steve diMaggio did. It was quite an impressive operation," Szent-Germain stared blankly at a space some six feet beyond Rogers' head. "I've put him on a weekly retainer, the way most of the Coven members have done. He has found bugs in highly unlikely places. Professor Treat is right: he's very good at what he does."

"What did he find? Where did he find it?" Rogers asked with an urgency he was unable to disguise. "And did he perhaps put it there himself?"

"He found them"—he gave subtle emphasis to *them*—"in the dining room, the drawing room, the reception room, and the library. I very much doubt he put them in place." He gestured toward the door. "We'd have noticed something."

"Ye gods," Rogers allowed himself to mutter. "When did this happen?"

"That he can't determine. He did say that they were probably installed over time, or when we were traveling and this flat was empty but for Fabert, though he thinks that is unlikely. He's left the bugs in place, but disabled. He believes that the listeners won't be aware of our cognizance of their devices. That will buy us a little time to try to discover who is listening, and why."

"You mean he thinks one of the servants helped?" Rogers demanded. "Fabert is the only one who lives in, and I can't see him being part of any such efforts."

"Apparently, according to him, since there is no evidence that the flat has been broken into. But diMaggio warned me not to jump to conclusions, which I wanted to do, though not in the way he supposed. He believes that if one of the servants is involved, he'll show his hand if we don't press him too much. If he goes to ground, we'll be in a real predicament." Szent-Germain rubbed his chin. "When you have time, I'll ask you for a shave."

"Certainly," said Rogers. "Tomorrow. This afternoon."

"This afternoon, late in the day," Szent-Germain said, as if trying to shake off the mass of unwelcome possibilities that were pressing at his thoughts. "I was hoping we were through with spies for a while."

"You're experienced with spies," Rogers reminded him.

"Oh, yes, but the more . . . traditional kind, the ones who watch and listen in the vicinity, not those who intrude from afar," he agreed. "But diMaggio has tried to explain matters to me: if I were to pursue the course that seems preferable to waiting, I could bring about just the kind of fracas that would lead to a host of legal complications and other disturbances. A very strange situation, isn't it?"

"Do you think he's right?" Rogers asked in surprise.

"I don't know, but it seems to be the wiser course to follow his instructions. He's done much for the Coven members, and I find them generally a reliable group."

"Has diMaggio shown any secondary purpose in his searches, do you know?"

"I've heard nothing to his discredit, but I'll ask Bethune when I see him, and trust him to be forthright." He paused, his expression troubled. "Apparently a Coven member who last year filed a complaint with the police when he found bugs in his home became enmeshed in some kind of intrigue he knew almost nothing about. He had a passing acquaintance with one of the agents involved, but nothing clandestine. Some of the others in the group were afraid that the Coven had been penetrated by US agents, and began a hunt of their own for the spy. There was an upheaval of some sort, and the Coven member who had made the original complaint had to flee to Spain in the night—"

"Not a pleasant task," Rogers said, thinking back to their own flight from Spain just as the Spanish Civil War broke out.

"The roads are paved now, most of the main ones, and the autos are better and faster," Szent-Germain said in French, then went on in Latin. "The man remains in Barcelona, and will not return to France for fear of ending up in prison on suspicion of espionage. He's invited the Coven to visit him when they like, but is staying as out of sight as he can, and has his house searched frequently for bugs. DiMaggio found the bugs that began the whole Sturm und Drang, only a day or two after he came to Paris from the US. There was an immediate demand for his services, and it hasn't diminished since."

"Interesting," Rogers said, and yawned again. "I'm sorry, my master, I need to get to bed. I may not need much sleep, but I've been up for over sixty-five hours and—"

"I understand, old friend," said Szent-Germain. "I'll see you during the day. I have to be at the press by noon, so plan accordingly."

"We've been spied on before," Rogers said.

"That we have, but not so persistently, nor so . . . ruthlessly."

"In what sense ruthlessly?" The bugs were unnerving, but now that they had been detected, there was no reason to be upset by their presence, Rogers thought.

Szent-Germain took several seconds to answer, and when he spoke, it was as much to clarify his thoughts as to answer Rogers' question. "We don't know who placed them, or why, and whether or not they will attempt to do it again. DiMaggio says two of them are American-made, and he thinks one of the others is German, probably from a black market supplier, but that's no guarantee that we know who is responsible. Anyone can get their hands on these devices, and there's no way to determine . . ." He gave a very quiet sigh. "They're so . . . competitive with one another, these nations calling themselves allies, although that appellation hardly applies to many of them now. It's not just the Soviets who have broken from Western European concerns, it is Greece, and in another sense, Spain, which was never an ally in the usual sense, or Switzerland, for that matter. All of them are eager to have knowledge of the greatest number of secrets, and they behave accordingly. So I cannot be sanguine when diMaggio tells me that two of the bugs he has found are of US origins, for the US supplies half the world with spying devices; it is a matter of knowing who ordered them put here, and why."

"Do you want to find out?" Rogers asked, snapping the clasp of his briefcase closed as he rose from the sofa.

"I doubt it, but I need to find out," said Szent-Germain, his tone sardonic. "Come, old friend; get some rest. We'll want to be out of the flat by half-eleven." He studied this room, trying to decide where he would look for bugs here, but realized he would need to learn more from Steve diMaggio before he would be able to check out his various homes for himself.

Rogers went to the door into the corridor. "Are you going out tonight?"

"I think not. It's much too late, and I'm not in need of sustenance just at present. I was planning to read."

"Then I'll wish you goodnight, for what's left of it," he said to Szent-Germain, and closed the study door behind him as he started off for his own quarters on the other side of the building.

When Rogers came into the drawing room the next day at twenty minutes past eleven, almost all signs of fatigue had vanished, though there was a little lingering shadow under his eyes. The draperies were pulled across the windows, shutting out the refulgent sun. He saw Szent-Germain put his finger to his lips, and turned so that he could see that his employer was on the telephone.

"Tell me as much as you know, Mielle, and send your report along at once." Szent-Germain's French was fluent, if a bit old-fashioned, and tinged by an unplaceable accent; Rogers realized the Grof was annoyed with the man at the other end of the line.

There was a vociferous outburst on the other end of the call; Rogers heard both indignation and fright in the tinny voice.

Szent-Germain was unmoved by whatever was said. "I'll expect your report by no later than Friday. No excuses, and nothing withheld."

Rogers could not make out the words, but he could hear the panicky outrage coming from the receiver. He regarded Szent-Germain curiously, but waited to speak until Szent-Germain hung up.

Szent-Germain repeated, "Friday, Mielle," and he put the receiver back in its cradle. "Good morning, Rogers. I trust you slept well."

"Well enough," he answered. "What was that about?"

"I was giving some instructions to a gentleman in Genova," said Szent-Germain.

"What kind of instructions? He didn't sound very pleased about it."

"No, he didn't, but he will do what I ask of him," said Szent-Germain. "He wants me to keep his secrets, and will do as I tell him."

"Are you certain? He didn't sound very cooperative."

"I am," said Szent-Germain, and although his manner remained genial, there was something at the back of his eyes that did not encourage Rogers to pursue it. "The Delahaye is in the alley; I brought it around an hour ago. If you're ready?" He indicated the hallway that led to the rear of the flat and the stairs to the alley. His pace was faster than it appeared, but Rogers was used to this after his almost two thousand years with the Grof, and he kept up without apparent effort. Szent-Germain took time to lock the back door before descending the staircase to the alley where the Delahaye waited.

"Is there someone coming by the press?" Rogers asked. "I know you've met with a few of the Coven members—"

"Yes, I have a couple of Coven members calling upon me, but about books, not about spies or other nefarious matters. Russell McCall wants to talk with me; I think he's after information about Bethune, although why McCall should think I would have anything beyond what he already knows is a mystery to me." He opened the passenger door, then went around to get into the driver's seat, settling himself behind the steering wheel.

"Why does he want it?" Rogers wondered aloud. "Don't tell me he's investigating the Coven."

"He's a reporter, so he is curious. He's one of the Coven who thinks there is still a mole in the group, and wants to bring him—or her—out into the open." He started the engine. "We'll need petrol later today."

"I thought you had an arrangement with—"

"I do, but I have to let him know I'm coming. He is afraid that the police may find out about his private reserves program." The Delahaye hummed along through the morning traffic, the engine operating reliably. "I had this to the mechanic last week. Pierpont's given it a thorough going-over."

"That's reassuring," Rogers said. "I think my Alfa Romeo is ready. I noticed I had a note from the dealer."

"Very good," said Szent-Germain. "Far better to have your own auto than have to resort to taxis and the Metro."

"Truly." He paused. "The 1900 isn't a very handsome vehicle, but it has an anonymity that is very useful."

"That it is," Szent-Germain responded. "Not like the Delahaye."

"No, but it is useful to have something less memorable," said Rogers. "Especially given what I have been doing of late."

Szent-Germain chuckled. "No doubt you're right I'd probably be well-advised to drive something a bit less distinctive than this." He avoided a large delivery wagon drawn by two massive Belgian Draft horses. "I do indulge myself in the matter of autos, as I used to do with horses, but I know the value of something functional and ordinary as much as I like fine design and careful engineering." He took stock of the round-about ahead of them, and slowed a little to time his entrance into the whirl. "If it bothers you to have such an auto as the Alfa Romeo 1900, you can get something flashier."

"No, thank you. I like my anonymity." He shifted in the seat, stretching out his legs a bit more.

"Then arrange for the delivery of your new auto," Szent-Germain recommended.

Rogers sighed, and ran his hands through his sandy hair. "Pay no attention to me; I'm out of patience with myself, and I'm taking it out on a blameless auto." This was a surprising admission from Rogers, who regularly kept his emotions hidden behind a demeanor of competence and integrity.

"And why is that?" Szent-Germain inquired, swinging into the first workable gap in the autos and lorries and vans and motorcycles. He heard something strike the rear window and shook his head once; he would have to arrange for the window to be replaced.

"You'll understand when you read my notes," said Rogers.

"I did read them. They're most comprehensive, and you describe a difficult situation that is going to take careful handling, but nothing about it is to your disrepute, or mine, for that matter. That was why I was on the telephone with Inspector Mielle this morning, and he, as you remarked, was not pleased." He jockeyed for position to leave the round-about, and was almost clear of it when he felt the Delahaye lurch, and the steering wheel became hard to use; a flapping noise came from the front of the auto. "Left front tire's blown."

"Are you sure?" Rogers asked.

"I am." He took a firm hold of the steering wheel and managed to get the auto to the side of the street he had just entered. As soon as he could, he turned off his engine, set the handbrake, and got out of the car, his mouth a grim line. He crouched down next to the tire and looked at it, noticing the smooth oval hole in the side of the white-wall tire. He rose and went to examine the rear window, and had his suspicions confirmed. "Who was shooting at us?" he asked the air in the vanished language of his people.

Rogers had got out of the passenger's seat and came up to the Grof. "Do you want me to call anyone? That bistro should have a telephone." He motioned to the small cafe across the street.

"I think that would be wise," said Szent-Germain. "Call Jean-Isaac at Pierpoint's, and ask him to bring his towing lorry. You have the number, I believe?"

"So I have," said Rogers. "What about the Gendarmes? Should I inform them?"

"I think not. I'll let Jean-Isaac do that." He nodded toward the bistro. "You might summon a taxi, though."

"Of course. I presume you want me to remain with the Delahaye until Jean-Isaac arrives?" said Rogers, and waited for a lorry laden with large crates to drive by before sprinting across the street.

The owner of the bistro—a bristly fellow with a look of doubt about him—demanded payment for the use of his telephone, and would not leave his post at the maitre d's desk, where he made a great display of not listening, which convinced Rogers that he was. When the second call was finished, he said, "You're a foreigner, aren't you? You sound like a foreigner."

"I am; from Cadiz," Rogers said, not mentioning that when he had lived there, it was a Roman outpost called Gades; he glanced at his wristwatch. "I'll need to go out shortly."

"Then go," the owner said, all his interest in Rogers suddenly vanished.

"I thank you for the use of your telephone," Rogers said, an expression of his customary good manners.

"You paid me to make it worthwhile," the bistro owner said. "If you plan to come back, plan to eat."

"As you wish," he said as he left the bistro to join Szent-Germain across the street. When he was once again next to the Grof, he said, "A taxi is coming to take you to the press; he has been told that you need to arrive there quickly; I have ordered a second in forty-five minutes," he informed his employer in Byzantine Greek.

"And Jean-Isaac?" Szent-Germain asked, using the same language. "Are you sure he will arrive before then?"

"He is on his way. He will examine the auto thoroughly, and report to you by tomorrow evening." Rogers frowned as he contemplated the Delahaye. "I suppose he will inform the Gendarmes of what he finds, as per your request."

"I trust he will. In the meantime, come to the press once you have turned this auto over to Jean-Isaac. We have to—" He went silent as another bullet went by his ear, knocking a small fragment of stone off the building next to where the two men stood. "By all the forgotten gods!" he exclaimed aloud, in his native tongue. "What is this about?" he continued in French.

"I think perhaps we should find shelter," Rogers said, then pointed to the same lorry he had waited to pass before crossing the street. "A rifle, there, in the back, among the crates."

Szent-Germain squinted, and moved back into the shadow of an awning over a front window of a haberdashery. He squinted. "I can't read the number on the—" and ducked as a final shot rang out just as the lorry put on a burst of speed and slipped into the maelstrom of the round-about, quickly becoming lost to sight. Szent-Germain stepped away from the awning's shadow. "He was hunting us."

"So it would seem," said Rogers.

"But why?" Szent-Germain asked, still in his ancient language, expecting no answer.

"How much should we tell Jean-Isaac?" Rogers did not appear to be distressed at what he might have to reveal to the mechanic.

"I don't know," Szent-Germain said, frustration making him brusque. "Don't volunteer anything," he warned. "Until we know more, we must keep close to the vest."

Rogers nodded. "Your taxi is arriving."

"So it is," said Szent-Germain, stepping out to the curb to signal to the cab. "Call me if you are going to be later than an hour."

"I will," said Rogers.

"Perhaps I should consider an auto like yours, after all," the Grof said as he opened the taxi door and stepped into the rear seat.

Watching the taxi pull away, Rogers had to take a moment to compose himself before he would have to explain to Jean-Isaac why there were bullet holes in the Delahaye.

June 18, 1950

My dearest Axel,

There is no easy way to tell you this, so I will not draw out the suspense or the pain that I know I will cause you: I am en route to Southampton to return to America on the ship Goodman Baynard which will leave in three days for New York. I will go from there to my sister's home in Colliersville, Vermont. You remember how pleasant her place is, I'm sure. I don't know how long I will remain there, but at least I will be home. In six months or so, I will set about establishing myself in some quiet little town where I will not raise any suspicions about my presence, and where you can live without undue attention in the years ahead.

You know how miserable I have been for the last two years, and I know you've done everything you can to comfort me, but the one thing I long for—a return to the US—you have not been willing to do. Your situation is a problem, of course, and I understand why you feel it is necessary for you to refuse to do the one thing I need to survive. You may think that such a statement is an exaggeration, but it is not. I need to be in my own country as I need food and drink, though I am certain you do not share my feelings. All I can ask is that you accept that I cannot continue to live away from my home.

I'm sorry to leave you in such a state as I have. If you decide to divorce me, I will not oppose it, but I hope with all my heart that this separation will end and we will be reunited with each other and our own people. It is more than I can bear to remain in a strange country for years and years with no hope of coming back to the US. You have shown me that you are *a man of stronger character than I can claim for myself, and I hope you can find it within your heart to forgive me for this hasty and secret departure. You may take comfort in knowing I will not assist in any prosecution of you during your absence: a wife may still refuse to testify against her husband, no matter what has passed between them.*

I hope you will write to me at Lois' house and let me know how you are faring. And may God bless you and keep you safe in the dangerous place where you have chosen to live.

Your most loving
Julia

❖ 3 ❖

SUMMER HEAT slowed the pace of everything and everyone along the Potomac River Basin and the fan of streets lined with imposing buildings dedicated to the workings of government; their magnificent facades enhanced the hotness, doubling the impact of the mid-day roasting. At the National Zoo, animals from the veldts of Africa drowsed under plane trees; others lounged in the ponds and streams that provided relief for hippos and crocodiles. Even the frenetic pace of the Washington traffic was slowed by the unrelenting sun that hung in the sky like an irate god, baking all he could see from his remote vantage point. Tourists plodded along the sidewalks, sweat on their faces and marking the necklines and underarms of their summery clothing, guidebooks used as fans, and bottles of diverse sodas marking every refuse container like religious offerings. Most of these visitors wandering in the heat carried cameras to use to commemorate their trip to Washington; it was two days before the Fourth of July, and President Truman had promised a memorable celebration for those in the city, beginning at four in the afternoon with a parade of states, with champion high-school bands from every part of the country, for which the Park Police had erected wooden sawhorse barriers next to the sidewalks: in tribute for Pearl Harbor, the parade would be led by the Peter Damien High School band, and many people wanted to see them, and applaud their work in the war; conservative columnists opined their disapproval but were shouted down with a blizzard of letters to the editors. As a result, there was a growing air of excitement in spite of the oppressive warmth. With the President's pledge to reassure them, tourists continued to descend on the capital, eager for good, old-fashioned, patriotic festivities that would begin tomorrow with a sunset concert by the Marine Band as well as a performance by Bud Abbott and Lou Costello, fireworks to follow. Already a large bandstand had been set up near the foot of the

Washington Monument, and the Park Police were on extra duty as the preparations continued. Plain-clothes District police meandered among the tourists, watching for pick-pockets and thugs; they would be tripling their numbers by tomorrow morning when the streets would be impassable with the crowd.

For those who worked in the government, all this excitement was more of an irritant than an occasion for festivities, an additional intrusion on the heavy industry of the city that stretched from the White House and Congress and spread out through agencies, services, departments, courts, archives, armed forces, cultural institutions, and all sorts of divisions and committees devoted to some aspect of the country's business. The look of the place was imposing, thought Broadstreet. As it ought to be.

Running almost five minutes late for his one P.M. appointment, Lydell Broadstreet searched for a parking space in the two-tiered lot behind the building in which Manfred Channing labored. At last he happened upon a space in the far corner of the structure, next to one of the massive cement piers that supported the upper level. Not a very promising omen, he told himself, but it could be worse. With a clicking of his tongue at the inconvenience of this location, Broadstreet pulled into the space, rolled up his windows but for the right side-wing, and got out, his briefcase in hand, and locked his three-year-old sedan, thinking he should hire the sixteen-year-old across the street from his home to wash and police the Frazer. But he could hear opportunity knocking and he would answer its call. Descending the cement stairs two at a time, he was sweating by the time he went out into the sunlight, and he swore fulsomely under his breath as he waited for the stoplight to change. He thought now that he should have worn something lighter than this heavy suit of navy mid-weight wool, which was proving more engulfing and stifling than Broadstreet had anticipated; he wondered if this were anything like an Indian sweat-lodge. At least his shirt was cotton, though he felt the collar wilting as he rushed across the street, his navy-and-gold silk tie beginning to feel like a noose—not the kind of omen he was looking for. Once inside the building, he was identified and Channing alerted to Broad-steet's arrival.

"You know the way?" asked the receptionist without interest; she had a voice that grated like a rake on concrete.

"Three flights up, room number 413," Broadstreet said, finally able to stop panting.

The receptionist waved him toward the bank of elevators and gave her attention to the man behind him.

The elevator was stuffy, the fan hardly stirring the air. The elevator operator—a chocolate-colored man with a fringe of hair that looked like cotton candy—nodded to Broadstreet. "Which floor, sir?"

"Fourth floor." He waited while two other men got into the elevator cab and requested floors five and eight. Now that he was on the last leg of his journey, Broadstreet began to worry in earnest, his early satisfaction at the summons from Channing no longer feeling as good as it had when it arrived yesterday. He had at first taken pride in the degree of attention that his superior paid to him, but that had drained away as he tried to imagine why Channing wanted to see him so soon after he submitted his last report. He could not help but fret over his account of the fictitious meeting with Baxter, an event that supposedly took place four days ago on the dock behind a crab-shack near Point Pleasant. Had he done too much in describing the private party in the main dining room that spilled out onto the deck from time to time? Might someone have checked his report, and found out that Broadstreet had dined inside, luxuriously and alone? Just the thought that he had been found out made him shrink inside his clothes. He took his wrinkled handkerchief from his trouser-pocket and wiped his face, as much to conceal his edginess as to blot away the moisture on his brow and cheeks.

"Fourth floor," said the operator, bringing the cab even with the floor.

"Good," said Broadstreet, pushing past the other two passengers bound for higher floors, out into the side hallway. He tried to quiz himself on the other two men in the elevator: one was in a navy-blue suit, but which one? One of the men had hazel eyes, but again, he could not decide which. There was so much to remember, so many things to notice, he chided and excused himself at the same time. He swung his briefcase as he walked, trying to infuse himself with the air of accomplishment he feared he lacked. He knew he would have to have a composed demeanor for his interview, and he did what he could to achieve it before he reached Channing's office. He began by slowing down the speed of his walk; it would not be good to arrive panting.

Channing's secretary was a new face to Broadstreet—a woman of about thirty, smallish, neat, with carefully subdued good looks, and an engaging charm about her as she took stock of Broadstreet, saying in answer to his question, "I'll be here until his usual secretary comes back from his assignment in three weeks with his brother, after spending most of that time in Italy, poor guys—it's much better there in the last couple years. Thank you for asking."—so he reached into his inner breast pocket for his wallet in order to identify himself with his credentials, striving to keep his anxiety at bay.

"It's all in order," she said after a cursory examination.

"Much appreciated, Miss Pierce."

"Missus Pierce," she corrected him with an easy smile. "Go on in, Mister Broadstreet. He's expecting you."

Two fans labored to cool off Manfred Channing's office, but they did little more than ruffle the pages under an ornate paper-weight in the middle of his desk-top blotter. The thermometer in the barometer display registered ninety-one degrees and the barometer was starting to fall. That would be a real problem, with all the preparations under way for the Fourth. There would be rain by sundown. Channing himself was a bit pink from the heat, but had no other direct sign of being too hot; his charcoal pin-stripe three-piece suit of lightweight Italian wool showed no sign of swelter, and his linen shirt appeared crisp; his tie had a regimental stripe and had not been loosened. He looked across the desk at his current visitor, and did his best to smile his approval. "I've read your most recent report on Baxter. It sounds as if you're making progress with him at last."

"So I hope," said Lydell Broadstreet. "He's not a man who is easy to pin down. He gets skittish when I've tried."

"That much is obvious," said Channing, and tapped his intercom. "Pierce, will you go get two large glasses of lemonade for me and my—?" He made no excuse for not using Broadstreet's name or position within the agency.

Opal Pierce, who was determined to gain the good opinion of Broadstreet, answered at once. "I'll be back in ten minutes at the most, if that's satisfactory." This was promised with a slight chuckle, as if the answer were obvious. "Will you want ice in the lemonade?"

"Ice for us both, a lot of it," said Channing, not bothering to ask Broadstreet which he would prefer. He toggled off the intercom, and gave most of his attention to Broadstreet. "I appreciate your care in seeking not to interject your opinion into your observations, but I think it would be best if you tell me at least this: what is your impression of Baxter?"

"You have it in my reports," Broadstreet said, and realized he had erred, that Channing was looking for something specific, and would fish for it as long as he had to. "But if you'd like me to enlarge upon what I have in the report, it will be my pleasure to do so; I have been reviewing my last meeting with him, and I think I might shed some light on the confusion around him. Or if you have questions requiring explication, ask me and I'll do what I can to answer." He told himself he had made a good recovery.

"Yes. I would like that." He shifted a little in his wheelchair, his brow furrowed. "You say you have tried to locate this man Baxter's place of employment among the marine engineering firms along the coast, but that you are beginning to think that he may be employed by the government, or working as an independent contractor for a government agency."

Broadstreet did his best to conceal his uneasiness. "It would account for a lot, either way. It would also explain why he is so circumspect."

"And why do you say that?" Channing asked.

"Well, I can find no record of him with any company that would give him access to what he claims to know from experience. But there can be good reasons for that: I have considered that he is using an alias, which, given the nature of his endeavors, is not unlikely, and that identifying him by his correct name could take time. As you see in my report, he says he has participated in trials of many kinds of marine structures as well as having a fair amount of knowledge about roads and bridges. To me this suggests that he has taken on a wider scope of—" He saw Channing lift his hand, and went silent.

"Yes, you made that clear in your report. I believe you may be onto something about the nature of his endeavors. What perplexes me is that you haven't been able to identify any single project on which he worked, and that troubles me."

Very gingerly, Broadstreet moved forward in his chair, knowing that his next explanation must be successful. "There is another possibility."

"And that is?"

This risky assertion he was about to make was the heart of the matter; he steadied himself for it. "He might have worked but been dismissed for activities that were questionable. He may also be bait for some sort of trap, a lure, but since I have no idea whom he might be allied with, I don't know if I should consider any of this in my evaluations. He might have been part of the war effort and now cannot find employment, so he is keeping body and soul together by selling what he knows to the Soviets or others who are seeking such information—or the Greeks and the Japanese, perhaps."

"How likely do you think any of this is?" Channing pulled a notebook out of his middle desk drawer and reached for a pencil. "That Baxter is a foil for another power? Have you any theory as to why that should be?"

"I have some ideas, none of them demonstrable at present, but I believe I should keep aware of these possibilities." He told himself that this was an excellent improvisation, and one he could use as needed.

"We'll consider his subterfuge a possibility, not a likelihood, but it would be folly to scratch it off the list entirely," said Channing, a warning in his voice. "I agree with you that it can't be ignored, but I believe that this is where we apply Occam's Razor and go with the simplest explanation first; it spares us the trouble of having to question what we have already established. But be aware that everything you're considering could be right. Don't waste too much time chasing wild geese if you can help it. I would assume that he is acting more like an amateur than a professional spy, which puts the focus on his occupation, not his ideology. How does that seem to you?"

Broadstreet blinked, surprised at being asked so directly. "I think it makes sense, but we haven't all the facts yet, and that makes going with the simplest explanation a bit premature. It is at least as likely that he has a secondary agenda as that he is some underling at an engineering firm with a present government contract, and that he is trying to turn that to his advantage," said Broadstreet, and watched as Channing wrote something down. "I still believe his area of endeavor is marine engineering, but I have become less certain on his specific employment because of his great understanding of roads and bridges. That could turn a man resentful, especially if he had participated in the early days of repairing harbors in Europe. Baxter is old enough that he might have been a civil service employee of the Navy, or perhaps even the Army Corps of Engineers, during the war. I'll check out the lists and see if someone stands out. He could have been among those contractors who worked on the rebuilding of parts of Europe, particularly where work included rebuilding and clearing harbors. On a broader front, he could also have worked along the major rivers, where restoring order meant rebuilding roads and bridges, and breakwaters, among other things."

Channing continued to scribble. "Do you have a plan regarding his present activities? When you first made contact with him, it would seem that he was reporting the machinations of others. Do you still think that?"

"I do, but with some modification of my position: I think he might have participated with others in dealing with our former allies and some of our enemies, and that for some reason, he decided to withdraw from their venture. It could be that he is in danger from more than one source, and that would explain his reluctance to deal with me directly, and why he chooses such out-of-the-way locales for our meetings—that he knows of these places at all."

"An interesting thesis," said Channing. "How do you intend to pursue it?"

"I haven't made up my mind. But I am aware that I will need time to work out how I will proceed to avoid going off on a wild goose chase." He regarded Channing, his expression hopeful.

"How soon do you think you will be able to undertake this next step in your investigation?" Channing returned Broadstreet's scrutiny. "Also, has it ever occurred to you that this Baxter might be lying?"

The challenge was so abrupt that it took Broadstreet almost a minute to summon up an answer. "At first, yes, I thought that was a possibility, but then I decided that it was better to learn as much as I could before determining if he were being truthful; I am trying to leave my mind open to the possibilities for a while longer; it would be intolerable to discover that in my zeal, I have neglected the obvious. I've been looking over my notes from our scheduled meetings—those that did and did not happen, which brought me back to that second time at the Helmsman, when he broke into my car and hid in the backseat until I finished my meal and your men ceased to watch me; that was when I decided that he had something to impart, if only I could persuade him to be candid in his revelations. He's not one to blurt out anything compromising, as I reiterated in my report." That sounded reasonable enough, he told himself, and waited for what Channing would ask next.

"But you suspect he has been engaging in espionage, is aware of the severity of his crimes, and is now trying to free himself from his comrades without endangering any lives, his own included?" He patted the papers under the paperweight. "You say that is your present stance: has it changed in any way?"

Broadstreet shook his head. "No. I stand by what is in that por-

tion of the report on that incident. I could make a few more sur-
mises to make the report longer, but it won't be any more accurate
than it is now. There are details I will want to flesh out in the next
few days, and a few matters that I'm doubtful about."

"And those matters—how important are they to your investigation?"

"I can't answer that until I know what they are." He hesitated. "I
don't mean that in any sarcastic way, of course; I haven't learned
enough to know what other answer to give." He would have gone
on, but Opal Pierce appeared in the outer door, carrying a tray
with two glasses almost filled with ice, and a large pitcher of lemonade.

Noticing her presence, Channing motioned to her to come in.
"This will help clear the head," he declared. "This heat saps the intellect."

Uncertain if Channing were expecting an agreement or other
observation, Broadstreet nodded.

"This should cool us both down," said Channing, signaling to
Pierce to pour for him and Broadstreet. "And buzz Alice for me
in about twenty minutes, if you would. She and I have something
to discuss today."

"Of course, Mister Channing," she said with a winsome smile as
she reached for the pitcher. "Half an inch from the top?"

"That sounds about perfect." When she was done, Opal Pierce
left the two men alone, going to the outer office and closing the
door between them. "She's a real asset to us."

"She seems very . . . amiable." Broadstreet wondered where this
discussion was going, and he listened closely in the hope that he
might learn something from Channing's tone or delivery that
would provide him some hint of Channing's objective in asking
him. He thought this was an encouraging omen, one that promised a good outcome. "I'll bet she's efficient—she has that look
about her."

"She is efficient," said Channing, smiling. "You might want to
see if she can be shifted to you when she's done here; keep her in
the family, you know. I gather your replacement secretary isn't

working out; I know you'd find Pierce very good at her job. She's smart but not too smart, if you know what I mean."

Looking out at the sky, Broadstreet was startled to see vast swaths of wispy, nacreous clouds as sheer as linen curtains, with the tell-tale lilac tinge that heralded the gathering of an electrical storm, which confused all the other omens of the day. Fireworks in the rain, he thought and was able not to laugh. But now Broadstreet was in a quandary: was Channing seeking to saddle him with a spy or was he actually recommending a good worker for another possible secretary? He missed Florence, and was sorry that she had followed her husband to Texas. Was this suggestion perhaps an indirect criticism against his temporary secretary, with whom he was not getting on, and who did not type as rapidly or accurately as he would have liked? "If you will, find out if she would like to work for me. She'll be taken down a notch in pay, won't she: I'm not as high-ranking as you are. That hardly seems fair."

"The pool secretaries—and she is part of it until she moves into a permanent position—get the same no matter for whom they work," said Channing. "If she is the only secretary you have, in a year she'll have an automatic upgrade in pay."

"I wasn't aware of that," said Broadstreet, though he dimly recalled hearing something of the sort when he was going through orientation. He took the proffered glass of lemonade and sipped a little of it from the glass; it was cold enough to make his fillings ache, but the ice made it chilly enough for him to cool off.

"Well, we owe it to our staff to be fair," said Channing. "I'm looking forward to hearing more from you, and shortly."

The bluntness of this statement startled Broadstreet, but he managed to nod twice and to say, "Yes. So am I."

"It is a very risky venture you're embarked upon, Dell," Channing continued. "You mustn't lose track of that. Bear in mind that the FBI is eager to discredit our work; Hoover wants to subsume the CIA under his command, though that could lead to more abuses of power on Hoover's part."

"Yes. I do understand that," Broadstreet assured Channing. "Atkins needs to be made to answer for his lack of loyalty to the country, and we need to know much more about Hapgood Nugent and his role in Atkins' disappearance. The Ex-Pats' Coven is likely to be providing a conduit for Communist sympathizers whose mixed alliances have brought about their various decisions to leave their place in American academia for the wide world. It's such an easy ploy: the members of the Coven passing along notes, just the sort of thing academics do, so no one takes the time to check out what is really being done. You hide a duck in a flock of ducks. So long as I am able to continue to focus on these interactions, we should be able to turn this potential embarrassment into a major accomplishment."

"Excellent," Channing approved. "I was right to rely on you."

"I'm honored to be worthy of your trust," said Broadstreet, hoping he was not fawning too obviously. "But what about this Grof Szent-Germain? Have you any more information about him?"

"Scotland Yard has a file on him: he has a shipping company and a publishing house in England, much as he has in France and Italy, and Amsterdam and Copenhagen for that matter, and probably in other places as well. His father or grandfather had a factory and a school in Russia, but he vanishes from the record before 1918; I can't tell you for certain if he got out ahead of the Cossacks, but I doubt it, which wouldn't incline Szent-Germain to help the Soviets, but might provide a means to contact anti-Soviet factions in the present government," said Channing, hoping he had covered all the bases on this case. "I was hoping the Soviets might be willing to pass on information on the fellow, if only because he has hereditary estates in Romania, but they're no longer willing to share information with us. If we can tie this Szent-Germain to Atkins, then we may have a valuable chip to play."

"That's an interesting response," said Broadstreet. "I'll have Rothcoe put one of his men on it and see if any of it dovetails with Atkins." The recent addition to being able to post no more than two spies to a case had caused Broadstreet his first sign of making progress in the Agency, though he was reluctant to discuss it for fear that someone as ambitious as he was himself might find a way to throw a monkey-wrench in everything he sought.

"Playing both ends against the middle?" Channing suggested. "It wouldn't surprise me."

Broadstreet was suddenly distracted by the first spangle of heat lightning—not the kind of omen he wanted on this occasion, he told himself. "It might all come to nothing," he said and coughed once.

"Leave your options open, Dell, that's the idea. Get as much confirmation as you can, from the most reliable sources." Channing made a grimace that passed for a smile. "I'll see if I can get you a couple more agents to pursue your case on-site." He blinked at the second squirt of heat lightning. "I believe it would make more sense for us to adjourn for now. You don't want to drive home in a summer storm."

"No, I don't," Broadstreet said with conviction. "I'll have more information for you by next Monday."

"That's excellent. Once you get the dice thrown, it's best to act quickly. Send a wire, don't bother with the evening courier."

"I'll provide you with a copy of what I put in motion before I leave tonight: nothing will get done tomorrow. I'll put the message to Rothcoe in an Agency bag no later than twelve, which should reach here by midnight." He tried to smile but got it wrong, and stopped still.

"That would be fine." He indicated the door. "Would you ask Pierce to come in as you go out?"

"Of course," said Broadstreet, encouraged by Channing's best efforts at geniality. Drinking the last of his lemonade, he set the glass down; he made a gesture that was half-wave, half-salute, and picked up his briefcase. He nodded to Channing and held out his hand. When they had shaken, Broadstreet picked up his briefcase. "If anything changes, I'll call you with a report as soon as I learn of it."

"Thank you," said Channing, and settled back in his wheelchair and watched Broadstreet depart. Then he rolled around his desk to go to the window, where three minutes later, he saw Broadstreet rush from the building, racing toward the crosswalk to catch the light, and honked at by a light-blue Nash for his pains.

A few minutes later, Opal Pierce knocked on the door and without being summoned, came in. "You sent for me?"

"Broadstreet took the bait," said Channing, rolling back toward his desk.

"Just like that? Hook, line, and sinker?" she asked, startled, and came up behind his chair, bending over to kiss Channing's ear.

"Not a quibble or a hesitation," Channing said, smiling in spite of his somber mood. "He'd fall on his sword in the Lincoln Memorial if we asked it."

"He may have to do that if this plan of yours doesn't work," Pierce told him, concern in her expertly shadowed eyes. "This is a big risk."

"I don't want to have to work for a glory-hog like Hoover; it would turn all of CIA into a tool for political sabotage—of this country," said Channing distantly. "The man would be Inquisitor General if we didn't have separation of Church and State."

"No; nor would I. Still, you will allow he's good at showing his Bureau to advantage," said Pierce.

"Give the devil his due, you mean?" Channing said, but not very generously. "So long as what is good for the Bureau also enhances the reputation of Hoover himself, yes, he does a great deal to reinforce the public understanding of G-men, especially those in the FBI. He and the Bureau are one in the same, I'd imagine, at least in his mind."

"I'll give you that, and at least Hoover is making himself an obvious target, if it all goes to hell in a handbasket," Pierce remarked. "Wild Bill told me Hoover was riding for a fall."

"It hasn't happened yet," said Channing morosely.

"Wild Bill had a pretty clear take on the man, and he said that Hoover is more like Stalin than FDR; that would be enough to make him fall."

"Eventually," Channing grumbled.

"It may take time," she conceded, "but—"

"We can but hope," said Channing.

Knowing this speculation would only upset him, Pierce changed the subject. "How much longer is this going to take, this investigation you've foisted on Broadstreet?" She sounded slightly amused, but Channing knew it was more complicated than that.

"That depends on him. He still has options, and a couple of them would advance him if he keeps his wits about him. I'll see to whom he assigns the next level of the case, and then I'll have a better idea. The good thing is that he may actually turn up something worthwhile if he goes about it right." He rolled his chair out from under the desk. "Either way, neither of us is in danger."

"And Alice? She's taking a risk signing on with you," Pierce reminded him.

"When we're done here, you can let Alice know what's been happening," he promised her as he unzipped his fly.

July 18th, 1950

Dear Kit;

God! I can't understand how those Scandinavians can stand it. It's light all day and most of the night. You can't sleep, you can't eat, you can't get any chance to sit and think. I know it's the opposite in winter, which I wouldn't like any better. Horrible things they do with fish, too, and present them as pate or something equally inedible.

All right, I've finished my ghastly bit and will try not to carry on too much more vociferously. I saw the head of Math here, and I'll say he has an ambitious program. There's plenty of opportunity to do new work without creating worries about Communists. He—the head of the Math Department—says he would be willing to take any flack that may come from having me teaching there—something new for a change—and could, in fact, turn my present problems to advantage: "Hounded out of his own country, this young mathematician, . . . etc. etc. etc." You know the drill. He's promised me a tutor so I can learn Swedish, and a translator so I can lecture until I do learn Swedish. I've accepted, of course, and I'll arrange to move before the new semester starts. At least that's my plan; I didn't actually ask what day they begin classes. As soon as I have a new address, I'll send it along to you, and you may pass it on—discreetly. Nothing specific said on any trans-Atlantic telephone calls, nothing spread too openly. I don't want the CIA appearing on my doorstep if I can avoid it.

Bethune has been saying that he's of the opinion that we have another mole in the Coven. I really hope Bethune is wrong. McCall has made an effort to find out, but there's nothing conclusive. McCall would like it to be Win Pomeroy—it would make a good movie that way—but there's nothing to point that way, and a lot of evidence against it, including that we might not have a mole at all. The whole thing is ridiculous. Wash Young is one of the few no one thinks is the mole, being colored and in the trades. Probably there are Negro Communists, but who knows if Wash is one of them? He seems content to keep up the work that Szent-Germain has offered him at his Paris printing plant. He does The Grimoire, as you might recall.

Boris King sends his regards to your father. He and Wilhelmina may be moving on to Tel Aviv as soon as things settle down there. His offer is a good one, not as remunerative as the old situation, but much more reward- ing. There is a group of people in Israel who are eager to keep all things Russian out of that coutnry, and Boris is not inclined to go where he isn't wanted. If all goes well, he'll be in charge of their Russian music archives, which will be as close to heaven as he's ever likely to come. He and Wil- helmina are planning to spend a month there in the autumn, looking for places to live, signing contracts, the whole kaboodle. He's had a raw deal all around if you ask me. I've promised to visit them in the winter, when every- thing is sere and dark—not this year, next year, we hope. Wilhelmina is being careful, in case something interferes in this encouraging develop- ment. I think she's being overcautious, but I can't dispute her concerns.

By the way, have you heard anything from George? I haven't, not even while Mimi was with me, in the south of France. That's puzzled me, it seeming to be unlike him. But how many of us are as we used to be? If you happen to get a line on him, pass on the new contact information; I'll thank you now. You're a good egg, Kit, and I hope Princeton knows it. They need more men like you working on their Maths programs.

We're going through some rough weather, and writing isn't easy. I'll try to send you another note in the next week, and catch you up with as much as I can. I hope our irregular correspondence doesn't get you into hot water.

Happy

THEY HAD tumbled into his bed more than an hour ago, and now her face was rosy, alight with her fading orgasm, and her lips still slightly swollen as she languorously half-sat-up in bed and turned her puzzled eyes on him. She disliked the sense that she was losing his total attention, a realization which caused her some embarrassment since she was the one committing adultery, not he. "Why do you do that?" she asked without any emotion beyond curiosity; she had not known there were so many ways to climax, nor had she felt so wholly content with herself as she was now—contented, and for the first time in four years, safe.

"Do what?" he asked, looking up at her from a mound of pillows.

"You know," she said, a dreamy note in her voice. "Everything short of . . . you know. Inside." She could feel the blush in her neck and face; she chided herself for prissiness, reminding herself that she was no child, not even a young maiden, but a woman with two sons, and a divorced woman at that. She knew about sex, she knew the words to use, and there was no reason not to use them. Yet she could not bring herself to say them. Her blush intensified and she remained tongue-tied.

He was enjoying the growing strength of night—in summer, they were all too brief—the return to full capabilities now that the sun was below the horizon, and he let himself smile as he answered, "What troubles you, Charis? That I am impotent? That you cannot change it? Or is it that my impotence does not restrict me from anything but the obvious?" The first time he had made such a direct admission, he had been in Egypt, a slave at the Temple of Imhotep; then, he had felt ashamed and abashed, but those emotions had faded over the centuries and now there was no distress left to color his statement. "I have discussed this with you. You assured me you understood."

"And I do," she said, trying not to be flustered. "It doesn't trouble me, actually, but"—she struggled to find the right word—"perplexes me."

"Why are you perplexed?" His faint smile had no suggestion of mockery in it. Touching her hand gently, he smoothed the sheet with the other and angled a large, overstuffed pillow against the headboard. "Lie back, and tell me what you want to know. I'll explain to the limits of my abilities."

She tossed the duvet back and stretched out beside him, her skin burnished by the last afterglow of sunset. What had been a sultry day was giving way to a warm, delightful night; Paris was beginning to sparkle, the City of Light showing off in grand style. "Why won't you . . ." She knew this was dangerous territory, and chose her words as carefully as her still-rapturous perceptions would bear ". . . undress for me? I do for you. Or let me undress you. What would be wrong in that, if you have undressed me? You say you want intimacy, and so leaving on your clothes is a . . . an apparent contradiction."

"The precision of the academic mind," he murmured, stroking her shoulder affectionately.

She would not allow his remark or his expert ministrations to distract her purpose. "It's . . . weird for me to be naked and you to be almost completely dressed." Now that the difficult part was over, she said the rest more quickly. "I mean, a silk shirt and summer-weight wool slacks! You see me naked. I haven't seen you naked. We could have more together if you—"

"We could," he agreed amiably, "but it brings us back to the four contacts again, and the fifth and sixth; you have said you think what little I've told you is illusion and lies. There is more to consider than this wonderful pleasure."

"I didn't use those words," she protested, her face going a bit pale.

"No, you didn't," he said, his gaze steady and affectionate. "But I know when someone is calling me a liar even when I do not speak their language. You are being most polite, and I appreciate that, but it means that I haven't your full trust, which saddens me for both our sakes." Szent-Germain ran his hand down from her shoulder to her hip, a light touch that made her skin tingle. "I do what I do within the restriction of my condition, so that you may cross the threshold of your fulfillment, and both of us be filled with gratification; yours is the only gratification I can have, and so I am joyous when you are willing to accept me. If we are very fortunate, there is a touching that goes beyond skin, a delicious transport that nourishes the soul," he went on gently, leaning over and kissing her shoulder where his fingers had been seconds ago. "Because you like your body so well, and that in itself is satisfying to me, though there is more—" His smile was quick and authentic. "Your satisfaction fulfills me as it does you."

"Don't dodge the question, Grof," she warned, almost as if he were a recalcitrant student; she struck at him affectionately with a small pillow. "Yes, what you do for me is . . . astonishing. But that's not the point: you've told me before it would trouble me to see you naked."

"I recall telling you that," he said without much emotion of any kind, thinking back to the many, many times he had told others the same thing. "Past experience has shown me that my scars are upsetting."

"Scars, is it?"

"Severe," he confirmed. "They're distressing to many who see them." He had seen strong men flinch at the sight of them, and women become nauseated.

"Do you still think I would be put off by them?" She was startled and saddened by the notion. "After all this? Whatever your scars are"—she privately thought it would turn out to be some kind of ritual scars or tattoos: she had heard that all manner of old noble families used to do things like that, and that perhaps some of them still did—"I don't think it would extinguish the torch I'm carrying for you."

"That does not perturb me; I am prepared to accept that if I must." To her surprise, he sighed. "No, I'm bothered by the sense that your curiosity is not likely to be satisfied with one or two simple explanations, and that could lead to more questions and more hazardous answers," he said.

"My curiosity is at the heart of me, Grof; I am an academic and the daughter of an academic, and I have cultivated skepticism most of my life," she said, pulling as far away from him as the bed would allow. "If that's a stumbling block, it is a major one."

"I like your curiosity, I like your capacity for thought, and I admire your academic work," he told her.

"Really? Doesn't my intelligence worry you? Don't you find it intimidating?" She had had that experience in the past, and had found it disquieting that so many men became defensive when dealing with a clever, well-educated woman. "I hadn't thought you had such a problem, but I am beginning to wonder."

"I hope I do not. Over the years I have found intelligent women wonderful companions." He thought of Olivia and Demetrice, of Hero and Padmiri, of Heugenet and Madelaine . . .

"You mean lovers?" There was a challenge in her question; her chin was raised and her face became more angular.

"In some instances," he said, "but not in all of them. When there is a . . . an allurement, shall I call it? then perhaps I will venture into amorous association, but only so long as it is welcome, and the hazards are understood."

"And you felt such an allurement from me?" she demanded. "Well?"

"Yes, I did. As did you."

The realization that he had been aware of her attraction from the first was disturbing for her. "So this ally talk was simply a device to get me here? A kind of lure?" She slapped the bedding with the flat of her hand. Suddenly she shook her head. "If I've overstepped the mark, just say so. I know I can get carried away with questions."

"Of course I didn't scheme to draw you in," he answered. "I am your ally whether you share my bed—"

"Your guest bed," she interjected.

"Yes. My guest bed: whether you shared it with me or not. It's not my practice to make my female authors show their appreciation by engaging in a dalliance as part of the publication process." He held out his hand to her. "One has very little to do with the other:

believe this. I would have responded to you if we shared a compartment on a train or attended the same lecture. And had there been no direct contact, I would not have sought you out."

"Not worth the trouble?" she asked.

"You wear a wedding ring," he answered. "I would prefer not to suborn infidelity. That does no one any good." His compelling gaze rested on her, his sincerity apparent in every aspect of his demeanor. "Please, Charis. If you have doubts, tell me and I will try to my utmost to answer your questions as fully as I can. I'd rather answer questions than have you come to your own conclusions."

She sat still, thinking for more than a minute, then straightened up and crossed her legs tailor-fashion and looked directly at him. "What I really like about you is that you don't try to jolly or . . . or belittle me out of my inquiry, no matter how much it annoys you. You discuss these things very well, as if we were both rational adults. You haven't called me silly—that's something." She touched his cheek. "Thank you for that."

He took her hand and kissed it. "Thank you for welcoming me in spite of all the questions you have, and the doubts. That's very brave of you; after all the coercion you have endured already, it must be doubly difficult to confront me about something so private." He saw her nod, and he felt a pang of grief for her. "I am not seeking to exploit you, not even in print. I am not interested in seducing you; I am interested in loving you. By the same token, I will not trivialize your work or your achievements, or claim credit for the work through publishing it. You've had to accept certain restrictions on your ambitions and your attainments well before the witch-hunt phase began. Unless you come across the lost books of the Etruscans or the fifth volume of the Athenian registry of plants, you will have few chances for advancement in the American academic world, more's the pity. Not that the Europeans are any better than the Americans in that context, and in some instances, worse." He shook his head. "And yet things are improved: since the turn of the century, women have had more opportunities than they have had in the Occident for almost two millennia. The most disheartening thing is not that it happened, but that it took so long to come about."

This basic summing up of the state of women's issues worried Charis, who drew away from him and no longer felt his presence in the same intense fascination she had experienced at first. She had not known any of her colleagues to discuss women's role in social developments beyond the Suffragettes, as if the vote were all that was needed. "You're right: there is still a long way to go." Her voice was subdued, and she rolled onto her side, drawing her legs upward against her chest as a barrier between her and Szent-Germain. "I want to tell you about my mother. My mother was a Flapper when she was young; she loved jazz and weekend parties in the country. She did sculpting in wood, and she was part of a show at a gallery in Chicago when she was in college. College was rare for women then, and still not common now. She had a little money from her grandmother so that she could wait to marry, and so she had a job decorating manikins in store windows for three years. She was good at it, I'm told. She was also good at designing games. But once she married—she was twenty-five when she did, and half her family had given up on her ever finding a man—the only enterprising thing she did was make bathtub gin. Once in a while, she would carve something in wood; she always gave the works away, but before she did, my father always displayed her work on the mantelpiece, and boasted of her talent to his friends. He stopped at that; he would not take a booth at the county fair to show her work, or suggest she visit an art gallery to find an exhibitor. That was too public an exhibit for him. By the time I went to college, my mother spent the afternoons playing mah-jongg and drinking tropical cocktails with three businessmen's wives, all in circumstances like her own." She was silent for almost three minutes, then shook herself. "Why are we talking about this? I accept that your interests are liberal. I believe you have my best interests at heart. I have realized that you are not a religious man. And you have a vast knowledge of history. All granted. All things I admire. I give you credit for taking on my books. But I am not without reservations. I might be more trusting if I were not in the process of getting divorced, but perhaps not. My ambivalence troubles me as much as I suspect it troubles you, but I cannot deny it. I may have too many questions about you. That remains to be seen. I apologize for my behavior, but I cannot give it up." She swung around to face him, speaking quickly so she would not run out of nerve before she had finished telling him what she wanted. "Will you, or will you not, let me see you naked?"

"I would prefer not, but if you insist, I will." He rose to his feet.

"I do insist." She stared directly into his dark, dark eyes that flickered with what looked like tangles of blue filaments. "You've warned me, and my reaction will be my concern." There was a slight qualm behind this assertion, but she overcame it.

"Since you are so determined, I'll ask Rogers to heat up the main bath. It's at the back of the flat, at right angles to the kitchen. In an hour and a half, it should be ready, and while we're waiting, I'll explain about the number of exposures you can have without risk, and why, and what that risk entails." He got out of bed. "I'll be back as soon as this is arranged; it'll take five minutes, no longer."

"You'll work something out with him—with Rogers—so that you won't have all your clothes off, won't you?" she began, only to have him interrupt her quietly.

"I gave you my Word, Charis. If that is insufficient—"

Something in his comportment showed her that she had gone too far. "No, no; I believe you." She drew the duvet up to her chin as Szent-Germain left the room, knowing he would find Rogers in his office. She found herself of two minds now that he had consented; whatever she saw, she could not unsee it, and if it really were dreadful, then she would have to deal with it as best she could. She lowered the duvet and stepped out of the bed, going to the armoire; it was an imposing structure from the earlier part of the last century, a three-part piece of furniture in elegant bird's-eye maple, with a full-length beveled mirror on the panel nearest the door. It was large enough to park a car in it, she thought as she opened the third panel. There were three Turkish cotton bathrobes of varying sizes hanging in the closet, and she decided to choose one to serve as covering until the bath.

Szent-Germain moved almost silently, his small, bare feet seeming to skim the floor. He hurried into the antechamber and knocked on the door of the office before opening it. "The main bath, ninety minutes from now. Robes, scented soap and shampoo, sponges, slippers. Cognac for after."

"Given how warm it is, do you want the floor-heating on?" Rogers asked at his most unflappable.

"Probably not, but if the wind picks up, then yes. Thank you, old friend."

Rogers waved the Grof away and closed his ledger book, a suggestion of a smile in the crinkle of his eyes.

Back in the guest bedroom, Szent-Germain said, "The main bath will be ready in ninety minutes. What would you like to do while we wait?"

"Get some answers; I don't mean this in any derogatory way, but I do have a great many questions. I've been asking questions all my life, you know," said Charis, trying to keep from reaching out to him. She had donned the bathrobe of middle size and length, so it hung on her a bit loosely. She had pulled up the duvet and was sitting atop it, reclining on the large pillow Szent-Germain had placed there for her.

"As you wish," he said, sitting back down on the side of the bed. "Where would you like to begin?" He straightened out the bedding on his side, tugging the folds out of the bedding, waiting for Charis to begin.

"How old are you?"

"I've lived thirty-three years," he said promptly.

This startled her, but she did her best to conceal it. "You look older."

"It was a long time ago."

She sat up. "No more games. Answer me. How old are you?"

He met her eyes directly. "I am thirty-three, but"—he held up his hand to forestall her outburst—"I was born over four thousand years ago to what was considered a royal family in the Carpathian Mountains, at the dark of the year. Today most people would probably consider my father a warlord at best, but the world was a very different place, back then. I was initiated into the priesthood of our people, which conveyed provisional immortality. I was captured by our enemies and executed when I was thirty-three, and since my death, very slowly, I have changed, grown older, yet my age is still thirty-three. I have been told I look, perhaps, forty-five. I don't know, for I have no reflection, and haven't had since I rose from the mass grave where my soldiers lay." Though the events that had brought about his transformation were in the distant past, they were still vivid in his memories, stark images against a backdrop that had lost all but its strongest outlines.

"That's impossible. You're not dead," she informed him stiffly. "You're nothing like dead."

"I'm not alive, either," he said, taking her hand. "There may be some scientific term for my state of existence, but I doubt it. I call myself a vampire."

"A vampire," she echoed.

"Most of the restrictions I must deal with are consistent with European legends. I cannot cross running or tidal water without pain, I am vitiated by sunlight, I survive on the blood I receive from those who provide me with nourishment. My native earth in my shoes and my furniture shields me from the worst of these limitations." He ticked off these items on his fingers. "I am not driven off by the Cross, and other religious paraphernalia has no effect on me, garlic does not drive me away, and neither I nor those of my blood are vassals of the devil. I have no compulsion to count millet-grains, and I am not afraid of white horses."

"More fables. I want the truth." She was precariously near tears. "You have promised me the truth."

"And I am telling you the truth insofar as I know it. This is one of the points you need to know if we are to continue as lovers. If we continue, what I am, you will become."

She flung up one arm. "This is like a bad movie. All that's lacking is a colony of bats and an ancient, ruined castle. Vampires! That's crazy!" She glowered in his direction and caught the reflection in the mirror on the armoire door. The bed was clearly visible, and she saw herself plainly, but where he sat, there was a kind of smudge, like a fuzzy cutout image of a man, tattered and thread-bare, no feature distinguishable. "How do you *do* that?" she yelled at him. "*Why* do you do it? You are . . ." She could find no words to describe him.

"It is my nature, as it is with all of my blood. I don't do any-thing."

She had never heard such kindness in his voice before, nor seen such an expression of longing in his attractive, irregular face. "Well," she said, a bit uncertainly, unwilling to meet his steady gaze. "I'll suspend my opinion for now." She stared at him, looking for some slight indication of deception; she found none. Maybe he was tell-ing her the truth as he knew it, she thought. Maybe this was all a delusion, one he embraced wholeheartedly. Maybe he had been hypnotized, or drugged, she thought, and was told this to cover what had really happened to him. Maybe he had some kind of men-tal condition that built up a fantasy world because his own experi-ence was too dreadful to remember; that didn't explain the missing reflection, but it accounted for his outlandish convictions. What-ever the case, she reminded herself, the man ran two large compa-nies working in many parts of the world, so he wasn't an emotional train-wreck. She had yet to think of an explanation for his lack of a reflection, but that would come. She made herself pay attention to him and ask, "You don't eat with other people. Is that really the custom of your people, or something else?"

"It depends on how you view the purpose of dining. I do not indulge in feasting, but I do take nourishment, as you should know, and I do it in privacy with one partner," he said, lifting her hand to his lips and kissing her palm. "What you give me not only con-firms our intimacy, it is the one source of nourishment I can toler-ate. Fortunately, my needs are not great: I take no more than would half-fill a wine-glass."

She tossed her head, missing her shoulder-length locks that had been pruned back to a sophisticated page-boy style. "You mean that 'taste of the blood' you do? You've had that from me?" She changed her position on the bed so she could not see the reflection directly.

"Yes. The taste of blood, as you call it, opens the way to the touching I've told you about, and it is the touching I seek."

"You really aren't making this easy, are you," she challenged.

"You mayn't believe it, but I am; this explanation could be much more complicated than it is," he told her gently. "I know it goes against the grain with you, all this illogical information, and I want to explain it all to you, but there are a few complex matters that go along with the answers you seek, and that may not work as you would like, for which I apologize." He patted the place next to him. "Lie down again, if you would. We have plenty of time to explore. We might as well make the most of this opportunity."

"That would make five, and I'd rather save it up, if you don't mind," she answered distantly, staring up at the painted ceiling, then asked, "Is it really true that this is your guest room, or is it something more intimate?" she asked while studying the cavorting angels that flocked from one side of the ceiling to the other, benignly mischievous in their capers.

"Yes, it is." He smiled a little. "My room is more . . . austere, not a place for guests." His room was a small alcove near his library, with a narrow desk ornamented with a simple brass library-lamp for writing, a low-backed stool, and a large iron-bound leather chest with a thin mattress on top of it, with a single blanket. "This is much more satisfactory, don't you think? It is designed for insouciance."

"So you have said," she told him as she suddenly yawned with her whole body, her sinuous movements revealing that her desire was still present within her. Now that she had opened this door with him, she was uncertain of how to proceed, and took refuge in her skill for seeking academic information. "I'm still at a loss to see how. If I understood that, perhaps I wouldn't feel that I've . . . oh, I don't know . . . *deprived* you in some way of what you give to me."

"I am not deprived, Charis," he assured her. "But I'm troubled that you're not happy."

"Oh, I'm happy about this, more than I can tell you," she said, indicating the confusion of the bed. "I don't think I could bear everything that Harold is doing if I couldn't have an occasional tryst with you. I'm depending on them to carry me through the whole divorce." She laughed sharply and grabbed his hand and brought it to her breast, sliding it under the bathrobe and holding it there. "Sometimes I wonder if I'm still a person. I feel as if I'm some kind of robot, going through the motions of life, but not actually living. When I look at where I started and where I am now, I can't see how everything changed so completely."

"You were not the one who chose the changes that happened. You did nothing to bring about your exile. You could only decide what to do after those changes had taken place. It is as if you had been caught in a tidal wave, and flung beyond the wreckage. I apologize for the image, if it troubles you, but I feel such turbulence in you . . . It would be most disturbing if you felt no strangeness in your circumstances. I am an exile, myself, and I know of old how often our situation in the world can change, and how that haunts us." He moved so that he could more easily kiss her shoulder.

"How do you stand it?" she demanded suddenly, the emphasis on the *you*. "From what I've heard from you, you've been through the mill for quite some time, though I hadn't realized for how long. I still don't believe it. I can't grasp the possibility of living for a century, though a few people do it." She gave an embarrassed little cough. "The other evening, when you were talking about the last Czar, it was almost as if you had been there—you, not your uncle." She fixed him with a penetrating stare. "Or do you have an appalling portrait in the attic?"

He chuckled once. "Wilde was always at his best when writing about mythic things. No portraits that I'm aware of."

Charis went silent, finally saying quietly, "I meant that, you know. I am depending on you. Not for forever, but until the divorce is finished, and perhaps beyond. Without you, I would flounder. I don't know how long it's going to take, but I believe it shouldn't be more than two years. Bethune thinks so, too. You can stand that, can't you?"

"Ah, Charis," he said, making her name a consolation. "Little as you may think you want it, you will want to know what I have to tell you if you seek my support—which you may have for as long as you require it."

"Those risks you keep mentioning," she said, shaking her head.

"They are very real," he told her.

"So you say." She rolled toward him. "Your silk shirt is all wrinkled," she remarked as if making an apology.

"It can be ironed," he told her. "Shirts are like that."

"You're making light of—" she began, starting to straighten herself up again, and her eyes glinted.

"No, I'm not. I am attempting to remind you that the shirt doesn't know or care if it's wrinkled: that is a human concern. It's really not a very good analogy," he told her, and felt her relax back down onto the bed. "Those who come to my life will have to learn how to conduct themselves, for their own sakes as well as mine and the rest of us."

"So there are more of you?" She concealed a sigh in a yawn. "Are there many of your kind?"

"No. Perhaps, at present, thirteen or fourteen in all the world," he answered.

"Thirteen or fourteen," she marveled. "Is that all?"

"Yes: one in Mexico, one in Canada, one in New Zealand, one in Kiev, one in France"—he pointed to himself—"one in Algeria, two in China, one in Rhodesia, one in the Argentine, one in Bombay, one in India, or so I assume, and one, perhaps, in Spain." As always, memories of Csimenae and Tulsi Kil saddened him.

"So a very select few," said Charis, her doubts burgeoning once again. "And far-flung at that."

"If you want to put it that way," he responded, and waited for her to continue.

"What has that to do with what you want to say to me?" She found herself curious about how he would respond. "What kind of association do you and these thirteen or fourteen have? Do you give parties, hold meetings, visit one another? I'm not applying to the Eastern Star. Am I? My father was a Mason, so I quali—"

"Nothing of the sort," he said. "I am not a Mason. I doubt they'd have me." He had belonged to a number of occult Lodges, Orders, and Brotherhoods over the centuries—including the Freemasons—but not for more than well over two hundred years.

The last traces of her ecstasy had faded and she could feel discontent welling up to take its place. "A group of ten or so, not a gathering like the Coven. Do you ever do that?" She stared at the ceiling again, wondering if the angels were listening to the two of them. "Why is this all so mysterious? Look, I have assumed that you are some kind of agent for one country or another, and I can live with that. You don't have to share particulars with me, or make something up. It bothers me when you say things that are more story-telling than real. You say you want to have experience of all of me, but you don't let me have all of you."

He could see by the faint vertical line between her brows that she was not convinced by what he had told her; she would not be persuaded without evidence. "I have no wish to discomfit you, Charis." He took a breath. "I know you are ill-at-ease now. Have I done something that offends you?"

"Not precisely," she said, staring at him.

"Will you explain it to me, whatever it is?" he asked, still sitting on the edge of the bed, his clothes—for although he had removed his jacket and tie, he still had on slacks and his silk shirt, just now open at the neck; his small feet were bare—surprisingly neat. He remained still while Charis lay back again, amid a cloud of cream-colored satin. The bathrobe she wore gaped open.

She reached out and touched his sleeve. "I think . . . in fact, I know you're holding things back from me. I can be specific, if you like. You tell me we are allies, but you keep secrets from me a lot more than I keep them from you." She did a half-roll and propped herself on her elbow. "And what about what you said earlier, that we can only make love another two times before it will be danger-ous for me? Do you carry some horrible disease? Why six times, since you don't . . . you know." She turned and stared at him. "I don't know what you're up to, Ragoczy Ferenz, Grof Szent-Germain, if that really is your name, and I need to find out."

"On that we agree," he said; he could feel her doubts growing during their times together, and had not yet decided how he might explain all she would need to know if they continued as lovers much longer. "Do you recall what I told you last month about my father's fiefdom?"

"Only that it's in the Carpathians," she responded as she thought about the wonderful, lazy evening they had spent at Longchene, in the shadows of birches and willows, and wreathed in the aroma of wild thyme. "The eastern hook, I think you said." She moved, her enticing smile holding his attention. "I know you told me more."

"And you didn't listen," he said, a philosophical smile brightening his face.

"No, I didn't." She looked away from him, then turned back. "It was such a delightful afternoon."

"Have you recalled any part of what I told you?" He did not sound disappointed.

"Incompletely," she said. "It was such a fine day, and the lunch you provided had been very good."

A pair of clear soft chimes sounded from the depths of the flat.

"The bath is ready, if you would care to come with me?" He held out his hand to her.

The lights in the flat were on low, providing a kind of half-light for them to use to get to the main bath. They spoke little, moving quickly past the dining room and the pantry, then into a corridor behind the kitchen, where Szent-Germain paused to open the door. Warm, scented steam wafted over them as he bowed Charis into the dressing room that fronted the bath itself. "Welcome," he murmured.

"Thank you," she replied.

"The tub is specially made, four feet deep in the center, with two sets of steps leading down into it. It is nine feet long and six feet wide," he told her. "You can hang your robe over there, on the padded hooks. Shall you undress me or would you prefer I do it?"

"I'll do it, and then I'll hang up my bathrobe." She did not want to admit that she found the bath a bit overwhelming. "If you'll stand over there, near the light-fixture, I'll take care of you."

"As you wish," he said, and approached the three sconces of frosted glass.

She came up to him, and began by pulling the tails of his shirt out of the waistband of his slacks. The shirt was open at the neck, so she took hold of the first secured button and unfastened it. This was strangely exciting to her, and she unbuttoned the other seven buttons as rapidly as she could, her attention on the silk and not the skin. She shoved the shirt back, and looked squarely at his broad chest. "Oh. Oh, God," she whispered, reaching for the shirt to pull it closed again. The scars began at the base of his sternum and followed the ribs down to his waist, then down beyond his waistband. The tissue was white and looked tautly stretched, with striations through it, testimony to a fatal injury.

"The scar goes all the way to my penis," he said, as she went still, unable to respond. "I was disemboweled."

"Good God," she exclaimed. "How could you survive something like that?"

"I didn't survive it," he reminded her; although he did not want to, he went on steadily, "I had been initiated into the priesthood, which was vampiric, and so the wounds that made these scars could not deliver the True Death, for they left my spine intact, and did not ruin my nerves. It took me almost a year to heal enough to be able to take my revenge on those who had ravaged my family." He turned away and unbuttoned his fly, then stepped out of the garment and his underwear. "I'm going to bathe. I hope you'll come with me."

She hesitated, her shock still fresh in her body. "All right," she heard herself say, "I will."

Szent-Germain gave her a measured stare. "If all this does not discompose you too greatly, I'll finish undressing." He pulled off his shirt and hung it on a hook.

"Would you stop if I asked you?" she inquired nervously.

"Of course," he said.

She got out of her bathrobe and hung it on one of the hooks. "It does discompose me, but not so greatly that I cannot bear to be in your company," she told him, and went to the far end of the bath.

He watched her take the railing that would help her to descend into the bath, and said, "This must be the reason I love you."

She managed a bark of laughter. "It must be," she concurred, and stepped down one stair, watching him as she did. "I'll listen this time, if you tell me how you came to be alive."

"You mean, how I came not to die," he said, and dropped into the bath.

August 16, 1950
Antwerp Station

Manfred Channing
Satellite E
Washington, DC

Dear Fred,
    What on earth is Broadstreet up to? I know you gave him free rein on whatever he's up to, but he's interfering with my work, and with Phil Rothcoe's. He's got six more field agents on his roster now, and has requested more. He's been leaning on the Coven members, especially the most problematic of the members, and has ordered more of our men to keep close watch on Ragoczy Ferenz, Grof Szent-Germain, as if he thinks the Grof is working for the other side. I shouldn't have to remind you that he's the one who has been carrying refugees to work and family all over the world, no charge to us or the refugees. He's even kept Inspector Mielle in line, which no one else has been able to do; Mielle is as corrupt as they come, but he stays bought, and right now, he's bought by useful people. I gather Ragoczy has similar arrangements in Venice and Athens. I've been trying to set up a meeting with him before I head for home, just to find out a little more about why he's doing this, but no luck so far. His manservant has politely turned down my invitation.
    Life here at the Antwerp Station has been surprisingly dull these last few months. I could almost think we were actually on the edge of peace,

but I can't make myself believe it. Lajos Hovarth keeps going on about the Soviets and Hungary, but we haven't seen anything specific in that regard; he keeps talking about the wheat harvests in Russia, saying that if that fails, the Russians will have to take their wheat from Eastern Europe, and that could turn ugly. Hovarth is reluctant to go back to Buda-Pest, and I can't say I blame him. I'd recommend we keep him on for a time. He can read the signs better than I can.

I gather you're interviewing replacements for me. I trust that does not include Broadstreet; he hasn't the temperament for this kind of work, little though he would admit it. He'd end up causing a host of problems, and it would be difficult to rein him in. I think you might want to look at some of the group that has come on board in the last four years. They know more about the current state of things and are not fighting the Nazis still. You'll want someone with field experience, I would think, someone with a good grasp of European politics. Ideally, you'll choose someone who speaks Russian, and maybe Czech or Serbian, or Romanian. We need that skill more than ever now, with the Communists attempting to infiltrate our intelligence operations everywhere, but not to the degree that Tail-Gunner Joe does. He's got a burr under his saddle on Communists; Hoover does, too, but he's slyer than McCarthy, and he is in a position to do us damage if he puts his mind to it. You might want someone less zealous than McCarthy for a Deputy Director or Station Chief.

When I get back, I'll set aside a week for debriefing, before I start looking for a place to live. My ex is letting me stay in her guest room while I go over things with you, but she wants me out from underfoot as soon as possible. I'm thinking of looking for something entirely different from spycraft: an apple orchard, perhaps, or a sportsmen's lodge. If you have any suggestions, let me know.

Sincerely.
Nate Waters

NW/hbr

❖ 5 ❖

LATE AUGUST heat had turned the sky bronze and the sun to an orb of molten gold that shimmered over the hills northeast of Paris, with only a hint of blue at the horizon. Like many others, the Ex-Pats' Coven had fled the city for the rural suburbs to find a break from the soaring temperatures. Hapgood Nugent was glad to welcome them to the Victorian cottage he had been leasing since he first arrived in France, and in preparation for this occasion, he had set up tables for a picnic in his rear garden. He was standing in the open gate, smiling under his wide-brimmed straw hat, waving to the various Coven members as they arrived, and directing them to a place to park. As Szent-Germain turned up the gravel drive in his Jaguar XK120, Nugent ambled out to greet him.

Szent-Germain brought the Jaguar to a halt in a cloud of dust, its top down and its two seats occupied. As soon as the engine was turned off, Nugent spoke up. "I like it better than the Delahaye."

"So do I," said Charis from the passenger seat.

"Yeah, that's a snazzy car you got there, all right," Nugent said, doing his best not to sound impressed by the elegant vehicle. "I like that maroon color. I'll bet that's a special order. And the roof is black?"

"It is," said Szent-Germain, getting out of the car and going around to open the passenger door for Charis, offering his hand to help her out.

"McCall's going to be jealous, and Jesse, too," Nugent said with a trace of begrudging admiration in his words. "And you might as well park it right where it is, so everyone can be flabbergasted, including the neighbors across the road." He nodded to another Victorian, this one looking more like a farmhouse than a toy box.

"Are we the first to arrive, then?" Charis inquired, looking at her wristwatch; they had arrived ten minutes late.

"No. Bjornson and the Praegers are in the back garden already. And Steve is checking out the cottage to be sure we aren't being eavesdropped upon. I had them park on the north side of the house; there's room for three cars under the sycamore. It's a little cooler than the south side, which has direct sun." He fiddled with the collar of his short-sleeved shirt, watching while Szent-Germain opened the boot and removed a large wicker basket from a nest of insulating blankets. He slammed it closed and bent to lock it.

"A contribution to the occasion," Szent-Germain said, lifting the basket.

"And a precaution, as well," said Nugent. "You're smart to lock it. A car like that could be a target, even out here at the edge of the country."

"My thought exactly," said Szent-Germain, coming back to Charis' side.

"We have three kinds of pate and fresh bread and crackers. There's also a tapenade of olives and figs." Charis grinned, and reached for her large bag in the well of the passenger seat. "And two bottles of wine. One red, one white." She smiled from under her elegant sunhat. "It's a lovely day, Happy." Kissing his cheek on only one side, she smiled and went on, "I know we'll have a good time. I'm just sorry it's because you're leaving. We'll miss you. You're sort of the last break with my past."

"Well, I haven't left yet, and I don't want the party to be dismal, so try to be glad for all of it," said Nugent, indicating the short walkway to the porch of the cottage. "I'll show you the way to the garden, and give you a look at the house at the same time." He moved ahead of his guests, pointing out the parlor, the dining room, the kitchen, the bedroom, the bathroom—"There are two more bedrooms upstairs, and a second toilet"—and the screened porch that projected over this end of the garden. "The steps are down the side of the cottage, right through that door. I've put in a hand-railing, so you shouldn't have any trouble."

"How many are you expecting?" Charis asked.

"Sixteen, counting me. Almost the whole Coven." Nugent sighed in contentment. "I hadn't thought so many would want to come." He smiled in a self-deprecating manner. "The weather probably has more to do with it than I do."

"That's doing it up too brown," Charis chided him affectionately.

"Me?" Nugent in mocked dismay. "I'm the soul of modesty, or I could have made the party sound far grander."

"Pretty large gathering," Charis said, summoning up a half-smile to answer his. "And a good turn-out for a bon voyage party. It makes for a good send-off." A sudden frown flashed over her features too quickly for Nugent to see it, but Szent-Germain did, and wondered what was bothering her.

Nugent opened the front door and indicated the stairs down to the garden. "They're a bit steep, so use the railing if you need it. I'm going back to the front of the house. Oh, there's a pond at the bottom of the garden; spring-fed, so it doesn't get brackish. It's pleasant, and a little cooler than most of the garden, and that might be important by mid-afternoon. Be careful at dusk, though. The pond gets swarms of some kind of midges, and they'll eat you alive. Until sundown, it's a nice place; there're a couple of benches near it, and some other features."

"We can manage from here," Charis called to him as he strolled away.

"Do you want to go down first?" Szent-Germain asked Charis, stepping aside to give her more room. The heat was unsettling to him, but he kept himself in order; he had attended occasions more demanding than this, that required more of him. He was wearing black slacks and a charcoal-gray linen shirt with long sleeves; he was relieved that Rogers had refilled the soles of his shoes with his native earth last night, for it provided some protection from the relentless sunlight.

"Thanks," she said, letting him hold the door open for her. It took her a step or two to become accustomed to the steepness of the stairs, but she made her way down all twelve of them without mishap. As she reached the foot of the stairs, she called out, "Hello, Coven!"

Axel Bjornson, in a khaki outfit more suited for fly-fishing than a picnic, rounded on her and waved. "Professor Treat," he greeted her. "Good to see you."

"Glad you're here, Doctor Bjornson," she responded.

"How's the work coming on your second book?" Bjornson asked, doing his best to be sociable.

"I have some new material that should create interest in it; I expect to have it completed in a year or so," she answered, a bit obliquely.

Elvira Praeger hurried up to Charis, bristling with enthusiasm. "I'm so glad you're here. I'm sorry I wasn't at the last Coven meeting. Couldn't be helped. We can talk now, though, can't we? You look wonderful. Come and let Jesse pour a drink for you." She took Charis' elbow and all but dragged her to the long table. "Doesn't it look wonderful?"

Charis studied the place for a couple of seconds, then said, "Let me put these down"—referring to the two bottles of wine in her large tote—"then we can talk." She handed the bottles one at a time to Jesse Praeger.

"'Thirty-five for the red, 'forty-five for the white. Someone knows the good vintages," Jesse approved.

"Talk to the Grof about it; he's providing them." Charis turned in time to see Elvira approaching again.

"Oh, good," said Elvira, now keeping close to Charis as she went along the outer side of the tables set up under the eaves of the screened porch above them. "We can have a glass of wine, and find a nice corner to sit. I'm afraid it's going to be hot in an hour or so. "

Charis did not look forward to either the conversation or the heat very eagerly, but she said, "If Jesse will open a bottle for us, we can have a little time to ourselves until the rest arrive."

"Very nice," Jesse said, inspecting the labels. "Red or white?" He managed a jaunty half-smile for Charis.

"White," said Elvira, looking at the array of glasses, tankards, and mugs at the end of the third table. "And that glass, please, the one like a balloon."

Jesse scowled, but picked up the glass. "And you?" he asked Charis. "Any preference in your glass?"

"The pear-shaped one would be nice, and red." She saw a look flare between husband and wife, and wondered why they were at odds; there were so many things that might account for it, it was impossible to settle on only one. "I'm not really finicky, if you think another would be better."

"The pear-shaped one is fine," said Jesse, not quite genially; he had the corkscrew in hand and was peeling the foil cap off the bottle of 1945 white Burgundy Szent-Germain had provided from his own vineyard. "It's going to be a long afternoon, honey," he said to Elvira, a hidden warning in his calm remark. "Don't wear yourself out too soon. You need to take care of yourself; your doctor said you shouldn't get overtired."

Elvira gave an angry giggle. "Good company with plenty of food. Just what the doctor ordered, don't you think, darling," Elvira said, then turned away to greet Russell McCall, who was making his way down the stairs, a large steel bowl in his arms. "After we eat, I'm going to spread a blanket in the sun and make the most of the day. How could I wear myself out?"

As soon as their glasses were filled, Elvira took Charis by the elbow once again and steered her to the bench at the edge of the overhang. "It's so good of you to do this. You have kids, so I know you'll understand." She was talking rapidly, glancing around to determine if they were overheard. "It's just that since the miscarriage, Jesse keeps putting limits on me, and it just drives me wild. I have to rest every afternoon, I'm not allowed to smoke, or go shopping without him. He wants me to stick to the regimen the doctor's provided, but I can't do it every day; it's just too boring." Her voice dropped to a near whisper. "I think I might be pregnant again, but I don't dare tell him: he'll wrap me in cotton batting and put me in a—"

"Do you really think you might be pregnant?" Charis asked, her voice lowered.

"Well, I'm more than two weeks late, and that doesn't happen to me." She took a long sip of wine. "I'm getting edgy, keeping the secret."

Charis looked at her, choosing her words with care. "Do you want to get pregnant now, so soon after your miscarriage?"

"Yes." Her nervous smile became a forlorn mask. "It's for Jesse, more than me. He wants kids, the sooner the better. I know I should be glad he does, but . . ." Her words faded away.

"What does your doctor say?" Charis asked.

"He doesn't know. I have an appointment with him the end of next week, and I don't know what I'll say to him."

Doing her best not to laugh, Charis said, "If he's any kind of doctor, he's going to figure it out, if you are actually pregnant, no matter what you say."

"That's what I think, too, and that scares me, because I know he'll tell Jesse, and then it's solitary confinement for me. I don't want that, but Jesse is worried, so I'm stuck." She took another long sip of wine; her glass was now half-empty. "Do you think the doctor should tell Jesse not to be so protective? I don't want him to think I'm ungrateful for his care."

"You can certainly ask him," Charis said, and turned on the bench as she heard the thud of footsteps descending the stairs.

"Greetings, Coveners," Boris King called out, waving, then resuming his descent behind Wilhelmina, who cradled a platter of deviled eggs in the crook of one arm. Both were dressed for this kind of day, he in slacks and a Hawaiian sport-shirt, she in a pin-tucked blouse and a twill walking-skirt. Both wore straw hats and rubber-soled shoes. "A fine day for a picnic!"

"Damn!" said Elvira, and muttered thanks to Charis, then rushed out to greet the latest arrivals.

"It could be a little cooler," said Nugent from the top of the stairs. "Those of you with hats, remember to keep them on. And if you want tanning lotion, I have a couple bottles in the bathroom; use some if you need it. Better embrocation than sunburn. If anyone wants a fan, I've got half a dozen of them." He grinned at his guests. "Steve's almost done with his checking. He brought a summer sausage with him."

"French?" Boris asked.

"Belgian. I don't know what the differences are. I have mustard in the ice-box, and mayonnaise—I'll bring it out shortly, with a carving knife and a serving fork." He waggled his long fingers, then went back to the front of his cottage.

"Willie," Elvira cried out to Wilhelmina King, and Charis watched Elvira pull Wilhelmina aside, and wondered how many of the women at the picnic would be privy to Elvira's secret by the end of the day.

Thirty minutes later, almost everyone had arrived, and Nugent asked Charis and Moira Frost to set about putting the various contributions to the feast on the table. "Remember, I have a cold ham to bring out, and a relish of sour cherries and prunes." He pointed to Wilhelmina. "If you'll supervise the plates and flatware and glasses, we can leave the potables to Jesse. You don't mind being cellar-master, do you?"

"It's fine with me," said Jesse, reaching into the ice-filled tub under the table for another bottle of beer.

Nugent gave him a thumbs-up sign and continued, "There are blankets under the middle table for those who would like to dine on the grass, and folding chairs are around the corner against the basement door, for those who'd rather be seated properly." He turned toward the hall through the cottage. "Win's here; I'd know that Citroen's engine anywhere. I'll go tell him where to park."

"We'll take care of setting it up," Charis told him. "But what about Tim?" She nodded toward where his wheelchair had been moved after it had been eased down the path on the south side of the cottage. "Where would you like us to put him?" Tim's coordination was lessening, and that meant he could not be left to fend for himself even in little things.

"I'll let Moira decide that," said Nugent, glancing at the thermometer. "Make sure he's in the shade, though. It's heating up."

"I'll manage that," said Washington Young, who had been in quiet discussion with Russell McCall. He had taken on the task of getting Tim about several months ago, and now was viewed by all the Coven as Tim's practical nurse.

"Excellent," Nugent approved, then hastened back through the cottage as he heard another car drive up.

"Bethune, let's hope," said Charis as she started to set out all the various contributions to the picnic, and moved around Wilhelmina as she set out forks and knives wrapped in serviettes. "Remember to leave an open place for the ham."

"Yes, we all hope it's Bethune, and not some pest from the CIA," said Wilhelmina, watching Moira slice white and rye breads, putting the slices into a large ceramic bowl decorated with low-relief birds and flowers.

"Hello, everyone," called Steve diMaggio from the top of the stairs. "Someone's got a fine car out there. Happy says it's yours, Grof."

"If you mean the maroon Jaguar, it is mine, and thanks for the notice." Szent-Germain stopped flapping out the blanket he was about to spread under a weeping willow.

"Who brought the Dutch salad?" Bjornson asked, looking at the steel bowl filled with chopped steamed potatoes, chopped steamed cauliflower, chopped sauteed onions, and chopped hard-boiled eggs, all in a dressing of Hollandaise sauce.

"Guilty," said McCall. "It's about the only picnic dish I know how to make."

"It should go well with the ham," said Wilhelmina.

Elvira raised her glass in a salute. "To the Dutch salad!"

"Amen," said Bjornson, reaching for his dark bottle of fruit-infused beer from Belgium.

Tim Frost made a sound that might have been a cheer or a rebuke. He had been wheeled to the far end of the three tables where the overhang of the porch provided him the shadow he needed; Moira went to him and offered him a half a croissant, which he mashed in his fist before carrying it to his mouth.

"Let me deal with this," said Young, taking Moira's place at Tim's side. "You give yourself a break."

"Thanks, Wash; you're a life-saver," said Moira, and went back to cutting up some round barley-rolls.

DiMaggio brought his summer sausage out of a cloth shopping bag; the skin of it glistened and smelled of summer herbs and garlic, a formidable creation as long and as thick as his forearm. "Where do you want me to put this?" he asked.

Mary Anne Triding, dressed more for a garden party than a picnic in a long flowered skirt and a peasant-style blouse, abandoned her contemplation of the pond, and came up the gradual slope of the lawn to the edge of the tables. "Anything I can do?" she asked of no one in particular.

"You can quarter the apples," Moira said. "There's another knife in that mug."

"Hot-diggity! Is there another cutting board?" Mary Anne asked, looking around for one. "I don't want to ruin the tablecloth."

"On the shelf," said Moira, and turned toward Washington Young, who came up beside her.

"Is there any juice or soft drink I can give Tim? He's getting restive."

Young looked around at the table. "I'll tell him it's almost time to eat, but he's thirsty now."

"I think Jesse has some lemonade," said Moira. "That should do."

"That sounds like a good choice," Young said, and went farther down the table to secure a bottle of lemonade for Tim.

Watching his guests, Nugent smiled and poured himself another glass of wine.

From his vantage-point under the willow where Szent-Germain had spread the blanket Nugent provided, he watched the Coven gather and talk. With the arrival of Bethune, the activities became more centralized at the table, now that the last guest had arrived. Charis came up to him, her face obscured by her hat, and took a second or two to study Szent-Germain, who was lying down on the blanket, his attention on the leaves above his head. To his surprise she asked, "Will I feel any different than I do now? After the sixth time?"

"Not immediately, no," he answered, sitting up to look at her. "But the requirements, later on, will impose some adjustments."

He saw her fretful expression. "You probably won't have to deal with it for a decade or two."

"And what will I be like then?"

His dark eyes glowed with compassion. "That is a matter for you and circumstances to determine. There is no set persona for a vampire, any more than there are those for the living."

"You mean, it depends on when I pass on, and how, I guess. Only I won't pass on, will I? I'll be somewhere between life and death. I understand that. You've told me the basics: line the soles of my shoes with my native earth, stay out of direct sunlight whenever possible, avoid running water in all its forms, including currents and tides, try not to travel by airplane. Fire can kill me, anything that breaks the spine above the heart can kill us," she said, making a recital of it. "I still have questions."

"Indeed," he said, lying back down as she started off toward the tables.

Jesse had opened another four bottles of wine, and was handing out more bottles of beer. "Those of you wanting blankets, now's a good time to get them," he said, nodding to where Szent-Germain sat in the shade of the willow tree. "The Grof's got the right idea; find a place that's out of the sun."

"I'll bear that in mind," said Mary Anne as she took one of the blankets. "I'm going down by the pond. There's an old arbor down there, with some grapes growing." She nodded to the others. "I'll be back for food. If anyone would like to join me?"

Pomeroy was taking off his jacket, his face ruddy in the heat. "If you'll wait a minute or two, I'll come with you, Mary Anne. So long as you choose a spot with some shade." He had a somber look about him, and he spoke with caution. "I think we're under observation; there's a black car parked just short of the drive up to this place. It's been there for an hour or so, according to Happy's neighbor—the one with the goats, a quarter mile along on the other side of the road. I spoke to him; he's been watching the car."

"That sounds pretty obvious to me," said McCall. "I'd expect more subtle surveillance."

"I think that's part of the plan, to be conspicuous, so that we'll know they're watching us, that they *can* watch us with impunity," said Pomeroy. "I'd like to be proved wrong."

"That's not the only thing you'd rather be wrong about." Bethune came down the stairs. "Sorry I'm late. Leeland and Rothcoe pulled me in again. I've come directly from the meeting. I asked them why they were harassing us in France, but they claimed not to be. They're just doing their jobs, their assignments, their duty— take your pick."

"Why did they want to question you?" Nugent was coming down the backstairs, bringing a bowl of cheese sauce.

"I don't know. They had a new round of questions for me, most of which I couldn't answer without betraying my canon of ethics, which I suppose they anticipated. It was a stalemate all around."

Mary Anne sighed and sat down on a small, convenient boulder; this would need more than ten minutes, she was sure. "You might as well tell us about it." She peered up at the sun through slitted, shaded eyes, feeling the day had lost some of its shine.

"In that case, how did it go?" Charis asked.

"About the same as last time. They might just want to rattle us. But I have to tell you, I don't trust them. They're after something, and they're being cagey about what it is. I did what I could to keep most of you out of it, but I don't know if it did much good. They might have some new information about us, or they're trying to get us to give in some way." He went and got a bottle of beer from Jesse, holding it carefully so as not to lose any of its contents. "Sorry to tell you this," he went on after taking a swig; he swung around, talking to Bjornson. "I learned one thing: your wife has been talking to the FBI about us. She's trying to make sure that she's doing what they want, so she won't be under suspicion."

Bjornson nodded heavily. "I'm not surprised."

"Is there any chance that you could persuade her to be more circumspect? The less she tells about us, the better." Bethune waited for Bjornson's answer, as did most of the others.

"I doubt she'll listen to me, not after she's made such a point of leaving me in order to return home." Bjornson sighed. "She's skit-

tish, and easily peeved. And that makes her manipulable, by everyone but me."

"But surely she writes to you? She must have mentioned this to
you?" Bethune exclaimed. "Can't you explain this to her?"

"Yes, she sends me monthly letters, and she tells me about the
canasta parties she has attended and what she has won, and if she
liked the leg-of-lamb at Sunday dinner. She's afraid her mail is being opened, and her telephone is tapped." Bjornson was obviously
uncomfortable discussing this so openly. "She's afraid of being de-
nounced as a Communist sympathizer. I can't blame her for that."

"She's probably scared: she won't pay attention to you, even if
you write to her—which I wouldn't recommend," Bethune admitted. "That won't stop the FBI, I'm afraid. It might make them push
harder."

"Would it help if one of us wrote to her on behalf of the Coven?"
Pomeroy volunteered.

"Good Lord, no," said Bjornson. "The greater the distance she
can create between herself and us, the happier she'll be."

There were murmurs of sympathy mixed with grumbles; Bethune abandoned his inquiry of Bjornson for the time being.

Mary Anne and Pomeroy collected a second blanket, then started
down the lawn toward the arbor. As they passed the willow tree
under which Szent-Germain was lying, Mary Anne said, a trifle
too loudly, "I think Bethune is right, and we still have a spy in our
midsts. Someone is passing on information about us."

"Mary Anne, don't fret," Pomeroy said, not wanting to argue
with her.

She glanced over her shoulder, her eyes fixed on Szent-Germain.
"Well, he isn't one of us, is he?" She walked more quickly, her skirts
bouncing as her stride got longer. "What's keeping him from spying on us? He's a foreigner."

From his place in the shadow of the willow, Szent-Germain remained still, as if he were napping. He could not blame any of the
Coven for having doubts about him; Mary Anne was right in saying he was not one of them, no matter how beneficial Eclipse Press

had been for seven of their numbers. He knew he was tolerated more than accepted; given the Coven's situation, he realized anything more would be an unreasonable expectation. Yet it saddened him to be regarded so mistrustfully. His long experience of exile made him especially sympathetic to the Coven's plight. He closed his eyes and waited for Charis to join him.

She walked up to him some ten minutes later, a plate of food in one hand, a glass of wine in the other. "McCall says he's going to London."

"That makes three times since April," said Szent-Germain, opening his eyes and propping himself on one elbow. "Are things looking up for him?"

"Who knows? I think he's looking for a job there; he surely isn't finding one here in France, unless he changes his mind about doing a book for Eclipse," said Charis, bending down to set her plate on the blanket, then hunkering on her heels in order to decide upon a position that would make her comfortable. "Axel Bjornson says his apartment has been bugged again. Steve confirms it, and is planning to get around to check all of us for bugs this next week." Gradually she sat down and put the plate on her thighs.

"I'm pleased to hear he's being so diligent." He shaded his eyes with his free hand. "I'll schedule a check on the print-shop as well. Anything else?" Szent-Germain asked, thinking he would do well to warn Rogers of these developments.

"Well, Elvira believes she's pregnant but hasn't told Jesse." She took a small sip of the white wine in her glass. "She told me shortly after we arrived, when she pulled me aside to talk. I know she's told Willie, and maybe even Mary Anne. I think she wants Jesse to find out from some source other than herself."

"How far along is she?"

"Not very; she's two weeks late with the curse." Charis picked up one of Wilhelmina's deviled eggs and ate half of it.

"Then she might not be pregnant; a miscarriage can throw the cycle off-schedule for some women." Memories of Zilphah and Orazia flitted through his mind, though only one had suffered a miscarriage.

"I don't think that would be any consolation to her," said Charis. "She wants a child and she's ignoring the risks. Jesse wants one more than she does, according to her."

Szent-Germain nodded once. "It's not an easy thing to get over." His eyes were fixed on the middle distance.

"A miscarriage or wanting a child?"

"Either, or both," he answered, and lay back again.

After a short silence while she nibbled at her food, she said, "I'm sorry you can't have any of this. It's pretty good, most of it."

"I'm glad you enjoy it," he said.

Another silence fell between them. Then she said, "How will I explain to Arthur and David, when I've Changed to your life?"

"You'll know better when the time comes," he said, not wanting to remind her yet again that she would have to die before the Change could occur. "It will depend on how old your boys are and how they feel about you when it happens."

"But they'll want some explanation, won't they? After the divorce, becoming like you will be difficult for them to accept, won't it? Worse than divorce, in a way. Who knows how long it will be until they and I meet again? They'll be curious, don't you think?"

"If any of these concerns distresses you, you can still change your mind and limit the risk that comes with revealing the nature of your . . . transformation. I won't hold that against you." He had a brief, intense recollection of Tulsi Kil, and of Gynethe Mehaut.

"But there could still be a risk of Changing, couldn't there?"

"A remote one," he said, then tried to quiet her consternation. "If you do not want to Change, you can order yourself embalmed, and you will die the True Death as surely as if your head were removed or your nervous system were destroyed."

She shivered a little. "That sounds so . . . so final: *head removed, nervous system destroyed.* Those are stark prospects."

"That they are. Bear in mind that once you Change, you will look the way you are when you die for a long time, and in time, as your sons become old men with children and grandchildren of their own, you will seem as young as the day you died. For we age very slowly, and that could make continuing contact with your boys awkward, not just for you—it could be troublesome for Arthur and David."

"I get that." She took up a round of bread with pate spread on it. "Do I have to tell them what I've become?"

"Do you mean a vampire?" he asked, and saw her cringe. "I wouldn't recommend it."

"I don't want to lie to my children," she said, indignation showing in her posture.

"You don't have to explain anything unless they insist, and even then, you may prefer to keep some details to yourself. You may tell them—and it is the truth, by the way—that you have received provisional immortality, or some other such definition. How and why this happened would be your choice to make."

"That's easy for you to say; you don't have children," she observed, and wished in the next second she had not spoken.

"No, I have no children. But I had a ward. She never knew what I am." His voice had dropped, and his enigmatic gaze struck her as deeply as the sight of his scars had done.

"And does she ask you nothing now?"

"She asks me nothing because she is dead," he said, his voice so flat that she felt more appalled than she thought was possible. "She was killed in Munchen more than twenty years ago. There was a large riot—broken windows and vandalized autos—and she was killed. There were others killed and many hurt; she probably hadn't been singled out, but she was still dead." He closed his eyes in a fruitless attempt to shut out the image of the five Brown Shirts who had attacked his ward, probably because she had a Russian accent, if they had any reason at all. He continued, "At least it was over quickly; she didn't have to suffer very long." His thoughts flooded with memories of Laisha Vlassevna, how cruelly she had been killed, and what he had done to her killers in retribution. "They used a rifle-butt to smash her skull."

"You *saw* it?" she asked, trying to imagine what that had meant to him.

"I wasn't near enough to stop it."

Charis finished her wine. "I'm sorry I brought it up. It never occurred to me that you might have been . . . like a parent."

"It surprised me, as well," he said, his tone becoming gentle again.

She moved a little nearer to him, as if consoling him with her presence. "I can't think how you stand it. I shouldn't have brought it up. I'm sorry—but I know I couldn't bear it if anything should happen to my boys."

There was a burst of laughter from the Coven members at the table under the porch, and Elvira shouted over the gaiety, "It won't take that long, it won't." She was moving around the table, sampling bits of what remained of the picnic. Nugent had brought half a dozen folding chairs from the side of the house, and now they were occupied by the Kings, diMaggio, McCall, Bjornson, and Nugent himself, where they were exchanging tales of faculty politics and student misbehavior with a kind of nostalgia that was painful to watch.

Charis did not allow herself to be distracted by the bittersweet jollity. "I . . . I'm sorry."

"So am I," he said, and went on as if unable to stop himself. "She was around thirteen when it happened; she had been orphaned by the Great War, or so it appeared. Whatever questions she may have had about my true nature, she never asked them." That was not quite true: Laisha had challenged him once; his chagrin from that confrontation was still with him; he had told Laisha that he was very old, and she accepted that for the time being, which was all the time they had had together.

Charis set her plate of food aside, her appetite reduced to nothing. "Would you have told her, if she didn't ask?"

"At some point, yes; I would have had to." He thought back to some of the explanations he had rehearsed in his mind but had never ventured to use.

"Do you miss her?" She held up one hand. "That's a foolish question. Of course you do. How could you not?" She drank some of her wine. "Does long life make it easier to bear, does it soften the blow?"

"No, but the passing of time does, or it always has before; I haven't lost anyone so young and so close to me, and it may take longer to release her than some memories."

"You must treasure your memories," she said by way of indirect apology.

"Memories are slippery things. There are decades of my vampire life from when it began that I am not at all certain are as accurate as I want to believe them to be. They are quite offensive, but not as profoundly atrocious as I fear my acts may have been. Who knows how those ancient recollections might have shifted if Rogers weren't with me to keep the memories clear for me." Rogers' predecessor, Aumtehoutep, had not known Szent-Germain until he had walked the earth for more than eleven hundred years, and he had not often challenged Szent-Germain on matters of his past.

She offered him a baffled stare. "How do you mean?"

"Rogers has been with me about half my undead years, and he remembers many things I might have forgotten, or that could shift in my mind, to spare myself the pain and ignominy of some of the things I did long ago—or a few more recent acts, for that matter—things that I cannot recall without distress; I sometimes believe that I have allowed the centuries to ameliorate the horror of what I did so that I can endure to revisit the past without untenable shame. Some capacity for that kind of murderous fury remains within me, whether I want to admit it or not."

"You couldn't have done anything . . . too reprehensible," she said, uncertainty coming over her.

"Why not?" There was something in his conduct—so remote that Charis felt chilled by it—that gave conviction to what he said. "They slaughtered my family, ran my people out of the Carpathians, and enslaved those of my people they were able to capture. It was a harsher time then, and I had not yet learned to honor the brevity of human life."

This time, when he stopped talking, she got up, saying, "I'll just go and have Jesse refill my glass," and did not wait for him to respond before she left him under the willow with only his memories for companions.

> *c/o Gemma McCrorie Literary Agency*
> *Suite 47, DeVere Building*
> *Queen Street at Edmonton Road*
> *Toronto, Ontario CANADA*
> *September 6, 1950*

Dear Saint-Germain,

I was pleased to hear from you last week, and having thought about your present difficulties, I'll now try to answer your questions: I have to admit I hadn't realized how far the current paranoia has spread.

So you have encountered the current zeal of US security: my sympathies. There is a fatal taint of Puritanism in a large portion of the US national character—I sometimes feel a touch of it myself—that sees argument with their position as heresy, and deliberate ignorance as purity. They proclaim their love of the Constitution without comprehending its principles, just as they seek to view the document as Christian Holy Writ, ignoring the First Amendment's provision regarding freedom of religion, and its reaffirmation in the decisions of the Supreme Court— off the top of my head I can't recall which decisions are crucial—which do not permit the establishing any state religion, and which also prohibit any religious test being a requirement for holding public office.

It is those links to Puritanism that present an opponent as a devil, not just a military or political adversary. As the Puritans justified hanging upstart women for being witches, so now the government uses the specter of

Communism to justify the expulsion of those whose opinions do not march with the majority of their countrymen. Not that most know anything more than the demonic interpretation of Communism. They have no knowledge of Marx's theories, and refuse to explore them for fear of contamination. They believe that Communism is soul-numbing, godless, and dehumanizing but that it is so highly contagious that anyone even remotely connected to it is in danger of being seduced by it. It pains me to speak so about US citizens, having been one myself, but it is apparent that they have been frightened into embracing the exaggerations and mythologies the so-called Right has been spreading since before the war ended.

You're correct, of course; I have had a few run-ins with the security division of the government, in my own name. As an overseas reporter, I was exposed to certain workings of the security agencies, and was put on a watch-list for endorsing some of the actions of the French Left, which in turn propelled me into other sorts of writing. No more reportage. T. J. Emmerson didn't come into being until I Changed during the war, and, as you know, T. J. Emmerson is a Canadian. Because James Emmerson Tree was "known" to have perished in France while covering the fighting for the Detroit Free Press, I had few options about returning. So rather than practice journalism, I now write juvenile adventures, and live a very quiet life here in Toronto. In this regard, I was most fortunate to have your good tutelage at Montalia, and although at the time I was let down by Madelaine's absence, I believe that the intervening eight years have brought me into a greater appreciation for what this Change has wrought in me, and what I will need to do to preserve myself from close scrutiny, which in these days of photography and fingerprints, is not readily avoidable.

If the foregoing seems too prejudiced to you, I ask you to wait another year before discounting my opinions. I believe you will find that the fear I mentioned is insidious as well as deplorable, and that you will need to be inclined to be cautious as well as alert.

Sincere good wishes,
T. J. Emmerson

❖ 6 ❖

LYDELL BROADSTREET's desk was laden with files, all conspicuously stamped SECRET in red ink, which, harried as he was, he regarded with pride, and a niggle of dismay. The last few weeks had seen a step-up in activity concerning the Ex-Pats' Coven in France, and all the efforts were starting to show how much his dedication had accomplished. Perhaps he was finally being given the credit he had earned in singling out this group for increased surveillance. He decided that it was a favorable omen to have submitted all his project summaries on the Equinox, two days in the past, for that would mean equal weight would be given to what he predicted was coming with what had already happened, which would give him six months to prove his case. And he knew he would need those six months. There was so much to *explain*, so much to *account for*. He raked his fingers through his light-blond hair, as if he could dredge up a solution from his brain through such action. He had, he reminded himself, delivered four large binders to Deputy Director Manfred Channing's home a little before nine P.M on the Autumnal Equinox, filled with information about Ex-Pats' Coven friends and relatives still living in the US, with recommendations as to how these connections could be used to Agency advantage. Then he had almost held his breath for a full day, but when no complaint was forthcoming, and no rescinding of his orders, Broadstreet felt the first, timid thrill of success. The completion of that phase of the project marked one conclusive event with another—one political, one astronomical—and though he still had an hour's work to finish up, he allowed himself the luxury of putting his feet up while he drank his coffee. It was a cool evening with the threat of rain in the air, the sky scumbled with leaden clouds, their lowering underbellies lit up by the lume of the city. He allowed himself ten minutes to luxuriate in the glow of his success.

There was a tap on his door, and before he could rise to open it, one of the night patrolmen came into his office, a flashlight in one hand, the other resting on his holster. "Working late again, I see."

"Just doing my job, like you," said Broadstreet with a modesty he did not feel; he glanced at his watch. "Nine-forty-eight," he said. "I won't stay much longer; probably about an hour or so." He had already decided to leave at eleven, but he wanted to know if the Guard would be here longer than he would.

"I'll be gone by then," the Guard said. "Shift change at ten."

"That's coming up fast," Broadstreet said. "And it's important that I get back to my reports. Thanks for checking on me. Who knows who might have been in here?"

"Well, you keep at it. And call down to the Guard Station when you're ready to leave; they'll tell you which door to use to get out." The Guard rubbed the stubble on his face. "You parked in the lot?"

"In Lot B, yes," said Broadstreet.

"I'll ask them to try to set up the north door, but it may have to be the east one: the cleaning crew is doing the floor in the north lobby." With that, the Guard touched the brim of his peaked cap, and stepped back into Broadstreet's outer office. Three seconds later, the outer door slammed.

What sort of omen was that? Broadstreet wondered when he was certain the patrolman had gone. Was he being warned not to be smug about what he had accomplished, or was it not connected to his achievement? But how could that be? To have a night patrolman enter his office without so much as a by-your-leave was unusual, and that stood out alone in his thoughts providing an alert, like a Civil Defense siren. He considered the possibilities as he left and locked his office in order to go thirty feet down the hallway to the men's room. He used the toilet, then threw cold water on his face and wiped it away with two stiff paper towels, all the while telling himself to calm down. "It's going to work. It's going to work," he muttered to his reflection, telling himself as he did that this room surely was not bugged. "It's going to work."

When he got back to his office, he was astonished to discover the door unlocked and Opal Pierce seated behind her desk, rolling a sheet of paper into the typewriter. "Missus Pierce," he said as if her being here were the most natural thing in the world. "How good of you to work late. I hadn't expected you." He wanted to know why she was here, but thought it was better if she volunteered the information than he demanded it.

"Oh, Mister Broadstreet, I didn't realize you were still in the building," she said in adorable, fallacious confusion, concealing her disappointment that he was here at all. Her smile was quick, with just enough seductive charm to ensure his attention. "I have about an hour's work I didn't finish earlier, and as this was on my way home, I thought I might as well . . ." She shrugged as her explanation fizzled. "So here I am." And now that he had seen her, she would need to spend some time on completing her assignment so he could see her do it.

He had noticed that she was dressed for a night out, in an evening suit of emerald-green peau-de-cygne with a high neck-line and an elaborate lace jabot to set off her face; she was wearing scent, something delicious and disturbing, and her mouth was painted deep-red. "You didn't have to do this," he told her, trying to decide if it would be proper to close the hall door with the two of them alone in the office together.

The strikers clacked on the paper. "But I do. I thought you were aware of the report I haven't completed; I'm sure I mentioned it to you. I don't want to leave you hanging because I lacked determination. This way, you won't have to be responsible for my error." She stopped typing long enough to pat her steno pad, just now open to a page that was filled with her meticulous shorthand. "I've had this on my mind all evening; I couldn't pay attention to the concert at all."

He felt himself nonplused. "I appreciate you doing this, Missus Pierce, but it isn't necessary that you . . . extend yourself in this way. You certainly didn't have to abandon your seat for the chamber music festival." He recalled vaguely that she had mentioned her anticipation of delight at an evening of Bach and Handel; it all seemed a little outre to him, too fussy and high-brow. Give him Louis Armstrong or the Dorsey Brothers any day, or Gershwin. He liked Gershwin—but he supposed it was a matter of taste. "I know how much you enjoy it." He was glad to see her, but she was a distraction, or perhaps an omen of ambiguous meaning. To have her so near, in the implied intimacy of night, engaged his fantasies much more than she did when she was working by the full light of day.

She finished typing the heading. "I promise I won't bother you while you work. Only you need to get this in to Deputy Director Channing before tomorrow night, and you'll need me to do it tonight if that's going to happen." All through the afternoon she had struggled to leave a small amount of work incomplete so that she could account for her presence in Broadstreet's office tonight; she had estimated to Channing that it would take a week to accustom Broadstreet to her after-hours presence; she wanted Broadstreet to go home, so she could do what Channing had charged her to do: slip two memos into specific SECRET flies among those stacked on Broadstreet's desk. She disliked working for Broadstreet, and this assignment was beginning to rankle, so the sooner she could accomplish this, the better. With any luck she would be out of here in under a month—two or three at the most. She had a brief moment to consider what Channing was doing to Broadstreet, but any compassion she might feel toward Broadstreet faded when she recalled his selfish clumsiness the first two times he tried to kiss her—the third time she let him, and that told her more than she wanted to know about him.

"I . . . I'm grateful. You don't have to do this," he said, more out of good manners than belief. "I was planning to work until eleven, but don't let that—"

"I have to get home before then," she said, and put him at something that was almost ease. "So I should get to work." And she would have to slip in the memos at another time, an aggravating thought.

He coughed diplomatically. "So must I. You'll want me to inform the Guard when you're ready to leave. I'll be in my office if you need anything." With that, he turned on his heel and went into the large, inner office, and sat down, staring at the stack of files, but trying to keep the image of Opal Pierce from his mind.

Twenty minutes later, while he fretted over how to show links and connections from known Communists with members of the Ex-Pats' Coven, he looked up at the dark windows, clapping his hand over his mouth to keep from shouting. "*Baxter!* That's it. Baxter." Baxter was clearly the solution to this coil; now he would have to decide how to go about bringing him into it. He wondered vaguely why he had not thought of Baxter before, but did not linger on that question as he considered the possibilities Baxter provided. Baxter could be invaluable if Broadstreet worked him right. He would come up with a trail that would lead from one of the Coven members—Hapgood Nugent would be a good choice, considering that Nugent's brother-in-law would help out—to suspected Communists in the US. He sat very still, weighing the omens, then he squinted his eyes and nodded. It would work. It had to work.

Goaded into action, he took his notepad and fountain-pen, and began to work out how he might construct a link from . . . which of the Coven members: that was the problem, he realized. Nugent was his choice, but mightn't Axel Bjornson be better? Or Charis Treat? Or Mary Anne Triding? Not Winston Pomeroy: he had a couple of good connections who might object, both of them in strong positions in the judiciary, including some kind of cousin newly appointed to the Ninth Circuit Court of Appeals—who could cause trouble, just as Russell McCall could, if he found an editor to back him. It would have to be one of the solos, anyway, that obviously was necessary. Stephen diMaggio, then? Probably not: his use to the Coven was very limited and specific. Same thing with Washington Young. He couldn't use Bethune, either; this wasn't the kind of game you played with a lawyer if you could avoid it. It might be best to look at the US families of the Coven members again, and work that angle. He could feel his mind racing, and he tried to jot down enough of what sped through his brain so that he could work it into a sensible plan, and quickly.

Fifteen minutes later, Missus Pierce rapped on the door. "Mister Broadstreet? The report is done, and I'll drop it off for Mister Channing, if you like. I'm leaving. I've cleared myself with the Guard and will be going out through the north door. See you in the morning."

Broadstreet looked up from the litter he had spread on his desk; he was glad now that he had closed the door between their offices, for he would not want anyone to see what he was working on. "Thank you for working late, Missus Pierce." He thought he should say something more, something that would show her that he valued her. "I appreciate your dedication. See you in the morning. Oh, and I may be out tomorrow afternoon," he added. "I'll phone in where I can be contacted. But that's for later."

"I gather it's important," she said, hoping to lure him into explaining to her.

"I'll know more tomorrow evening, when the meeting is over," he said. "It may be the break I've been looking for." He had stumbled upon a possible tie-in between Hapgood Nugent's sister and Szent-Germain's publishing company in Amsterdam; on one of her madcap rambles through Europe, she had kept a journal, which Eclipse Press had published for the American market with some success. If that was too flimsy, he could cobble together a tie-in with Baxter. He frowned as he reminded himself that he needed to find a Social Security number for Baxter, or Channing would have more questions to ask.

"Then I hope it pans out," she said, eager to leave.

"Thank you, Missus Pierce," he told her, for once wanting to get to his work more than he wanted to talk to her. "Good night, then."

"Good night," she said, and went away.

Broadstreet looked at the clock and tried to make up his mind if he should call the Guard Station and tell them he would be leaving later than he anticipated, and decided against it. He would book a call to Phil Rothcoe on his way out; the night desk would do it for him. He needed to get some absolutely current information, and Rothcoe should have it. He picked up his pad of paper, shoved it in his briefcase, closed his pen, and made a cursory effort at stacking up all the material he had strewn across his desk, making it look much more organized than it was. He turned off his desk-lamp. After ringing the Guard Station and announcing he was on the way out in ten minutes, he sighed. This was going to be a real drag to get through, but once it was over, he would have a much stronger position in the Agency, and would be in line for a promotion. He gathered up his hat and coat, turned out the lights, and locked his office, checking twice to be sure the door was secure. He then locked the outer office and trod off to the elevators to get down to the main floor.

"Telephone call to France," he said, handing a request form to the clerk on the night desk. "Ten-forty A.M., local time for me. It won't be too late in France then, and I won't have to get up at the crack of dawn, hoping to catch him before lunch."

"Ten-forty, to France for L. Broadstreet," said the clerk, dutifully entering it in the master-schedule. "Got it."

"Thanks," said Broadstreet, and hurried off toward the eastern lobby to be let out into the blustery streets, his mind already working out plots and possibilities for shoring up his investigation.

Driving home, Broadstreet decided he would have to get some more anonymous paper for the Baxter note he planned to compose. And pens that were untraceable: the sleuths in the analysis unit of the CIA could find out amazing things from pens and paper. So he would have to have an excuse to be out of town for a day or two. That would mean a drive of some distance, which he could tie into making contact with Baxter. He wanted to choose another location for the event, one he had not used before. He would have to take a look at his road atlas at home, and work out a route he could take that would not suggest he was trying to cover his tracks. There had to be someone he could visit, or an event he could attend. He continued to mull over the possibilities as a mist gathered more closely along the road. So preoccupied with these plans was he that he paid no attention to the blue Nash that followed him, two cars back, all the way home; only when Broadstreet was locked in for the night, the two FBI agents found a telephone and reported back to their superiors, telling the night-clerk that Broadstreet had made no stops going home and was in for the night. They were allowed to call it a night, since Broadstreet was known to be a heavy sleeper.

Missus Pierce was at her desk when Broadstreet approached his office the next morning; she was in a neat dress—fashionable but not daring—that showed her figure to advantage; it was made of rayon so it was nearly as clingy as silk, and the color, a very sub-dued persimmony orange that hinted at banked fires, comple-mented her hair and her slightly olive skin tone, and reflected the fading summer. Her scent was lighter than what she had worn the night before, but Broadstreet noticed it anyway, and smiled appre-ciatively. "Good morning, Missus Pierce. I know I'm a little late, but it is in a good cause. I'll tell you all about it this afternoon."

"You don't have to explain any of this to me," she said, offering him another tantalizing smile.

He paid no attention to her remark, fixing his attention on a place just above her head so he would not be distracted by her mes-merizing presence. "I'll be talking to one of our people in Paris this morning, at ten-forty, and that should provide a crucial piece of the puzzle—that is, if I have reason to sum up all these disparate fac-tors in the way I think they should be viewed, so that the treachery is visible and not hidden in a number of—" He realized he was blathering, and made himself stop; clearing his throat, he went on, "I'll ask you to go on your coffee-break while I make the call; it needs to be private." He grinned, and held up his briefcase. "It's taken months to follow all the ins and outs of this investigation. Finally my work is paying off."

"That's good news," said Pierce, intending to pass this informa-tion on to Channing while on her coffee-break. She smiled as she caught sight of two little iodine spots on his jaw, where he had cut himself shaving that morning. "I put the report I completed last night in Mister Channing's delivery box before I went home, so he should be in line with your progress first thing today." She man-aged a supportive smile.

"Yes; you said you would," he said, and then decided to add, "Thank you for that." He waited for her to speak, then added, "I'm most grateful."

"All part of my duties, Mister Broadstreet," she said.

"Um," said Broadstreet, pulling his office-door key from his pocket. "I'll be available for calls until ten-twenty," he said, want-ing to get away from her, and the power she had to command his attention.

"Ten-twenty," Pierce said, and gave a sigh of relief when Broad-street entered his office, leaving her to her current chores, which required very little concentration; she rolled paper into her type-writer and filled in the first three lines of the form in front of her while she did her best to work out what Broadstreet was up to, all the while puzzling over his uncharacteristic exuberance that had marked him this morning. She had to decide what she would tell Channing. It would probably be best to wait until Broadstreet had made his call to Paris, for then she could describe to Channing how Broadstreet reacted to the call, and how much he was willing to tell her of his plans. She had a new envelope purse with her, in good leather, dyed a rich walnut-brown, and matching her shoes, she thought, and he had hardly noticed. She was only slightly aware that Broadstreet could not stop staring at her.

It was going to be an important day—every omen confirmed it. He leaned on the door for a few seconds, trying to gather his thoughts for his coming talk with Rothcoe. To his astonishment, he was shaking. He made himself breathe slowly, and repeated softly, "it's going to work, it's going to work, it's going to work," as he made his way to his desk and sat down, opening his briefcase as he did. He pulled out five files and placed them at various intervals in the stacks he had already made. No one would notice that there were five files with their spines to the right rather than the left, he promised himself as he looked at the clock on the wall. "Nine-fifty-two," he murmured, and tried to make up his mind how he would spend the next half-hour. At last he pulled his personal note-book out of the briefcase and began to review his plan for the next week. He took time to try to decide how long it would take him to bring about the results he was seeking. Ideally, it would not require more than a few days, but he knew that was an unrealistic goal. As much as he liked to believe that it could be accomplished quickly, and that he would have all the weight of the Agency behind him, he knew that was not going to happen. Under the current con-straints of his position, he would have to be willing to go slowly, so as not to exceed his authority, and to be sure that no informa-tion leaked before he wanted it to.

A tap on the door pulled him out of his musing. "Yes?"

"Your coffee," said Opal Pierce.

"Oh, yes. Bring it in. Please." He sat up and folded his hands on top of the files he needed the most. "Very good. Thank you, Missus Pierce."

Making no effort to be convincing, she said, "My pleasure." She set the cup-and-saucer down on the clear space next to his lamp, and was about to leave when Broadstreet spoke again.

"You're very helpful, Missus Pierce. I should thank you more often than I do, but it is true."

"It's part of my job to be helpful," said Pierce, adjusting her stance so that her dress made her bust glow like ripe fruit; she saw the flare of lust in his eyes that she knew he did not recognize for what it was. "If there's anything more you need, Mister Broadstreet?" she asked with a deferent smile.

"Nothing just now. Probably later."

"I'll do my best," she assured him.

"And you do it excellently," said Broadstreet, handing her a dollar. "For the coffee. Keep the change."

She wanted so much to slap his face for that casual, smug gesture that put her on the par with a servant, but she swallowed hard and said, "Thank you," before she hastened out of his office, closing the door between them with more than usual force.

Broadstreet was too preoccupied thinking about his call to Rothcoe to notice that Pierce was upset. He slipped his notebook out of his briefcase and went over the points he wanted to discuss with Rothcoe. It would not do to falter in his conversation, given what he would be asking. He would destroy these notes later, of course, but just now he found it deeply reassuring, a vindication of all his plans. He sat back and drank a little of the coffee Pierce had brought him, thinking about the non-fraternization policy that would frown upon an open flirtation with his attractive secretary; he would have to find a way to work around those strictures, but that could be an intriguing challenge in itself. He drank more coffee, considering the omens he had observed that morning, and so far felt that the tide was with him. He picked up the receiver of his telephone and dialed for the international operator, then gave her his name, and the number in Paris he wanted to reach. It was tempting to mention how important the call was, but he kept that to himself: there would be plenty of time for boasting later on, when he had resolved the case and received his recognition. He listened to the telephone ring.

"A call for Philetus Rothcoe," said the operator as soon as the ring was answered.

"I'm Rothcoe. I'm expecting a call from Lydell Broadstreet."

"I have your party," said the operator. "Go ahead, Mister Broadstreet," she told him before she clicked off.

There was a brief silence, then Broadstreet said, "How's it going in Paris, you lucky stiff?"

"Well enough," said Rothcoe carefully. "The Gendarmes picked up another Nazi camp guard a couple days ago, small fry, really, but he knows where some of the big fish have gone."

"Is a prosecution likely?" Broadstreet asked, although he was not much interested.

"Depends on how many survivors there are who can identify him, and how willing they are to testify," said Rothcoe. "For now, it's hurry up and wait."

"Well, even if you're marking time, what a great place to do it," said Broadstreet with false enthusiasm. "How are matters going with the Coven?" He could hear Rothcoe's cigarette lighter flare on, and a second later, Rothcoe's long exhale. "I ask, because I think I may have found an interesting link among the members, and I'd like your insights on that group. Their dynamics are a little . . . confusing from here."

"You mean dynamics beyond being virtual exiles?" Rothcoe asked. "They're academics: there's bound to be some connections. That world's a pretty exclusive club, even now."

"No, more than that," said Broadstreet, reminding himself not to plunge into his case right off the bat. "I think I may have found the underlying—"

"About half of them publish through Eclipse Press," Rothcoe interrupted deliberately. "They have that in common."

"That's not what I mean," said Broadstreet, knowing he was being needled and growing testy because of it. "This is something that goes back a while, to the Thirties, when Szent-Germain was in America." He let this sink in. "You didn't know about that, did you?"

"No," said Rothcoe. "I can't say that I did. Tell me more."

"It's a little strange, but I believe I may have found the way in which these people may all be attached as more than Communist-sympathizing university instructors." He paused long enough to let Rothcoe think about it. "It began when the Spanish government seized Szent-Germain's aircraft-manufacturing business. It seems they left his trading company intact—probably not big or strategic enough to worry about."

"When was this?" Rothcoe asked, sounding impatient.

"Back in the Thirties." He glanced at his notepad though he had memorized the information several days since. "He vanished from Spain around the end of June in 1936."

"That's fourteen years ago. He must have been just a little more than a kid," Rothco remarked, then his tone changed. "You needn't remind me that the men who took Omaha Beach were little more than kids, too, for the most part."

"All of them were kids, but the officers," said Broadstreet, pleased that Rothcoe saw the importance on his own, and needed no careful leading. "But, as I said, he vanished from Spain, by which I mean *poof!* No one in his airplane company knew what had happened, except that his business affairs were all in order. And no one in his trading company had any knowledge of him. His manservant was seen—perhaps—the day that the Spanish Civil War began, but no one can confirm it, so that leads nowhere. The next place he crops up is in Boston, and it turns out someone has set a hired killer on him, although who or why, I have yet to find out." He could feel Rothcoe wrestling mentally with this knowledge, and he paused to light up his pipe. "So you see, there are factors here neither of us have considered. I believe that if Szent-Germain were gotten rid of—very discreetly this time; nothing like those two thugs you hired to discourage him from helping the Ex-Pats' Coven—we could tidy up that organization without fuss. And we could find out where D. G. Atkins is without resorting to . . . intrusive tactics to do it."

"The report on what he has done for refugees and displaced persons is truly admirable," said Rothcoe uneasily. "Why should we repay his generosity and care so . . . ?"

"Shabbily?" Broadstreet suggested. "What if all those so-called good works of his are only a smokescreen, to keep governments from asking the very things you are asking me? He is a very crafty fellow, this Grof Szent-Germain, if he is a Grof at all."

"He's got some kind of title, that's certain," said Rothcoe, wanting to be able to demonstrate his knowledge of the man. "The family has been in Romania and Hungary for centuries, and not one of the present generation has spoken out against this man. They defer to him."

Unwilling to concede the point, Broadstreet said, "Well, considering the chaos in Eastern Europe generally, and the hostilities in the Carpathians in particular, all manner of rag-tag opportunists may claim a noble ancestor or two. Have you sent anyone to question the family? I should have thought that would be first thing on your list."

"No, we haven't done that; we're not allowed to," said Rothcoe, sounding a bit morose. "If you have nothing against Szent-Germain you can prove, present it to Channing. I think it would be wise to be rid of him, but I lack the means to make an accusation stick." He cleared his throat. "I know you have strong opinions about Szent-Germain, but unless you have facts to back you up . . . This part of the CIA has to operate on demonstrable evidence or we will shortly be unable to function at all. Innuendo may work to discourage Communists at home, but here in Europe we are obliged to proceed on proof."

"And you never bend the rules, do you?" Broadstreet asked, his smile worthy of a bad-tempered alligator.

"Of course not," said Rothcoe, a shade too quickly; he took a long, steadying breath and went on, doing his best to sound calm.

"Tell me what you'd like to know about Szent-Germain and I'll do what I can to authenticate the charges against him. Until you can do this, it would be a good idea if you don't let—" He stopped abruptly. "The assassin sent after Szent-Germain to America might not be an isolated incident."

Broadstreet sat up slowly, his pipe clutched in his teeth. "Are you suggesting anything?" he demanded quietly.

"No. I'm warning you," said Rothcoe.

"Don't get caught. I realize that," said Broadstreet.

"No. Don't do anything at all." Rothcoe's voice was more urgent. "Stay away from Szent-Germain."

Broadstreet chuckled. "I wasn't planning on involving you," said Broadstreet and hung up, savoring his sense of accomplishment; he pulled out his notebook and began to check off points in preparation for the next phase of his plan.

24 September, 1950

L. G. Broadstreet
P.O. Box 251
Madison Station
Baltimore, Maryland, USA

Dear Mister Broadstreet,
I heard you're looking for a man with my talents, and I was wondering when you would get around to me. It sounds like the sort of job I wouldn't mind doing. One event, a Jaguar XK120, in a public street. A pity to destroy such a handsome auto, but you say it can't be helped. The cost would be $20,000 up front, in cash, delivery of which we will arrange if we have a deal. I will also require a round-trip airplane ticket from Mexico City to Brussels and back, for the week of 3 December or 10 December, whichever is more convenient to you, so that I may acquaint myself with the target, and then one round trip for the middle of February, a four-day trip, preferably beginning on a Sunday. I will arrange my housing, and I will add the price of it to the second installment of your payment, $30,000 in cash within ten days of the completion of the event. Failure to deliver the full amount would result in my turning over all evidence I am able to supply to the American Embassy in Paris, where I am sure there will be someone who will find it most interesting. I will be out of France by then, and not easily located, so do not suppose you will be able to turn me in to avoid payment. I do not haggle about

price, nor the terms of delivery, so I will expect nothing more than your acceptance of terms and payments as scheduled, or I will arrange a demonstration for you that will teach you the error of your ways, however briefly.

The event you are seeking to accomplish will occur on or before the end of next February, or you will owe me nothing more than the initial payment of $20,000, and I will account for my failure in a letter, which it would be wise not to keep. You state you would prefer I use American components to encourage the authorities to search out Americans as primary suspects. You do not need to inform me why you ask for this—far be it from me to discourage business—but I draw the line at planting socalled evidence of any kind. I prefer to use components from the place the event is supposed to take place. I have connections for such materiel as I will require in Paris, the cost of which will be added to the final payment.

I will expect to hear from you before 8 October; if I have nothing from you by then, I will assume the project you propose has been delayed or canceled.

> I have the honor to be
> At your service,
> Jimmy Riggs O'Hanraghan

Part Four

❖ ❖ ❖

RAGOCZY FERENZ
GROF SZENT-GERMAIN

1 October, 1950

Robert E. Price, Attorney-at-Law
Makepeace, Taylor, van Amzel, and Price
748 Chandler Court
Suite 3G
Philadelphia, Pennsylvania, USA

Dear Bob,

Let me begin by apologizing for putting you in an awkward situation again, but I know this is not the sort of thing any of us would want outside the family. It may not be possible to keep some of what I hope you'll do for me—for Tim, actually—from becoming known, but not as a scandal. Yet I can understand if you feel I must retain other counsel for this matter. I come to you, Cousin, rather than Uncle Owen, because you are more sympathetic to Tim's and my situation than many of our relations are. I've never heard you condemn me for my opinions, or believed the gossip that so many of our other relatives have taken as gospel, for which I am truly grateful. You've been helpful to me and to Tim before, so I come to you as the most likely person to be willing to assist us this time. I am still glad that you were able to find a college that will take Regina when the time comes, and although Oregon is a long way from Paris, she wants to do undergraduate work at home, and you are the one who made it possible. It lessens the burdens we have at present, which is above-and-beyond a cousin's familial duty. So, naturally, I'm going to add to our indebtedness to you. I trust you will understand my reasons.

As I mentioned last month, Tim's condition is continuing to deteriorate, and the doctors here tell us that there still is much to be done to slow it down, if I can afford it. As a US citizen, I am likely to have to pay for some or all of his treatment. I have been in touch with a clinic in Switzerland that has made some progress in cases like Tim's, but the results are uncertain and the costs are far beyond our means. If I had the money from our grandfather's trust, we might be able to buy him six months of treatment before we ran out of rent money, so I'm not going to ask you for anything so potentially divisive, but I am going to ask you to see if there is any way for him to collect on any of his veteran's benefits, or other possible benefits we haven't considered. His family has washed their hands of him since his first questions from the FBI, so now I am faced with a predicament that I cannot extricate myself on my own, as things stand now. The last time you mentioned this, you said the red tape was endless and that I should prepare a report for you on the state of Tim's health and how he got that way. Tim refused, but now he has reached a state where he cannot comprehend anything that he cannot see or touch or taste. His vocabulary is minimal, and he is very reluctant to see anyone other than me and Washington Young, who has been kind enough to help me with all the chores that come with a disabled husband. I think I've mentioned Wash to you: he's one of the Coven—in fact, he's the one who puts out The Grimoire *four times a year. I don't know if I've mentioned that he's a colored man whose family is in St. Louis. He has been a printer for more than twenty years, and has kept Tim and me in food more than once. I don't know what I'd do without him. Tim would certainly be a lot worse off than he is now if Wash Young weren't willing to help out.*

We aren't paupers—I don't want you to think that we are. My practice covers most of our expenses, including the rent, most of the time, and for the most part, we're as comfortable as it is possible for us to be, but I am aware that those times are ending, and Tim is going to need more, either in treatment or simple maintenance, and that has me very troubled. I still have over thirty thousand in my savings account; not a vast amount, but better than what most people have, and I haven't touched the money from Great Aunt Clodette. The firm you recommended has managed the money well, but as little as I want to admit it, I'm going to need the money, and I know there will be obstacles to achieving that, which is why I am hoping you will find some way to shake the money out of that account and transfer it to me here without too much interference from the government, so that I can continue to take care of Tim without being crushed by the rising costs of his care.

And with Regina at a good girls' school in England now, I'll have those expenses to meet as well. I am willing to pay for her education, especially away from the acrimonious tenor of schools in the US; it would be most unkind to thrust Regina into the midst of the increasing intolerance of political dissidence in America. While he could still do it, Tim set up an education fund for Regina, and she is going to be able to do two years at Saint-Catherine's without having to scrape and scratch; she lives in at the school; there are several girls who do. Truth to tell, Regina is glad to be away from us, and not just because she's just turned sixteen: Tim's continuing problems upset her very much, and she is inclined to view what is happening as grotesque and just more of the same kind of misfortune that has followed us since the accusations against Tim began. She's a Daddy's Girl, and she is very much aware of how Tim was hailed as a hero in the war, as we all are, and she feels that the government has cheated him out of the rewards he had earned. I understand her feelings and I sympathize with her, yet I know she will manage better away from us just now. I would like to think that Regina will emerge from this relatively unscathed.

It's not my intention to load you up with good deeds to do; I'm prepared to pay you the going rate for your services, particularly if I can get my hands on some of my money. I do realize that once it is gone, it is gone, and that cannot be changed. I'm not expecting any special consideration just because we're cousins. Writing that last, I realized it's not true. I am expecting you to understand my predicament and to be willing to put up with being questioned by the Committee, or Hoover's Hounds, in order to help me out. That may be unkind of me, but I look at Tim and there is so little I can do for him, and without Wash Young, I wouldn't be able to manage the things he does for Tim. Much as I would like to, I can't pick Tim up and carry him to his wheelchair, or the bathtub, or his chaise in the garden. Those sound like minor things, but you *must believe me when I tell you they are not minor at all. Tim is probably not going to last much longer—two years at most, his doctors say—and I don't want him to have to face them as a bedded invalid.*

After Tim is gone—and it is unrealistic not to be prepared for his death—I will probably remain here in Paris for a year or two at least, longer if conditions at home warrant it. I've learned to like this place, and how to get along with the French. I'll have the house, and my practice, and I don't want to try to survive in the US as long as my reputation is smirched. I don't want the Committee to subpoena my patients and question them on how much Marxism I work in with my psychology. You recall they did that when I was practicing in Silver Springs. I would not want to be party to such a lapse in ethics—exposing my clients to more stress than what drove them to me in the first place—not even the guilt-by-association way I would be in a case like that. Just thinking about it distresses me. There are times I worry about that here, since most of my patients are American or Canadian, and I have warned them that they may be approached by governmental investigators when they return to the US. A few have decided to find another therapist, so even here, worry about matters of sustenance, and what I learn from my patients make it clear to me that I am not being paranoid about my situation. So I will be here until I can be confident that I can do my job properly in the US, without government interference or the FBI pestering my patients. On the other hand, I would not object if you and Jeanne wanted to come for a visit and a vacation. I may not be a friendly native guide, but I've learned my way around—I've had to. Regina's room is available if you would like to stay here, but if not, there is a very good small hotel two blocks away, and a more than acceptable four-star restaurant in the same block. It would be a pleasure to see you again. It's been much too long, and caring for Tim has taught me that time slips away from us much faster than any of us realizes.

Will you please give my warm regards to Jeanne, and to Howard and Dorothy, and to your mother, if she'll allow you to mention my name? I think of all of you often, and I look forward to the time when all this unpleasantness is behind us. I'm assuming you and Jeanne still spend Sundays with your mother, and may run into other relatives there. If you have the opportunity, I'd appreciate it if you would bring them up-to-

date on Tim's condition; I only wish the news were better. I know you'll handle all of this as diplomatically as possible, and I thank you for all you're doing for us here in Europe.

Your loving cousin,
Moira Frost

P.S.
If your mother wants to tell the story of how she and Uncle Harry met in Social Studies class in the ninth grade and were sweethearts for forty-one years, let her. I thought I had heard it enough to last me a lifetime, but I was wrong. I wish I could hear it again. It's funny, the things you miss. This is one of them.

❖ 1 ❖

"So what do you think of Samuel Effering?" Axel Bjornson asked Winston Pomeroy as they sat hunched over the right angle at the end of the bar at Chez Rosalie, an open bottle of decent Burgundy between them; both of their glasses were nearly empty; the bottle was slightly more than half-full. It was getting on toward sundown, and although it was not yet seventeen hundred hours, it felt as if night were already upon them; masses of dark clouds hovered in the sky, waiting for an opportunity to rain, eerie beams of sunlight sliding under the clouds to lend a wan, yellow light to the end of the day. Regular customers would not arrive until later, which gave the two men the privacy they sought; the bar portion of the restaurant was all but empty but for these two, Dudon himself being occupied in the kitchen with preparations for the evening meals, and Olivier, the taciturn bartender, was not due for another half-hour.

"It's a hell of a name to go through high school with," Pomeroy quipped.

"No doubt," Axel said without a trace of humor. "It's just the kind of name that kids can turn to all kinds of objectionable phrases." He finished the wine in his glass. "Do you think he's legitimate? How does he appear to you?"

"He sounds like most of our members," said Pomeroy somberly after a thoughtful silence. "I think he's in a pretty bad mess, just like the rest of us."

"But is he credible? Does his story hold up? Well?" Bjornson propped his elbow on the bar. "We can't have another spy in our Coven. So you tell me—do we let him join or not?"

"What do I think about the good Doctor Effering?" Pomeroy asked back, as if they had anything else to discuss at this meeting. "Well, Praeger and Mary Anne both vouch for him, and that's reassuring. Mary Anne knows him by reputation, which I'd expect of her. But I don't like to think of us closing ranks automatically. There might be something we're missing. I'd like to get the Grof's take on him, but he's out of town just now, I think: travels a lot, Szent-Germain does. He's supposed to be back tonight."

"Why consult him? He isn't one of us."

Pomeroy snapped his fingers. "That's my point. He can study Effering without bias. He's an outsider and that makes him aware of things we might not notice."

"Because we're all academics," said Bjornson as if pronouncing sentence on a miscreant.

"Yes. Because of that. Oh, I'm convinced that Effering is one of us that way, but we don't know whether what he's given us here"—he patted the binder containing Effering's CV—"is biography or legend."

"We don't know what to ask him. None of us is a physician, let alone a virologist. I wish we had someone who could vet him on his medical skills." Bjornson sighed and stood up. "Very specialized field, virology."

Pomeroy remained seated. "We can probably get some information for him from his medical school. It should be listed in his CV." Again he patted the three-ring binder on the bar next to him. "Stanford means money somewhere, so this isn't a job for McCall, or diMaggio. People with money can cover their tracks if they want to." He took the last sip of wine in his glass. "We just have to choose which of our group would be likely to get the most information for us. Sit down, Axel. We aren't through with this."

"I realize that," said Bjornson, scowling. "I'm going to the bog; along the way, I'll have a look-see, in case someone follows me, or is watching this place."

"Go to the bog if you must, but who's going to follow you? And why? We're alone in here." He could feel the flesh on the back of his neck tighten.

Outside a chorus of brakes and hooters followed by curses and imprecations in French, identifying a near-miss in traffic.

"I understand that," Bjornson said. "But I will feel less uneasy if you permit this."

Pomeroy shrugged. "Go ahead. I'll top off our glasses for when you return."

Bjornson nodded and stepped into the corridor, his scowl becoming more distressed. He was convinced they were under observation; there was a very unscientific sensation on the back of his neck that warned him, and after two decades of ignoring its promptings, he now paid close attention to such esoteric signals. At this moment, he was almost completely certain that he was being watched. The last year had been exhausting for him, what with Julia agreeing to testify before the Committee, and his notice that his teaching contract would not be renewed at Columbia, which said that Bjornson's wife had made his presence on the faculty an embarrassment to the Regents and the academic reputation of the university. He had no doubt that Julia had held nothing back, and was proud of doing what she saw as her civic duty. It was troubling to reflect on the things she might tell the Representatives if they asked the right questions. He went past the double-doors that led to the kitchen, and made his way to the latrine, looking around with care before he let himself into the small chamber, then hurriedly bolted the door.

In the bar, Pomeroy turned around in his long-legged chair to look out through the arch in front of the dining room. He liked this place, he liked Dudon, he liked the building, and he was very determined not to sacrifice the few real enjoyments he had come upon since he arrived in France simply because he and the rest of the Coven might be under scrutiny. He knew Bjornson wanted to find another meeting place for the Ex-Pats' Coven, but Pomeroy could not agree; the Coven needed a place everyone knew, a Parisian place, where the Americans would be safer than if they kept themselves isolated in the Ex-Pats' communities in the city. *You hide ducks among other ducks, not in a flock of chickens*, reminding himself of one of his grandfather's favorite aphorisms. The occasional meetings at members' houses continued sporadically, and that was all the risk he wanted to assume as a distinct group. The Coven's meetings here had worked well for almost two years, and there was no reason the arrangement could not continue. He took a sip of wine, rolling it around in his mouth before swallowing. He liked the Burgundy. He was beginning to think that Praeger was right, and it would be years still before it would be safe for any of them to set foot on American soil. He sighed, and took the last sip in his glass. And, he reminded himself, as long as he was the leader of the Coven, he would continue to encourage the group to meet here rather than at any of the members' homes, so they could enjoy the ambience and food as well as one another's company. Asking everyone to stand the expense of a dinner was beyond what most of them could afford to do more than once in a year, and the exposure of such meetings had troubled him from the first: it allowed those who might be watching the Coven to see too much of their group, to discover more about them than they already knew. With Steve diMaggio to watch out for bugs, old-fashioned snooping could be used by government agents to keep track of them, and that idea bothered Pomeroy more than he wanted to admit.

"Did you notice anyone?" Bjornson asked as he came back into the bar.

"Not really," said Pomeroy, not wanting to tell Bjornson that he had not bothered to look. "Nothing much going on yet."

"In an hour or so it will be busy." Bjornson nodded and picked up his wine-glass. "This Samuel Effering. To return to our discussion: what do you make of him?"

"Well, virology is a hot topic these days, and not everything being done in it is for the public good. There are labs working on making super-strong strains of diseases as military weapons almost as fast as there are men trying to find a cure or a vaccine for everything from polio to mumps." Pomeroy realized he had raised his voice. "Sit down, Axel. We don't want all Paris to know what we're doing."

"All Paris doesn't speak English," Bjornson reminded him, but got back onto his high-perch chair. When he spoke again, it was softly. "I'm sorry that I'm being so abrupt. It's been a hard couple of weeks, ever since diMaggio found bugs in Charis Treat's flat, and in McCall's apartment. I'm afraid that we're still under scrutiny. I have no proof," *except for the feeling on the back of my neck*, he added to himself, "but I don't think we should ignore the possibility."

"Indeed, no," said Pomeroy. "Effering has some of the same concerns; he said so."

"It's either the truth or a clever ploy to make us think he's truthful." Bjornson took a swig of the Burgundy.

"The question is, which one," said Pomeroy, and poured the last of the wine in the bottle into Bjornson's glass. "Unwind, Axel. You're going to get the job; they need your experience. As you said, there's no one with a background as thorough in recovering from natural disaster as what you have, and that's certain."

"We'll see," said Axel gloomily. "There are a lot of matters to consider, you know. I don't want to get my hopes up."

"You provided your degrees, your CV, four analyses of your rebuilding plan—what else can they want?" Pomeroy asked, signaling Olivier for a second bottle. So far the wine had had little impact on him, and he was mildly disappointed.

"A Frenchman?" Axel suggested, and reached into his pocket for his pipe, and realized his tobacco pouch was almost empty; he put his pipe back in his pocket. "Sorry—that sounded surly, didn't it? It's nothing to do with you, it's—I had another dispatch from Mother today. Julia is supposed to testify in Washington, DC, next week. That makes the third time she'll be in front of them."

"So they wore her down; that's unfortunate, but you said they would," said Pomeroy, looking up as he saw Samuel Effering coming up to them, looking a little worn-out and bedraggled. "You know how they do it. They lean and lean and lean until their target can't support their push anymore."

"No disagreement," said Bjornson, adding, a bit guiltily, "Julia loves to dish it out, but she can't take it."

"I have a cousin like that," said Pomeroy in commiseration.

"Mind if I join you, gentlemen? I won't stay long. I know you have things to discuss about what I've told you." He looked around. "It's just so nice to speak English again. I'm getting so tired of French."

Pomeroy hooked a long-legged chair, and pulled it nearer to them. "Olivier, another glass while you're at it," he called in passable Parisian French.

The man who had just taken up his post behind the bar reached for another wine-glass and set it where Effering could reach it. "More Burgundy, or would you like something else?" He spoke in heavily French-accented English, wondering how much longer Pomeroy would insist on Burgundy.

"A Cotes du Rhone, perhaps," said Bjornson, adjusting his face to a smile. "Pull up one of these bar chairs, Effering."

"I don't mean to be pushy, but I have to know your decision as soon as possible. If I can't join the Coven, then I'll have to look elsewhere for work, and Americans. I've already tried England, you know, which was hard enough, but Paris!—and the language barrier gets more imposing with every move I make. But I can't sit around doing nothing, letting my imagination run wild and getting more broke by the minute." He watched Olivier open a bottle and pour a taste for Axel Bjornson so he wouldn't have to look the two Americans in the eyes. He had mixed feelings about the Ex-Pats' Coven and wished that Dudon would not encourage them to meet here. He thought it would be easier to serve the members by keeping as much secret as they could, but it was too late to reclaim that privacy in Paris, not after more than a year of even-numbered months' meetings.

"Very pleasant," Bjornson pronounced. "We'll have some." He indicated Pomeroy and Effering. "If you'll leave the bottle for us?"

"Bien sur," said Olivier, and went back to preparing for the evening crowd.

"You say you worked with Salk," said Pomeroy as soon as Olivier was out of ear-shot.

"Yes. I still think he's on the right track. I expect him to release a vaccine in the next three years. He's had encouraging results." His smile lessened. "I've got a half-brother in an iron lung. It matters to me, this vaccine."

"Would you be able to teach in any language but English?" Bjornson asked.

"Not virology; basic high school science, perhaps, but nothing more complex," said Effering.

"But you are conversant with other languages, aren't you?" Pomeroy inquired.

"How do you mean, conversant?" Effering regarded the other two men with a slight sign of unease.

"You say you spent two years in Czechoslovakia after the war," Bjornson prompted.

"In refugee camps, for the most part. The conditions were pretty primitive there, and almost everyone living in the Army tents we provided needed more food and shelter and medical care than we were in any position to give them. We had a translator with us, sometimes two of them."

"A group of you were tracing break-outs of diseases as part of a United Nations effort to keep from a repeat of the Spanish 'Flu after the First World War, according to what you've said in your CV," Bjornson said quietly with an obvious glance at the three-ring binder.

"United Nations, you say. So you weren't all Americans, then?" Pomeroy asked.

"No. We had a Scot, a Belgian, a Pole, a Swiss, and a Ukranian. Six of us in all. I was the only American." He took another sip. "It was over in 'forty-eight, and I went to work with Salk and his team."

"Not letting any grass grow under your feet, were you?" Bjornson remarked.

Effering sighed. "That's why the Committee began investigating me. I'd done some work with the Red Cross during the war, and the Committee thought I might pass on information to the Russians because we had worked together as the war was ending. I told them that even if I had done that, the USSR was in no position to develop a polio vaccine at present, with or without our help. They didn't like that, and so I ended up out of work, and no one was willing to hire me." He took another sip of the wine and smiled. "Very nice."

"Truly," said Pomeroy, pointing to the ring binder Effering had supplied to the Coven. "It says here you're divorced. When did that happen?"

"In 'forty-three. Ellie didn't like me being gone so often, and not allowed to talk about my work when I came home. I can't say I blame her. She wanted a social life with a genial man, and with me she had neither. I don't condemn her for that. I didn't oppose her suit, and I gave her as much of what we had together as my lawyer would let me. I didn't need it, and being gone meant that I'd have to sell the house in any case—I let her have it, and the car. I'm lucky. I could afford to do that much for her."

"Very generous of you," said Bjornson.

"I was making good money doing epidemiological studies on viruses, and I have a good-sized trust fund—that I cannot easily draw upon while I'm here, but I was in a position to use to help my ex-wife. I arranged for reasonable alimony, and agreed to keep my life insurance paid up, and have her remain the beneficiary." He tried to chuckle. "I didn't think any of this would happen. Not this whole witch-hunt."

"No kids?" Pomeroy asked, deliberately blunt.

"None planned, either." Effering put his wine-glass on the bar. "She still sends me Christmas cards, Ellie does. She's a good gal."

"That's nice," said Pomeroy, to encourage Effering to go on.

"How much time have you spent in Paris?" Bjornson pursued.

"About four months this time. Maybe a couple more if my previous visits were added up. I'd be happy about it if the circumstances were different." He turned to Pomeroy. "You're from Cal Davis, or so I've heard. You worked with the Russians on improving their food supply during the war, didn't you?"

"Yes," said Pomeroy, a bit remotely.

"The Russians had a hard time of it, trying to maintain their farming during the war, from what I've read."

Pomeroy stared past Effering. "They did."

"Did you think the war changed anything for them?" Effering asked.

"I don't know." Pomeroy shook his head. "You know what it was like. My . . . Comrades weren't encouraged to communicate with me, nor I with them once the war was over. They say Stalin sent a couple of them to the Gulag."

"You're in a kind of exile, aren't you? We all are," Effering said.

"My situation is unpleasant; the Russians in the Gulag are as wretched as all those Jews and Gypsies and Catholics in Hitler's concentration camps," said Pomeroy with unusual force.

Undaunted, Effering went on. "Still, I guess Oppie's reputation hurt you, too, after the war."

"Oppie had nothing to do with it. Cal Berkeley has its own agricultural department, with greenhouses on Oxford Street at the north edge of the campus. Robert Oppenheimer might have hurt the work they do in Berkeley, but Cal Davis is not that kind of university. The two campuses are nearly a two-hour drive apart." He realized that Effering was goading him, and made himself calm down. "I doubt the Committee understands that difference in campuses—that's more apt to be the reason for coming after me rather than the work on the atom bomb. Besides, most of that was done in New Mexico."

"And the scientists who worked on it came from all over, not only New Mexico," added Effering with a nod. "Oak Ridge, Chicago, Princeton. Everywhere."

All three men drank more of their Cotes du Rhone and kept their thoughts silent for a short while as a light spatter of rain dashed against the two large windows at the front of Chez Rosalie.

"DiMaggio's going to scan the meeting room for us tomorrow afternoon," said Pomeroy as if that had been the subject of their discussion all along. "Tomorrow night, we'll make our recommendation to the Coven, Effering."

"I guess that'll have to do," said Effering. "The thing is, if I'm going to be part of this group, I want to find something more than a tourist hotel to live in, and I'd like to have my situation set before I sign a lease or arrange to move my things again." He watched as Bjornson poured more wine into his glass and then topped off Pomeroy's and his own. "I don't like having to push, but you see my predicament."

"That we do," said Bjornson before Pomeroy started up again. He held out his hand to Effering. "We'll be back in touch with you in two days, to discuss your background one last time."

Pomeroy gave him a startled look. "Are you certain?"

"I believe so," said Bjornson for both Pomeroy's and Effering's benefit. "We do have an associate who should be able to get us the information we need, and quickly."

"Do you mean the Grof?" Pomeroy asked, too startled to show it. "Are you sure we need to approach him?"

"Yes. We have too little time to address these questions. If Szent-Germain can't provide the information himself, he'll know who it is we should contact," he said, and gave Effering a brief scrutiny. "I will use your own CV, if you don't mind?" He indicated the three-ring binder. "You have a great deal of information for us to digest. We'll call upon the Grof first thing in the morning."

"Is he one of those wild noblemen? The kind that are all over Monte Carlo?" Effering asked skeptically, paying no attention to the wine Bjornson was pouring into his half-empty glass. "Paint-the-town-red exile?"

"He does not gamble that I know of," said Bjornson. "If he does, he chooses private clubs and not the glamour of Monte Carlo."

Pomeroy gave a snort of derisive laughter. "Bjornson has a book with the Grof's publishing company. So do about half the Coven."

"Does that present a problem?" Effering was being cautious now, aware he was on uncertain ground.

"He's been most reliable," said Bjornson. "I've liked doing business with him so far, and yes, that contributes to my generally good opinion of him."

"Okay." Effering drank about a third of the wine in his glass. "If you trust him, I suppose I must do so as well."

"He's been reliable in all other matters," said Pomeroy. "I can think of no reason he would play us false on such a question as this."

"That's not very reassuring," said Effering.

"Probably not," Bjornson agreed. "But it will speed up your answer, Mister Effering, and I would encourage you to wait two days in patience. Otherwise, it will take us three or four weeks to find our if your claims are true and you are who you say you are, and that will be a long time to set your membership before the Coven."

"Fine," said Effering. "I'll try to hold body and soul together as long as I can."

"Does that mean you are short of funds?" Pomeroy asked, sounding a bit sympathetic for the first time. "If you are, we can extend a small loan to you, to tide you over. We've done it before." He did not add that some of those loans came from Szent-Germain, not the Coven.

Effering looked astonished, but the expression faded quickly and he nodded. "If you're willing, I'm in no position to refuse. Thank you very much for anything you can spare. As soon as I have work, I'll pay you back, with interest."

"That's agreeable," said Pomeroy with a supporting gesture from Bjornson.

Effering drank the last of his wine. "Thanks for this, too. I hope your meeting goes well on Friday."

Pomeroy bit back a sharp remark. "We all know it's not easy, once you're on the outside like this; we all went through what you're going through."

"You can say that again," Effering declared, a trifle too loudly.

"Are you completely on your own? No money from home in any way? No relatives still living in the Old Country to help you out?" Bjornson asked in sardonic amusement.

"No. Not really," said Effering. "I have some war bonds back home in a safe deposit box, and they'll be mature in 1961, as I recall. It seems strange to have to be careful with money—we came through the Depression without significant losses, and we have significant inheritances from our father and grandfather."

"We?" Pomeroy inquired.

"My sisters and step-brothers. Three sisters, two step-brothers."

"And one in an iron lung?" Bjornson asked.

A couple entered the restaurant and were escorted to a table by Gaspard, who served as head waiter and maitre d'; Pomeroy, Bjornson, and Effering went quiet, and when they began to speak again, did so in lowered voices.

"That sounds like a goodly sum to me, right about now," said Pomeroy, sympathy returning to his manner. "It wouldn't hold you out for much more than a year, if it's all you have, but it's enough to keep the wolf from the door, even here in Paris, if you don't mind being frugal. If you were in a smaller city, it would go a little further."

"I was able to get some money out of my ordinary savings before I left, but not as much as I wanted." Effering shook his head, the vein in his neck showing that his pulse had increased. "I don't dare to try to touch any other money from here, not the way the Committee has been poisoning the well for me."

"For all of us," said Bjornson, a suggestion of bitterness in his tone.

"You're right about that," said Pomeroy.

"I've exhausted almost all my contacts here in France, yet I can't think of where else to go. I don't speak German or Italian or Spanish or Portuguese, or Dutch and Danish, for that matter, at least not at a level that would get me hired. I don't know that the English would be eager for someone like me with a cloud over his head."

"And what do you make of your chances of getting work just now?" Bjornson asked as politely as he could.

"In finding work in my own field?—few to none." He drank down the rest of his wine and put the glass on the bar. "That should hold me until I get back to my hotel. Thank you for giving me some." He got down from the tall chair. "I'll call you day after tomorrow, around noon, if that's satisfactory," he said to Pomeroy.

"Please do," said Pomeroy. "I'll tell you anything that might affect the Coven's willingness to include you in the group." He gave an automatic smile. "And I'll let you know how much we can loan you. That's assuming you can make it for three more days on what you have."

Effering sighed. "Thank you. You're being very kind."

Bjornson barked out two abrupt laughs, then said, "Wait to see what the Coven decides before you thank anyone."

Effering nodded as if his neck hurt. "Yes. You're right." He went toward the door, not quite steady on his feet. He paused to wave, then stepped out into the bustle and rain.

The bar was quiet for almost a minute; it was Pomeroy who broke it first. "Well, you sure put the fear of God into him," he said.

"I wanted to make sure he understood we won't be made fools

of," Bjornson declared as he emptied the second bottle into their two glasses.

"Why don't we wait to see what Szent-Germain discovers for us?" Pomeroy asked. "We have no reason to suspect Effering, given what he has provided us."

"Right you are," said Bjornson. "But I want to have real confirmation on those various points before I recommend him to the group." He rested one elbow on the bar and said with growing fatigue, "We already have one mole in the Coven, and we can't afford a second mole. We have to be very careful about Effering, or don't you agree?"

"But what if there isn't a mole at all? Maybe it's just paranoia for all we've been through in the last three years?" Pomeroy said, his face showing a sadness that unnerved Bjornson. "I don't want to think we have to contend with any of that here, but we're in the habit now, and we might be seeing ghosts because of—"

"Our experiences," said Bjornson, ending their discussion. "Were you thinking of having dinner here, or going somewhere else?"

"I'm staying here," said Pomeroy. "I've got to get something to soak up the wine, little as I feel it right now."

"That's as good an excuse as any," said Bjornson, reaching for the open bottle and pouring more wine for himself. "It's irrational, I know, but I would like it if he weren't quite so ready with his answers. It's his story, I understand that, but if only he would stumble over some minor fact of it, or would correct himself on a little error, I would feel far more confident about him. He's too pat, and that bothers me."

Pomeroy shook his head. "It's the opposite for me: I like his forthcoming way. Some of it is probably the result of having money—all his life by the sound of it—and having received a very good education."

"Well, we would value that, wouldn't we?" Bjornson almost giggled. "Oh, damn. I should not have had that last glass."

"We would," Pomeroy agreed. "Why don't we have Gaspard seat us? We could both do with some dinner, don't you think?" He could feel the wine sneaking up on him, and thought that at home, his parents would have condemned him for drinking anything alcoholic, though they grew grapes for vintners when Prohibition was repealed. He forced his thoughts back to here and now. "My treat."

"Can you afford it?" Bjornson asked.

"I hope so," Pomeroy said, and got down from his tall chair. "Come on, Axel. We'll both feel better for it."

"But the Grof . . . aren't we expected at his flat at seven?" He found his edginess returning twofold, and took a last swig of wine to quiet his nerves.

Pomeroy grinned. "I'll call him and tell him we'll be by a little later. In case you haven't noticed, Szent-Germain is a night-owl. We could probably arrive at midnight and not intrude."

Bjornson permitted Pomeroy to convince him. "All right. Let's have dinner," he said, then added, "I don't think he's the sort of man to excuse an intrusion."

As Gaspard led them to a table, Pomeroy said, "I never thought about it before, but you're probably right. Courteous as he is, he's not very hail-fellow-well-met, is he?"

October 28th, 1950

Ragoczy Ferenz, Grof Szent-Germain
Eclipse Trading and Shipping Company
No. 14, Quai Serie d'Ouvert
Paris, France

My dear Grof,
    Let me point out at the first that I am most displeased by the havey-cavey manner that you have insisted we observe for this interaction, but pursuant to your instructions, I have, as you see, not used our letterhead nor my title and position within the company itself. You have assured me that this precaution is not contrary to any laws, either of this country or state, or to those laws and regulations pertaining to this issue in France. Should any misfortune befall this company as a result of your require-ments or any action be taken against us, we will sue you for whatever damage you do us, in this country and any country in which Eclipse Trading and Shipping is licensed to operate.
    We assigned two of our investigators to your case, and they spent almost all of yesterday making telephone calls to verify the claims made by Saumel V. Effering, PhD in virology and internal medicine. The information, as far as we could determine within the time constraints you imposed, is cor-rect and complete. His father was a gunnery captain who lost an eye in combat; he returned home to his wife and family, and a year later, lost her

and two children to the Influenza epidemic. The father married a widow with two boys. Samuel V. Effering was born in Eugene, Oregon, attended Stanford University and its medical school, as claimed, and worked in Europe during the end of the last war and well into the decade. He married Eleanore Heckley in 1939; they were divorced in 1946, no children, and a settlement favorable to the wife's interests. What he does not mention in his CV is that he was a capable pianist in his youth and showed great promise in that skill, observations we heard several times during our initial contacts. Neither his sister nor his step-brother knew why he had given it up, only that he went to science camp when he was fifteen or sixteen, and soon after stopped playing the piano. You asked for inconsistencies in his accounts of himself, and this was the only one we can verify, although there are very likely others. Had we more time, we could probably uncover more of them, but you were willing to pay not only for the time gathering what they did learn required, but for the courier service to deliver this document to you. There is a detailed invoice attached explaining all the work done to comply with your orders. If you have any question in regard to any of the charges, please address your inquiries to me.

If you have decided to pursue your investigation through our office, please advise us of that as soon as possible; we will estimate the length of time our efforts will take, and what the costs are likely to be for our work. You will receive all our supporting information in our transcripts so that you may be able to reach an informed decision about Dr. Effering. If you want to expand your probing, we will require the names and possible employment records, along with any military service or work that supported the US's war efforts. We pledge to strive to achieve an unbiased assessment of the persons and activities you seek to know more about; you may rely on our continued confidentiality and discretion.

If there are any other services you require of us, do not hesitate to contact us. We look forward to being of service to you.

Sincerely,
JKG/MTTC

Nota Bene: Full transcripts of all interviews will be complete by this time next week, when a copy of all pertinent documents will be sent to you for your files.

❖ 2 ❖

Sleet was slowing traffic to an uncharacteristic crawl, and most of the sidewalks were empty of the strolling masses of Parisians, who often began the Christmas season by calling on friends for pastries and cognac, but were today for the most part keeping within doors. Drivers showed more caution as they made their way along slippery streets than they did on most days, and lorries delivering goods for the holiday markets went gingerly to their destinations.

Tolliver Bethune inspected the meeting room the parties involved had finally agreed upon for this unofficial inquiry into the activities of Ragoczy Ferenz, Grof Szent-Germain; the building was used for meetings, seminars, and lectures, a far more neutral setting than any embassy would be. Bethune looked about, taking stock of the room: it was large enough for twenty people, but set up for a dozen with a polished table at one end of the room, just in front of the plush, spruce-green velvet curtains drawn across the wide bay that faced southeast toward the river. The meeting room was paneled in burled oak and buffed to a subdued shine. The room was lit by a pair of chandeliers of polished brass that suggested lotuses floating on ponds of light; these Art Nouveau masterpieces looked a bit dated now, but they were so well cared-for that their age did not seem to be a fault. It was ten after three in the afternoon—fifteen hundred ten hours, he reminded himself—and the evening seemed to be already upon them; the meeting was to begin at half-three, or fifteen thirty hours—he hoped he had that right, and stifled the urge to look at his watch. He did his best to conceal the agitation that had taken hold of him soon after this meeting was proposed.

"We'll want coffee, and perhaps something stronger, in such raw weather," he said to the waiter who had come into the room behind him.

"Will cognac or sherry be preferred?" the waiter asked, his accent still tinged with the vowels of his native Cornwall.

"Must it be one or the other?" Bethune asked.

"Not if you would prefer both," the waiter said.

"Both, then, if there's no objection." Bethune had removed his coat and set his briefcase on one of the chairs at the table. He was in a suit of English cut in Prussian blue, a white-linen shirt, and a foulard tie in a muted puce with subtle highlights in gold; his tie-clasp was also gold and had a dime-sized version of the Great Seal of the State of Virginia incised upon it. He carried his hat in his hand, as if uncertain what to do with it. "The rest should be here in a quarter of an hour, if you could make sure everything is ready by then."

"That is my understanding," said the waiter, and took Bethune's coat. "It will be in the cloakroom on the landing, sir."

"Oh. Thanks." Bethune took another turn around the room, taking stock of it and trying to familiarize himself with the chamber. "This place is wonderfully restored, isn't it?"

"That was Lord Weldon's intention when he purchased the place; he selected this building among many, and gave it his full attention," said the waiter, falling silent for a short while. "Will you require anything more of me now, Mister Bethune?"

Bethune went on as if he had not heard the waiter's question. "I've seen another building Lord Weldon owns. It is as handsome as this one, and perhaps a decade younger than this is. It's an apartment building, about fifty years old, I would guess. Rumor has it that some high-ranking Nazis put their mistresses up in those apartments during the occupation." He was briefly silent, and when the waiter had nothing more to say, he went on, "This Lord Weldon is a curious fellow, isn't he . . . ?" He faltered.

"Medwyn, sir," the waiter informed him.

"Medwyn. Sounds Welsh. Are you Welsh, Medwyn?"

The waiter responded obliquely. "I'll get your refreshments order, Mister Bethune, and man the front door."

Uncertain how to respond, Bethune nodded. "Thank you, Medwyn."

"I'm pleased to be of service, Mister Bethune."

"And one more thing? about Lord Weldon: does he rebuild any-where else, or is all his effort in Paris?"

"I understand there are five buildings in Paris, a few in the countryside within two hours' drive. His friend, the Grof, has a horse-farm near Orleans, so Lord Weldon isn't the only man from outside France who is helping the recovery from the war. I've been told that Lord Weldon has two buildings in Denmark, and one in Antwerp that is being restored even now. Lord Weldon and Grof Szent-Germain often work together on projects: there is one in Milan and one in Lisbon that I'm aware of. There may be more." He took a step toward the door, his demeanor unchanged by so many questions. "I don't know where else Lord Weldon might have buildings; they could be almost anywhere, just like Lord Weldon himself."

"Yes; I understand he travels extensively." Bethune was prod-ding for answers now, determined to make the most of his oppor-tunity.

"You could say that, Mister Bethune. Goes everywhere, Lord Weldon does. They say he's in Tibet at present, but who knows."

"He must fly under the radar when he travels," said Bethune, turning the brim of his hat through his thumb and finger and, as he did, realizing he had overplayed his hand, so he was doubly sur-prised when Medwyn replied. "He goes places where there is no radar to . . . um . . . fly under."

"Do you worry about him?" Bethune was careful to maintain an air of geniality, and to smile when he spoke.

"He's told us not to, that worry doesn't fix anything, and it makes you ill half the time." Medwyn nodded toward the L-shaped extension of this meeting room that served as a study for the larger part of the room. "There's a globe in there, if you want to give it a squint. Go through the study if we have a fire: the backstairs are through the ironwood door."

"Thank you," said Bethune, and this time he made a point of looking at his wristwatch. "The rest will be here shortly. You'd best go and see to the refreshments."

"Of course. Do you want the coffee in the Italian, French, or English style?"

"The Italian comes in those little cups, doesn't it? With lemon peel." Bethune shook his head. "Better make it the English style, or the French. Use one of those glass-tube coffee-makers with the seal to press the grounds to the bottom of the tube. And both milk and cream, if you would." He checked his wristwatch—only eleven minutes to go; he was certain that Szent-Germain would be on time.

"You've asked for sherry and cognac, and now coffee. Is there anything more you would like me to bring you?"

"Tea, I guess," said Bethune, handing his hat to the waiting Medwyn.

"Black or green?" Medwyn asked, so politely that Bethune had to keep from making a sharp retort.

"Black, probably. I don't know much about tea." His mother had served tea often, and to Bethune it represented a time that was gone from the US.

"I'll arrange things as you like them," Medwyn told him with a nice mix of confidence and diffidence. "We'll bring up the trays in twenty minutes. Would you like us to provide a few Bic pens and a few notebooks?"

"Bic? Those throw-away pens? Sure. Why not?" He made a yawn that was more of a sigh, and wondered if the room were bugged, and if so, why, and by whom?

"Very good, sir." Medwyn nodded to Bethune, and left him alone; he had seen the way Bethune looked at the chandeliers, and the waiter laughed silently. "Wrong direction to find bugs," he whispered as he opened the cloakroom door on the landing to hang up the coat he held; he heard the sound of the door-chimes on the floor below. He hurried down to answer it.

Philetus Rothcoe stood on the broad top step, his expression purposefully blank, his hat pulled down on his head in an unbecoming fashion, his coat-collar turned up and wet from the storm. He came into the lobby quickly, and pulled off his topcoat and handed it, with his hat, to Medwyn. "If you'll take these? Put them where they can dry properly. It's miserable out there." He carried a small valise which he clasped to his chest as if Paris were the ocean and the valise a floating spar. "I'll keep this with me." He was afraid he was talking too fast. "I'm sorry. I should have told you that I'm here for a meeting with—"

"—Ragoczy Ferenz, Grof Szent-Germain," Medwyn finished for him. "There will be ten attending the meeting, with the possibility of an eleventh. Yours is the only meeting being held here today, and I am in charge of serving you. My name is Medwyn, and I have familiarized myself with your files." He saw the shocked look in Rothcoe's eyes. "Not political files; your alien resident's files; the police provide them for meetings when more than half those attending are not French. We have one file for everyone who will be here today, except for Hawsmede, of course. We do the same for every group meeting here. Tomorrow there is a conference of engineers, most of them civil or electrical; they'll take over the whole building for four days. In all, we're expecting thirteen hundred participants for tomorrow, so this is hardly a major occasion for us. You might think of it as a warm-up exercise, one that will get us ready for tomorrow." He pointed upward. "First floor. As you leave the elevator, turn left, and go to the end of the hall. The meeting-room door should be open on your left. One of your company is already here." With that, he nodded and went toward the angled staircase.

Two discreet lighted signs directed Rothcoe to the elevators. He got into the nearer one, thinking he would never get used to the phone-booth-sized Continental elevators. He closed the door and pushed the button for the first floor; he was relieved when the cab moved upward at once and without protest. He held his valise more tightly, his face set in hewn lines from ill-defined dread. As he stepped out of the elevator, he heard the front door chime on the floor below, announcing the next arrival; mindful of Medwyn's information, Rothcoe reached in and pressed the floor-button for G, the ground floor, as courtesy demanded, then hurried along to the meeting room.

"Hello, Rothcoe," said Bethune as Rothcoe came into their meeting room. "You're here in good time."

"Hello, Bethune," said Rothcoe with no attempt to match Bethune's impeccable manners. "I wondered if you'd be here early." Expecting no answer, he turned to the polished oval table. "That briefcase is yours?"

"Yes." Giving Rothcoe no time to comment, he barreled on. "I think you and I should take the right side of the table—the right side from where we stand now—the other side can be reserved for Szent-Germain and his group. We can present our material more . . . unitedly. You and Leeland, your Embassy observer, and whomever the French are sending can take up the remaining seats. That way, Szent-Germain can have the head of the table, which is only courtesy, since he's paying for this meeting."

"Because he wouldn't come to the American Embassy, and the English refused to provide space," said Rothcoe critically as he placed his valise carefully on the chair next to the one holding Bethune's briefcase.

"I think it was wise, his insistence that we meet on neutral ground." Bethune took care not to sound critical; he did not want Rothcoe to get his back up any more than it already was.

"You would," Rothcoe said mordantly.

They both looked up as Rogers, in an Oxford-gray suit, came into the room, followed closely by a lanky, sharp-featured man in his mid-thirties, dressed in superbly tailored charcoal pin-striped worsted; his tie alone, in the color of Brasenose College, was worth twenty pounds. "Gentlemen," said Rogers. "This is Everett Hawsmede of Eisley Butterthorn & Hawsmede, with chambers in London and Greenwich, a law firm specializing in international law. He's here to protect Grof Szent-Germain's business interests."

"And why is that?" Rothcoe asked. "Why should he have a business lawyer attend this meeting?"

"Is there a reason he should not?" Rogers asked the air.

"He does not know what issues are to be discussed, and he prefers to be prepared," said Bethune, who had wondered about the Grof's reasoning when he had been informed of Hawsmede's inclusion.

Rothcoe nodded to Bethune. "I believe you and Mister Hawsmede might want to take a little time to agree on your points of law, Mister Bethune," he suggested with exaggerated courtesy.

Bethune stepped forward. "Tolliver Bethune, in private practice here in Par—"

"Rogers told me about you," said Hawsmede, taking Bethune's proffered hand.

"Where is Szent-Germain?" Rothcoe demanded as Hawsmede moved aside to have a sotto voce conversation with Bethune.

Rogers answered before either Bethune or Hawsmede could speak.

"In traffic, no doubt," said Rogers, and motioned to Bethune and Hawsmede to continue with their discussion.

Next to arrive was Edward Merryman, sent over from the American Embassy to observe the negotiations, an unfailingly polite man in his forties who walked with a cane and who wore a hearing aid in his left ear; he told Bethune and Hawsmede that he had entered the diplomatic corps shortly after receiving his doctoral degree from Princeton, and had been there ever since. He had spent the war advising General de Gaulle on the ways of Americans. He went about the room introducing himself as the Embassy observer, and informing the men there before him that the US Ambassador was sending a second observer to this meeting, an officer from Naval Intelligence who had information to offer that had bearings on this case. "I offered a deposition instead, but the Ambassador refused. He said he wants everyone in the same room."

Rothcoe glowered at Merryman, but managed to keep his mouth shut. He took a warning stance behind the chair that held his valise, and watched the door, his expression daring anyone to address them.

The next arrival was Gui Saint-Michel Terrascote, the French observer, who spoke English with a Canadian accent, which he learned in Winnipeg in the eight years before he entered the university in Montreal. "I'm regarded as neutral enough for the assignment. I'm a translator: English, French, German, and Dutch."

Rogers had just finished introducing Terrascote around when Peter Leeland came in. "Good afternoon, gentlemen. What say we get this over with?"

"Not everyone is here yet," said Rogers, earning a sharp look from Rothcoe. "We have to have everyone here in order to make our agreements official."

"So how long do we wait?" Rothcoe demanded, as if he had no idea.

"Our instructions say we wait ninety minutes beyond the stated meeting time for everyone to gather," said Bethune. "It's in the memo each of you received last week."

"Ninety minutes! Ridiculous!" Rothcoe scoffed.

"Phil," Leeland said, making the name almost a rebuke. "We might as well wait. I don't want to go out in this weather until I have to."

Rogers glanced at the clock in the corridor, and noticed the elevator was moving again. He hoped it would be Szent-Germain, but saw Medwyn emerge, rolling a cart laden with trays ahead of him. He stepped back into the room and motioned to Rothcoe and Leeland to help him hang up the coats on the sideboard to make room for the coffee-urn and a dozen pastry plates. "I think this will help," he said, wondering where his usually prompt employer was.

Rothcoe shook his head. "The butler will take care of it. He doesn't need any help from us." His stare at Rogers showed his contempt. "Or you may want to help out of habit."

The doorbell chimed again; Merryman jumped a little, startled by its suddenness. The elevator descended again, and then moved up.

"Szent-Germain?" Rothcoe asked Leeland, cocking his head in the direction of the elevator.

"No," said a voice from the study at the back of the meeting room, "I'm here." He came out of the small chamber holding a newly revised atlas of Europe in his hands; he was dressed in his usual black three-piece suit with an ivory silk shirt, a tie that was of so dark a red that it looked almost black. As usual, he did not wear a hat. On the first finger of his right hand, he had a platinum ring set with a black sapphire and incised with raised, displayed wings: his sigil. "I came up the backstairs; I parked in the alley behind this place." He looked around the room. "I see we're all here, and it's not quite half-three."

"Two minutes of," said Bethune, a great portion of his nervousness fading as he went to the table and the chair that had his briefcase on it.

The others took their places around the table while Medwyn set out the various items on the racks of his rolling tray-cart, working as if he were completely alone in the room; he went to turn up the brightness on the two chandeliers, stacked his trays on the tray-cart, and whisked it and himself out of the door, leaving the remaining nine men in silence.

"The room was scanned for bugs not two hours ago," Szent-Germain said as the quiet became oppressive. "You may speak freely."

Bethune almost chuckled, wishing he had such sangfroid. "There are cups for twelve, and we're only eight."

"One of us is still missing," said Rothcoe, staring in Szent-Germain's direction as if Rothcoe suspected the Grof of doing something to delay the meeting.

"The fellow from Naval Intelligence," said Bethune. "I don't know him."

"Nor I," said Rothcoe.

"The terms of this meeting require we not discuss anything bearing on this case until and unless all parties are present," Merryman reminded them in his most diplomatic voice. "Perhaps we should choose what we wish to drink."

"Lord, what fun you must be at diplomatic receptions," Leeland muttered.

"More so than you would be in the same circumstances," Merryman rejoined as he got up and made for the sideboard where coffee, tea, milk-jug, creamer, sugar-bowls, pastries, sherry, and cognac were set out with appropriate bone china, napery, and utensils.

SUSTENANCE 403

"I guess we might as well," said Bethune, rising and going to pour out some coffee.

"Please, all of you, help yourselves," said Szent-Germain. "If nothing else, you will have something to sustain you while we wait."

Over the next ten minutes, all the men but one went to choose something to refresh them; they spoke little, not wanting to say anything that could compromise the purpose of the meeting.

"—and furthermore, the man was a haberdasher, not a good training job for someone who was going to be President of the United States," Merryman was saying to Rogers and Hawsmede as the door-chime sounded with the demand of attention that might have been in preparation for the Last Trumpet. Hasty footsteps on the stairs served to announce the arrival of Lieutenant William C. Bereston of US Naval Intelligence.

He was an impressive figure in his uniform, his close-clipped tawny hair looking more blond than it had when he had met Szent-Germain before. He came to the head of the table where there was an unoccupied chair. "Good afternoon, Grof, gentlemen." He very nearly saluted, but instead remarked, "I extend my apologies to all of you. I was unavoidably delayed."

"That's the Navy for you," Merryman mumbled.

Watching Lieutenant Bereston attentively, Szent-Germain nodded once, certain that he recognized the man. "I must suppose you do not really arrange film and publishing ventures for the US Department of State, or if you do, it is only a side-issue for your assignment. I have your card somewhere in my study in Venice."

"It's old information now, Grof; you don't need to keep it." He put his leather portfolio down in front of the chair and said, "I hope you don't mind, but I'm famished. Haven't had anything since zero-five-thirty. I've been traveling to get here, and there were delays." He went to the sideboard and selected a round pastry about the size of a baseball and poured himself a large cup of coffee, carried them back to the table, and sat down. "I love these sweet grenades. I don't know what their proper name is, but they're wonderful, with sweetened cream cheese inside." Three of the men at the table were finishing up their pastries and coffee or tea, and one of them—Terrascote—signaled to Bereston.

"Why did you rush to come here?" asked Hawsmede.

"To provide you with some intelligence about Szent-Germain you may not have discovered for yourself." He took his fork and carefully, deliberately stabbed it, and was rewarded with a small explosion of soft, white cheese. He grinned as he cut the half in half again.

"Why would the Department of State—or the Navy, for that matter—be watching a man like the Grof?" Bethune inquired patiently.

"I'll explain that shortly. First, there are a few misconceptions about—"

"What do you mean, *a few misconceptions?*" Leeland demanded, seeking to keep Rothcoe from entering the fray as much as he wanted to have some answers; Rothcoe was in it for the kill, he thought, not the information.

Bereston took a sip of coffee and put his cup back in the saucer. "I am about to tell you something, but you never heard it from me. My superiors will not look kindly on any discussion outside of this room. Do you understand me?"

Terrascote bristled. "You cannot make such demands on us as this. You have not the authority."

Merryman coughed delicately. "Actually, he has. His information impacts the French as well as it impacts the US." He had been holding a zippered portfolio. "The authorizations are all in this, if you want to examine it."

"By all the forgotten gods, what is this nonsense all about?" Szent-Germain asked in a firm voice. "And before you speculate, I work for no government other than my own."

"You're an exile," Rothcoe said as if he meant something contagious.

"I am, but I still honor the ties of blood. I transmit nothing from Western Europeans to the Soviet Union, nothing from the US to the Soviets, nothing from Europe to anywhere, unless you would call cargo a transmission, which I admit to doing on a regular basis." He saw Bethune's urgent gesture to stop talking; he folded his arms and looked at Rothcoe. "Your turn."

Rothcoe leaned forward on his elbows, his hands gathered into fists. "So you want to play clever, do you?"

"I want all this rumor-mongering to stop. I am not a Communist. I do not work for Communists. I am not involved in espionage. I do not produce nor do I trade in military weapons. Believe this. I am here with two attorneys, as are you, and there are observers as we agreed upon. You obviously have something you want to know. Ask me and if my attorneys agree, I will answer. If they refuse to allow me to answer, they will tell you why." For half a second, he appeared to be exhausted, ancient, and incapable. Then it was gone and his elegance and self-possession had returned, so the five men who noticed Szent-Germain's change wondered if they had seen anything at all; the most perplexed of the four was Edward Merryman, and it took him marginally longer than it took the rest to shake off the odd sensation that had come with that instant.

"Is that true?" Rothcoe challenged. "Because I have it on good authority that the group known as the Ex-Pats' Coven is under your patronage, and they're all notorious Communist sympathizers."

"May I answer?" Szent-Germain asked Bethune.

"Carefully," Bethune replied.

Szent-Germain thought for almost a minute. "To the extent that I publish books some of the members of that group have written, I suppose I do—patronize them. But not for their politics: I publish scholarly works for the most part, and the Coven members are almost all scholars. I have no group agreement with them: each book is contracted individually, and I put no money into the group per se, I only pay those who are my company's authors." He looked to Bethune and nodded once; Bethune made a gesture suggesting that Szent-Germain had just parried a sword-blow.

"You may say so, but where is your proof?" Rothcoe pursued, and then wanted to call his words back as he looked at Hawsmede, who was wearing a lupine smile. "My firm handles Grof Szent-Germain's international businesses: we keep copies of all contracts, scheduled

meetings, tax filings, customs forms, as well as all secondary trans-
actions. We have records of all his dealings, and if you require it,
we can arrange a time for you to come to our chambers and examine what we have on hand. You'll have to allocate some time for
that project. I should warn you, there is a great deal of it." He
leaned back in his chair and had the last of his tea. "I would need
the Grof's permission to show you anything, of course."

Rothcoe shook his head. "You want to drown me in paper, is
that it?"

"No. I want you to have an appreciation for what this man does,"
he said as if addressing a difficult child. "My obligation is to my
client to the limits of the law."

"Very noble, for a lawyer," Rothcoe sneered.

"Gentlemen, please," Merryman interrupted. "Shall we stick to
the point of this meeting?"

Szent-Germain spoke up again. "If you feel you must see these
records, Mister Rothcoe, then we will make an arrangement that
will accomplish your wish. But I think that in pursuing me, you are
ignoring the obvious targets of this whispering campaign: the
members of the Ex-Pats' Coven, I am, at best, a secondary casual-
ity." He saw Leeland flush. "They're trying to salvage their reputa-
tions and their livelihoods from here, and there are those in the US
that do not want them to succeed. By dragging me into the conflict, the waters are muddied, because my presence gives the appearance of foreign intrigue, which does not exist. I do not want to
cause any of the Coven distress, but I think, for their sake, I must
lessen my involvement with some of its members." He had talked
to Charis about this, and would shortly discuss the matter with the
rest of the Coven.

"They aren't useful?" Rothcoe asked.

This time it was Rogers who answered. "What is it you seek in
this investigation? Do you want to provide political entertainment
for your citizens? Do you think this is some sort of film, one that is
designed to show the vigilance of your security forces against a
system the leaders fear and dislike?" He directed his gaze to Rothcoe. "Are you crying wolf? If you are, the wolf is a puppet of your

own making. You have imbued Communism as Catholics believed Protestants were diabolic; by magnifying the nefarious deeds and intentions of Communists with the same malign intent, you make your hunters of them more powerful and heroic than they would be were you more realistic in your depiction of an economic system that does not coincide with your own." He paused. "I have known the Grof for a great many years"—roughly two thousand years, he silently reminded himself—"and I know he is not involved in anything clandestine."

"You work for him," Rothcoe said, dismissing Rogers' remarks. "What else would you say?"

"And he is right, Ragoczy Ferenz is a humanitarian, from all our records on him, and his uncle before him," Bereston added, and went on a bit more rapidly. "I have official records that he"—he inclined his head in Szent-Germain's direction—"helped Cardinal Roncale get Jewish children out of Bulgaria during the war; he provided transportation for many of them to safe locales. The Grof has also established a school for refugees in Hungary. There are persistent rumors he provided a kind of way-station for the Resistance during the war, as well, but if he did, he covered his tracks completely. For a wealthy man, he is remarkably uninvolved in politics."

"Thank you, Lieutenant," said Szent-Germain.

"Can all these claims be established?" Leeland asked.

"How do we know you're not lying?" Rothcoe moved in his chair as if he might try to pounce on Szent-Germain.

Szent-Germain regarded him steadily. "Because I give you my Word I am not."

"Sweet fucking Jesus," said Leeland, his patience finally gone. "Give it a rest, Phil. It's settled that this guy isn't a Communist. We'll check out his proofs of it after the first of the year."

Merryman made a sound that might have been a *tut-tut* but was more likely a swallowed chuckle.

"What more do you want to ask my client?" Bethune inquired personably, directing his question to Rothcoe.

"I want him to tell the truth," said Rothcoe, his eyes accusing. "I want him to say who he's working for."

Bethune started to speak, but Szent-Germain waved him to silence. "I work for those of my blood, not as their servant, but as their . . . protector, I guess you would call it. It's a bit old-fashioned these days, but I keep to the old ways where blood is concerned."

"You say that so easily," Rothcoe complained.

"I say it readily, not easily, but I doubt you would understand the difference," Szent-Germain told him.

Bethune straightened his back. "Is there any other question you want to put to my client?"

Rothcoe swore.

Merryman rose. "I think we're done for now. Something may arise later, but I don't believe we will need anything more today. I don't know why we should continue this—it is degenerating into unfounded opinion, and that should worry some of you." He went to the far end of the sideboard and examined the labels on the three bottles that stood there. "There's some excellent cognac set out for us, and a very acceptable sherry. And some kind of Romanian liquor I am not familiar with. Tell me which you would like."

"We can't stop now!" Rothcoe exclaimed.

"We can, and we will. As the senior representative of the US government present, I am adjourning this meeting, and unless I receive a request from President Truman himself to schedule a new meeting, then we will regard the matter settled." Merryman's air of bumbly preoccupation had gone and in its place was a decisiveness that surprised everyone but Hawsmede. "Come, gentlemen. It's dark and cold outside. Have a little something to help you keep warm."

"You *bastard*!" Rothcoe blared. "He's *conning* you. Can't you see? And you're lapping it up by the spoonful."

"If you are displeased, you may leave, Mister Rothcoe. I'm tempted to tell you that you owe the Grof an apology, but I fear that would be useless." Merryman opened the bottle of cognac.

Terrascote got up and went to join Merryman at the end of the sideboard. "Thank you, Mister Merryman."

While the two men found the glasses for the sherry and the cognac, Rothcoe gathered up his things, and glared at Szent-Germain and then Merryman before he flung himself out of the room, leaving the door open.

Merryman held out a small balloon glass of cognac. "Grof?"

"No. Thank you. Rogers and I have another engagement tonight." He rose. "I am grateful to you, Lieutenant Bereston. If ever I can be of service to you—for anything other than politics—please do not hesitate to ask." He held out his hand to Bethune, who had got up and was talking quietly with Hawsmede.

"Is this actually over? Is it really so simple?" Bethune was asking Hawsmede, who answered, "Probably not. It is usually just the first salvo." With that comforting statement, he turned to Szent-Germain. "A well-played opening round, Grof."

"Then you should be doubly pleased. You have both been most helpful," he said, shaking hands with them in turn.

From the study door, Rogers called out, "It is getting late."

"Yes. Gentlemen, excuse me." He raised his voice a little. "Thanks to all of you."

"Grof," said Merryman as Szent-Germain went toward the study and the rear stairs, "I don't want to belabor the obvious, but you have some very powerful enemies."

"Yes; and I thought I knew them all," he replied before Rogers closed the door.

October 21ˢᵗ, 1950

Dear David,

Thanks for the Christmas invitation. Please tell Tamsin that I say
thank you, yes, I'd love to come. Most of the Coven this year is having
Christmases away from Paris, and I was feeling very much rootless. I
had an invitation to dine with the Kings on Christmas Day, but they're
glad that you sent your invitation. Tell all your family for me I will be
happy to bring along some fine French vintages, a wheel or two of cheese,
and a brace of smoked ducks; if they have any other favorites, they should
let me know. You English have been on short rations for far too long: live
a little.

The weather has been miserable here—cold, damp, and foggy. You
know how dreary Paris can be in the winter—it's almost as bad as
London. I was ready to drive all the way to Switzerland just to see the
sun, but I couldn't summon up the enthusiasm. The prediction promises
warming, but you know how unreliable the weather reports are. I'll make
arrangements for the ferry. I think I'll want to have my car with me, just
in case. I'll plan to arrive a day after you and the family motor down to
Oakley Green. I'll plan to be with you for ten days, if that's convenient.

I am still working on that book for Eclipse Press. I find it harder to do
than I thought it would be. So much of what I want to describe turns out
to be difficult to communicate. I've been trying to figure out how I work
out reporting on a riot or a battle so that it doesn't seem as chaotic as it
actually is. Experience has a lot to do with it, but there's more to it than
that, and it's important to recognize the hubs that develop during such

events. But how to distinguish between a true hub, where those with an agenda in the fight make every effort to see that it goes their way, and a group of men driven together by circumstances, whose only purpose is to get out whole and alive.

Perhaps you can tell me if there is a library in the west of London that has information on your various nobles. I'd like to do a little more research on that Lord Weldon fellow. He has me puzzled. Szent-Germain told me, when I asked him about Weldon, that he was given to taking risks, and that considering how things stand in China now, it might not be a very safe place for him to visit. Szent-Germain is probably going to send an inquiry to the British and the Chinese ministries in charge of keeping track of travelers. There may be a story in this, but I'm not holding my breath. I'd just like to know more about the guy. He sounds like the very model of a modern English eccentric (sorry to mess up the meter). I won't let it eat up all my time, but enough to get the basics.

I'm looking forward to seeing you and Tamsin and the kids. It sounds as if you're all getting back to relative normal. It's good to know that your town house can be safely rebuilt and that the insurance will actually pay for it. If the bomb that wrecked your neighbor's house had fallen on yours instead, you might not be so lucky. I'd be delighted to have a tour of the town house, to see how the work is coming. I hope you find some way to restore your garden, as well. It was lovely.

I'll send you a wire when I'm en route to the coast; it should give you sufficient warning.

Cordially,
Russell McCall

❖ 3 ❖

SZENT-GERMAIN LAY stretched out on top of the bed, his white silk shirt open at the neck, his slacks of gray flannel only slightly wrinkled. Despite the chill in the room, his small feet were bare and he showed no sign of being cold; not even his breath steamed in the frosty dawn light. Their long night of opulent love-making had left him wonderfully restored; he was also keenly aware that Charis was less gratified with the vampire life that lay ahead of her than she claimed to be, and that niggled at him, robbing him of the sweet lassitude he usually experienced after such a night as they had had. Too many questions churned within her for their intimacy to have been unmitigated rapture for either of them, a realization that troubled him. He braced himself for more questions when she woke, certain that she would want more explanations from him than she had gained so far.

Beside him, under the duvet, Charis was asleep, although the sky was growing bright in the east and the sounds of the Orleans horse farm that had once been Olivia's were beginning to fill the morning; as if to prove the point, a cock offered his doodle-doo fanfare to the coming sun from the courtyard of the ancient holding. The ground floor had been built a millennium ago and, despite attempts to modernize it, was dark and inconvenient in about half the rooms. The upper floor of the house had been rebuilt after a regional skirmish a century before, and could boast this bedroom, a much smaller bedroom, a library, a laboratory, and a lavish bathroom that had been refitted three years ago, something which made the staff very proud. Although it was cold and there was a biting wind blowing, there was a festive spirit in the air; it was the last day of 1950. Szent-Germain and Charis had driven down from Paris the evening before—Charis had driven the Jaguar most of the way—and were planning to spend a day or two enjoying the countryside before returning to their respective flats in Paris. It would be a pleasant way to welcome in the New Year, away from the holiday chaos, assuming the clear weather held. All but two of the household staff would be gathering with their families in four hours' time, leaving La Belle Romaine to the two of them. He would order a meal for Charis, one that cooked slowly and would be ready by sundown, since he knew only the rudiments of cooking.

Charis woke suddenly, sleep-flustered and groggy. "So we did come here," she said after looking around the room and out the window. "I thought perhaps I'd dreamed it." She looked over at him. "Thanks for letting me drive."

"My pleasure," he said at once.

"That was what made me think it was a dream—that you let me drive."

"As to that, I can't say: you may very well have dreamed about it, but yes, we are at La Belle Romaine, and the staff will soon be up. There is a kind of fete that La Belle Romaine provides for the staff and their families at home on New Year's Eve, and the staff will be busy with it this afternoon. Don't worry, though, Valerot will have issued instructions that we're not to be disturbed, and we will enjoy our own celebration."

"Just like that?" she asked, surprised at his confidence. She snapped her fingers. "Just this, and it's done?"

"You seem startled," he said, a bit astonished at her question.

"Well, you aren't here very often, and servants can be unreliable when that happens, or so I've read; folk-tales are full of them, and so is history. How do you maintain this kind of loyalty? You know, all those weasels and martens in folk-tales, the ones in the households of lions and bears? You know what delight the weasels and martens take in getting the best of their masters, but you are confident that your staff will uphold you, in spite of all the caution-ary tales you must have heard through the centuries you say you've lived. And the history of Western Europe in the Dark Ages." She did not speak to ameliorate the alarm she might have caused him, but added only, "Don't you ever worry about your servants? If noth-ing else, aren't you worried they might find out about you?"

A streak of a memory brought the Vidame de Silenrieux's pages, which he quickly banished from his thoughts. "Not Valerot and Pensjour and Chansant: they are as staunch as Horatius at the bridge. I and my . . . family have been their employers for generations. If they have suspicions of me, they keep them to themselves. They are well-paid and they uphold the standards of earlier times by being steadfast." Seven generations so far, he reminded himself, had served Olivia's place, but many, many decades since she had died the True Death in Roma. "Beyond that, Valerot worked with me during the war, while I was at Montalia; he ran a group of locals who had hiding places for those escaping from the Nazis. Orleans was a central place for escapees and refugees to come, and the Nazis had other demands on their time than chasing down the people outside of the cities. Depending on where the refugees were bound, Valerot would pass them on to me or to Castelene in Toulouse. We'd had a man in Nice, but he was discovered and took poison before he could be interrogated. There are narrow pathways through the mountains—hunters and herders use them, and smugglers—that the Nazis could not locate effectively, and that helped all of us. We're not quite five miles from Orleans here, and there are a dozen large farms near here that provide a sort of protective barricade around La Belle Romaine, which made sudden aggress on this place . . . shall we say impracticable? Between Valerot and me, we must have had over a hundred people through here by war's end. I'd hoped it would be more, but Valerot was satisfied, for we only lost one. For those bound south, coming in from Austria, I kept in contact with Genova and Venezia and Trieste, making arrangements so that there would be safe places to escape *to*. So, yes, I trust my servants." He leaned over and kissed her upper lip, slowly and deliciously. "For now, let us devote our thoughts to the future."

She reached out and touched his face. "I'm sorry to have wakened in such a mood. I think it must be holiday blues. I can't help being homesick."

"No apology necessary," he assured her.

Another cock, this one farther away than the first, heralded the morning energetically, and this time, a chorus of doodle-doos answered him.

"They'll probably crow all day. My grandfather's certainly did," said Charis. "The country's so quiet, the roosters are loud by comparison."

"There are other sounds to listen to: you can hear the horses starting to move in their stalls. They're hungry and restless. So a handful of grain now, and a turn-out in the central arena will allow them to get the fidgets out of their feet before breakfast. They have a light grooming before their breakfast. It's frosty out, and the grooms will have to watch them so the cold doesn't cause problems for them. Once they're back in their stalls, they'll be groomed again, and given a mixture of chopped apples, hay, and crimped oats."

"Do you blanket them? My grandfather—the same one with the chickens—who lived near the New Mexico border in Colorado, thought blanketing was being too cautious, that it softened up the horses and kept them from growing a good winter coat. He was of the opinion that horses need their winter coats for more reasons than cold. He got snow every winter, but he kept the horses in the barn and the barn in good repair. He thought that was enough warmth for them. His horses were shaggy from the beginning of October until the end of April." She did her best to smile. "I'm sorry. I guess I'm trying to make up for being silent while I drove."

"You have no reason to be sorry. About the horses: it seems to me that if you put an extra blanket on your bed to sleep, you should show the same courtesy to your horse." He touched her hair, which made a tangled halo around her smiling face.

"I don't think you could change his mind," she said, rubbing sleep from her eyes. "Are you really going to have a sip of champagne tonight? You did tell Valerot you might."

"Probably not. I like the ceremony of it more than the taste, or the results of the taste." He tweaked a stray strand out of his way and kissed her again, deeply, lingeringly; she gave him a muzzy smile as she moved back from him, using her pillows to prop her up.

"Is M'sieur Valerot preparing breakfast for . . . me?" she asked as she yawned.

"The cook, Sibelle, will be making breakfast for the staff, but if you like, I'll send down an order now; it will take a while to get here. You may want to put on your peignoir for it; Valerot can serve it to you here, if you like. You needn't dress or neaten up beyond that unless you want to." He waited for her to respond.

"Oh. Oh, yes; the staff eats first, don't they? Of course. You said they have a celebration later that they need to prepare for. No problem, I'll be happy to wait." She offered him a slow, provocative smile. "I'm sure we'll find something to do."

He returned the smile. "Very good." He turned his head toward the window, where the morning light was much brighter: the sun was rising. "By the way, unless you mean to insult him, call him either Valerot, which is his first name, or M'sieur Bartimy. He's very old-fashioned about that." He looked around, and considered the Franklin stove that fronted the much older fireplace. "Would you like some heat? I can have a fire going in a short while."

She sat up in bed, and almost at once pulled the duvet around her as gooseflesh sprang up on her shoulders and arms. "Yes, please. It must be about fifty degrees in here—Fahrenheit. I don't see how you can stand it. It feels like it's freezing, and you aren't bothered." Then, before he could speak, she said, "That's right: it's one of those things, isn't it? One of those things that vampires do, like having a faint smudge for a reflection."

"Yes."

She dropped back down on the pillow, pulling the duvet with her. "I'd like it if you'd take off your clothes when you come back to bed."

"You know I cannot do it," he said, rising and going toward the stove.

"I know you *will* not do it," she countered. "The scarring is bad, and I don't like to think how you came to have so much, but it doesn't ruin the mood for me," she went on, more gently.

"I can't risk having any of the staff see them: they know my supposed great-uncle had severe scars, and so they mustn't see these.

That would lead to comparisons that would not be helpful; I am inclined to err on the side of caution, as the previous owner did."

"Olivia," said Charis.

"No. She died the True Death in 1658, in early December. When Niklos Aulirios, who had been her bondsman—"

"Like Rogers?" she interjected.

"Yes. Like Rogers. When he inherited this place from Olivia, he ordered a number of changes made, including hiring many new servants and pensioning off the old, and I have followed his example when I was left Olivia's estates by Niklos. He didn't stay here often— too many memories—but he kept it up to honor her."

"What became of him?" Charis asked, interested in spite of the pang of jealousy she felt toward the long-dead Olivia.

"He was executed by Napoleon's soldiers after the Egyptian campaign. He was accused of robbing the old tombs."

"And was he? robbing the old tombs?" she asked before she could stop the words.

"No, he was not. He was helping to show Madelaine where the tombs were." He shook his head once, sadly. "He was serving as her scout, preparing maps for her before she arrived."

"It sounds pretty weird to me," she said, reaching out and taking his hand.

"It's a reasonable precaution."

"Like lining the soles of your shoes with your native earth," she said.

"Very similar. I recommend it to all vampires who want to be part of humanity."

"Which you do."

"Which I do," he confirmed.

"But that requires many disguises over time, doesn't it? You're at risk if you don't come up with plausible identities." She held his hand more tightly, thinking for the first time that this was how she would have to live when she became what he was.

"I have found it prudent to make preparations for the next . . . manifestation. Madelaine always has wills drawn up leaving her property to her niece or cousin, so that the new identity is established before she needs it. I often do similar things, as do almost all those of my blood who survive."

"Is that what you're doing here? Are you preparing to go away? Are you teaching me how to prepare another . . . persona?" Charis asked, repelled and fascinated at the same time.

"Yes, in part," he said, and was drowned out by a sudden eruption of doodle-doos. "I can show you various ways to achieve this," he offered. "I've had a long time to get used to making such changes." He lifted her hand to his lips and kissed it, then rose to attend to the stove. "If there's anything else?"

"Rogers tells me you change your name from time to time. Why?"

"So that I can create a smokescreen for my existence, so that I will not have to vanish into the wilderness of Russia or Africa or America, or spend a generation or so in a remote—" He thought back to Lo-Yang, to Upper Egypt, to Delhi, to—

"Or your cover would be blown? Does that bother you, like Rumpelstiltskin?" Charis suggested, cutting into his memories.

"I have no skill to turn straw into gold," he admitted with a wry smile, "but I comprehend his predicament."

"It's Rumpelstiltskin or the King of Elfland, I suppose." She paused, shocked at her accusation, then went on plaintively. "But when we first got here, you were speaking of touching, the touching we shared last night. I would like so much to be touched. All of me this time."

He paused in stoking the stove with the cut trunks of ancient trees, atop a kindling bed of dry leaves and clusters of twigs. "You know that is impossible," he said flatly. "All of you . . . with one exception can be done, this evening."

"You can't do the act of life. I'm beginning to appreciate that you weren't kidding when you told me, though it seems a pretty big stretch to me, to be so sensual and not ever be hard. But that was my mistake; you weren't exaggerating to make a point. I thought it meant that you needed special circumstances to perform, and that they might not be as pleasant as what we do now." Her perplexity was apparent now as she pressed on. "The blood remains in your veins, however slowly it may flow, and that . . . incapacitates you, according to what you've told me. I understand all that. I get it. Dead-but-not-dead, alive-but-not-alive. I get it. It's just so unfair."

"Are you changing your mind about becoming what I am?" he asked, thinking of Susanna, who had changed her mind when it was too late, and who had tried to end his undead life because of it.

"I don't know," she said petulantly. "Sometimes, when I'm feeling on my own a bit too much, I can see the advantage of not going on."

"It's likely you'll have a decade or more before you have to make up your mind," he said, favoring her with a sad smile. "I don't ask you to do it for me, but for yourself. If you do not want to live as those of my blood must, then I can tell you how to arrange matters."

"You're having doubts, too?" she asked.

"Ah, Charis, you have enough for the both of us," he said, a bit sadly. The fire in the stove had taken hold; the smell of burning apple-wood filled the room before he finished closing the tinderbox. He went back to the bed and slipped under the duvet.

"Under the cover. Now that's unusual," she said, trying to figure out what he meant by it. "You usually lie on top, don't you."

"As you say, the room is chilly, and I'm tired of wrestling with the bedding." He turned to her, smiling.

"But you're still dressed." She plucked at his sleeve to underscore her complaint. "I'd like you naked."

"Not at present, I think."

"The scars still?"

He shook his head. "The sunlight. I'm not lying on my native earth, and I'm barefoot. The sun can be painful if I'm not dressed, or unless I close all the shutters, which would be a pity on such a fine morning." He turned to her. "If you would rather put something on, to establish parity, please do."

She tugged the duvet more closely around her. "That's not what I had in mind, and you know it." Her eyes were shining, but not entirely from desire; she was eager to force him to admit that much of what he told her was untrue; the prospect of having to live with such . . . ancient restrictions on her activities was beginning to rankle. "Native earth. Sunlight. Running water. It's like something out of a Medieval romance. Do you have to count grains of millet or sunflower seeds? Do white horses seek out your resting places? Do flowers wither where you tread? I know that last is nonsense."

"No, not nonsense. That is a creation of storytellers, like the belief that you can stop a charging tiger by throwing a glass ball at it, which is supposed to make the tiger think that it is seeing its cub reflected in the glass. I have no idea how that one originated." He trailed his finger along her brow, her nose, the curve of her lips. "The cross is no problem for vampires, nor the Star of David, nor the crescent of Islam, or the wheel of the religions of India. Garlic will not prevent us from entering a room—although it does tend to keep off mosquitos. We can cross thresholds without invitation. We can say the names of deities without hazard." He looked at her steadily. "Fire can kill us if it reaches the spine. Anything that destroys the nervous system will destroy us."

"Yes, you've told me this before. I'm aware of all the dangers."

"I surmise that; you've paid attention," he said, taking her hand in his. "But you will need to remember these things until you accustom yourself to them: daylight, as I've said, can be enervating to vampires; water is enervating unless contained in our native earth. So no passion on the beach or in the desert before sundown." His attempt at a chuckle fell flat. "I would like full concentration and energy when we enjoy our explorations."

She gave an acrimonious sigh. "Can you at least snuggle?"

"With pleasure," he said, turning on his side and drawing her close to him spoon-fashion; he could feel tension in her that was not the product of unaddressed desire, but of some greater vexation. "What's on your mind, Charis. You aren't simply worried about how you'll manage things in the future."

"Why can't I be worried about that?" she demanded.

"You can, if that pleases you, but I am aware that there is sorrow in you, and dismay. I believe something has happened that is eating at you, in a very personal, present way. Are you having more trouble with Harold?"

"With Arthur. He wants to come here when he's eighteen: he's 4F, of course; he'll still be on crutches then. David might not be so lucky. Arthur won't be drafted, and he wants to spend some time with me, or so he's told me in a long letter." She sighed heavily. "I don't know how to respond."

"See him before you change, if that will heal some of your wounds; I might not be the only one who can see them," he said, making no apology for his language. "By then you might have reached detente with your husband, and this would cause no additional hostilities."

"You think you know everything," she said in a small voice. "Harold is being himself, and for the first time, I know him for what he is."

"I have tasted your blood, Charis: I know you, and I will know you until the True Death comes. Everything else is beyond me, but you, and everyone I have loved will be with me, a part of me, until the True Death." He said it tenderly, but he could feel her flinch. "If you would prefer not to tell me, so be it, but I cannot be unaware of your state of mind."

She rolled over to face him. "Maybe later," she conceded.

"As you like." He kissed her forehead.

She took one of the pillows and swung it at his head. "You are the most *aggravating* man!" she announced as the pillow struck.

He made no attempt to block the blow, and used no counter-measures to disarm her. "It isn't my intention to seem so, nor do I want to distress you," he said, tossing the pillow across the room as soon as she released it, watching a trail of feather float from the rent in the pillow's side. He considered her briefly. "If you decide vam-pirism is not to your liking, there are many ways you can—"

"Die the True Death? Be sure of not rising to your life? Without rousing suspicion?" She turned to face him directly. "Do you think I'll need to know?"

"I think all of us should know these things. All those alive of my blood know how to end vampire non-life, or how to create a believ-able vanishing that would permit any one of us to use that device to move on to our next . . . version of ourselves. It is harder now than it used to be. I still use my waxwork for identifying photographs, and in time I will find other ways to make what I am less obvious. I have yet to arrive at a method for dealing with fingerprints. As the world changes, so must we." He could see the troubled expression in her eyes. "These days many people no longer believe in such creatures as vampires, which is useful, in its way."

"But why? What makes it necessary that we not remain as we are? Will we cease to be allies when I come to your life?"

"That will be up to you," he said gently. "Because nothing stays the same as long as it is alive. We age much more slowly than the living do. Being undead, we have a portion of ourselves that remains fixed at the moment of our first death and—"

"That's why we age very, very slowly," she filled in for him. "I do listen to what you tell me."

"I know you do, because you question everything I tell you. You analyze what I say, subject it to skeptical examination until you are satisfied that it has been broken down into acceptable and unacceptable parts. With so much of your life gone askew, it is not remarkable that you are inclined to question more of your life than you had done before you left New Orleans. It's your training as well as your natural inclination to question. I understand that, too. And I agree with you to a point: logic has its place, and in its place it is invaluable, but I have come to the conclusion that we do not have nearly enough knowledge of the nature of existence to be able to use logic alone to achieve the level of understanding we would like to have in dealing with the rudiments of existence. You will need time to weigh your experience with your logic and decide where the crux lies." He slid a hand's-breadth away from her so she could lie back and stare at the painted beams of the ceiling. "Religions—all religions, like all philosophies—offer their explanations of existence, as well as setting standards of conduct for a praiseworthy life, but all of them are subject to the human view of their own importance—"

"Humans, you say, are limited to the human view of *their* own existence? You don't count yourself among the human beings?" Her snapping eyes dared him to answer her. "You're not human?"

"I began human, but with as long a life as I have had I have found it difficult to sustain—"

"I reckon it's been about two thousand years that you've been your sort of alive, and I can't believe it; not even tortoises live so long," she said, reaching for his hand. "This is flesh. A little cool, I grant you, but flesh. How can you be two thousand years old?"

"I am somewhat older than that," he said apologetically.

"Be serious," she said.

"I am being serious." He nodded. "The urge to keep my humanity has shaped my behavior a bit less than three thousand years of my after-death life; for the first thousand years, I considered myself as much a demon as those I hunted. While I was held in prison, I began to grasp the loneliness of my circumstances, and that compelled me to manage my non-life in another way. I seek to retain my link with humankind, which is no easy thing, but I abhor what I was before I learned that, so I continue to strive for the human part in myself, no matter how difficult a task that may be. There is something monstrous in me that is quiescent most of the time; hundreds of years can pass and I will have nothing more than a faint distaste for the memories associated with it. Still, I know it is within me, but I rarely respond to its impetus. A little more than twenty years ago I had a taste of what it had been like for me all those centuries ago when I . . . dealt with the men who killed my ward. I had not summoned up my capacity for havoc for a very long time, yet it was as devastating as I remembered it." He had killed all five of them with his bare hands in a single hour of fighting, and for a moment he was tempted to taste their blood as a vindication of Laisha. Their dreadful act ought to be acknowledged; if only by him. But the thought of having anything of them in him had stopped him from even licking their blood off his hands.

"That sounds a bit facile to me," she said, feeling a quiver of unease stir deep within her.

"We need to be aware of the monster we can be," he said, a bit distantly. "If for no other reason than to be able to hold that savagery at bay."

"Yes, I know it's dangerous to give free rein to that fury you tell me is part of what we are. You've told me at least five times before now."

"And you still do not believe it is a real part of how you will change when you come to my life." He spoke tenderly, and with such sadness in his blue-shot dark eyes that she began to wonder if his warning really were truthful.

"I'll bear it in mind; I promise you." She lifted a corner of the duvet and thrust her arm out into the morning. "A little warmer. Do you happen to remember where my bathrobe is?"

"On the back of the bathroom door," he said, accepting that she would not discuss these various matters for the time being. "Would you like me to go and fetch it for you?"

"Yes," she said. "Not because it's cold, but with the servants moving about . . ."

"I do understand," he said. "It won't take me more than a couple of minutes." He got out of the bed, and paying no heed to the cold floors, let himself through the door into the hallway, then padded down to the elegant bathroom. He took Charis' bathrobe from the peg on the back of the door, and started back to his guest bedroom only to find Valerot waiting at the top of the stairs. "Good morning," he said to his steward in French.

"To you as well, Comte," said Valerot. "Are you and your guest up yet?"

"Not yet. Is there something that needs my attention?" His manner was courteous, but now his senses were on the alert.

"Oh, no; not yet. We'll want to see you in the Great Hall at mid-day, but for now, I wanted to know if your guest is ready for breakfast."

"In half an hour, I should guess. We'll come down to the morning room." He smiled. "Thank you, Valerot."

Valerot ducked his head as a sign of appreciation. "Half an hour in the morning room. I will meet you there."

"Very good," said Szent-Germain and passed on to the guest room, saying as he entered, "Breakfast in half an hour in the morning room."

"I suppose I should get dressed," Charis said, watching him.

"No need. You might want to brush your hair." He tossed her bathrobe to her. "Otherwise, you will not shock the staff."

"My overnight bag is on the straight-backed chair," she said, pulling on the bathrobe while sitting up straight in the bed.

He reached it and handed it to her. "Here you are." While she opened the herringbone-patterned hard-sided case, he went on, "The celebration begins at noon: you'll want to dress for that. Nothing too fancy."

"I brought the mulberry skirt and the embroidered jacket," she said as she took out her boar-bristle brush and set to work on restoring order to her hair.

"That will do well." He held out his arm to assist her to stand, but she ignored the gesture, and went on brushing her hair.

"Give me ten minutes and I'll be ready, if I can find my slippers." She went from stiff-bristle brush to comb.

Szent-Germain looked under the bed and retrieved her pair of red satin slippers, which he silently offered to her. "Am I neat enough for joining you at table?" he asked when he was on his feet once again.

"If you want to," she said. "I have to make an appointment with Celeste; my hair's getting unruly."

"As soon as we get back to Paris, telephone her shop." He opened the small closet and removed a black brocade smoking jacket which he donned, taking care to make sure the wide silken belt lay smoothly around his waist.

"Are you ready?" she asked as she came down from the bed. This time when he proffered his arm, she took it with a slight toss of her head.

"If you are," he said as he opened the door and bowed her through it.

Feb. 16th. 51

Hapgood Nugent
Department of Mathematics
Uppsala, 036
Sweden

My good friend Happy,
    *I have written to your sister to inform Uncle Freddie that this project
to which he assigned me is completed, and I am pleased to say that my
skin is intact. My reputation is another matter, but the possibility that I
might find myself turned away from the company of honest patriots was
explained to me at the first, and the pension that has been arranged
should provide for my basic wants. It has occurred to me that I will need
to make arrangements to find other housing before I set foot in my native
land again, if, in fact, I ever do. I still have that place in British Honduras, and I may go there for a while. You'll pardon me if I believe you
got the luckier result from the coin-toss that said you would align yourself
with the Ex-Pats' Coven for the purpose of learning who among them
might be in active cahoots with the Reds, and the course I was set upon:
following the traffic in human beings out of the refugee and displaced
persons' camps into the Third World, as well as authenticating the missions authorized by men working with Uncle Freddie. The Limeys would
say he has a couple rum blokes working for him, and they'd be right. Still,
I wanted adventure, and you may rest assured that I got it. You will*

have to remain in Sweden for another five years at a minimum, and that can't be easy for you.

I hope you'll be able to find some way to tell your sister thank you for me—short of showing her this letter—she was a most effective go-between; but she'd better be careful of your brother-in-law: he would be appalled to learn that she was doing more than sending you the occasional money order. The reports she carried home after visiting you last summer give me the opportunities I had been seeking. I got two years' worth of investigation documents past Hoover's Hounds; using Dave Wissart's address for the reports gave an added level of protection: who in the FBI would suspect a Republican Congressman's campaign planner of helping a real Communist Sympathizer? Hoover's a vainglorious buffoon, but we're stuck with him at the FBI for the time being.

Uncle Freddie has ordered me to create a legend for myself to account for the years that I was officially missing, and I think I may have the first outline of one. I'll fill you in if it turns out to meet Uncle Freddie's standards. Do you happen to recall that paper I gave in '39? The one about the universe not being static? The one all the Einsteinians found so objectionable? I may be using that as a jumping off place, as an academic argument that put my name on the mathematics landscape with a warning that I was worse than a union fink for doubting Papa Albert. It moves me away from the mess of the HUAC—not even Dave Wisssart could protect me from that stench—and puts me in with those whose hubris lost them all righteous mathematical chairs at respectable universities anywhere in the civilized world.

You tell me you like Uppsala, and I wish I could believe you, but I know the Swedes—stiff-rumped, inhospitable, and proud. Thar's not like you, Happy, and I can't believe your work for Uncle Freddie has made you so cynical that you're willing to take on protective coloration with your sister and me. You're there because you either feel some loyalty to Uncle Freddie or you've been painted into a corner and you want to keep your friends and family away from CIA attention. You're being cautious, and that is very good of you, as I am in preferring British Honduras to the US of A. My place is pleasant enough to provide you an amusing visit, but I'm prepared to wait until it's safe. When it is, we can make our plans.

D. G. A.

❖ 4 ❖

WINTER WAS making a last bid for attention, sending gouts of wind along the Parisian streets and over the waters of the Seine, whipping the surface into a grayish froth that made the wan light seeping through the lowering clouds seem even more threatening than it was in a city drained of color. From his small office in the Eclipse Press building, Szent-Germain stared out into the afternoon, a distracted air about him as he found himself recalling his stay in the city some two centuries ago when he was first introduced to Madelaine de Montalia: it was at a ball, and her aunt had introduced them; he clearly recalled how she had met his gaze directly, no sign of fear or dubiety in her knowing eyes. From that night until her death, she knew him for what he was and did not despise him for it, nor see him as the monster so many would do if they knew his true nature; he had not needed to tell her anything about his undead state, and yet she came to him willingly, eagerly. This recollection was anodyne to him, soothing his anxiety and giving him a clearer vision of his situation. The problems within his own company required immediate attention, he knew. "Back to the present," he told himself in his native tongue. He had more urgent—and less pleasant—matters to attend to than memories of Madelaine in her breathing days: he concentrated on the last year, trying to sort through the most recent changes in his plans that the latest news from Cecil Tommerson would require; this was not the kind of misunderstanding that could be worked out over time: he needed to address it promptly. To add fuel to Tommerson's accusations, Szent-Germain had received a letter from the factor in his South African office that left him troubled, and although the cold of his office did not bother him, he suppressed a shudder; he had already put in a telephone call to Hawsmede and would meet with him on Thursday in London, and he would need a day or two to assemble his records here in Paris as well as requesting information from Copenhagen, Amsterdam, Lisboa, Barcelona, Genova, and Venezia before he took the next step. Then there was the more delicate matter of Lord Weldon; he had let it be known that he had been trying to get news of him, and was considering venturing into Central Asia to find him, a prospect that gave him sardonic amusement. "A man in search of himself. How twentieth century of me." An emotion compounded of despair and vast loneliness that was only slightly relieved by irony and mourning enveloped him, but he quivered it off him. A small electric heater provided a little warmth to the room, but he paid no attention to it, for the cold he felt was not the result of the weather.

"Grof?" came Washington Young's voice from the other side of the door.

Szent-Germain shook himself mentally, and called out, "Come in, Young."

"I've just sent out the last *Grimoire*," he said as he came through the door. "We're planning a last meeting for mid-March, so you have a month to decide if you want to attend. Do you have any preferences for the date?"

"Not at the moment, and it shouldn't matter in any case; I've never been a member of your group, officially," said Szent-Germain, indicating the chair on the far side of the desk from him. "But thank you for thinking of me. I'm glad you've come in; I know you're busy." He cocked his head in the direction of the sound of the big presses clanking away in the main room. "I have a proposition to put to you, and I trust you'll consider it. A loyal Wobbly like you should find the opportunity acceptable."

"What kind of proposition?" Young asked, trying not to sound suspicious. "Are you going to include any others in the Coven in this offer?"

"No; this is specific to you, having to do with these presses, and others like them, and the Guttenburgs especially. I hope that won't be a problem for you with the Coven? I can see no reason why it should be, but if there is one, I hope you'll let me know now."

"I'm the only printer in the group—that's obvious. Okay, I'll consider it, so long it's none of your *divide and conquer* methods."

He realized what he had said, and changed his demeanor to something less confrontational. "I don't mean *your* methods but that's how some businesses go about union-busting."

"I'm aware of that, and I have nothing against unions; in fact, I think they're beneficial." He thought back to his centuries of dealing with working-men's organizations: guilds in the Middle Ages, Artei in Fiorenze, Brotherhoods in France and Germany, Companies in Eastern Europe . . . He made himself address the present. "If the shops want to organize, they may do so, with my blessing, if they need it."

"That's good to know," said Young, not entirely convinced. "But about the Coven—"

"I won't know my schedule for another two to three weeks, but remind me, if you would, and I'll ask Charis what she thinks."

"There aren't likely to be many of us still here by the last meeting," said Young, a little sadly as he sat down. "I don't believe it'll be much of a crowd."

"Very likely not," said Szent-Germain. "The Praegers have already left, and Russ McCall; Mary Anne is pleased in her new work and, I think, tired of Paris, so she may not attend. I think she's doing her best to break with the past, and that includes the Coven. We know Happy is set in Uppsala, and Win Pomeroy is out of the country," said Szent-Germain, agreeing with Young as a way to show his concern more than to reiterate shared knowledge. "The rest aren't likely to linger unless they have work here—"

"Like I do, thanks to you," said Young, a touch of anxiety in his voice. "Moira wants to stay here, and so do I."

"Then have Bethune review the contract and remain where you are, with my thanks." He leaned back in his chair, wanting to put Young more at his ease. "Not all the Coven is gone; I'm assuming that now Boris King has opened his record shop in Rue de les Faisans, he and his wife will attend anything linked to the Coven. Happy says any of you who want to visit are welcome in Sweden, but he has no intention of coming back here except on holiday. Steve diMaggio's business is flourishing, so he'll be here for some time. Sam Effering doesn't want the group broken up entirely—he was just getting used to it when it began to unravel—and is willing to come in from Luxembourg to help keep it going on a social level if nothing else, but he is in the minority. Axel Bjornson is bound for Kenya; maybe this time he'll find what he's looking for; the English don't seem worried about his politics the way the Americans are." He paused to allow Young to ask the question that was clearly burgeoning in his mind.

Young coughed diplomatically. "What about Charis? Do you think she'll join us at Chez Rosalie one last time?"

"I don't know," said Szent-Germain, and wondered if he should ask her or advise her to decide for herself; she would get Young's notice in a day or two, and would have many questions, provided she did not run into Young when she came to this office later this afternoon, in which case he would expect an immediate battery of questions.

"Okay," said Young. "She'll follow your lead, I suppose."

For an instant Szent-Germain looked startled, but then achieved a neutral smile. "Why do you assume that?"

"Cause that's what women do. They let the man rule the roost. It's what everyone expects." He shrugged. "Moira isn't like that, not after all those years taking care of Tim, but she's told me how hard it was to stand against him, when he first started downhill, and would not deal with his condition. Her family kept telling her to do what Tim thought best, and for a while she did, until it became obvious he wasn't improving, no matter that he said it was nothing to worry about, according to him. And he's right—it's nothing to him anymore." He watched Szent-Germain out of the tail of his eye to see if this last observation had given offense.

"It must have been very difficult, watching him fade away as he did," said Szent-Germain as he took a large manila envelope from his central desk drawer, stood up, and held it out to Young. "The specifics are spelled out in the contract. It will give you authority to coordinate all my European printing and distribution standards, essentially putting all the branches under one publishing house, as well as establishing one standard of conduct and procedure and an equivalency scale of pay for all employees." He saw Young's black

eyes light up, and knew he had made the right choice. "I'd appreciate an answer in a week, if that's convenient."

"I can't see any problem with that unless Bethune finds something wrong with the offer, and I don't think he will; he says you're
a fair man—more than fair," said Young, taking the envelope from
him, hesitating as he tucked it under his arm. "You know, Grof,
back home this wouldn't be as easy to do. Putting a Negro in charge
of so many branches of a business that isn't a Negro business . . . it
wouldn't be welcome."

"Is that why you're staying in France?" Szent-Germain inquired.

"It's part of it," he said, and added thoughtfully, "More than
that, most people back home wouldn't like the idea of Moira and
me as a couple. It's illegal for blacks and whites to marry in a lot of
states, and we're still thinking about possibly getting married one
of these days. I'd like it, and some days, so would Moira, but she's
close to her family and that makes for problems. The regular folk
here in Paris don't seem to mind so much here. We get strange
looks now and then, and Regina isn't very happy about it, but that's
not surprising: I doubt my kids will like it much when they find
out." He sighed.

"Mightn't it be easier to face them now rather than years from
now, when they've locked themselves into position?" Szent-Germain
remembered how dismayed Rakhel had been, twelve hundred years
ago, when she had been expected to accept a step-family into her
life.

"Hell, Grof, they've all been locked into position since they were
two—Negroes as well as whites." He looked about nervously as if
he still thought the room might be bugged. "You know why I want
to stay, really? It's not Moira, though I'd go with her to the ends of
the earth or even Alabama. The reason is no one here calls me *nig-
ger*." Then, as if this admission had exposed a rift between them, he
took a step back. "So do you think it likely that you'll be here for
the last meeting?"

Szent-Germain looked about the room. "I may be away when the
meeting happens." He saw Young flinch, and added, "You needn't
worry. This has nothing to do with my publishing houses. There

are some questions about what's happening in one of my shipping offices."

"Venice again?"

"No, not this time." He shook his head for emphasis.

"Then I won't count on you." He chuckled to cover his nervousness. "Count—Grof." He opened the door. "Steve diMaggio's going to visit Happy next weekend. He said he'd be . . . uh . . . happy to carry galleys to him if you'd like."

"Thank you; I'll telephone him tonight and make arrangements." He took a slow breath, and then said, "I trust you and Moira will be happy together, in spite of the difficulties you're apt to encounter."

"Much appreciated, Grof; at least we both got our eyes open." He went out and closed the door behind him, leaving Szent-Germain in the chilly isolation of his office.

"It always bothers me when I talk to myself," Szent-Germain remarked to the air. He was speaking his own tongue, relishing the rhythm of it, and the rolling cadences of its structure. "Sometimes I wonder why I bother; only Rogerian understands the language, and not very well. Who knows how much of it I have forgotten." Even as he said it, he knew he continued to use the long-vanished tongue of his people as a gesture of continuity, a tie beyond blood that gave him a sense of endurance to serve as a tribute to his blood and his god. The loss of his language would be as great a sacrifice as the loss of Laisha had been. "Come, Ragoczy, you have work to do. There are more things to put in motion. Lord Weldon must vanish officially, and I must make the first statements of my intention to find him." He reached into the top drawer on his right and pulled out a pad of lined paper, which he set in the center of his desk while he removed his fountain-pen from the small box containing several kinds of writing implements. Then he sat down and began to write in a small, precise hand. He would begin with Rowena Saxon in New Zealand, then James Emmerson Tree in Canada, and then Madelaine de Montalia in Central America; Rowena and James he addressed in English, Madelaine in slightly archaic French, telling them all of his plans for the next year or so, and reassuring them that the Blood Bond would keep them aware of one another and him. They were to pay no attention to any rumors of his death, or of his disappearance, for that was all they would be: rumors and gossip. If anything seriously wrong happened, Roger would notify them personally. He was in the middle of the last paragraph to Madelaine when there was an urgent knock on his door; he folded the letters and slipped them under the large, fresh blotter. "Yes?"

"Szent-Germain, it's me," Charis called out somewhat unsteadily. "I'm a little early."

"Charis. Come in." He rose and stepped out from behind the desk just as she flung open the door and rushed in.

She was neatly dressed, but her well-cut simple page-boy hairdo was slightly awry, with tendrils twisted around her face—a sure sign of anxiety. She had not bothered to put on lipstick, which made her look paler than she was. "Thank God you're already here. I thought I'd have to track you down all over the city." She came up to him, embraced him hastily, and leaned her head against his shoulder.

"Why? What's the matter?" He guided her to his visitor's chair. "Sit down, won't you? and tell me what this is all about."

"It's about that . . . that *toad* from the Embassy," she exclaimed.

"And which toad would that be?" he asked politely.

In spite of her fury, she coughed up a chuckle. "You know him. Peter Leeland's his name. I hate the sight of him." Now that she had spoken the worst, she continued more companionably. "You're right. They do have a lot of toads at the Embassy. Do they choose them for being like that, or is it an accident? Rothcoe is cut from the same cloth, only not so smooth a customer. There's something ophidic about Leeland, and something—I don't know what—about Rothcoe." She pulled a handkerchief from her purse and dabbed at her eyes with it; her hand was shaking.

"I have no idea how they select them," said Szent-Germain, half-sitting on the edge of the desk and taking her hand. "What has Leeland done now?"

"He's been at my flat, asking questions about where all the Coven members are—I don't think he believes I don't really know, but

I don't, and some of what I've been told is wrong on purpose." She shook her head. "Today I realized he's a lot like Harold—quiet and polite and scarey; not the way you are when you want to settle something that annoys you, or you distrust the person with whom you're dealing. Leeland's like Basil Rathbone: like a sharp knife on a whetstone: Rothcoe's more like a rake on concrete. He—Leeland—tells me what happens to people who don't cooperate with the US government. I wanted to scream. I know what happens. It's happened to me. I'm not going to let it happen again."

"That is uncalled-for: Leeland's conduct, not yours," said Szent-Germain. "I'll ask Bethune to have a word with him, and with Rothcoe, just in case. Bethune's signing on with Eisley Butterthorn & Hawsmede; he'll be able to handle Leeland, and probably any other . . . shall we say toads?"

"He also wants to see pages from the book I'm working on," she declared, her indignation returning. "He's threatening to subpoena the manuscript, and any carbons. I put them in the safe in the bedroom closet before I left. Not the obvious one, the one behind the shoe-racks. I don't think they'll find it on a regular search."

"Well, he can't see them, whether he finds them or not, so there's an end to it." Szent-Germain leaned over and kissed her gently, taking his time about it.

"I'll ask Bethune to handle it," she said when the kiss ended, and took hold of his hand. "You don't have to get involved with any of this."

"I'm your publisher; like it or not, I am involved." He looked toward the window, and saw that the day had darkened. "How did you get here?"

"I hailed a cab," she answered. "I figure Leeland's got someone watching the car, and I didn't want to make things easy for him."

"He probably does," Szent-Germain said with a world-weary sigh, continuing, "Have someone watching you."

"He's probably got someone watching you and your Jaguar, too." She bit the inside of her cheeks to keep from weeping. "I'm so sorry, Grof."

"You have no reason to be sorry, and an excellent reason to be angry," he said, laying his small hand on her shoulder. "You've done nothing to bring any of this about, so you owe no one an apology. Leeland and Rothcoe certainly owe you one."

"I don't want to see either of them ever again," she informed him, beginning to feel cold now that her immediate anger was fading. "The Committee was bad enough: those two are like lethal kewpie dolls."

He got off the desk and went to his side-cabinet, taking out a beautiful glass bottle filled with a bright-yellow liquid. "May I ply you with some Strega? And then some advice?"

"Yes please to the Strega; I gather that's it in the bottle? Very pretty. I'm not so sure about the advice." She tried to smile but it did not quite work.

"As you wish," he said, and filled a tulip-shaped liqueur-glass halfway. "There is more if you want it."

"I haven't tried it yet," she reminded him, accepting the glass. She tasted the buttery liquid, opened her mouth in surprise and in response to the intensity of the flavor. "Wow. That's almost electric. That's something else again," she said, and put the glass down on the desk. "I'll go at it slowly, I think. I can tell it'll knock you endways." She almost laughed. "Well, not *you*, specifically, but most simple mortals."

"Perhaps the advice will be more to your taste?" he ventured. "The weather isn't very enjoyable, but what do you say to the plan that we go down to La Belle Romaine? We needn't stay for more than a day or two, but it would give you some time to recover from the Embassy's tricks. I'll make a few calls, and the thing is done. We can come back to less hassle than we've endured the last six months." He would have Rogers do a little snooping in his absence so that there would be necessary information waiting upon their return from Orleans.

She tried the Strega again, this time with more preparation. When she put the glass down a second time, she said, "I don't like running away."

"This would be a strategic withdrawal, not a rout," he said. "The last thing you need to do when you're worn out is take on a larger foe. Give yourself a chance to recuperate and then set Bethune on Leeland and Rothcoe."

"Why? If I don't react quickly, they'll think they've won, won't they?"

"Only if they are fools," he answered, his voice low and caressing.

She studied his face but saw nothing that helped her to decide what to do. "Oh, God, Grof. I don't want to talk about this. I want to bash them on their heads with Dutch ovens. I want to hang them by their heels from the Eiffel Tower. I want them to leave me alone!" she said audaciously. "I just want it to be over."

"That makes sense to me, but it can't happen by wishing," he said, his voice gentle as he came back to hitch one leg onto his desk.

"I knew you'd say something like that," she complained. "It's worse that you're right, I know you're right."

He studied her, wondering if she were letting him lead her as Young had suggested. "If you go away for a few days, they will tend to think they've done well, and they will begin to underestimate you."

"That's just what I'm afraid of," she said at once.

"And it's completely understandable that you are. But think a moment." He held up his first finger. Not in an admonitory way, but to gain her attention. "If they underestimate you, you gain an advantage over them at once. If they believe you have lost your nerve and are retreating in disorder, they will not be prepared to deal with you when you return, ready to enter the second phase of your campaign against them. With you away from Paris, they won't know what you're doing, and may think they needn't care. They will have dropped their guard and will not be looking for indications of your next step. Gather your thoughts and define your goals while we're at La Belle Romaine, and when I go to London to see Hawsmede, come with me and let him discuss the problem with Bethune. Between them and you, it should be possible to come up with a way to get these toads out of your life for good."

She considered this carefully, saying quietly, "Will they believe I've fled? Won't they think I'm up to something? *I'd* think I'm up to something."

"Ah, but you know yourself, they don't; they believe that females do not plan ahead, and that they are easily intimidated, which you and I know is untrue," he said, reaching into his pocket to pull out a folded key-wallet. "The Jaguar is over on the other side of the park behind this building, in an access-alley. It's near the Boulevard Deux Mintoux; the second access-alley." The old potholed roadway had been very grand two centuries ago, with a history going back nine hundred years; now it was a handy parking place for those in the neighborhood who did not mind poor paving and few lights.

"That's the one with the seventeenth-century house with new bay windows on the first house?" she asked, being cautious.

"Yes. I need about ten minutes to finish up here, and then I'll join you." He offered her a look that was both supportive and encouraging.

"Does this mean you'll let me drive?" She took the key from him, and slipped it into the small pocket on the sleeve of her dress.

"If you want to. But don't start the engine until I arrive: I don't want to waste fuel." It was less than the truth, but he did not want to upset her by implying that there might be people listening for the Jaguar's engine. If he was being followed, he wanted to get away from his watchers with as little notification as possible.

"Okay," she said, setting the one-third-full small glass on the end of his desk. "But don't be too long. That car of yours is really tempting. I might end up tooling it around the block."

"I like the XK," he concurred. "Go on. I'll be out shortly. No more than ten minutes." He took her hand and kissed it. "We'll find a way to end this, Charis. It won't hang over your head much longer."

Her expression drooped for a fraction of a second, and then she smiled—perhaps a little too broadly and brightly, but it was better than a scowl. "I'm counting on you, Grof. If anyone can do it, you can."

"With the help from several others." He reached for his telephone. "Now go. Ten minutes. Remember."

"I'll check my watch," she said. "Four-twenty-three. You have until four-thirty-three," she informed him as she picked up her purse and reached for the door. She waved as she left him alone; he remained still for nearly three minutes, then took a deep breath and began to dial, one eye on the clock on his desk.

Szent-Germain's first call was to Rogers, and it lasted no longer than three minutes: "Charis and I will be going to Orleans tonight. While we're away, have Steve diMaggio come and do a very thorough search of her flat, this office, and our flat. There's something amiss going on."

"You'll pardon me if I say there has been something amiss since we got here," Rogers answered abruptly; as a precaution he spoke in Byzantine Greek.

Szent-Germain went on in the same tongue. "I want a complete report by the time we return, which should be Saturday afternoon; I'll let you know if we decide to stay the whole weekend. Leeland and Rothcoe have been pestering Charis again, and it's wearing on her. Please pass on the report to Bethune. Use a messenger and not the post office. It's important that we keep our effort under the rose."

"I'll attend to it. Are you coming back here this evening?"

"Yes, I think so. Charis left her auto at her flat in the hope that she wouldn't be followed, and so it may be better to have her stay the night. We'll pick up her things in the morning, on our way to La Belle Romaine. If you would, call Valerot and tell him we're coming."

"Of course."

"I'll want an appointment next Monday, as early as you can get, with Edward Merryman at the Embassy. Impress upon him that it is serious and urgent. He only looks harmless, so don't hesitate to tell him everything he wants to know." His demeanor softened. "Thank you, old friend. I'll gladly answer your questions later."

"When should I expect you?" Rogers asked.

"A little after five, or maybe a bit later. It depends upon whether or not we're being followed."

"I'll bear that in mind," said Rogers, and hung up.

Szent-Germain's second call was to the overseas operator. He booked several telephone calls for the next week, asked that the bookings be confirmed by Saturday, and made notes to himself in his pocket memorandum. The most clamant of the new array of problems would be addressed as soon as he got back, and at least he had done the initial work for counter-measures. He took his coat from the peg on the back of the door, then turned off the light in his office, and the heater. As he left, he called out over the clank of the presses, "Mister Young! I'm leaving now. I'll return on Monday." He thought as he closed the outer door that it was time to get a secretary. He would ask Young if he would like to have one when he came in on Tuesday. As he checked his watch, he saw he was on time. He entered the park, holding his coat closed against the wind, and caught sight of the grounds-keeper attempting to water a bed of emerging hyacinths; he slowed briefly, wondering if the man might be watching them, considering how poor the weather was for gardening. Satisfied that neither he nor the Jaguar was being surveilled, he moved on. He could just make out the bumper of his Jaguar in the anemic afternoon light. He lifted his hand to signal he was coming.

Charis rolled down the window and waved, then held up the key. "I'm ready!" she called to him.

He reached the edge of the park and stepped over the low brick fence and onto the aged paving of the Boulevard Deux Mintoux; he increased his pace as he heard the key turn in the ignition.

There was an unfamiliar second sound, unrecognizable, and then fire erupted with volcanic ferocity; Szent-Germain stopped moving. In an instant the flames caught up with him; they lapped his clothes and much of his skin off him before being quenched by the first blast of water from the nearby emergency cistern being manned by the horrified grounds-keeper, who sprayed water in all directions, from the ruined vehicle to the burning trees, to the collapsing figure framed in fire. Smoke came suddenly in blinding clouds, and when that had cleared, what was left behind was a mass of bone and raw tissue heaped in the road and an ugly black burn-scar topped by lumps of blasted metal sunk into the new pothole in the pavement along with shattered glass and bits of bone, which, until not quite three seconds ago, had been a 1949 maroon Jaguar XK120 with a woman in her late thirties who had been preparing to drive it away.

18 February, 1951

Hotel Felicidad
Plaza de los Evangelistas
Caracas, Venezuela

My dear friend,
    *To enlarge upon what we discussed on the telephone the other night, let
me say that I have been able to get Saint-Germain's body away from the
authorities here, thanks to the document the Comte constructed before he
left for America, almost twenty years ago. At present, I have brought him
to his estate at Lecco. I have him safe in the guest-house on the knoll behind
the main house. Only you, Mister Tree, and Miss Saxon will know of this
until the Comte begins to recover. The French have him listed as dead,
which is acceptable to all of us. When the Comte is stronger, I will take him
into Romania, to his native earth, so that his recovery may be complete
and as rapid as possible. From there, he can proclaim his new identity and
pursue a course of retribution on behalf of the man he will present as his
cousin. For now, the Comte is in a stupor, of course, almost as profound as
he was after hanging on that cross in Mexico. Here, at least, he can be kept
in isolation until he has regrown some muscle and skin.*
    *The grounds-keeper who witnessed the explosion was very much
overset by it, and, it turns out, somewhat mentally handicapped. He has
only been able to say that he saw a man with reddish hair near the automobile, but paid no attention to him—so many people stopped to stare at*

the handsome auto. Luckily he was not immobilized by panic, but turned his water on high as soon as he realized something dreadful had happened. It is unlikely that he will ever be called to give testimony.

I have spoken with Inspector Mielle in Genova, asking for what the French police—all their police; Gendarmes, Surete, and local authorities—have learned, and what has been told to me indicates that they agree this was a targeted killing; it took place away from most public attention, and was set off in all likelihood by the turning of the key in the ignition. Whoever set the bomb was clearly experienced in such tasks, and none of the radical groups have claimed credit for the act. Mister Bethune is talking to the US Embassy about Professor Treat and so far has learned very little. No doubt he will persevere.

The Comte will need a month or two before he can travel any distance, and at present, entering Romania would be too much of a risk, so it is likely that we will go along the southern shore of the Black Sea into Turkey. The Comte has a small estate there, and it is known that many of his relatives have lived there over the last hundred years. You may have been one of them. In any case, he will have time to himself and will not be found easily without his encouragement.

He has said that he looks forward to seeing you next year in Roma, when you give your paper. As burned as he is, he can still speak enough to make his wishes known. He will appear as his cousin, of course, and will be glad of your company whenever it can be arranged. I admit that this is a relief to me, for I have worried that the murder of Charis so soon after the loss of his ward Laisha might impel him into a melancholy that would complicate his recovery from his burns.

I will call you on the telephone in a week and tell you what progress we have made—if any—so that you may decide how you wish to proceed. I should warn you that the Comte does not want any visitors for at least two months, when his features and his eyes should be nearly healed, and I know he would rather delay meeting with you until your conference brings you to Roma; he wishes to quiet all speculation about his identity. He has told me you would understand.

With deep respect,
Rogers
(Roger)

❖ 5 ❖

LYDELL BROADSTREET put the receiver into its cradle with more force than he intended, and then muttered a curse under his breath. "So the report was right. He killed two people. In Paris. I never asked him to do that. The French don't like having bombs go off in their cities." He got to his feet and began to pace, and expostulated to the room as he moved, "He's made a mess of it. A whole cock-up. A man with his reputation. Just goes to show." He stopped at the window and stared out into the waning February light; Baltimore seemed melancholy in the pale winter sunshine, like an old hand-tinted photograph that had faded to nacreous shades. "Riggs, Riggs, Riggs, I made it plain that you were to implicate the Ex-Pats' Coven," he added, reassuring himself, for thinking back on his instructions, he had to admit they were deliberately vague, and because of that might be subject to misinterpretation, a realization that he resisted. "Forty thousand is more than enough." He had hired a professional, a man known throughout the covert world as reliable, who knew how the game was played, no matter how Broadstreet had expressed it in his first telegram. Still, Riggs knew what he wanted, and now the man was asking for more money since two people were killed in the blast he had set under Szent-Germain's Jaguar. The foreign Szent-Germain was an unfortunate accident, but the American woman meant that the CIA would be doubly vigilant in their participation in the investigation, and that caused him consternation. He had applied for money to pay Baxter two weeks ago: half of it had gone to Riggs; Broadstreet could not ask for more without some results from the first payment, which could lead to questions being asked. And it all came down to this: Riggs wanted more money. "I won't stand for it. It's damned blackmail. Another ten thousand dollars, because of the killings. Ridiculous. He's had two payments of twenty, and that's going to be the end of it. He won't sue me."

A gentle tap on the door made him jump in his chair. "Mister Broadstreet?" Opal Pierce called out softly. "Are you busy?"

Broadstreet collected his thoughts, and reminded himself not to speak aloud when he was alone. "Come in, Opal. Please," he said, standing straighter in the window, and staring at the far wall. He turned to smile at Pierce as she came through the door. "What is it? Anything from Baxter?" He had taken to asking frequently about Baxter as if he had some genuine cause for worry; it gave him satisfaction to continue the deception, making him feel clever and capable. "I wish we knew what had silenced him so suddenly." He knew he sounded odd; he was amazed at the immediate effect she had on him: he dared not look down in case his growing erection was visible in the front of his trousers. She smelled of expensive perfume, and the way she moved was hypnotic. He realized he was staring and looked away.

"Are you afraid something may have happened to him?" she asked, coming to his side and putting her hand into his.

He strove for the proper tone. "I'd be irresponsible if I weren't concerned. A man in Baxter's position can be exposed by hundreds of little things, and then . . . well, who knows?" He rubbed his chin. "I wish I knew who he really is. I could do more to protect him."

Pierce knew Broadstreet was working himself into a state, and decided that she had to calm him down. "Baxter will turn up. You said so yourself." She slipped her arm around him. "Don't worry; you'll get through this. So will Baxter."

He stared at her gratefully. "It's not easy, handling a case with such far-reaching elements." With a short, abrupt sigh, he turned to her, kissing her bluntly.

As soon as she could, she ended the kiss. "It's still working hours and there are people about," she said quietly. "You don't want to draw attention to yourself."

"No, I don't," he agreed. "There's so much at stake."

She moved away from him, her face revealing nothing but concern for him. "You can show them how useful you are, right now. Especially now. If you can avert a crisis, it will go down in your record, and that will bolster your position. Don't let yourself get flummoxed, not when you're so close." She saw him wince at her choice of words. "Just think what you have endured so far. Surely you can stand a little more."

He nodded appreciatively. "There has been a lot to do." He was certain that he would have to find a way to shore up the appearance of blame for the two deaths on the Ex-Pats' Coven. "Baxter might know something about the explosion. He has a connection to them, as I recall." As soon as he said it, he wished he had not; he could not remember if he had linked Baxter and the Ex-Pats' Coven in any of his reports. Now he was committed to providing an explanation about the two deaths that might in some way lead to Baxter. He would need some means of shoring up such a suspicion, but it could be too little, too late. He would not get through this without too many questions being asked.

She put a little pressure on his back and guided him back to his desk. "There are many things you'll need to do overnight. You need to get ahead of the herd or it'll stampede right over you."

A phone in the next office shrilled and after four insistent rings was picked up; the steady clack of typewriters continued.

He sat down, once again feeling bewildered. "What things?"

She sat on the arm of his chair, perching carefully. "There was a call from Mister Channing's office a short while ago," she said. "He'd like you to come there at ten tomorrow morning. There are some questions he would like to go over with you."

Broadstreet took a deep breath as if he had been doused with ice–water. "Ten? In his Washington office? All right." He thought he sounded stilted and unconvincing, so he added, "What more can you tell me? Did he happen to mention what concerns him?"

"His current secretary didn't say," she told him, not mentioning that she had not asked; she was relishing the discomfort she was causing him; it was precisely what Channing had told her to do. "There's been some talk about closing some of the satellite offices in favor of putting them all under one roof." There had been a lot of gossip about that possibility, and thus far no final decision had been made.

"We're not actively at war now. Why shouldn't we put us all in one place? I think the satellites were sensible during the war, but now?" He was speaking too loudly. "We can maintain better control of our information if we have a . . . a central office for central intelligence." It was a feeble joke. "It's not as if anyone's going to blow it up during the peace. It could have happened during the war, but not now." He cleared his throat. "You know how the upper directors have been pushing for a proper office, somewhere close enough to Washington to be useful for all of us, but away from the hustle and bustle of the city. We ought to include everyone who handles classified information."

"Mister Channing will want to hear your opinion," said Pierce as an encouragement. She bent and kissed him. "Have you had your lunch yet?"

"No. I've been busy."

"It's about two, isn't it?" She slipped off the arm of the chair and stood, half-facing him. "Why not leave early, have a real lunch away from here, do some thinking, and then go home and organize yourself for tomorrow? Bring everything that's even marginally connected to that explosion in Paris, then figure out which of the field agents you think should work on this."

Broadstreet nodded several times. "I don't have any appointments this afternoon. I guess I could do that," he said slowly, still feeling nervous but beginning to think that he might have happened upon an out. He stared hungrily at her. "I'd rather spend it with you."

"We'll put our minds to that later," she said, all brisk efficiency. She had her own appointment with Channing in less than two hours, and would have to leave shortly. "Remember, if you're worn out tomorrow, Channing will notice. He might hold it against you, to see you unrested."

"I know, I know," said Broadstreet, sounding ill-used.

Pierce regarded him very somberly. "You want that promotion, don't you? You want to be head of a foreign office?" She felt more than saw Broadstreet nod. "Then don't carp about the rules of the game you're playing."

"I won't," he promised, surprised at her brusque recommendations.

He knew Channing could make or break him now, and after all he had done to gain a promotion to the *real* work of the CIA, he was determined not to throw it all away on a point of pride. "I get your point. I'm going to study up on everything I've been working on. Particularly Baxter. And I'll have a plan or two to show Manfred Channing, as well."

"That's the spirit," she said, and started toward the door. "Go on, now. I'll notify the front desk that you're out the rest of today and all of tomorrow."

"Thank you," said Broadstreet in a tone that was precariously close to being humble.

"You get on it," she told him as she let herself out.

"Right you are," Broadstreet called after her, then loaded up his briefcase and went to find his coat. He was already thinking where he should go and what he should do about Baxter. He was out of the building in three minutes and in his new Nash in another two, so he did not see Pierce leave through the north door ten minutes later. He drove through the city paying little heed to the traffic; he was trying to decide if he had failed with his Baxter ploy, and if so, how. He drove steadily for almost an hour, preoccupied, trying to ease the desperation that welled deep within him while he searched for an out-of-the-way place to eat. He knew that whatever he decided before his meeting tomorrow would have to be the story that he would make into the truth if he were ever to get his promotion. "And I *will* get a promotion," he said, leaning toward the steering wheel. "I've earned it."

After a little less than an hour of driving, Broadstreet pulled in at the Blue Crab, out on the county road that led to Little Macklin, a small fishing village that had been slowly dying for a century. The Blue Crab was at the head of a pier where crabbing boats would tie up and make their first sales. It was frequented by people from the village and the faculty and staff from a junior college located a mile away. The tables were covered in newspapers, and the waitresses wore sensible slacks and shirts, and thick-soled boots because of the bits and pieces of soft-shelled crabs that littered the floor. The place was not very busy this afternoon, and the owner, who served as his own maitre d', was more than glad to seat Broadstreet at a table for four, giving the main dining room the air of more business than was the case. Broadstreet ordered a local beer and a bucket of blue and golden crabs in butter and onions, and encouraged his thoughts to drift. He glanced around the room with its decoration of nets and old crab-traps. Was this the kind of place Baxter might suggest as a meeting place? Was this too ordinary? Not ordinary enough? Was the Helmsman a better choice? He thought about that as a possibility and rejected it. Baxter might prefer a place like this, catering to the working class and where strangers were always remembered. That realization almost made him get up and leave, but that would make him more obvious than if he had a meal. He would take the time to consider how to go about bringing Baxter back into the case. It was time Baxter left the scene, Broadstreet saw it clearly. But to do that, he had to bring Baxter back long enough to resolve the case. He would need to show some activity from Baxter by the end of the month, so that Channing would continue to authorize payments for him. It would have to be another ten days before the next communication arrived, so that it would not appear too coincidental to have the inquiry begin at almost the same time as the newest letter arrived. He would have to receive something from Baxter that was useful as well as serious. He would have to go through many of his files to see what could be tied to Baxter. Broadstreet signaled to a waiter to bring one of the large bibs the restaurant provided its patrons. He slipped the loop over his head and tied the waistbands behind him. Now he felt less conspicuous than he had before. He smiled as he reached for a crab and the mallet that served as flatware. There was something so satisfying about smashing crabs, he thought as he broke the shell in a single, well-placed blow. One of the crab's claws spun halfway across the table, so Broadstreet reached for it first.

Pierce, too, was preparing for an afternoon light meal, what Channing called a French Tea, with an array of sweet pastries and a bowl of brandied whipped cream as well as tea. She sat on the sofa away from his desk, the coffee-table providing a small barrier between her and Channing, who had rolled his chair over to face her, his full attention being on her. "It's good to see you, Opal." His very cordiality put her on guard, although she was careful not to show it.

"Well, Fred, I have to thank you: this is a luxury, an absolute luxury." She poured a cup of strong English Breakfast tea, and held it out to him. "I think I'll save the eclairs for last. They'd ruin everything else if I had them first."

"Whatever will please you, Opal," he said, accepting the cup.

"I suppose you ordered this from a bakery. They didn't do it up in the lunchroom." She was relieved to see him smile.

"No, the most I could get from the lunchroom is crackers and cheese and maybe a dozen smoked baby clams."

"Or an assortment of store-bought cookies," she suggested, and made a face at the prospect.

"Something of the sort," he agreed, locking the wheels on his chair before leaning forward to take a paper napkin and a cream-puff. "Go on; help yourself."

"This is a wonderful treat; I'm going to make the most of it," she declared, contemplating a napoleon. "Napoleons, babas-au-rhum, eclairs, cream-puffs, and lemon squares." She was about to reach for one of the display when his question stopped her.

"How's Broadstreet doing these days?"

Her answer to that was the reason for this meeting. She took the teapot and filled her own cup, using the time to frame her answer; it was a large, stoneware pot, and quite heavy. "He's getting worried, and that's upsetting his work. There's been no further contact from Baxter—nothing. I think Baxter's left town, or someone else has found him and he's run off or maybe we'll find him floating in a marsh in a month or so. I'll bet, if he's running, he went out through Canada and then on to Europe. I've already checked with the overseas airlines, and there's no record of a Baxter leaving from this area in the last two months."

"National airlines carry more passengers, and the search would be more complex," Channing said. "And, as you know, if he's left the country, there are a number of airports he might choose. He could take a train to Chicago and fly from there."

"Yes, he could," Pierce agreed. "But did he?" He took a bite of the cream-puff. "Seems a bit unlikely, under the circumstances," he said, then wiped away the whipped cream and confectioner's sugar that framed his mouth.

"I doubt it," she told him, frowning. "I think that Broadstreet has a plan in place with him."

"Have you seen anything that supports your theory?" he asked calmly. "Or is this your woman's intuition working overtime?"

"It's not intuition, Fred. I wouldn't bother you with that." She did her best not to sound annoyed at such an accusation, and very nearly succeeded.

"Don't get your feathers ruffled," he admonished her, smiling to make it all right. "You're a sharp-eyed girl, and I respect that. So what makes you think Baxter might have flown the coop? at least temporarily."

"The way Broadstreet's acting," she said at once, striving to order her thoughts on the matter. "He's paid little attention to Baxter for three or four months, almost as if he knew that Baxter wouldn't be around, or that he didn't expect to hear from him. I didn't put much stock in that, assuming the two had worked something out between them. Someone might be closing in on Baxter—the FBI, Army or Navy Intelligence—and so he's gone to ground. But a couple of weeks ago, Broadstreet started getting . . . I don't know . . . nervous. Not for any reason in particular, but enough for me to notice it. I thought maybe there'd been new information on that group in Paris, or maybe D. G. Atkins had been located, but it wasn't specific enough to know what had set him off." She looked away from him, her face set with exasperation. "I couldn't get much out of him, except he said that he was worried about a case."

"What made you think it was Baxter?" Channing persisted. "Broadstreet has other cases to worry about."

"He made a joke about Baxter, about how we should be looking at mother's maiden names among those we've been checking out. He said Freud was right—mothers were at the heart of men's problems. It wasn't funny, really, but it was clear that he had something in mind about Baxter, something that was bothering him. I followed up on the mother's maiden names search, but didn't find anyone with that name among close relatives. I don't want to spend the next six months tracking down family names for all the possible suspects." She flushed a little, knowing that Channing was running out of patience; she spoke faster. "And he's been getting more distressed. Broadstreet is doing a more extensive follow-up than is necessary, under the circumstances." She waited a few seconds while Channing consumed the rest of the cream-puff, then went on. "That bomb in Paris upset him. He's been brooding about it since it happened."

"Do you think there's a connection to Baxter? That explosion is worrying the French. Broadstreet's doing the smart thing with his follow-up: it shows the right attitude." Channing sounded more forceful now, pressing her with his stance and the tone of his voice; the rest of the pastries went untouched.

"He'd probably like it, to connect them, but about the only thing they have in common is Broadstreet himself. If the two cases intersect, it may be only through him." This was the meat of her burgeoning notion, and she decided to make the most of it. "Something in his earlier investigation of the Paris group could have set off the Baxter case. I don't know what it is, but it would explain what we're finding out." She chose her words carefully, to show Channing that she considered herself involved.

Channing was about to upbraid her for that remark, but then sat back in his chair, musing. "That's an interesting theory. Tell me more."

Pierce drank her rapidly cooling tea and looked directly at him. "It didn't occur to me until just now: but I can't remember how he decided that there might be a connection to the group in Paris. I didn't start to work for him until after the Baxter business began, remember. Nothing he said to me seemed to support it. I make full allowance for secretive plans, but there are secrets and then there are secrets. And the care that Baxter went to to hide himself made me think he might be an agent of some kind, himself—maybe FBI, maybe someone foreign—because everything Broadstreet reported about Baxter suggested a professional."

"That's interesting," said Channing, softening his approach to Pierce.

"I can't figure out what Baxter is up to. If he were MI6, we could approach the Limeys, but he's not English—I can tell by the spelling and the grammar. He's American."

"You're certain of that." Channing waited for her to explain herself.

She paused. "He could be a Canadian, but they're still very British."

"Could he be working for a foreign power?" Channing asked.

"So you can keep the Agency out of the spotlight?" she countered. "I don't know enough about Baxter to make a guess." She wondered if she dared to light up a cigarette.

"Don't make up what you don't know, but is it possible that Baxter is selling what he has to the highest bidder?"

"Yes, it's possible, I suppose." To gain herself a little time, she reached for the teapot once more, offering him a fill-up, which he declined, before pouring more into her cup. "I thought it might be an FBI operation—trying to set us up for Hoover, so he can take us over."

"Truman won't let that happen," said Channing, his confidence apparent in every line of his body. "Truman knows why we need a foreign intelligence agency that is not part of domestic intelligence."

"He doesn't trust Hoover." Pierce looked toward the window, doing her best to ignore Channing's scrutiny.

"Who does?" Channing asked. "Besides Walter Winchell."

It was almost as feeble a joke as Broadstreet's about mother's maiden name had been, but Pierce laughed dutifully, feeling that she had avoided something dreadful. She reached for her purse and took out a pack of cigarettes, selecting one and removing it. She was about to pull out her book of matches but saw that Channing had his lighter out. "Oh. Thanks, Fred." She leaned over the table so he could apply the little flame to her Lucky Strike.

"Always a pleasure to be of service to a lady," he said as he snapped the lid closed and returned it to his pocket. "Tell me more about your reason for—"

To her dismay, Pierce suddenly sneezed. Mortified, she put her cigarette in the ashtray at the end of the coffee-table, then she set her cup down and reached for her purse again for her handkerchief. "I'm so sorry," she said. "It's this hay fever. Smoking's supposed to calm it down, but . . ." She turned away to blow her nose.

"Have some more tea," Channing recommended.

In order to turn attention away from her hay fever, she said, "I thought you had a waiter. Didn't you have one the last time I came in to discuss Broadstreet?"

"Yes. He left two months ago. I'll have to find a new one." He drank a little tea.

"What happened to him?" It was an innocent inquiry, not intended to require an extended answer.

"He's gone back to J. Edgar, a little the worse for wear now, I trust." There was malice in his smile.

She was folding her handkerchief, but looked up at him. "Good Lord. There's going to be a scandal."

Channing chuckled. "No, there isn't."

"Why not?" Pierce asked.

"Because neither we nor the FBI want to be too closely scrutinized by anyone, including our own leaders. The more closely we're monitored, the less effective we can be. Too many people will know what we're doing, and that can't be allowed." Channing sighed. "It's an awkward situation. They and we have taken advantage of the fear of Communist infiltrators, and have extended our activities beyond the limits of the law, and neither they nor we can afford to have these . . . lapses exposed. We're in the more marginal position, because we aren't supposed to deal inside the US, and to find out what we've been doing in some cases would really be a scandal. So, like the FBI, we'll handle our internal peccadillos internally."

"How?" Pierce asked, then stifled another sneeze.

"The way we have avoided scandal before: Hoover's man will be given a technical promotion and then be posted to some place like Fargo or, if he's really screwed up, Guam, and his career will stagnate. We do the same thing here, and we have more out-of-the-way places to send our embarrassments. There's an opening in Singapore, and another in Bratislava. And one coming up in Jakarta."

For a chaotic moment, Pierce thought this warning was for her—that she might be posted to Papua in New Guinea, or Vladivostok in the Soviet Union. "Oh," she said, to let him know she understood. She picked up her cigarette, tapped off the ash, and took a drag on it.

Channing shook his head. "Don't worry, Opal; I need you here to help me keep an eye on our people. I was referring—a bit too obliquely—to Broadstreet. As much as this business can be secure, your position is. You can buy a town house in Alexandria, if you like, and know you'll still live there when it's paid for." He picked up a small bowl holding three babas-au-rhum, took a spoon from the goblet full of flatware, and cut off a bite-sized bit.

Or until you're gone from the Agency, she thought as she fought down a third sneeze. "Job security?" she suggested, wishing she had a plausible reason to leave.

"You know more about the Agency than most of the people working for it. You have a reputation for not listening to gossip, and you're loyal—to me."

She could think of nothing to say, so she bowed her head, trying to decide as she did if she should warn Broadstreet of what might be facing him by summer.

"Penny," he said, cutting short her reverie.

"What? For my thoughts?" she asked, hoping she had made a good recovery.

"What else?" He maneuvered his chair a little nearer the table, picked up the teapot and refilled her cup. "I'll call up for more, if you'd like."

"Not for me, thanks," she said, already anticipating a dash to the ladies' room even as she drank half the cup.

"About your thoughts," he prompted, his face once again in neutral lines.

"I think Broadstreet may be in over his head. The Baxter case has got away from him, and he's floundering." This was as direct as she was prepared to be; the whole mess might still blow up in Baxter's face, and Pierce wanted to catch no shrapnel from the blast.

"Would you think that having an assistant would help? I could assign another agent to the case, to work with him." His ingenuous smile might have fooled someone who did not know Channing, but Pierce was not fooled.

"You mean you want to put another spy on him?"

"In a sense," said Channing at his most bland.

"I think it wouldn't be wise. I think that could lead to public attention and more publicity than would be good for us." She picked up her purse and stood up suddenly. "Excuse me. I'll be back shortly." With that, she bolted for the door, hoping she could make it to the rest room in time. When she returned to Channing's office less than ten minutes later, the profusion of pastries had been whisked away and in its place was a bottle of whisky.

"I don't want to ruin your appetite for dinner," Channing said by way of explanation.

Pierce shook her head. "Don't worry. I'm not hungry."

TEXT OF AN AIR LETTER FROM JIMMY RIGGS
O'HANRAGHAN IN JESUALBO, SONORA, MEXICO, TO LYDELL
G. BROADSTREET IN BALTIMORE, MARYLAND, USA, SENT
RAPID DELIVERY AND IN BROADSTREET'S HANDS
TWO DAYS AFTER IT WAS MAILED.

19 May, 1951

Lydell G. Broadstreet
139 Roanoke Way
Baltimore, Maryland, USA

Dear Broadstreet,
Let me be among the first to congratulate you on your promotion. I'm sure that being attached to the US Embassy's trade ministry in Jakarta will be filled with opportunities for you.
Let me remind you that you owe me $50,000. Next month, the sum will be $60,000. In your new post you should be able to purloin that amount by the end of the year.

Be careful where you park.
Riggs

❖ 6 ❖

HEAVY SHUTTERS on the tall windows blocked the view of the Black Sea now shining darkly in the coppery August sunlight beyond this building that housed the Istanbul office of the Eclipse Trading Company. Sounds in the street announced increasing activity as the day slipped toward the delights of evening; it had cooled a little in the last hour, though where the sun struck, the heat of the day still lingered, and with it the spicy, salty odor of the city itself.

Germyn Rakoczy sat alone in the pleasant gloom of his office; his skin was still intensely sensitive to sunlight, and had the same stretched appearance as the scars on his torso—but unlike the tokens of his execution, the burn-scars would fade. To protect his skin, he only opened the shutters after sunset, when the lights of the city shone like fireflies in the night. In the last week, he had started coming to his office during the day, and occasionally had good reason to regret it, for he had not fully regrown his skin, and exposure to sunlight at mid-day was particularly enervating. His brief sojourn in the Carpathians had sped up his recovery, but he had not remained there long; there was too much political foment in Transylvania for him to feel safe. Constantinople had seemed a reasonable choice—near to Romania, but not too near; Eclipse Trading and Eclipse Publishing both had offices in the city, and his presence was beginning to attract attention. He set himself up at his desk and prepared for his visitor, the third one he had had since his arrival in Istanbul a month ago. During that time since Hrogre had wheeled him off the train from Bucharesti, he had claimed and occupied the house in Bistrita of his supposedly late cousin, and with Hrogre's help had ventured deep into the mountains to fill several chests with his native earth, some of which he added to the crawl-space above the concrete foundation of his elegant house here in Constantinople. He was now into the last stage of his healing from the burns the explosion had ravaged upon him, and settling into his latest identity.

There was a noise from the intercom that connected the front office with Rakoczy's own. "He's here again, sir; the same request for an hour of your time," said Hrogre in Imperial Latin, the intercom's speaker adding an electronic squeal to this announcement. "That makes four days in a row. You had better see him."

"No doubt you're right, old friend. But I am nervous; I don't want him to start asking questions about me." Rakoczy sighed; it was apparent that Hrogre had assessed the situation, and it would be prudent for Rakoczy to receive this fellow from the American Embassy; yes, it would be better off seeing his caller than refusing him admittance yet again. "You might as well send him in," he went on in Turkish. "He'll only be more persistent until we meet."

"I'm afraid so," said Hrogre. His disguise was more comprehensive: he wore Turkish garments; he had dyed his hair a walnut-brown and had let it grow so that it brushed his shoulders; to complete his transformation, he had fashioned a wen with undertaker's putty and placed it high on his cheek, making his face look lopsided.

"Then let us be done with it." Rakoczy adjusted the open collar of his black silk shirt so that it looked a bit more formal; his visitor from the American Embassy was used to a certain level of decorum in his work. The rest of his clothing—the black Italian-silk suit he wore, and the Florentine shoes on his small feet—were not only fashionable, they were obviously expensive.

"Right you are," said Hrogre, and clicked off the intercom. A few seconds later, the door opened and Edward Merryman stepped into the half-light of Rakoczy's office. "Mister Merryman, sir," said Hrogre in English.

"Good afternoon, Mister Merryman," said Rakoczy in the same language, rising and extending his hand. "Forgive me for not seeing you sooner; I'm just becoming acquainted with my cousin's business. How can I be of help to you?"

Merryman, very natty in a summer-weight linen suit of pale blue with a handsome straw hat, and carrying a chestnut leather briefcase, took Rakoczy's hand. "Thank you for agreeing to talk with me, Mister—is it Mister, or is it Grof?—Rakoczy. One never knows how these things work within the Soviet hegemony." He had not changed much in the months that had passed since Ragoczy left Paris, but Rakoczy would not mention that, for it was Ferenz Ragoczy, not Germyn Rakoczy, who had seen Merryman there.

"It is whichever you prefer," said Rakoczy. "I am more familiar with Mister."

"Then let us stick with Mister for now; I can't make sense of the systems of nobility in this part of the world. My failing, I know, but better to admit it than become more confused than I am already," Merryman remarked with the same slightly fusty ease he had shown in Paris, which Rakoczy knew was a mendacity: Merryman was keenly observing everything he saw and heard, starting with Rakoczy himself. Seemingly relaxed, Merryman was doing his best not to stare too closely at Rakoczy, but still ended up peering at him as much as the low light would allow. "There's a remarkable resemblance."

"So I have been told; I don't see it, myself," he said with complete honesty, taking care to speak English with a Romanian accent.

"Well, that's often the way, isn't it?" Merryman offered a genial smile. "You're a bit younger than your cousin, I would guess. And perhaps a little taller?" He pursed his lips to show he was mentally comparing the two men.

"So you met him?" Rakoczy asked, to see how Merryman would respond to the question.

Merryman ignored this conversational feint, and offered his own. "There was a lot of talk when his Jaguar was blown up, with Professor Treat in it."

"A very bad business," Rakoczy said darkly.

"That it was." Merryman shook his head. "And I am sorry if I am causing you distress, but the sooner we get through this in-quiry, the sooner all those pesky questions can be put to rest. You know how these things go."

"I gathered when you first came here that the reason for your visit is my cousin; shall we get on with it," said Rakoczy with ur-bane ease, avoiding the implied question in Merryman's observa-tion. "I will tell you what I can, but I did not know him very well, as you are no doubt aware."

"Cousin, is it?" Merryman asked.

"The one from whom I inherited the title, my cousin Ferenz, who died in Paris earlier this year, my cousin—second cousin, actually, if you want to be specific," said Rakoczy, knowing what Merryman would find in the Rakoczy/Ragoczy family records that he and Hrogre had just revised; he gestured to the two chairs that faced his desk.

"Your great-grandparents were siblings?" Merryman asked tentatively as if he knew little about genealogy.

"That is my understanding," Rakoczy said. "Sit, please. Would you like something to drink on this hot afternoon? We have coffee, tea, and for Europeans, brandy, gin, and ice."

"Whatever you're having," said Merryman with the practiced ease of one used to diplomatic maneuvering. "I appreciate your willingness to see me, and I hope my purpose will make this worth your while." He went to the sofa and sat down on it; he removed his hat and used it for a fan for a short time. "I am glad for this opportunity to speak to you. There are a number of questions surrounding your . . . second cousin, is it?"

"Second cousin," Rakoczy confirmed again, coming to the Turkish armchair at right angles to the sofa.

"Second cousin, then; I won't expect to hear family secrets; you rarely find them beyond the first-cousin tier." He fiddled with his tie. "This call is pro forma—nothing too drastic, just a few loose ends," Merryman said, and blinked to keep from staring. "I have to tell you, the resemblance between you and your late second cousin *is* astounding. I don't mean to goggle, but it is . . ." He sat up a little straighter. "If you didn't have that scar on your cheek, in this low light I would think I was speaking to Ferenz Ragoczy, Grof Szent-Germain, rather than Germyn Rakoczy, his heir. But this is often the case with these old families—in-breeding makes for these marked resemblances, don't you think?"

Rakoczy, who had had Hrogre apply the scar on his face with theatrical collodion before he left his house this morning, as he had every morning since his arrival in Istanbul, gave Merryman a diplomatic nod. "I have heard the same things many times myself. A number of us are readily identified by our faces as relatives; I will allow that the family has a stamp set upon it long ago, luckily rather better-looking than the Hapsburg jaw."

"Yes, Good Lord, yes, poor fellows," said Merryman, chuckling. "They all ended up looking like old-fashioned nut-crackers, didn't they? Lower jaw ahead of the upper one, isn't that it?" he added, to show he got the joke, then reached for one of the pillows to put behind his shoulders. "I wish I could tell you that I knew your cousin well and could recount some personal recollections of the man, but, alas, we met only twice—once in connection with an investigation, and once at a reception he gave for his authors. He had an air of command about him, which many short men strive for, but which he achieved. A very personable fellow in a slightly stand-offish way."

"That sounds like him." It was also an accurate recollection; they had met on those two occasions but no others.

"I'm not only acting on instructions from the State Department, I am here to deliver a report on the progress of this investigation being conducted by the CIA, pursuant to your request for information on the inquiry into your cousin's death. Ordinarily such access would not be granted, but under the circumstances . . . I hope the news I have won't disturb you—" Merryman said, sitting up enough to rest his shoulder on the bolster of the sofa.

"What information is that?" Rakoczy prodded gently.

Merryman waved his hand. "It appears"—he put subtle emphasis on *appears*—"that the Grof was not actively the target of the explosion. This was simply a case of being in the wrong place at the wrong time."

"Do you mean the bomb was an accident?" Rakoczy asked, struggling to keep his tone even.

"I said it appears; we're seeking confirmation on this, which means asking about your second cousin; you know, I would suppose, that he was engaged actively in anti-Nazi activities during the war?" He saw Rakoczy nod. "If I can confirm a few things with you—similar to what I just asked—I can turn my attention to more troubling developments in this investigation. I don't mean to sound like a broken record, but I wouldn't have bothered to seek you out unless the event didn't *appear* to be associated with a rather more important investigation currently under way; your . . . second cousin's activities can be set aside from the suspicions that might linger around his businesses, given the terrible business of last February."

"If it will help end the rumors of spies and assassins, I am delighted to help."

Merryman stretched a little trying to adjust to the depth of seat on the sofa. "I can't promise to rid the event from spies and assassins, for they are the very ones most likely to be involved, but I can make it clear that he was an unlucky target—if that's what he was."

"I appreciate your service on behalf of my second cousin, whatever it is, and for telling me what your progress is." Germyn Rakoczy nodded to Merryman with sardonic gravity. "I hope that once you have your answers, there are no more suspicions from Paris. I am hardly in a position to be much help with the French, you know. And I hope that there are no more persons who are seeking to bring about the ruin of our family, if that accounts in any part for the explosion. There's been far too much of that already; no matter what happens in Korea, we are not presently at war." His smile had more sadness than warmth, but Rakoczy went on. "We have been in the Carpathians for many generations, as I must suppose you are aware—you Americans seem to be relentless in your pursuit of information—that our family has long striven to maintain our autonomy among our various national leaders we have had to accommodate. You must have some sympathy for us."

"Some—yes. But not all," said Merryman. "Over time, I hope you and yours will establish links with me and mine, in the name of international good will, although I realize that isn't likely to happen."

"No," said Rakoczy. "Probably not."

"There are a few puzzling aspects of the . . . incident which I hope we can resolve so that our inquiries in your regard may be concluded, assuming you know anything useful." He held up an admonitory finger. "But I am not here just to demand an answer, as I said, I am here to inform you as to how matters stand for you and your House in relation to the bomb in Paris." He looked steadily at Rakoczy. "Will you let me present you with a report?"

"Of course, and welcome," said Rakoczy; it was more than he

had expected. He rose and turned on the standing electric fan in the corner. "This should make the room more comfortable; the heat has made the air stale."

"It does have a cooling effect," Merryman said, pushing another pillow into position behind his back, then pulling his briefcase into his lap and opening it. "Thanks for turning it on. Your second cousin was punctilious about the comforts of his guests."

Rakoczy inclined his head. "What are your questions?" He came back to his chair and sank into it as Merryman handed him a two-inch-thick folder. "Unless you want any of the refreshments I mentioned?"

Merryman smiled. "Very generous of you, Mister Rakoczy, but for the time being, I'm not looking to have a drink, of anything, with or without alcohol. I have heard that you do not drink wine." He made an unconcerned gesture. "Do you want to go over the file now?"

"Do you think it is necessary?" Rakoczy asked, anticipating the answer; he was not disappointed.

"I would have to return next week rather than conclude my questions now if you believe you need to know all that is contained in that file."

Again, Rakoczy shrugged. "Then let's get on with it." He folded his hands and looked at Merryman, an expectant shine in his dark eyes.

"Excellent," Merryman approved, and took a notebook and pen from his inner jacket-pocket. "Do you mind if I take notes?"

"Not at all," Rakoczy said, making himself a bit more comfortable. "Ask away, Mister Merryman, and I will do all I can to answer you."

Merryman opened his pen and tested it, making sure the nib was clean and the ink-chamber full. He cleared his throat and prepared to write. "Are you aware of a group calling itself the Ex-Pats' Coven?"

The room was a bit cooler; the light through the slats in the shutters was becoming blue. At the docks some distance below Eclipse Shipping bright lights came on, and were greeted by the hoots of tug-boats.

"You mean the one in Paris? To a degree, yes. I have seen several copies of a publication called *The Grimoire;* Rogers, my cousin's manservant, told me a fair amount about them."

"Are you aware that all the group's members were considered to be sympathetic to the Soviets and Communism?"

"I have become aware of that, yes," Rakoczy answered. "I have encountered correspondence between him and his authors within the group."

"Have you contacted any of those group members? The ones published by Eclipse Press?"

"No. My cousin's attorneys have done so, in accord with his instructions. Thus far, no emendation to the contracts is required."

"Do you know that your cousin—second cousin—and Professor Treat were having an affaire? at the time of the bomb-blast?"

"Rogers said something of the sort, in passing." Rakoczy rubbed his chin, trying to determine what Merryman was looking for.

"No doubt you have an opinion?"

An abrupt, intense memory of his time with Charis in Orleans came back to him, vivid and evocative. "I do, but it is not a fact, and would not help your investigation in any way." He waited for Merryman to respond.

Merryman leaned forward. "Why not?"

"All right, if you want it. My second cousin liked intelligent women. It would have been surprising if he weren't pursuing Professor Treat." He offered a quick half-smile. "There, you see? Nothing useful for you."

"Um. Speaking of Rogers, can you put me in contact with him? He seems to have disappeared."

Rakoczy knew at once that this question was crucial to Merryman. "I have surmised from the carbons of some recent letters that Rogers had been preparing to accompany my cousin in a hunt for Lord Weldon, who has been missing for more than a year. My cousin was planning to go in search of him. Rogers undertook the mission as soon as he saw my cousin to his resting place."

"Any idea where this Rogers is?"

"There was a letter at the end of May, sent from Karaganda, say-ing he was pressing on to Pavlodar—they're in the Soviet Un—"

"Union. Yes, I know. Those are pretty remote places."

"That they are; if I understand what Rogers told me, Lord Wel-don prefers remote places," Rakoczy agreed. "I would recommend sending word to the police in Pavlodar if you feel you must reach him. They will know of any foreigners in the city; Russian police are like that. I don't know if they will help you, but the police in Karaganda were very helpful when I wrote to them. I can show you the letter, if you'd like."

"I doubt I'll need it. I can have the CIA handle it." He cleared his throat. "How long do you reckon Rogers will be gone?"

"No idea," said Rakoczy. "We never discussed that." He felt a poignant sadness come over him; he disliked the need to lie, even as insignificant as these lies were. But the truth would lead to more questions and revelations that he and Hrogre would not want to endure, as had almost happened in Marin County on the day the Golden Gate Bridge was opened; nor did he want to have to vanish again, not so soon, not in this world of telephones and photographs and fingerprints and medical innovations with more of the same to come, so he offered a tight smile. "Or *I* could send him a note, via the police of Pavlodar."

"That won't be necessary. We learned a bit from Tolliver Bethune, who was a member of the Ex-Pats' Coven, and who was involved in several legal issues on behalf of the Coven members. He pointed out a few buildings in Paris that Weldon owns, or owned." He gave a diplomatic cough. "Your cousin lived in one of them; a handsome apartment building, about forty years old, in excellent condition."

"That may well be," said Rakoczy with a hint of boredom in his manner; he realized the last had been a test of his veracity, so he said nothing more.

"Bethune doesn't think your cousin was a target of the bomb, and neither was Missus Treat," Merryman went on. "Bethune thinks that it had to do with the Coven, to warn them away from Eclipse and to keep you from helping them by publishing them." His voice rose at the end of this statement as if it were a question.

"I understand that the bomb's trigger was linked to the ignition, which suggests that my cousin was the target, wouldn't you think? The explosion was intended to kill anyone who turned the key in the ignition, and almost all the time, it would be he who turned it." He said it more brusquely than he had intended, but saw that this had not bothered Merryman.

"How could the bomb-maker know whose car it was?"

Nettled, Rakoczy answered unceremoniously, "My second cousin liked fine automobiles. The drop-nose black Bugatti Typo 101 in front of this building is one of several bequests from him. The car that was blown up was a Jaguar XK120. Not many of those in Paris, or anywhere else."

"That does make it unlikely that there had been a mistake." Merryman paused. "Would any of the Coven be able to plant such a bomb?"

"I suppose so," said Rakoczy, remembering Steve diMaggio's skill with electronics, and Hapgood Nugent's reputed familiarity with ordnance. "But I can't think why any of them would do such a thing."

"Political reasons?" Merryman inquired.

"Because they left America due to political pressure?" Rakoczy paused in a show of thought. "I never met any of them, but I have seen a few issues of *The Grimoire*. All political material in its pages related to the American anti-Communist craze. My second cousin was not much involved in politics once the war ended."

"He worked with—"

"—refugees, during the war. People wanting to get away from the Nazis. He occasionally worked with the Resistance, but not politically." He folded his arms.

"You seem to believe he was a humanitarian," said Merryman.

"Indeed: I was aware it was his goal to be one."

"Do you know if Rogers had any political affiliations?" Merryman asked almost as an afterthought.

"I wouldn't have thought so. My cousin never mentioned that in his few letters, and given my cousin's stance in such matters, you'd think he would. He and Rogers agreed more often than not. Neither was inclined to participate in politics; it is not wise for foreigners to do so." Rakoczy had a valise that contained a great deal of communication to and from his various heirs, establishing their identity for the purpose of being able to settle estates quickly, as he had done for establishing his claim when he went from being Ferenz Ragoczy to Germyn Rakoczy. He had already created two possible heirs for his present self. "Let me ask you something, Merryman."

"Of course, Rakoczy," he exclaimed eagerly. "What do you want to know?"

"Do you think there could be a connection between the bombing of my second cousin and any American intelligence organization? One of the Coven members mentioned it to Rogers, I'm told. Would such a thing be possible?" He stopped, and continued, more circumspectly, "I know this is what some of the Coven think. Most of the Coven knows of instances when such interference has occurred, and are inclined to see this as another such example."

Merryman gave the idea some thought. "That seems a little convoluted to me."

"But not impossible."

"No." Merryman shook his head heavily. "No, not impossible."

"Ah." Rakoczy made himself hitch up his shoulders. "In your opinion, would there be any point in pursuing such a possibility?"

"I wouldn't bother. Even if such a foolish endeavor were associated with the bomb, you are in no position to discover it."

"I have dealt with bureaucracies in Italy and India and China," he said, not mentioning that he had done so for nearly three thousand years. "I ought to be able to function with the Americans."

"It is apt to be more trouble than it is worth, for if you should unearth a scandal like that, one that would implicate men in high places, it—and very likely you—would be buried deeper than a uranium mine." He patted the file. "Have a look at what we've gathered, and you and I will talk again."

"Thank you, I will." To emphasize his determination, he stood up, picked up the file, and carried it to his desk. "Do you have any more questions for me, Mister Merryman?"

"Not just at present. I'll make an appointment with your secretary for next week." He offered a good-natured smile as he got to his feet. "I'll have a few more questions, and I believe you will have some for me, too. Do me a favor and don't let anyone know I've loaned you this."

"Does that mean you want it back?"

"Naturally. I couldn't do this if the file had been logged into the archives, but it will take another six weeks before that happens, so we have a few days to take advantage of what it has to say. I imagine you can get through in two or three days."

Rakoczy put his hand on the file, snapping one of the two rubber bands that held the sheets of paper within it. "That is a likely guess," he said as he got to his feet in order to escort Merryman to the door.

"No need to stand on ceremony with me, Rakoczy," Merryman said, waving him back to his chair. As he reached the door, he turned back to scrutinize Rakoczy's face. "Your resemblance to your cousin . . . second cousin is really quite uncanny. I would have believed you were twins, had you made such a claim." He pressed down the latch and let himself out; the door banged behind him.

Sitting behind his desk, Rakoczy turned on the reading lamp that stood at the top of the blotter-pad; the small pool of light was briefly dazzling, then resolved to a sharp-edged type on the outside of the file:

CAR BOMB
1 FATALITY
PARIS, FRANCE

There was a stamp of the American flag in the upper right corner of the file.

Rakoczy removed the rubber bands and put them in the empty ashtray on the desk, then opened the file. The first page was an account of the event. It was accurate as far as it went, offering no theories or opinions, simply reciting the facts of the explosion to the extent they were known. Rakoczy read it carefully, and set it down to the left of the file. The second page was the report of the first policeman on the scene, and after that was a chemist's report on the bomb, running three typewritten and stapled pages. What came next were photographs. Rakoczy swallowed hard against the sudden knot at the base of his sternum as he saw the glass tray with the recovered bits of bone and clothing that were all that was left of Charis Treat. A scrap of her handbag was set at the end of the tray, and at the other end was half a shoe. There were three photographs from various points around the explosion; in one there was a heap of blurry, unshapen tissue, shiny, slick, and red. He realized it was a photograph of himself, lying where he had fallen after the fireball engulfed him. He stared at it, though it remained out of focus, and the shine from the flashbulb created stark shadows around the place where the Jaguar had been, making the burn-scar seem ominously larger. He put the photographs, face down, next to the reading lamp. Then he sat for a while, unbreathing, his gaze fixed on distant places and times. He could sense a smoldering urge to take vengeance for Charis, if only he could learn who had made the bomb, and who ordered it made, but could not forget what killing the five men who murdered Laisha had cost him, and he told himself that neither vengeance nor justice would return Charis to life; with all the death he had seen over the millennia, he had never grown used to it, and could not bring himself to add to the carnage by continuing the killing; it had robbed him of his humanity for a time, after the slaughter of his family, leaving him indifferent to his life and refusing to engage in the touching love provided. This had happened occasionally during his long, long undead life. The last had been a quarter-century ago, and he felt its lure now, but knew he would not risk so much—it would be an appalling tribute to Charis, as it had proved to be for his ward Laisha—for until he was in America, and had once again seen his American friends, and the gulf of sorrow began to close, he had had to fight the impulse within him to cut himself off from humanity, since that was the truth of his existence. Vengeance was a most seductive solution to the pain that gripped him, but it would also prolong the alienation. He shook his head and turned up the desk-lamp, making the room a little brighter; he shook himself mentally and looked at the file.

For as long as he walked the earth, he told himself, there would be irrevocable loss, and knowing that could ease his anguish, restoring the bonds he had with the living and lessening the unspeakable loneliness that had transfixed him while he healed.

More than half an hour had passed before he shook himself and resumed his examination of the file. He was methodical, steady, all emotion carefully banked though he felt as if his skin had been newly seared by his healing burns.

There was a tap on the door, and Hrogre asked in Medieval Spanish, "It is full dark, master. Do you wish to leave?"

The question took a few seconds to penetrate his concentration; Rakoczy blinked and glanced toward the windows. "Oh. You're right. Yes, it would probably be best. Give me a moment or two and I'll join you."

"I'll go check the Bugatti," said Hrogre.

Rakoczy paper-clipped what he had already seen of the file and put the papers back in their original place, then used the rubber bands to secure it all. This done, he pulled a sueded mail-sack out from under his desk, deposited the file in it, and turned out his reading lamp before he left his office, taking care to lock it as he left.

Hrogre was holding the Bugatti's driver's door open. "Nothing underneath that shouldn't be there," he assured Rakoczy. "The fuses are all in the right place, the seats are as we left them."

"Fine. Thank you, old friend," said Rakoczy as he climbed into the elegant automobile.

"Do you think we'll ever reach a time when you won't have to bother with such precautions?" Hrogre asked, not yet closing the door.

"I would like to think so," Rakoczy answered, then frowned. "But I am not sanguine about it; I am not sanguine at all."

Sept 27th, 1951

Peter Leeland
Thermopile Ranch
Chugwater, Wyoming, USA

Dear Peter,

I don't know if you've heard, but I've been officially demoted. Singapore may be a hotspot for espionage, but if you ask me, it's just another small office in a place that gets too hot to think. I'm beginning to see why you decided to resign—but Chugwater, Wyoming? You might as well have stayed in the Agency; they might have sent you somewhere exotic. Okay: your salary is better than what the government pays, a lot better, and you say there are plenty of chances to provide intelligence for the big companies with projects abroad. You said you've already done a security survey on a US company's oil-drilling installation in Siberia, and that all went well. I'll take your word for it, but I can understand your leaving. There was too much gossip about Broadstreet. I don't know what Jimmy Riggs told them, but it screwed up Broadstreet's career, and that got us out from under the merde we were in.

Speaking of Broadstreet, did you hear he had a lucky escape last week? He's on assignment in Ulaanbaatar—and we both know what that means to a career officer like Broadstreet—working on interceptions and transmissions: he went out of the city in response to a report that sounds a little peculiar. He followed the directions he had been given and ended up on some kind of remote back-road, and at that point his car apparently broke down—out in the wastes of Mongolia. So he, knowing he was on a lightly traveled road, started back on foot toward Ulaanbaatar, and in three miles was picked up by a farmer with a load of ducks and chickens bound for market, who came along, and carried him back to Ulaanbaatar. When they found the remains of his car, it was riddled with bullet-holes, and the tracks of at least six Mongol ponies around the car. There were paint-scrawls on the car, anti–US slogans and such. Apparently Broadstreet wants to hunt the group down that did it, and would, but I'm told that he's been spooked and is talking about resigning from the Agency. I can understand why someone in his position might want to get of the target area, but given Jimmy Riggs' testimony, I have to accept that what happened to Missus Treat and the Grof was by design at the demand of someone in the intelligence business. To be sure, much of this remains speculation, but Channing has accepted that Broadstreet is most likely responsible for the Paris bombings, and possibly for the destruction of his car in Mongolia, pony hoof-prints notwithstanding. Channing's still trying to locate this Baxter fellow whom Broadstreet was using as an informant. I've requested an opportunity to call upon Channing when I am next in Washington. I would like to know everything he knows.

You have been wise to get out with only a few unhappy notes in your file. If I had the chance to join you, I might well do so, no matter how demanding it is to be in your company. The industrial sector of our economy is demanding of the support we are trained to provide. No dispute on that point. I would welcome even Chugwater, Wyoming, over my current work here in Singapore. If you will tell me where to send for an application, I would be grateful. I'll have a break at Christmas, and would like to get together then, if that's possible. I think it's time for me to absquatulate.

October 2nd, 1951

Sorry for the break. I had a call that took me out of my apartment for a couple of days. Nasty business. I was working with an Australian guy who's fluent in several Oriental languages, and thank God for it. My

Chinese—Mandarin and Cantonese—is good enough, but Douglas Brenner has Thai and VietNamese and Laotian. I think we've scotched the chance of a large, meaning multi-ton, shipment of the stuff to get out of Singapore, bound for the US and Europe. I'm getting reassigned next week. They tell me I'm a marked man, so I might end up on your doorstep by Hallowe'en.

More in a week or so, when I know what the next step is.

Sincerely,
Phil Rothcoe

P. S. I just got a letter from Channing: Broadstreet is missing, and there was blood in his bathroom, Channing says a lot of blood.

Epilogue

Two days out of Tashkent
on the road to Frunze
11 April 1952

Madelaine de Montalia
University of Grenoble
Grenoble, France

Madelaine my heart,
This letter will probably be opened and read on its way to you, so I ask you to forgive the lack of familiarities as well as personal endearments I might otherwise send you.

The weather has been wretched—either pouring rain and washing away sections of road, or the sun has come out and baked us during the day, and then, as we are in the mountains, we'll then be half-frozen at night by the wind off the snow. My auto has been holding up quite well, but I have taken the precaution of carrying as many replacements for it as we may need on this journey. It is my plan to meet up with Roger there next Tuesday or Wednesday at Frunze. I'll hand him several letters and reports which he will carry to Paris for posting. He will then fly to Delhi and wait for further instructions from me. I believe it is time for me to return to what is called civilization. When and where I will do this, Roger will know and he will keep you informed. I will need to stay away from areas where hostilities are taking place.

I have seen several orphans of memory, as the Khazars called them, on this expedition, abandoned towns from long, long ago that no one now remembers, except perhaps in folk-tales. These reminders of your work leave me apologetic to have missed your paper at the conference. How have you enjoyed Grenoble? Has the conference been a success? You told me there would be papers on discoveries in the Americas as well as the Middle East, and a few on the trouble of attempting an archeo-logical dig in the middle of a modern city. That sounds most challeng-ing, though I have been told that there are parts of Rome that have been successfully excavated without destroying what stands above them.

I'll write more tomorrow. StG Weldon

13 April, 1952

As it turned out, we were detained yesterday at Cimkent, and so to-day, I will try to make up for the lapse. Two of the men accompanying me have decided to leave, which means that I am going to have to find at least one local person to take their places, a man the other two of my guides will work with and respect. My old friend Olivia taught me the importance of that many years ago. The police asked if I intended to press on alone, but I told them I would not; Olivia having chided me for that. It would be foolish for a foreigner like me to go about wholly on my own in these remote regions. Occasionally the guides I have used have played me false, but that must be expected from time to time. I do not take guides in a group—another of Olivia's dicta—but singly, for that reduces the chance that I will fall into the hands of rogues and outlaws.

These mountains are most impressive, not unlike the mountains of Peru, having many long, narrowing valleys with a few high plateaus. As you know, it is my preference to travel at night, but this is not advis-able in these mountains, and so I have spent hours in the auto, as much out of the sun as possible, and have taken my rest at night, on the back-seat, which, though hard, is exactly what I want. Buka, my chief guide, sleeps on the floor of the backseat, to protect me. He is planning to con-tinue on with me. We rarely see any persons along the road, and the few *we do encounter are most often one or two in number, some on Bactrian camels, some on ponies. I don't think I have seen more than five autos between here and Tashkent, and only a few lorries. Malyk, the other guide who will remain with me, has said that the war is still being fought in this region, by which he seems to mean that there is an uprising by the people of the region against the Soviet government. If so, it is a most unhappy turn.*

It is often difficult to find adequate sustenance, and I have more than once been hungry. But this should not concern you. Worry more for my guides than me, if you must worry. And forgive me for having to withhold the personal exchanges that usually mark our correspondance.

I will hope to see you in Roma, where there are plentiful means of alleviating hunger of all sorts, and no need to sleep in autos, with or without guides. StG Weldon

16 April, 1952

A note from Roger tells me he is delayed for a week at least, so I am taking a chance and posting this here in Frunze. All being well, this should reach you in two or three weeks. I have taken Roger's recommendation to heart and will be returning to England as soon as transportation may be arranged. There is more turmoil growing in these regions, so I'll have to be careful while making plans to go west. I will sign over my auto to Buka so that he may make more money as a guide by providing transport.

It is time I return to cities and libraries and what we call culture, to regain my footing. Too often the events we encounter in life convince us that changing our environment will change the experience, but I have learned that it rarely does more than provide a new context in which to interpret the experience, and I am of such an age now that I would like to attempt to accomplish this in elegant surroundings and with companions who share my love of art and learning. You and I rarely see the same thing the same way, but that does not mean that I will reject your insights; in fact, I will welcome the insight they provide. I will agree not to challenge the fools who have only greed and dread within them, no matter how high they may rise; unless they endanger what and whom I hold dear, including you, my heart. I will let them claim victory in a fight that is more for form's sake than to demonstrate any other advantage. I can hope only to see you again while you continue your archeological work. One way or another, even we will not always live alone.

My life-long devotion,
StG Weldon